This book should be returned to any Lancashire County Council Library on or before the date shown

Lancashire County Council Library Service,
County Hall Complex,
2nd floor Christ Church Precinct,
Preston, PR1 0LD

www.lancashire.gov.uk/libraries

Lancashire
County
Council

D0420013

SECOND CHANCE WITH HIS PRINCESS

REBECCA WINTERS

WHISKED INTO THE BILLIONAIRE'S WORLD

NINA SINGH

MILLS & BOON

First Published in Great Britain 2022
by Mills & Boon, an imprint of HarperCollins*Publishers* Ltd,
1 London Bridge Street, London, SE1 9GF

www.harpercollins.co.uk

HarperCollins*Publishers*
1st Floor, Watermarque Building,
Ringsend Road, Dublin 4, Ireland

ISBN: 978-0-263-30217-2

05/22

MIX
Paper from
responsible sources
FSC™ C007454

This book is produced from independently certified FSC™ paper
to ensure responsible forest management.
For more information visit www.harpercollins.co.uk/green.

Printed and Bound in Spain using 100% Renewable Electricity
at CPI Black Print, Barcelona

SECOND CHANCE WITH HIS PRINCESS

REBECCA WINTERS

MILLS & BOON

I've dedicated this novel to my dearest,
sweetest nana, Alice Vivia Driggs Brown,
my beloved father's mother.

She was an angel in my life and taught me
everything from Bible stories to the stories of kings.

I can't wait to see her again one day
and let her know how much she enriched my life!

PROLOGUE

Scuol, Graubunden Canton, Switzerland, the end of April

THE LAST FRIDAY morning announcement came over the high school's PA system. "Hey, all you ski bums—don't forget when the bell rings in a few minutes, come straight out to the back of the school where the bus is waiting. We want to get up on the mountain fast before the sun makes things slushy."

Just the sound of Luca Torriani's deep voice excited sixteen-year-old Bella Baldasseri to her core. Not only was he a brilliant student, he was president of their school and ski club. His expertise on the slopes had caught the attention of the ski world. Already becoming famous at eighteen, he'd won a place on the Swiss men's ski team to train for the Olympics.

Luca had been her brother Vincenzo's best friend for as long as she could remember. Over the years he'd been a constant visitor to the palace. She'd spent most of her free time with them, preferring to be with dark-haired Luca more than any guy alive. In truth, she loved him heart and soul. There would never be anyone else for her. *Not ever.*

"Bella? Can I sit on the bus with you?" Deep in thoughts about him, her friend Margite's question startled her. She hadn't noticed the bell had rung, but the students were running around. Bella had hopes that when Luca came on board, he'd sit by her. But she couldn't say no to her friend. Margite had a hopeless crush on Vincenzo.

"Sure. We've got to hurry and grab our skis." Like Margite, she was already dressed in ski clothes. Before long they took their equipment outside in back where the driver loaded their gear on the side of the bus. She deliberately chose a seat near the back where she knew her brother and Luca liked to sit.

The bus filled up fast and soon she spotted the two of them coming down the aisle, talking to everybody. When Luca drew close, his emerald eyes fastened on her. They looked like the green in the stained-glass windows going up the stairs to her room. She was mesmerized by the way they penetrated.

"Is the Princess ready to tackle Devil's Gulch?"

She winced, wishing he wouldn't call her Princess. Bella wanted him to think of her as an ordinary girl like all the others. "Just watch me."

"I plan to." His dashing smile got to her before he moved to the back seat. Her brother greeted Margite, but he kept going.

Twenty minutes later they'd arrived at the ski resort and climbed out under a full sun, ready to tackle the slopes. To her joy, Luca pulled his skis and hers off the rack. Together they put them on. "This is going to be fun," she said as he handed her the poles she'd brought. Slipping on goggles and a helmet over her jaw-length hair, she was ready.

Luca pulled on his gloves. "All right, let's push off so you can show me your latest technique." She chuckled because she didn't have one and he knew it.

Her brother had been distracted by some guys and didn't join them. That was an answer to prayer. Bella was dying to be alone with Luca. Every feminine eye was envious as they struck out for the Devil's Gulch trail.

To her surprise a sign had been erected she hadn't seen all winter. *Danger of avalanche.* No one else would try it now, but she would prove to be the exception. "Are you game?" She looked back at him, daring him.

He studied her through narrowed eyes, as if trying to see inside her. "It's not safe. Let's ski Bishop's Cauldron."

"I prefer the Gulch." She knew he favored it too. In the next breath she took off and shushed down the trail.

"Bella—" he shouted. "Stop and come back here!"

"You'll have to catch me!" She laughed, confident in her own abilities.

She'd been skiing with Vincenzo and Luca since she was nine and knew this mountain well. Now that spring had come, the snow was heavier, but just as divine as always. Her euphoria knew no bounds as he came after her.

To know that the great Luca Torriani was chasing her made Bella's mad dash down the face ten times more exhilarating. Seconds later she heard an ear-splitting crack from above. The ground trembled beneath her skis. "Bella!" he shouted at the top of his lungs. *"Avalanche!"*

She slowed to a stop and looked up in time to see a

chute of snow full of trees cascading from the summit. Luca reached her and pulled her down to remove her skis and his. "We can't outrun this avalanche, Bella. When it covers us, try to swim up and out of it. Don't forget to raise your arms."

It was getting closer. She grabbed onto him. "If we're going to die, I'm thankful I'm with you. I love you, Luca."

He pulled her close and kissed her mouth. "I love you, too, Bella. Always will. Brace yourself. Here it comes!"

Snow filled her nostrils like dust. She felt herself being buried. "Luca—" she screamed before she couldn't breathe.

The next time she had cognizance of her surroundings, it was night. She'd awakened in the hospital in Scuol with an IV in her arm. "Luca? Luca?"

"No, darling. You're awake, thank heaven." Her mother stood at the side of the hospital bed with a pallor she'd never seen before.

"Don't look so worried, Mamma. I feel fine."

"It's a miracle you escaped without injury."

"That's because of Luca."

Her mother leaned over her. "We've been waiting for you to fully awaken. The doctor says you can go home in the morning. Your father is out in the hall with him."

"Where's Vincenzo?"

"Leonardo asked him to fly to San Vitano on a special assignment. I don't know how long he'll be gone. The doctor wants to keep you here overnight just to be certain there are no compli—"

"How's Luca?" she interrupted her. He was all she

cared about now that she was conscious. "Please tell me he wasn't injured. I couldn't bear it if—"

"He's alive," her mother responded. "He was in surgery all afternoon."

All afternoon? She'd lost hours. "What happened to him? Tell me!"

"It's his right leg. A snapped tree slammed into him, but the search and rescue teams got to the two of you in record time. You were airlifted here."

Bella groaned, wanting to die. "Do you think he'll be able to ski again?"

"No." The news dropped like a bomb, horrifying her. "But the doctor believes he might be able to walk."

"Might?" Filled with gut-wrenching guilt and pain, Bella buried her face in the pillow. "Luca warned me not to go down the Gulch. He tried to stop me. When I kept going, it forced him to follow me." Bella started sobbing. "It's my fault he got injured, Mamma. He wanted to ski Bishop's Cauldron. I wouldn't listen and he came after me."

"Don't blame yourself. Spring skiing is dangerous. You shouldn't have gone in the first place."

Bella lifted her head. "But I *did* go. Luca saved my life and told me what to do. He kept *me* alive!" She broke down completely. "I love him so much, you'll never know."

"I've always known how you felt about him," she murmured.

Of course. Her mother knew everything. "How soon can I see him?"

"You can't."

Her unequivocal answer surprised her. "What do you mean?"

"He's been flown to England so a specialist can try to put his leg back together, but that will take another miracle."

"Luca is in England?" she cried in panic. "How long will he be gone?"

"From what I understand it could be a year considering he'll have to undergo physical rehabilitation and all that entails."

The revelation crushed her. "His condition is much worse than what you've told me, isn't it?"

"That's as much as I know."

"Then I'll text him and ask him to phone me when he's able."

"Right now you need to concentrate on your recovery and put the past behind you." Her mother got that steely look on her face.

"What are you saying?"

"It's time you understood what's expected of you, Bella. You are Princess Baldasseri, destined to marry the right prince. You've always known what your future would be. Surely you realize there can be no more Lucas of this world for you."

Bella felt like she'd just been tossed into a void from which there was no return. "You mean—"

"You know exactly what I'm telling you."

Despite weakness, Bella sat up, clutching the sheet. "In other words, you and father are forbidding me to see Luca again."

A strange smile broke out on her mother's face. "Good. I'm glad we finally understand each other. He's not a prince. Now I'll find your father and tell him and the doctor to come in."

Smoldering in pain and rage, Bella stared at her mother's retreating back.

What her parents were doing was *evil*. Barbaric! She wasn't even allowed to get in touch with Luca and confess that the tragedy was all her fault? She needed to ask his forgiveness.

I must help him. I love him.

Where was Vincenzo? She needed to get a message to Luca through her brother. How soon would he be back to the palace? The doctor and her parents came in the hospital room, but all she could think about was Luca. She fell back against the pillow in agony.

CHAPTER ONE

Bern, Switzerland, ten years later

FOR THE FIRST time in a decade, twenty-six-year-old Princess Bella Baldasseri of Scuol, Switzerland, was finally going to lay eyes on Luca Torriani, the man whose life she'd ruined ten years ago.

Not a day had gone by in all these years that she hadn't suffered over her thoughtlessness. A fleeting moment of throwing caution to the wind to prove her bravery had smashed his dreams forever. Hers too, because she'd never been allowed to talk to him and ask his forgiveness.

After leaving the hospital, she'd tried to reach him on the phone. When she couldn't, she'd sent him letter after letter, begging him to call her so she could ask for his forgiveness. The fact that he never answered one of them proved how much he hated her, and he would have had every right.

She'd pestered her brother to find out what was going on with Luca, but when Vincenzo got back from San Vitano a week later, he had no answer. With his friend in England, they'd had no contact either. Bella believed him implicitly and had to accept the fact that Luca wanted nothing more to do with her.

Perhaps today—the wedding day Vincenzo had planned with his beloved Francesca Visconti—meant that Bella would finally be able to see Luca. He would be standing up for her brother. The two men had been best friends, but after Luca went to England, everything changed. Vincenzo attended college and said they only kept in touch by phone when they could. Today might be her only chance to tell Luca of her deep sorrow.

She thanked God every day and night that Luca *could* stand on both his legs. The surgeon in England must have done spectacular work. But until she could unburden herself to Luca, she'd stay locked in a prison.

Her brother had been living in a prison all his adult life too. Their parents had arranged his engagement to a princess he didn't love. When she broke the engagement, he was free at last to marry the woman *he* chose. But until their mother knew the reason for the break, it took a miracle for Vincenzo's world to change and their mother to give her blessing.

Bella knew Francesca was her brother's whole world, and she couldn't be happier for them. Her soon-to-be sister-in-law had asked her to be a bridesmaid. Bella loved her already. She and her mother, along with Francesca, her mom and Princess Luna, went shopping. After finding the perfect wedding dress, they picked out filmy gowns of pink, purple, lavender and blue chiffon with lace. It had been a lovely day.

Since the death of Bella's father almost a year ago, she'd done what she could to get along with her mother. She'd dated several princes and had even gone along with her parent's idea to spend time with Prince Antoine Beaufort of Orleans, France. Antoine was a very attractive man who'd been pursuing her for the last few months. Four nights ago, they'd met in Geneva for dinner and dancing. He'd taken her out on the terrace overlooking the lake and admitted that he'd fallen in love with her.

"Will you marry me, Bella?"

As she looked into his anxious eyes, she realized how very much she cared for him.

"Oh, Tonio. I didn't expect a proposal this soon, but I know you'll make a wonderful husband. Will you give me time to think about it? My brother's wedding is coming up this next weekend. After that I have a week of charity commitments taking me out of town. When it's over, I'll phone you and we'll meet wherever you'd like so we can really talk about our feelings and everything else."

"I admit I'm disappointed, but I can wait another week. No longer."

The Beaufort family had been friends of her parents for years. Bella knew both mothers wanted the relationship to end in marriage. He deserved her full attention, but until she'd seen Luca again and had said a final goodbye with her heartfelt apology, she couldn't think clearly.

"I hear you, Tonio, and I promise I'll call. You're everything a woman could want." She meant those words and she knew he could be her future husband if she wanted it to happen.

The next day she left Geneva to fly back to Scuol. But instead of dwelling on Antonio's proposal, her mind was elsewhere. Bella had never forgiven her mother and father for causing the permanent separation between her and Luca. The hole in her heart had never closed. Worse, the avalanche that had ruined Luca's dreams for Olympic greatness had also changed Bella's life. *Irrevocably.*

Today she would seek him out after the ceremony and bare her soul to him. This might be her one and only chance to talk to him and beg his forgiveness. It was something she had to do, even if she knew he hated her for what she'd done. Then maybe she could push past her feelings of guilt and loss in order to say yes to Tonio. The media had already hinted there might be another wedding in the future following in the wake of her brother's.

She hoped that seeing Luca again would at last allow her to put the past to bed so she could fall deeply in love with Tonio. Right now Bella needed reassurance that her feelings for Luca had been nothing more than a residual teenaged crush. It couldn't be anything else. The fact that he'd never reached out to her in ten years *had* to mean that the only feelings of attraction and longing had come from her side. She'd been a fool to think otherwise. That kiss they'd shared that day on the mountain had been nothing more than a reaction to a life-or-death crisis.

Bella drove in a limo from the Bellevue Palace Hotel to the cathedral with her mother and grandparents on her father's side ahead of time. She was sorry that her grandparents on her mother's side couldn't be here to see Vincenzo married.

They used to come to Scuol often. Bella loved them very much.

But her grandmother, Princess Caderina Melis

Cossu, had been in a tragic car accident four years earlier. It had killed Bella's grandfather, Prince Alfonsu Cossu, and had left Caderina paralyzed from the waist down. She'd become an invalid and was ill. Since his death, their family flew to the palace in Sardinia to see her when they could. It was a shame her *nonna* was missing this event since she adored Vincenzo and Bella, and they adored her.

With the aid of umbrellas, the family avoided most of the summer rain. They hurried inside and sat on a pew near the altar while they waited. In a few minutes Princess Luna, the darling, pregnant wife of Bella and Vincenzo's cousin Prince Rinieri, joined them dressed in pink chiffon.

But Bella had a problem. Sounds of the organ began to permeate the interior. The church had filled and she couldn't sit still. Any second now the rest of the wedding party would assemble and she'd catch her first sight of Luca.

Her heart jumped when the Bishop in ceremonial robes entered from a side door. Following him came four men all looking magnificent. Vincenzo and Rinieri wore the royal navy dress and gold braid of the House of Baldasseri. Francesca's brother, Rolf, and Luca walked in wearing black tuxes with a white rose in the lapel to match Francesca's bouquet. Again Bella thanked God Luca *could* walk. Tears trickled down her cheeks as they stood on one side of the aisle.

Luca, the eighteen-year-old skier she'd loved and dreamed about all these years, had turned into a tall, virile male with a five-o'clock shadow and dark wavy hair. He was so visibly gorgeous he took her breath and she froze at the sight of him.

The Bishop nodded to the women to come forward. Thank goodness Princess Luna had the wits to give Bella a slight nudge, otherwise she would have remained sitting there in a trance.

If Luca saw her get up, he gave no indication. She felt sick to her stomach to realize this moment had come. Her brother had indicated that he liked Tonio and hoped something might come of that relationship. But other than to tell her that Luca wasn't married yet, Vincenzo kept his silence about everything else.

That vital piece of news didn't mean Luca wasn't involved with some beauty. All the girls at school had been crazy about him. From this brief glimpse of the full-grown man, Bella knew he could have his pick. It killed her to think of him with another woman. She had no idea where he lived, what he'd been doing all these years, what he did for a living. Nothing!

At the sound of the wedding march, she watched Francesca walk down the aisle on the arm of her father. To see father and daughter together so happy sent a fresh pain through Bella. What she would have given to have her own father alive, walking her down the aisle toward Luca. But it could never be. Her mother's words of ten years ago had scarred her soul.

You are Princess Baldasseri, destined to marry the right prince.

The Bishop began speaking. "If the couple will clasp hands, please come before me while the others take their seats and we'll begin with a prayer."

Francesca's mother took the flowers from her daughter and the three women sat down again on the bride's side of the aisle. Bella's eyes followed Luca, who sat on the other side. No longer a simple crush of a sixteen-year-old girl, one sight of Luca and he was still the epitome of Bella's womanly dreams. Yet there was no way she could see more of him right now unless she leaned forward. She would have to wait until the reception at the Visconti villa after they all left the cathedral.

The beautiful ceremony touched her heart when she heard Francesca vow to love and honor Vincenzo for as long as they lived. At that moment her brother added the unscripted words, "And after." He truly was in love with the veterinarian commoner. His joy had begun.

But at the sight of Luca, a new kind of turmoil for Bella was just beginning.

As the beaming bride and groom started down the aisle to greet everyone, Luca Torriani followed the Bishop out the side door to the anteroom. From there he could exit the cathedral from a rear door to a taxi and avoid everyone.

After Vincenzo had begged Luca to stand up for him at his wedding, he'd promised to be there for him. But it had been at a huge cost to him personally. One look at Princess Bella Baldasseri gowned in heavenly blue had destroyed every defense he'd erected to shut her out of his consciousness. Ten years of being away from Scuol hadn't helped anything. The beautiful, fun-loving sixteen-year-old teenager had grown up all right.

She'd become a breathtaking, voluptuous woman. Her hair, a swirling mixture of vanilla and café-au-lait, cascaded over her shoulders. Over the years he'd seen her in the news. Vincenzo had mentioned her during several phone conversations having to do with Prince Antonio. More recently there'd been pictures of her with the Prince. The thought of them together twisted his insides.

Bella had a sensual beauty beyond the physical. It eclipsed that of every woman he'd ever met or dated. While colleagues his age were married and having children, he couldn't be further from that situation. For her to have this effect on Luca when she hadn't reached out to him in all these years made him want to escape Bern right now.

He'd thought she would at least have contacted him after the avalanche, but he never saw or heard from her again. Vincenzo had never volunteered any information. It seemed her interest in Luca had been the simple infatuation of a sixteen-year-old after all. That's how little he'd meant to her and Vincenzo's silence on the subject said it all.

The last thing he'd wanted to do was participate in Vincenzo's wedding because it meant seeing her again. But the two men had been like blood brothers in their teenage years. Luca had to put in an appearance at his friend's reception before leaving.

The only thing that helped was Vincenzo's promise he would arrange for Luca to sit at a table with Daniel Zoller and his wife. Luca had always enjoyed the well-known vet. Over the years Vincenzo had visited Daniel at the vet clinic in Zernez many times. First there was his golden retriever, Rex, and then his Bernese mountain dog puppy he'd named Karl. Luca had loved both of Vincenzo's dogs, not being able to have one of his own.

By an amazing stroke of fate, seven years later Francesca Visconti, first known as Dr. Linard, had been hired as a new vet at the Zoller clinic. She'd looked after a dying Karl when Vincenzo had taken him in. Talk about love at first sight for Vincenzo, even though he was engaged to Princess Valentina at the time! He deserved this happiness after years of doing the princely duty he was born to. What a hell of a life it had been for him until now.

When the taxi reached the Visconti villa, Luca noticed a dozen or more photographers from various news outlets and tabloids already covering the Baldasseri wedding. Following the rumors of another Baldasseri marriage about to take place, they were eager to capture photos of Bella with her future prince. The thought gutted him.

Luca told the chauffeur to drive around the side where he slipped out of the taxi. While he waited for Dr. Zoller to arrive in one of the limos, he made some phone calls. Anything to avoid seeing Bella until he had cover.

The guests began to show up. Luca could pretend he was looking for Daniel, but his heart raced out of rhythm while he watched for the one woman who'd dominated his existence since he was ten. He'd never forget the moment he'd met her.

Vincenzo had invited him to the palace after school. They ran out in back to play and found his eight-year-old sister, Bella. Luca noticed her sitting on the grass with a golden retriever. She was sobbing her heart out.

When she saw them coming, she lifted her pretty blonde head. Her eyes looked like beautiful wet violets. "There's something wrong with Rex's left leg, Vincenzo. I found him lying here. We have to help him! I know *you* can fix him."

"I'll ask Papa to drive us to the vet. Be right back, Bella."

He raced off, leaving the two of them alone.

She stared at him. "Who are you?"

"Luca."

"Do you like dogs?"

"I'd love one of my own, but my mother is allergic to them so we can't have one."

"That's sad. You can come over here any time and play with Rex when he's better."

He'd been touched by her friendliness and that she loved her brother and dog so much. Luca didn't have siblings. The meeting that day was the beginning of a three-way friendship that didn't end until the two of them were caught in the avalanche.

His thoughts had taken him back so far, he hadn't been watching for Dr. Zoller. By now most of the guests, if not all, would have arrived. That meant Bella was here too. He took a deep breath and walked around to the front of the villa to face a barrage of cameras he ignored. Signora Visconti, Francesca's mother, greeted him at the door.

"Come in, Luca."

"It was a beautiful ceremony, *signora*."

"I agree, and your being here for Vincenzo means everything to him. He told me you'd be sitting with Dr. Zoller and his wife since you know him. Walk through the foyer to the left."

A dozen tables decorated with linen cloths and flowers filled the room. The guests had found their places. Luca made straight for the vet's table situated near the back. He had one friend here. Being with Daniel and his wife helped him to relax.

They'd just started to relive memories of Vincenzo and his dogs when Francesca's father stood up to make a speech. It forced Luca to look in that direction. He dreaded the sight of Bella sitting next to Prince Antonio. Out of the corner of his eye he saw her seated at a table with her cousin Prince Rinieri and his wife, Princess Luna. For some reason Prince Antonio wasn't with her. He wondered why, but figured the man had other princely duties to attend to.

The three of them radiated a kind of royal splendor that cut through him like a knife. Bella had matured into her princess world and had lost interest in Luca years ago. What an idiot to believe she'd ever yearned to see him again.

Just last evening Vincenzo had indicated that the Prince would be a great catch for his sister. He really liked him. That did it. Right now Luca had to force himself to concentrate on the meal being served.

Before long everyone made toasts, then it came Luca's inevitable turn. He'd come prepared and got to his feet with his champagne glass in hand.

"Dante once wrote that a great flame follows a little spark. Apparently there was more than a little spark the day Vincenzo took his sick dog, Karl, to the vet. One look at the gorgeous Dr. Linard and he was lit by the brightest light in the firmament."

"Francesca is that," Daniel whispered with a smile as Luca sat back down. "The clinic can't do without her. It's going to be a fight between me and Vince for her attention. We know who will win."

Luca nodded. Francesca adored her new husband. Lucky man.

Before long the ecstatic couple was ready to leave. Francesca turned and threw the bouquet behind her.

It fell into the hands of… Bella. Intentional or otherwise, that did it for Luca.

With his stomach churning, he left the room and hurried out to the side of the villa to call for a taxi. The rain had turned to drizzle. As soon as he could return to the hotel where he'd stayed the night, he would change his clothes and head for the airport.

Five minutes later he walked around to the front. The taxi turned into the drive at the same time. But before he could climb in the back, he felt a hand on his arm.

"May I ride with you?" sounded a trembling voice he would never forget.

CHAPTER TWO

BELLA HELD HER breath waiting for Luca to answer.

He turned, impaling her with those stunning green eyes that had haunted her dreams for years. "Is it allowed, Princess?" His cold, deep voice permeated to her insides, cutting her to the core.

She shivered, realizing how much he despised her, but she refused to run from him until she'd bared her soul. "After I ruined your life, you have every right to tell me to go to blazes."

His dark brows furrowed. "What are you talking about?"

"You know exactly what I did, Luca, and I've never gotten over it. Please hear me out," she begged. "I—"

"Signorina!" the driver exclaimed, interrupting her. "Are you coming or not?"

"Quick, Bella. We're blocking the other cars. Get in the taxi." Luca helped her with her gown and slid in next to her before closing the door. After telling the driver where to take them, he turned to her. "Start again from the beginning. Explain to me how you ruined my life. Whatever gave you that idea?" He sounded so matter-of-fact, she didn't know what to think.

"You don't have to pretend, Luca. We both know

you warned me not to go down Devil's Gulch, but I did it anyway to show off in front of you and prove I wasn't afraid."

"Wait a minute. *That's* what you're talking about? Something that happened so long ago I hardly remember?"

Tears gushed from her eyes. "How can you say that when I think about it every day!" she exploded in pain.

"Why?"

"Because of me you got caught in the avalanche that ended your skiing career. I'll never forgive myself for what I did."

"As I recall, I admired your fearlessness."

"You *couldn't* have. It was a facade anyway." Scalding tears kept running down her face, but she couldn't hold them back and needed to finish this apology. "When we heard the crack and saw what was coming from above, you skied down to help me. It was *my* willfulness that put your life in danger. I understand why you hate me so terribly and never came near."

"Never came near—" he murmured as if deep in thought. She thought he sounded bewildered. "Blame didn't come into it."

She heard the old caring Luca in his voice. Her heart wanted to believe him. "Of course it did. What I did ended your chance to ski in the Olympics. I'm *so* sorry." Bella forgot they weren't teenagers. She sobbed and buried her wet face in her hands, oblivious to everything but her need to ask his forgiveness.

"It was my choice to come after you."

"And look what happened—Mother told me they operated on your right leg all day, hoping to save it, but you would never ski again. You can't imagine the depth of my agony when I heard that. I tried to visit you while we were both in the hospital, but I wasn't allowed."

In the semidarkness, a look of real anger darkened those green orbs. "Who prevented you from coming to my room?"

Surprised at his fierce change in tone, she wiped her eyes. "Mother. She said—"

"We've arrived!" The driver broke in once again, sounding impatient. She hadn't realized they'd stopped in front of a hotel.

Luca grasped her hand. "Come on, Bella. We need privacy to talk."

She got out the best she could in her long brides-maid gown, breathing in the warm night air. Every-one outside stared at the two of them while he paid the driver. A few people took pictures with their phones. Still clutching her hand, they walked inside the hotel to the elevator. The guests stopped talking to watch them.

The elevator couldn't enclose them fast enough. Lu-ca's eyes played over her. "Don't be surprised if a pic-ture of us coming into the hotel is on the front page of tomorrow's news. How will you explain this to Prince Antonio? The news has hinted at a marriage between the two of you."

"We're not engaged yet, Luca. The journalists get away with speculation all the time, the way they al-ways do," she bit out. "Because of Vincenzo's wedding, today's pictures will be splashed all over anyway. I couldn't care less. My life has been a nightmare. What else is new?"

Not engaged yet? Why in heaven's name had Bella's life been a nightmare? It made no sense.

Luca took her to his suite on the third floor and shut the door. "The restroom is down the hall. While you freshen up, I'll get us something to drink. Do you still like cola?" They used to drink it when they went on picnics in the mountains.

She smiled at him. It lit up the dark places in his soul. "Always."

"It's nice to know some things don't change. Two colas coming up. Then we'll talk." He needed answers to questions he'd been waiting for all these years.

"Thank you. I'll be right back."

The fact that she'd never come near him or talked to him since that fateful day pretty well told its own story. He hadn't been on her mind, and it was a fact she *was* involved with a prince Vincenzo approved of. Despite her denials, there wasn't much more to be said. It shocked Luca that he could feel such jealousy at this point.

Impatient with himself, he disappeared into the bedroom and changed into a navy pullover and jeans. After a trip to the kitchenette for drinks, he went in the living room and sat down on the couch to wait for her.

When she came in, she stopped in her tracks. "It's not fair that you've changed into something comfortable."

"You're welcome to put on my robe. It's hanging on the back of the bathroom door." He hadn't meant it to sound provocative.

She flashed him a surprising grin. "I better not. What if there's a house fire and we have to evacuate? Imagine the shocking images spread all over the media."

He laughed. Bella's spirit was like no one else's and

she seemed surprisingly unchanged. More like the girl he'd once known and loved. She sat down in one of the upholstered chairs and put her small jeweled purse on the nearby end table. He'd placed her cola there and they both drank a little.

"Where's that fearlessness you displayed years ago?"

"I lost it on the day my actions meant you might not ever walk again. When I saw you enter the cathedral earlier today, I thanked God all over again that you could still stand on your own two legs. Your recovery is an answer to prayer."

Her anguish tore him up. He'd never forget how she'd broken down in the taxi. To be that close to her had been a torment for him. "What exactly did your mother say to prevent you from coming into my hospital room?"

"She said you'd been flown to England where a specialist could work on your leg and try to put it back together. The implication was that you still might lose it."

"Your mother told you *what*?" Luca shot to his feet, incredulous. "That was a lie!"

She stared up at him. "I—I don't understand," her voice faltered. "You weren't flown there?"

"Hell, no. I was right there in the hospital, frantically trying to call you from the pay phone since I'd lost my cell."

"*You* tried to phone me?"

"Of course. I wanted to know how you were. The doctor said you escaped with no broken bones, but I wanted to hear it from you. Unfortunately your phone wasn't working. I almost went out of my mind." When she didn't try to reach him, he'd assumed he wasn't that important to her. When he'd eventually talked to Vincenzo, he'd deflected any inquiries about his sister, until Luca finally got the message. It hurt soul deep.

"That's because I lost my cell in the avalanche too and my parents bought me a new one. I kept trying to phone you, but there was no service. My mind melted down completely," she lamented. "In desperation, I started writing you letters, but you never answered. I must have written sixty of them."

"Sixty—but then what...?"

"Yes. Finally I had to realize you despised me for what I'd done and so I stopped trying to reach you."

Luca stopped pacing because he believed her. "It's all starting to make a ghastly kind of sense."

"What do you mean?"

Over all these years, nothing was as he'd imagined. He turned to her. "Please go on. I want to hear the rest before I explain this riddle."

"Riddle?"

She really didn't know?

"Maybe *mystery* would be a better word."

Bella stared up at him. "When I asked mother how long you would have to be in England, she said you could be gone a year. She explained you would have to undergo rehabilitation."

"For a whole year?" He was incredulous.

"Yes," her voice quavered. "But when school ended in May and there was still no word from you, I believed you hated me for what I'd done. I couldn't bear it and believed that was why I never heard from you."

Luca bit out an epithet. "I could never hate you, Bella."

"Even so, I—I went into a depression," she stammered. "My parents booked a suite at the Chateau d'Ouchy on Lake Geneva and we vacationed there for a month with their friends. I spent time with Princess Constanza in Lausanne. They hoped the vacation would help, but it didn't."

"So *that's* where you went." His words sounded more like a hiss. "I saw one of the kitchen boys from the palace in town. He said you'd all gone on vacation, but he didn't know where."

Tears filled her eyes again. "The second we returned to Scuol, I sneaked out of the palace and went straight to the health clinic to see your father in the allergy department. Though I was forbidden to see you again and knew you hated me, I was determined to get answers about you even though I'd never met him."

So Bella *had* tried to see him too! His mind reeled. These revelations changed so many things for him, he was stunned. "What did you find out?" He held his breath.

"It turned out to be a very short trip because…because I learned that your family had *moved* from Scuol! No one in Dr. Torriani's old office knew where he'd gone. He'd left his practice with no forwarding address. It was as if you'd vanished off the face of the earth! I decided you wanted to get away from me after what I'd done."

Luca heard her agony, but didn't dare sweep her in his arms. If he did that, he'd never let her go. "I had no idea."

The sobs kept coming. She clutched at her gown. "After I went home to the palace in devastation, I ran to my parents' bedroom and demanded they tell me the truth. Do you know what Papa said?

"Bella, sweetheart—you must remember what we've told you. You are Princess Baldasseri, destined to marry the right prince. You're an adult now and must accept your fate."

A groan came out of Luca.

"From that moment on I realized my parents were in total charge and I wouldn't be allowed to see you ever again. I began to understand that Vincenzo must have been warned off too. It explained his silence. With Papa's words, it was as if the world I thought I'd known had blown up in my face."

"And mine," Luca whispered, needing desperately to comfort her. "There's no question we were both betrayed, but not by Vincenzo. No better man on earth exists. I have the gut feeling your parents and my father decided to intervene in our lives to get the job done."

"*Your* father—"

He nodded. "It took teamwork and had to be him. You never knew him. He's a good man who did everything for me. But if he'd been born royal, he would have invented the divine right of kings."

A half smile broke the corner of her delectable mouth. "I heard a lot of emotion behind that statement. Tell me."

"My *papa* married late and dominated my sweet mother, who couldn't have more children after I was born. His father was a doctor too. They made a good living. Papa was determined to support me to the best advantage—the best schools, the best education, the best friends.

"Everything went along fine until I met Vincenzo. Papa had an innate revulsion toward royalty and was furious that you and your brother were attending public school. He didn't consider royals to be a useful part of society."

"Your father had a point, Luca."

"Papa wouldn't believe it if he heard you say that."

"Not all of us are prigs."

Deep laughter came out of him. "The last thing he wanted was for me to have anything to do with your brother. But he couldn't stop me from being friends with him at school.

"One day I brought your brother to the house on his eleventh birthday. My father took one look at him and turned into someone I didn't know. It hurt me that he left the room without saying anything to him."

"How awful."

"It was. Mamma baked a cake for him as a favor to me. The three of us had a little party. She told me later that he didn't act like a prince and she loved him. In fact, she said that if she could have more children, she'd like one just like Vincenzo."

More tears came to Bella's eyes. "I love your mother without meeting her, Luca. She sounds wonderful."

"She is, and she would love you because you're like Vincenzo in many ways. But because of my father, you'll understand why I always played at the palace. Meeting you made it even more fun. I had the happiest childhood memories there that anyone could have had."

Bella sucked in her breath. "So did I. But it all ended on that horrible day." She looked into his eyes. "Tell me everything from the moment you got home from the hospital."

He checked his watch. Luca didn't know where to start and now wasn't the moment. "That'll take some time and I have a plane to catch. I should already have left for the airport. Vincenzo told me you're staying with the Visconti family so I need to take you back there on the way."

"Can't you stay until tomorrow?"

"I wish I could, but I have to be back for work in the morning."

"You work on a Sunday?"

"Sometimes. Tomorrow is one of those days. Why don't you finish your drink while I grab my suitcase. Then we'll go."

Bella walked over to the end table for her cola. She should be grateful to have had this much time to apologize to him. Her prayers had been answered. But the teenage Bella would have begged him to take her with him.

Except that you're not sixteen anymore, and Luca has been playing by the rules for the last ten years.

He'd stopped thinking about her a long time ago. She imagined he was involved with a gorgeous woman right now and anxious to get back to her. The lucky man didn't have photographers following his every step.

They took a taxi for the short trip back to the Visconti villa.

She couldn't stand it that he was leaving, but his reasons were none of her business. "Luca? Before you go, I have to know about your leg. How bad was it? I want the truth."

"It did require some surgery but my surgeon was a genius and I recovered quickly. I can still ski if I want to, just not competition."

"Honestly?" she cried for joy. "You have no idea

how happy that makes me. If you'd had the opportunity, I know you would have become an Olympian."

"It would have been exciting for a while, yet it was more my father's dream than mine."

"You're his only son."

"Just as you are your mother's only daughter. We both know her dream for you. Maybe you're not engaged to Prince Antonio yet, but I imagine it will happen any time soon. Vincenzo says he's a good man. That means a lot. And I noticed Francesca's bridal bouquet was tossed at you."

Trying to convince Luca of anything was like talking to a rock wall. "That was bad aim on her part since it was meant for Gina, not me." They reached the villa way too soon and she was frantic. "There are still so many questions I want to ask you, but I know I should be grateful you've given me this much of your time."

"I'm sorry I have to rush away, Bella."

"Please don't apologize."

After the driver pulled to a stop, Luca told him to wait while he helped Bella get out. They walked to the entrance. She wanted to fling herself in his arms and never let him go.

To her surprise, he suddenly reached in his wallet and pulled out a business card he handed to her. "Perhaps this will answer some of those questions. *Adia*, Bella," he said in Romansh. *"Buna fortuna."*

Good luck in the future?

Clearly he didn't expect them to meet again. He'd moved on with his life.

Dying inside, she watched him stride on those long powerful legs to the taxi and get in. After it drove away taking her heart, she rang the bell. Rolf, Francesca's brother, opened the door with his usual smile.

"Bella—come on in. Gina and I wondered where you disappeared to."

"I spent a little time with Luca. He just brought me back on his way to the airport. Where's Gina?"

"In the study. My parents have gone to bed."

"That sounds good to me too. You go back to Gina. I'm going upstairs to change out of this gown."

Once in her room, she sat down on the side of the bed to look at the card clutched in her hand.

Luca Torriani, MD
Sports Medicine
Julier Medical Clinic
Suite 6
Saint Moritz, Switzerland

It gave the clinic's business number.

All this time Luca had only been an hour away, and he'd become a doctor, *just like his father.* She felt like she'd been stabbed all over again.

After these many years of wondering, the card did answer where Luca lived and worked, but she knew nothing about his personal life. She spent the rest of the night in utter turmoil.

The chauffeur drove Luca to the Bern Belp Airport. It had done wonders for him that Bella had appeared upset because he'd been forced to leave. Those violet eyes of hers had pled with him to stay. The drive away from her constituted a fresh new agony.

During his flight back to Saint Moritz, Switzerland,

he went over every detail of their conversation in his mind. Luca now understood the cruel thing their families had done to keep them apart. When he'd never heard from Bella again, he'd been forced to accept what had happened. He was a commoner and could never be Bella's choice. She'd been forced to accept the situation too. Since the avalanche, they hadn't seen or talked to each other. *Not until tonight.*

It tugged at him that she'd wanted to keep talking, but he'd had to pull away to catch this flight. The pain in her eyes had prompted him to give her his business card. What she did or didn't do with it was up to her.

He drove back to his apartment and checked his messages before going to bed. But getting any sleep was futile while he tried to fit the missing pieces of a ten-year puzzle together. They all led back to their parents' subterfuge. By morning he'd reached the boiling point.

After getting through his hospital rounds, he received a text from his mother. His parents expected him for Sunday dinner that evening. He knew what his father wanted. Luca was sick to death of his watchdog tactics. The bullying and rage may have subsided to some degree, but his father was like a hunting dog, always on point.

His parent had been furious that Luca had agreed to be part of Vincenzo's wedding party. It didn't take a genius to realize what was really going on in the older man's mind. His fears of Luca and Bella getting together had dominated his father's life ever since Luca had met Vincenzo in grade school. Luca decided to drive over to their house now and have it out with them.

"Mamma?" he called out after letting himself in.

"Ah, Luca—you're back from Bern!" She came running into the living room from the kitchen to hug him. "This is much better than a text. Come in the kitchen and I'll fix you some lunch."

"I'd rather stay right here." He drew her to the couch. "Where's Papa?"

"He ran to the store for some pipe tobacco after I got home from church. He'll be back soon. How was the wedding?"

"Incredible, but right now the three of us need to talk about what happened ten years ago."

Her smile faded and a haunted look crossed over her face, but she said nothing.

"After the wedding, I spent time with Bella. We pieced everything together. I now know that our two families purposely kept us apart all these years."

Tears filled her eyes. "Luca—" She pressed his arm. "I didn't know anything about what your father and Bella's mother did until Vincenzo came to see me a few years after you left for the States. He loves you and felt it wrong that I never knew. I loved him for telling me the truth, but by then the damage had been done to you and Bella. I didn't want to dredge it all up for you then, not after so much time had passed."

Luca hugged her against him. "I couldn't believe you had any part in it."

"What the two of them did went against God. Your father did a terrible thing by tearing up the letters Bella wrote to you. He told Bella's mother triumphantly—that's how Vincenzo found out about it. I am so ashamed of his actions. He never learned about Vincenzo's visit, but I've been in pain ever since. You know I love you heart and soul and have only wanted your happiness."

"Grazie Dio." He rocked her in his arms. His father had torn up Bella's heart and Luca's. "You have to know how much I love you. Thank you for telling me about the letters and Vincenzo, but you need to understand I'm not letting Papa or Bella's mother rule my life ever again."

"That's good, *figlio mio*. It's wonderful that you and Bella have reconnected. Live your life the way God intended—the way *I* always wanted you to live it." She kissed his cheek.

"That I plan to do. Forgive me if I don't come for dinner. I have other plans for today. I'll call you tomorrow." After another hug, he left the house and drove to his apartment to change clothes. The thought of being inside four walls would be unbearable.

CHAPTER THREE

THE BRIGHT SUN practically blinded Luca as he headed for the mountains. He reached for his sunglasses and took off. As he turned onto the main road, his phone rang. No doubt his father wanted to know why he wasn't coming for dinner and would insist Luca drop by at some point.

Luca had anticipated this latest response and let his phone ring.

Though seeing Bella again had turned Luca inside out, the truth remained that she'd moved on. For that reason, his father's worries made no sense, yet the ringing didn't stop. He reached for the phone to decline the call. But he caught himself in time when he saw the caller ID. It was the clinic's answering service. He clicked on. "This is Dr. Torriani."

"I have a patient needing to talk to you. She said it's an emergency, yet hung up before leaving her name. Here's the number."

He made a note and phoned it. One of his patients had to be in trouble.

"Luca?" a familiar voice sounded.

His heart leaped into his throat. "Bella?" Handing

her his card had been an experiment of sorts. He hadn't expected a response this fast.

"Yes! I'm so glad you answered. I'm in Saint Moritz at the train station."

She was here? He shook his head in disbelief. "Say that again."

"I know this is a surprise. I flew to Chur early this morning, then took the Bernina Express, knowing it would pass through Saint Moritz. It'll be leaving to go on to Pontresina in about fifteen minutes. I wondered if you have enough time to take the train with me that far so we can talk. We didn't have enough time last night. Would it be possible, or do you have other plans?"

Luca was so blown away to hear from her, he didn't stop to consider anything else. "I will leave for the station now."

"That's wonderful!" she cried. "When you walk through the train car, you'll see me wearing a slouchy black winter hat and sunglasses." All that glorious blond hair covered up made sense. Otherwise, the photojournalists would notice her immediately. She thought of everything!

"I'll be in a sage-colored crew neck sweater."

"I'd know you anywhere."

Bella. "See you soon." He clicked off, stunned that she was in Saint Moritz, that she'd dared to reach out to him knowing what could happen. He'd thought she'd be traveling back to the palace with her family once they left Bern.

After he'd parked at the station, he went inside and bought a first-class round-trip ticket. He had no idea where to find her as he hurried out to the platform.

The only thing to do was climb on board and walk from car to car.

In the next-to-the-last car, he spotted her. No matter how she'd disguised herself, Bella was an absolute knockout and every male eye noticed her. She wore black pants and a fitted short-sleeved black top with gold buttons that hugged her waist. If she saw him, she gave no indication. He knew her bodyguard from the palace followed her everywhere, day or night.

The car was full except for one vacant seat opposite her on the side of the aisle. Somehow, she'd arranged it. He sat down and the train took off for Pontresina. Outside the window he saw the passing landscape of the Engadin.

She sat forward. "I'm so thrilled you answered your phone and could come with me. It was a chance in a million."

"It worked." He smiled at her breathlessness. "You know, of course, your mother will be told what you're doing."

"That doesn't matter. Why don't we sit back and enjoy the scenery out of these gigantic windows? A trolley is coming by if you want a drink."

"I'm not thirsty yet. I thought you'd still be with your family."

"After being with you such a short time last night, Luca, I needed more time to talk with you. I had to hope that your business card meant you might want to talk too. But if this causes complications for you because of a woman you're involved with, I totally understand."

Luca had never known anyone more honest. He sucked in his breath, ignoring her comment about another woman. "I did hope we could talk again down the road."

"But you didn't expect me to take it several forbidden steps further. Today is a case in point, and now that I've come, you don't know what to do with me."

Her frankness took his breath. If only she knew what was going on inside of him. "How did you happen to fly to Chur?"

"It's a long story. I'll tell you everything later. Here comes the trolley. I'll grab a cola."

Out of the corner of Luca's eye, he watched her drink. Everything she said and did had always fascinated him. Nothing had changed for him where she was concerned. Ten years had turned her from the girl he'd loved into the woman he desired beyond all else.

"Let's hear your long story."

She still wore her sunglasses, but he knew she was staring at him. "I wanted to see you again, so I convinced the family that I had important work to do and took a roundabout way of meeting you."

What important work?

"It was a risk to myself, of course, but by some miracle you were available. I don't think my bodyguard has figured it out quite yet. He's assuming I have business in Pontresina as well as Chur. What's nice is that I have friends there I've done business with before."

That sounded like the adventurous and creative Bella he'd always been crazy about. "So what's the plan?"

"When we reach Pontresina, I'm taking a taxi to Oberengadin Hospital, where I've met people in the past. You come in the front entrance after I've been inside a few minutes. There's a drinking fountain around the corner to the left on the ground floor. I'll send someone to show you where I'll be."

She recrossed her long legs, drawing his attention to the fabulous way she looked. "I think it's time to change the subject to something happy. What were you going to do today?"

"Go for a hike."

"That sounds like heaven."

"I'm perfectly content to be here with you, Bella."

"I feel the same way. We'll be getting off any second now."

Luca had been in Pontresina before, hiking with friends. As they arrived in the alpine village surrounded by pine trees giving off a pungent scent, the train slowed to a stop.

Bella got up. "See you in a few minutes."

Luca couldn't take his eyes off her womanly figure. He waited until she'd disappeared from sight before leaving the car himself. After looking around outside, there was no sign of Bella. Most likely her bodyguard had already followed her to the hospital. Luca found a taxi that drove him there.

A smile broke out on his face. Even though he knew she was being watched, this cloak-and-dagger stuff had started to appeal to him. Luca hadn't had this much fun in ages. When his father heard about it, he'd erupt, but Luca was impervious to him. He walked inside and found the drinking fountain around the corner.

"Dr. Torriani?" He turned to the thirtyish female wearing a white hospital coat. "If you'll follow this hallway to the end and turn to the left, there's an examination room on your right where your party is waiting."

"Thank you."

When he reached the said room, he knocked on the door and Bella let him inside. He shut the door and they sat down. "You know we're not fooling anyone, don't you, Princess? Word will get back to Prince Antonio that you've been with me twice since the wedding. Isn't that living a little dangerously, even for you?"

The moment the words came out, she stiffened and he knew he'd offended her.

"Maybe, but it gives security something to do. I'll face the consequences later."

"How will you get to Scuol?"

Her softly rounded chin lifted. "In my royal helicopter waiting here in back for me."

He grimaced. "I've upset you. You know I didn't mean to and I apologize."

She stared at him, but he could see her lower lip trembling and wanted to kiss it quiet.

"You can't help it can you, Luca. You haven't forgiven me, and my title is so ingrained in you, I'm lit up in neon lights where you're concerned. Unfortunately, this foolish escapade of mine will cause you more distress once your father hears about it, and he will."

"Bella—" he said on a groan. "Forget my father and listen to me. I could have refused to meet you at the station and that would have been the end of it. After seeing each other last night, we both know we need to talk again."

"Really? Or are you just here because you and Vincenzo are blood brothers? You don't want to upset me because you know it will upset him."

His jaw tautened. "This isn't about Vincenzo."

"I hardly think it's about me, his little sister. You're too saintly for that."

He cringed. "Saintly? Be honest. You and I have always had a special connection."

"Maybe *gentlemanly* would be the better word. You see me as a 'special' friend. I threw myself at you in high school and you handled it with mastery. How you must have dreaded Vincenzo's wedding! You knew I'd be there. Only your love for my brother would have caused you to put up with me again. I'm the woman who ruined your chances for Olympic fame, let alone damaged your leg forever. You'll never get over it."

He couldn't believe they were having this conversation again. "I thought we'd resolved all that." He shook his head. "You have a picture of our situation that's completely wrong." Her lack of interest in him after the avalanche had kept him away from her, nothing else.

"I don't think so," she came back. "Your father was right to move your family to Saint Moritz without telling a single soul. He knew what he was doing so the princess couldn't find you. *I* am that said princess, my most hated word in any language. From the moment I was conceived, it became a birthright I haven't been able to escape."

"Stop, Bella—" he blurted in frustration.

"I *can't* stop. Hear me out, Luca. You were born a Torriani, with the title of doctor, son of a doctor. Our two paths were never meant to cross, let alone converge. Forgive me for having phoned you. It was a mistake."

"Why would I have to forgive you for anything when *I* was the one who gave you *my* card?"

"It doesn't matter."

"But it does, and I have something vital to tell you." In fact the matter of the destroyed letters would crucify her.

She shook her head. "It's too late. Goodbye, Luca."

Bella jumped up to leave, but Luca grabbed her and pulled her close. "If you won't listen to words, maybe you'll understand this." He lowered his head and his mouth closed over hers in a long passionate kiss. He'd dreamed of this moment for so long, he refused to let her go. She eventually pulled out of his arms, leaving both of them breathless. "Think about that while you're in flight, Bella."

She flew out of the room. Luca could have run after her, but there were people in the hall. This hospital was no place for the no-holds-barred conversation he needed to have with her. Bella's white-hot pain had been building since the avalanche. He understood it because his pain had also reached its zenith.

He heard the helicopter lift off. When it was out of ear sound, he took the short train trip back to Saint Moritz. It gave him time to plan his next move. She needed to know what his mother had verified about the letters, including Vincenzo's visit with the truth. Now would be a good time to send her a text.

The helicopter flew Bella back to the palace that evening. Luca's unexpected, consuming kiss had turned her world inside out. She trembled the whole way home, trying to understand where it had come from.

As she hurried into the palace and raced up the stairs, her mother called to her. No... Not now. But she had to kiss her and the grandparents good-night.

As soon as she could, she hurried to her suite to get ready for bed.

Before climbing under the covers, she reached for her phone. Her heart almost jumped out of her chest when she saw a text from Luca.

When she'd left his arms and had run outside the hospital to the helicopter, she hadn't known what to expect. With hands shaking, she clicked on his text.

Bella. I believe you meant it when you said goodbye to me today. I also meant it when I said you have a picture of our situation that's completely wrong. Of course I think of you as a special friend, but there's a lot more to it than that. That kiss should have told you something! If you ever *want* to know more, you know where to find me.

Bella read and reread it. Did she truly have a faulty picture of their relationship? His kiss had felt so real, she knew she'd never get to sleep and decided to call her *nonna* in Sardinia. It wasn't too late.

"I'm so happy you've phoned me, *bimba*." That was the Italian endearment she'd always used with Bella. "I want to hear about the wedding," she said between deep coughs Bella didn't like.

They talked for a while, but her grandmother Caderina's voice sounded trembly and feeble. Maybe she shouldn't have called her. "I wish you could have been there and I miss you, Nonna. How are you? You don't sound well."

"I'm all right. Don't worry about me." More coughing ensued. "What's going on to cause the deep pain I hear in your voice? Problems with Prince Antonio?"

"No. Nothing like that. After Vincenzo's wedding

reception at the Visconti villa, I met with Luca last night, and again today in Saint Moritz."

"Ah."

Yes, ah. "It's been ten years and—" But that was all Bella managed to get out before she broke down sobbing. "Oh, Nonna—I've made such a fool of myself I want to die.

"We had enough time to figure out my parents and his father purposely kept us apart for the last ten years. But as for everything else, my head is a mess. Mother wants me to marry Antonio. He's a wonderful man, but I can't say yes to his proposal yet. Not when I feel the way I do over Luca." Her whole face glistened with moisture.

"And how *do* you feel?"

"The truth is, if I can't be with him, I'll never be happy again."

"Does Luca feel the same about you?"

"I don't know. He kissed me, really kissed for the first time this afternoon. Now I'm in agony."

"Why?"

"Because I don't know if it meant to him what it meant to me. I engineered both meetings. Luca thinks I'm marrying Tonio. I'm so confused I could die."

"But remember, *bimba*—" Bella had to wait for another coughing spasm from her grandmother to subside. "He was willing to risk seeing you twice since the ceremony. Doesn't that tell you anything?"

"Yes, that he doesn't want to offend me. I would give anything on earth if I hadn't been born a princess. You probably think I'm horrible to say that."

"Of course I don't. If you dislike it that much, then do something about it."

Bella swallowed hard. "You wouldn't hate me for it?"

Her grandmother laughed and coughed. "I love you no matter what. You're in charge of your own life, *bimba*. As for Luca, if his kiss made your dreams come true, he meant it. I liked him very much during the times I met him at the palace with your brother. He has a strength about him I admire. Why don't you put him to the ultimate test and see what happens?"

Bella sat up in the bed. "What kind?"

"That's for you to figure out." There was too much coughing now. "You're a clever girl and will find a way." At this point her grandmother could hardly speak.

"Nonna? We've talked too long and you're ill. I'll call you again soon. Right now you need to rest your voice. I love you more than you know. God keep you."

Worried about her grandmother's health, she clicked off before getting under the covers. But in the back of her mind, her *nonna's* admonitions kept taunting her. *Put Luca to the ultimate test.* What kind? What did she mean?

For the rest of the night she tossed and turned reliving their kiss, and trying to figure out what Luca had really meant. At five in the morning, she got out of bed and wrote a special email to her great uncle King Leonardo. Her *nonna* had given her the courage.

As for Luca, she would seek him out again, but this time new tactics were called for. Her grandmother had challenged her to put Luca to the ultimate test. That was exactly when she intended to do.

On Friday of that week, Luca had just finished up with his last patient and was dreading the empty weekend when there was a knock on the door. "Dr. Torriani?"

He recognized the voice of the receptionist who'd

been hired four months ago. Luca had lost count of the times she'd come back to his office when she knew he was alone. It couldn't go on. He felt minus zero attraction. "*Si*, Adele?"

"I can come again if you're still busy."

"I'm afraid I am. Next time, just buzz me if there's an emergency."

"I don't know if there is one or not." He blinked. "A woman came into the office just now. She doesn't have an appointment and didn't give her name. Dr. Glatz upstairs is still in the building and would be willing to see her, but this woman was insistent it had to be the sports medicine doctor."

Could it possibly be Bella? His heart raced. "I'll come."

Luca got up from his desk and walked out of his office to reception. The second his eyes fastened on Bella standing there, his heart rocked him like a sledgehammer. After that fiery kiss, it had only taken her five days to respond to his text in person. He could breathe again, but for her sake he needed to keep up the pretense of knowing nothing in front of the receptionist.

She had pulled her glorious dark blond hair back and tied it at the nape with a brown-and-white-print scarf. The style revealed her oval face and high cheekbones. With eyes the color of the sweet violets that grew above the palace in Scuol, she was beauty personified.

Her scarf matched the white blouse with its elbow-length sleeves and chocolate brown linen pants. Brown leather sandals adorned her feet. At five foot seven, Bella was a picture of casual elegance only she could carry off. He feared he might need Dr. Glatz in cardiology.

"I remember seeing you at the wedding," he exclaimed in front of Adele, who stared with a mutinous expression at the two of them.

Bella flashed an illuminating smile. "We were never introduced. I'm Alectrona Cossu." *What?* The sun goddess in Greek mythology? He'd seen paintings of her. Bella looked a lot like her with her long blond hair, and was a hundred times more breathtaking. "Rolf told me you worked here, but I couldn't recall your name."

Pay attention, Luca. "Dr. Torriani."

"From the prominent nobles of the Torriani family in Piedmont?"

"Not the same patriarchal line."

"That explains why you're not an architect or sculptor. But I'm thrilled you're the renowned doctor Rolf told me about."

"He's paid to say that."

Her familiar chuckle delighted him. "I happened to be in this area on business and know a child who's in dire need of your particular skills." The reference to business intrigued him. "Will you forgive me for intruding on your work long enough to make an appointment?"

Luca spread his arms. "As you can see, there are no more patients. Come in my office and we'll talk about it."

He glanced at the receptionist. *"Buon weekend, Adele."*

"E tu, Dottore," she said through gritted teeth.

They walked down the hall to his office. Once inside, he shut the door hardly able to believe she'd come. "Finally we have the time and space to talk about the things we didn't have time for last weekend, Bella."

She walked around studying his diplomas on the wall while he studied her tantalizing figure. "Columbus, Ohio. You spent all those years in the States studying medicine. You were so far away," her voice trembled. He felt it to his bones.

"Not all. If you'll notice the document behind my desk, I ended up in Freiburg, Germany, to do my residency."

She turned to him. "How long have you practiced here?"

"A year and a half."

She gave him a searching gaze. "What brought you to Saint Moritz?"

"You mean *who*. As soon as I was ready to go into practice, my father suggested I join a medical group here looking for a sports medicine doctor."

He heard her mind working. "Don't tell me. Your parents moved to Saint Moritz ten years ago."

Luca nodded. "He and Mamma bought a home with an office where he sees patients. But enough about me. Why don't you sit down and tell me what you've been doing all these years while I've been away from my favorite place on earth."

She subsided into a chair near his desk. "You mean our own Garden of Eden?"

Their eyes fused. "Where else?"

"It's still my favorite place too, Luca."

The two of them loved to hike to a special grassy spot above the palace beneath arching tree branches full of leaves. Walking underneath made them feel like they'd entered a cathedral. There'd been something magical, even spiritual about it where they'd seen red deer wander through.

His brows arched. "Have you gone there often?"

She gazed at him through half-veiled lids. "Not since the last time you and I saw two adorable mountain hares living there."

Cherished memories made this conversation hurt too much. He perched on a corner of his desk. "What's the latest news from the palace?"

"Well, the honeymooners are in paradise, and Vincenzo's former intended is going to marry the palace guard with whom she fell in love."

"Sometimes good things do happen to the right people."

She nodded. "*Sometimes* being the operative word."

Bella, Bella. "Getting back to you, I want to catch up. I take it you finished high school. So, what did you do next?"

"Princess Constanza and I grew closer. Our parents had fits when we told them we wanted to attend college in Geneva to learn marketing management. They said a princess didn't do that kind of work. We told them we were living in the modern age and needed some skills in case the revolution came."

Luca burst into laughter. "I can hear you saying it. Only you would think of it. Did you prevail?"

"Yes, but we couldn't neglect our princess duties or avoid meeting suitable future husbands."

His lungs froze. "Prince Antonio for example."

"Yes. Among others."

Of course. Bella's comment did nothing to help his troubled state of mind. "Tell me what you did after graduation."

"We went to work for a regional manufacturing company."

Incredibile. "You're a wonder, Bella. I'm totally impressed. Are you still working there?"

"No. After a while we both turned in our resignations. She wanted to work in her family's robotic business. I planned to work for my family's timber company. I talked it over with Vincenzo and learned we Swiss don't really export wood, so there was no market for me to build or expand the business outside the country. By then my parents insisted I head some charities and put my new skills to work organizing fundraising events."

She'd aroused his curiosity. "You mentioned you were here on business. Last weekend you indicated the same thing."

"*Princess* business, but I didn't want to draw attention in front of your fascinated receptionist."

"Your instincts were right on. Several days a week my father drops in to see me on my lunch hour and has developed a friendship with Adele. His motives are embarrassingly transparent."

Bella's eyes flashed purple. "I can see why. She's a lovely brunette who couldn't take her eyes off you. It wouldn't surprise me if he's hoping to get the two of you together."

"It'll never happen."

"Because someone else has captured your heart?"

His pulse raced. "Could be."

An impish smile broke the corner of her luscious mouth. "All your father needs to hear is that I paid you a visit today."

His father would find out before long. He had the instincts of a bloodhound. Luca got to his feet. "That reminds me. How did you come to be Alectrona Cossu?"

"I'm amazed Vincenzo never let it slip."

"What do you mean?"

"I was named Princess Bella Alectrona Cossu Baldasseri. My grandmother on my mother's side is a princess from the House of Cossu on Sardinia."

"I know," Luca murmured. "Vincenzo and I talked to her on several occasions when she visited with your family. She had a warmth that made it fun to be with her."

"Now you know why I love her so much. She's been an invalid and isn't expected to live much longer. I talked to her last week and she has a horrible cough that means she could be verging on pneumonia."

"I'm sorry to hear that."

"It really frightened me."

He heard the concern in her voice. "Maybe you need to fly there and see her."

"I plan to."

He cocked his head. "You still haven't explained about Alectrona."

"My mother wanted me to have the name Alectrona because she loves Greek mythology. My father wanted to call me Bella."

"I don't know why *you* couldn't have told me all that years ago."

"Because it's too many names and ghastly. I'd rather be Bella, plain and simple. You should hear Constanza's royal name. It's longer and worse than mine."

Bella had always made him laugh. Every time he was with her, he felt a renewal of life. "When did you get here?"

"I flew in on the helicopter this afternoon. The family thinks I flew to Lausanne to see Constanza. Once

I checked into a hotel, I took a taxi here not knowing if you'd be available."

Maybe he was dreaming, "How long can you stay?"

"I have to fly back to the palace tomorrow morning. I'm helping Mamma with my grandfather's eighty-eighth birthday party."

The weekend he'd been dreading was back on again. Luca only had tonight to be with her and explain certain facts. He removed his white coat and hung it in the closet. "We haven't begun to talk. Are you hungry?"

"I am now."

"I'll drive us to a place outside town. They serve skewered beef, *pizzocheri* and truffle fondue to die for. We'll leave by the rear entrance. My car is parked in the private lot in back."

CHAPTER FOUR

BELLA HAD TAKEN up Luca's offer to contact him. Now she intended to find out what had been behind that kiss.

She followed him out to his car, an older-model blue Alpha Romeo sedan. "I remember you and Vincenzo always loved talking about Italian cars like this one. You've remained loyal."

"It's been a reliable car." He helped her in the passenger side. Once she'd buckled up, he drove them out of the alpine resort town of five thousand to a tiny village higher up in the mountains.

Saint Moritz had always been known as a winter paradise, but September had to be the perfect time of year to enjoy the fall before snow started to appear. Being alone with Luca like this was so exciting, she felt feverish.

They wound around a more isolated area and pulled up to a small off-road restaurant that looked more like a cottage. Half a dozen cars were clustered around. He parked the car.

"This is a surprise, Luca. You would never know it's here."

"Alf's is Saint Moritz's best-kept secret. Most tourists don't know about it. That's why I like it."

Her gaze swerved to his. "How did you find it?"

"I've had a patient whose parents own it. When I can't stand my own cooking, I eat at the hospital cafeteria, drop in at the folks or come here."

"Where do you live?"

"In an apartment near my office."

Bella would give anything to see it, but he would have to ask her. They both got out of the car and walked to the entrance. She ached for him to take her arm, anything—but he was careful not to touch her. All she could think about now was Luca's mouth on hers with nothing to prompt it except years of suppressed desire on her part. And his? She needed to find out.

"Luca? *Bainvegni! Co voi?*" A welcoming male voice spoke Romansh as they walked inside. Bella watched a bearded, middle-aged man wearing an apron hurry over and hug Luca hard. A pair of warm blue eyes stared at Bella. "Aren't you Pri—"

"A business associate," Luca cut in. "Alf Engen, meet Signorina Cossu. She's here on important business. Is your truffle fondue on tonight's menu?"

"Always for you, along with Barolo wine. Come with me."

The diners ate in booths shaped like horse-drawn sleighs. Bella smiled at Luca. "This place is as charming as the owner. No wonder you like to come here. He cares for you very much. Tell me about your patient."

"Alf Jr. is a star hockey player. Last year he incurred an AC shoulder injury and the doctor wanted to operate. I was consulted and worked with him. No operation was needed and now he's ready to play this season."

"You worked your magic."

"Dr. Torriani!" another male voice broke in on them.

She turned her head to see an attractive dark blond guy in his twenties headed for their booth with their wine and fondue. "Papa said you were here with a blonde goddess. For once he wasn't exaggerating."

His eyes, a sea blue like his father's, studied her with embarrassing male interest before serving them. "I understand you're here on business. How long are you going to be in Saint Moritz? I'm free every night."

Luca actually frowned. "Slow down, Alf. I'm afraid Signorina Cossu has other calls on her time."

"I don't doubt it, but since I have an in with you, how about cutting me a break. What are you doing tomorrow, *signorina*?"

"Tomorrow she'll be busy." Luca's quick, less-friendly answer sent darts of delight through her body.

Alf grinned. "As long as it's not with you, Doc, I can handle it until she's free." His gaze swerved to hers once more. "Where are you staying?"

"With her associates," came the pointed answer.

"Okay, Doc. I was only asking. *Guten appetit.*" He winked at Bella.

When he'd disappeared, she looked at Luca. "He's a handful."

Luca swallowed his wine. "Does this happen with every male you meet?"

She took a sip of hers. He sounded jealous. "I was going to ask you a similar question. In case you didn't know, I planned my visit to your office hoping you'd still be there, and alone. Does every good-looking female staff member stick around after hours, praying you'll take them home?"

"Praying? Your choice of words breaks me up, Bella. Why don't we change the subject? If you were able to stay in Saint Moritz tomorrow, I'd ask you to take a hike with me. I thought we'd follow the Fuorcla Surlej trail. You'd love all the meadows and wildflowers. Further up you'd see the Tschierva glacier."

"Stop!" she cried with a smile. "You're torturing me." It *was* torture to hear his plans for them if she could stay. She ate the last of her food and finished her wine. "Please tell the owners that's the best fondue I've ever eaten."

"I'm glad you enjoyed it." He put some money on the table. "Let's go while it's still busy around here. Otherwise, I won't be able to get rid of you-know-who so easily."

Bella noticed that since Luca's former patient hadn't returned, it appeared he'd gotten the message. You didn't mess with Luca.

Relieved to be back in the car, Luca drove them into Saint Moritz, the playground of athletes and the affluent including royals like Bella's family. Night had fallen. He chose an isolated spot along the shore of Lake Saint Moritz.

"I brought you here because we can't go to my apartment or your hotel room. The pictures of you with me would be plastered all over the news tomorrow. I don't want to be the man to upset the royal family."

"And your father."

"He doesn't run my life any longer. That's all over. I had a private talk with my mother last Sunday. She had no idea what my father and your mother did until Vincenzo told her."

"*My* brother?"

"Yes. While I was in Ohio, he went to her out of love

for all of us. I knew deep down she wasn't responsible. She admitted she's been very unhappy with my father ever since." He had yet to tell Bella about the letters his father had torn up. Luca didn't have the heart to tell her that yet.

"Oh, Luca. The poor thing."

"It's a great relief to know the truth. That's why a day in the mountains would have been the prescription for what ails us."

"Except we don't have a disease that can be fixed that way," she reasoned. "We were cruelly torn apart by forces beyond our control at the time so we couldn't even say goodbye. But that doesn't have to be the case now, does it?"

His heart thudded. "What's on your mind?"

"We're both over twenty-one and in charge of our own lives. We're free to live the way we want. Do you think you could get away from your work next weekend? At least for one night?"

"You mean like old times," he murmured.

"Not exactly like that since Vincenzo won't be with us. I always wanted to camp out alone with you." Something was going on with Bella he didn't understand, but he was excited about it. "We'll eat the fish we catch, study the constellations with your telescope and visit our own Garden of Eden to see if the mountain hares are still living there."

Good heavens… This woman had turned into temptation itself, heedless of the consequences to her. He had no magic power to erase her from his consciousness and didn't want to. Over those early years Bella had become part of his DNA.

He turned to her. "I'll come to Scuol next Saturday and go home Sunday." It was only a fifty-five-mile drive. "If you can find a way to meet me at the Garage Lishana on La Via de la Staziun at nine a.m., we'll leave for the mountains from there."

"Isn't that where you had a part-time job?"

"You know it is. For a couple of years, yes. I'll bring all the gear we'll need."

Her eyes glowed purple fire. "I'll tell Mother I have to be away overnight on official business. Then I'll leave my car for a checkup and get in your car."

"Official business, eh? I'm waiting to be enlightened."

"Have you got all night?" She sounded serious rather than playful, arousing his curiosity no end.

"Unfortunately, no. I still have patients I need to call before it gets any later. But next Saturday I want to hear it all."

"You may be sorry. Please don't let me hold you up any longer, Luca. I'm staying at the Badrutt's Palace Hotel."

He started the car again and drove to the center of the town. "A ton of journalists hang around there waiting for celebrities to show up and make their day. One sight of Princess Baldasseri with a local will create a frenzy."

"Which is why I'll ask you to drop me off at that next corner. I'll walk the rest of the way."

"I'll follow you in the car until I see you're safely inside."

"Don't worry about me. My bodyguard is always following me, and I carry this in my purse for protection." She pulled out a pocket-sized version of bear spray even though there weren't any.

She needed that kind of protection. "Whoa." Luca laughed. "If Alf Jr. had any idea." He pulled over to the curb.

Bella put it back in her purse with a smile and looked over at him. "I've had the most wonderful evening in ten years. Thank you from the bottom of my heart. You'll never know how much I've needed to see you for closure."

But Luca *did* know, having suffered from the same agony. He leaned across her to open the passenger door. Her fragrance assailed him. "I'll see you next Saturday." On their campout he'd tell her what happened to the letters.

She rolled those fabulous violet eyes. "We can hope, but after our history, there could be interference. I won't believe it until I see you again face-to-face."

He couldn't let her go like this, not after remembering what had happened ten years ago. "I'll give you a call if something untoward comes up."

She placed her hand in his, he lightly touched his lips to the top of it. Releasing her fingers, he continued, "If both our phones are stolen for some inexplicable reason, we know where to find each other." He sat back, loving it that he could just look at her after all these years.

"*Arrivederci*, Luca."

Once she crossed the street, every male in sight watched her as she headed for the famous old hotel. He kept driving and heard wolf whistles until she'd disappeared inside, then he headed for his apartment.

After returning some calls to patients, he opened his storage unit and took inventory of his camping equipment. Most weekends he stayed up in the mountains.

He had a double sleeping bag, but would buy a new one for her. Everything else he had on hand. The question now was how to stand it until he saw her again next Saturday.

At noon on Wednesday, Luca went to the sporting goods store he often frequented, this time to check out sleeping bags engineered for women. He found a quilted rectangular bag that could turn into a down-filled blanket. Bella would love it. He carried it down the aisle to the sales guy at the counter who usually waited on him.

"Hey, Doc. Nice choice in blue," he commented and wrapped it up. "For your girlfriend?"

Luca gave him his credit card. "For a friend."

"Yeah?" The other guy's eyes twinkled as he put in the numbers and handed it back to him. "Have fun."

He walked out to the car with his purchase and headed for the office. When he pulled into his space, he carried the bag inside just to keep it safe in case someone broke into his car. It had happened before when someone was looking for drugs.

Adele eyed him immediately. "Your father is in your office. He's been waiting for you," she said in an accusatory manner.

"Thank you."

He strode down the hall and entered his office. His dark-haired father with silver showing at the temples glanced at the purchase. "It looks like you've been shopping at Wasescha Sport. I thought we had a lunch date."

Luca put the bag in the corner by his desk. "So we did, Papa. I forgot it was Wednesday. I'm sorry."

"Your mother and I hope you'll come over for dinner tonight."

"I will if I can." He knew his father would ask him what he'd done on the weekend.

The older man sat forward. Lines creased his face. "What's going on, son?"

"I'm sorry. I'm afraid I've been preoccupied with a couple of my patients."

"Maybe a particular woman too?"

"That sounds like something you know about that I don't."

His father grimaced. "According to Adele, you left the office with one last Friday after work. I've the feeling Adele has been hoping you would ask her out. I didn't know you were seeing anyone special."

Luca sat back in his chair. The receptionist had taken one look at Bella, whose beauty was exceptional along with everything else, and had understood that she was outmatched. It was possible she'd recognized Princess Baldasseri. With his parent giving him the steely eye, he'd had enough.

"Father? You know how much I love you and Mother, how grateful I am for all you've done for me. But it's obvious you've forgotten I'm a grown man living my own life. Please understand I have to follow my own path."

The older Dr. Torriani scowled and got to his feet. "There's something you're not telling me."

"But I *have* told you," he said, barely concealing his rage, "and now there's a patient waiting for me."

"This isn't the end of our conversation."

It was as far as Luca was concerned. "I'll let Mamma know if I'm free tonight."

His father left the office like a bear coming out of hibernation. In a sense, Luca felt like he'd come out of one that had lasted a decade. Certain comments Bella had made ran through his mind. He'd always loved this daring side of Bella, but feared it could cause real damage with her mother.

We're both over twenty-one and in charge of our own lives. We're free to live the way we want.

Yes, they were, even if it meant real trouble. He was ready for it, and Bella seemed willing.

Elated for the weekend coming up, he sailed through the rest of his workweek. As Saturday dawned, he was up with the birds and left for Scuol in jeans and a T-shirt. When he saw a creamy Kimera Lancia that had to be Bella's parked at Lishana's Garage, a sense of homecoming almost overpowered him.

Luca drove in and stopped near the side of the building, but he didn't shut off the engine. Through his rearview mirror he watched Bella, also clad in jeans, T-shirt and hiking boots, walk around holding a small duffel bag. She'd put her hair into a braid and wore a baseball cap. The cap brought back dozens of memories.

He reached over to open the passenger door and put the bag in the back seat before she slid in. "Hurry and drive away before Dizo sees you."

Luca took off. Dizo had been Luca's mentor. Now the master mechanic ran the garage. No guy was a bigger gossip and she knew it. Luca headed for the road that led up into the mountains.

She looked back. "I think we escaped before he realized what was happening."

He flashed her a sideward glance. "I thought we'd

escaped the evil eye last Friday night. But thanks to the receptionist, this week my father let me know he'd heard I'd left the office with an unknown woman. He wanted to know what was going on. Knowing how his mind works, he has to be thinking you and I reconnected at the wedding."

She groaned. "I'm way ahead of you there. Mother expected I would stay with her and the grandparents at the hotel in Bern after the wedding. But Francesca asked me to stay at her parents' home. Mother couldn't say no, but she didn't like it.

"And earlier this morning her maid saw me slip out with my duffel bag. I'll be facing an interrogation tomorrow, considering I'm supposed to be leaving on official business."

"I'm afraid we can't elude palace security, Bella. We're being followed and you know it."

"I do, and today I don't care."

"Neither do I." They smiled at each other. She looked adorable in that same baseball cap of the Swiss Alpine Club she used to wear years ago. "How was the party for your grandfather?"

"Mother invited their best friends, a married couple. I'm sure you've heard of them, Prince and Princess Renaldo, my friend Constanza's parents. She came with them. We ate out on the terrace. I gave him a 1560 Romansh translation of the New Testament. I had to hunt for a copy."

"I bet he was thrilled."

"I think so. He and Nonna are deeply religious, but in a good way."

"What do you mean by that?"

"In a word, they don't judge people."

Luca sat forward. "That makes them very good people. The world needs more of them. Now I want to talk about that business you're in that brought you to my office in Saint Moritz."

"First you need to understand about the pain I suffered over the separation from you a decade ago. It affected my whole life. Finally I made an appointment to see my lifelong physician, Dr. Pendergast. He sat me down and asked me to tell him my whole story from the beginning in order to understand my depression. When I finished, he had one suggestion for me. I'll quote him.

"Bella? Since you'll never be able to be with Luca again, never be able to say you're sorry and help him, then find a way to help others who suffer from a similar injury. It could ease this pain of guilt you've been carrying around far too long to be healthy."

To hear this sadness coming from Bella ignited Luca's anger. His father had destroyed all her letters where she'd poured out her pain. How did Luca get beyond it?

All those years he'd thought she'd lost total interest in him. After they'd been manipulated and permanently separated by their families, he hadn't realized that Bella had gone through the same horrific kind of trauma he'd experienced over the years. All of it had been so unnecessary, even criminal in his eyes.

Yet you didn't do anything about it, Luca. You didn't fight for her. No matter your reasons for holding back, you didn't go after her. You've been a coward and unworthy of her. But not any longer.

"Bella? There's something you need to know. I only found out about it last week. My father intercepted all the letters you wrote to me the second they came to house. He ripped up every one of them."

"What?"

"It's true."

"How could your father, or any father, do that? Why was he so intent on keeping us apart?"

"I don't know, but I'm going to find out."

"You were right, Luca. Your father and my mother made a formidable team."

"Formidable is the right word. More than ever, I'm convinced that the help your Dr. Pendergast gave you makes him one brilliant doctor, Bella."

"He's wonderful and his advice helped me get through the last year with new purpose. Since there was no place for my marketing skills at our family's timber office, I decided to do what my mother had been begging me to do."

"Charity work?" By now they were climbing higher in the mountains above the palace, and she had him riveted.

"Yes. That's the proper job for a princess to do. After a lot of contemplation, I did research on children with all kinds of physical disadvantages because of accidents and injuries like yours."

"The need for help in that department is staggering, as you quickly found out."

She nodded. "I'm no doctor like you, but for once I felt that a royal *could* be useful."

Oh, Bella… "How did you get started? When? I can't even imagine it."

A sigh escaped her lips. "I couldn't either. It was like eating an elephant one bite at a time. About a year ago I decided to contact various service organizations around Graubunden and Eastern Switzerland first. I spent hours on the phone finding the right people to talk to.

"One man in Arosa asked me to meet him. After I explained what I wanted to do, he got excited. I told him I didn't want the Baldasseri name mentioned, only that I wanted to help. I went with Alectrona Cossu and it stuck."

Luca just shook his head. "I'm in awe of your industry and perseverance."

"He put me in touch with some health care workers and came up with a list of two children—one needed a hand, the other an arm. I investigated the cost of a prosthesis. The amount is astronomical to a poor family with little or no insurance. On a burst of inspiration, I wrote letters to my family's friends asking for a donation to help those two children.

"To my joy, money came in. The thought of an injured child had touched their heartstrings. When those two children had undergone their operations and were functioning, I sent the donors some before-and-after pictures to thank them for their contributions."

Her eyes filled with tears. "You'll never know how much it meant to receive letters from the donors who were thrilled to have helped. What else could they do, they asked. My experimental project had been a success and gave me more reason to keep on going. I'm not saying that what I did made my pain over you go away miraculously, but I've been happier."

"You're one remarkable woman." Bella had always been kind and generous, but this side of her proved she had a heart of pure gold. He loved her beyond life itself.

"Not remarkable. I just wanted to get rid of my guilt

over what I did to you ten years ago. Every time a child is helped, it takes a little more of that guilt away."

He groaned. "You've paid for a crime you didn't commit a thousand times over. Let it go now, Bella."

"Being with you again has helped me more than you know. I consider it a job now, one that's worthy."

"I'm so glad it's fulfilling you, Bella," Luca sighed. "When you came to my office, you mentioned a boy in need…?"

"Yes. One eleven-year-old named Hasper Bazzell. He lost his left leg below the knee a month ago when he took the tractor out to the field. His father had forbidden him ever to touch it. He was years too young to drive it." She choked up and tears trickled down her cheeks. "His father had died earlier and he was trying to do a man's work when it tipped over and the accident occurred. The mother has little money and doesn't know what to do to help her son."

Bella's compassion for the boy touched his heart. Luca was humbled by what she'd told him. "I'm impressed beyond words and want to be able to help your cause."

"I didn't tell you this so you would feel obligated, Luca."

"You think I don't know that?" he emoted. "We're coming to our favorite spot by the river to camp." So far he hadn't seen any other hikers or campers. They had the place to themselves. "Later tonight we'll talk more about this boy."

CHAPTER FIVE

IT MAY HAVE been ten years, but for Bella it was like yesterday the minute they parked and started to set up their camp. They both knew their duties. Luca got busy putting up their three-man tent. The sight of his tall, rock-hard body driving in the stakes made it difficult for her to concentrate on her job.

She reached for the cinder blocks he kept in the trunk to form a small keyhole firepit on the spot where they'd made one many times before. After arranging them, she carried the kindling and placed it inside. The grate and charcoal could come out later when they decided to cook their dinner. By now their tent had been erected and Luca had taken their duffel bags inside.

"Let there be light." Bella walked in with the lanterns, then stopped in her tracks. "What's this?" His double sleeping bag had been placed on one side, but there was something new and blue on the other side beneath the small window with the netting.

His enticing smile made her body tremble. "*Your* sleeping bag."

"It's so plush! I brought my old one, but it doesn't compare to this." She sank down on it. "Ooh, down filled. Luca?" She looked up into those glinting green eyes. "You didn't need to do this."

"I wanted to."

"This is so fun I think I must be dreaming." More than anything in this world she wanted him to join her on the plump sleeping bag. She had to remember it was a miracle he'd even agreed to spend this day and night with her, but just being with him again now was no longer enough for her. Possibly he felt nothing deeper for her beneath the surface but that's what she had to find out on this trip.

"Come on, Bella. What do you say we visit the Garden of Eden, then come back and fish for our dinner? I'm hungry for perch."

She got to her feet. "That or trout sounds wonderful!" She tossed her cap on the sleeping bag, not wanting to hike with it. Once out of the tent, he zipped the entrance closed. Before locking up the car, he pulled out water bottles already filled for them. They hooked them to their belts. Now they were ready.

Between the mountain peaks and birdsong, Bella felt they'd come to the land of enchantment. The fragrant scent of pine intoxicated her. If she only had this one weekend with him, she would treasure it forever.

They started to forge their own trail through a meadow full of thousands of yellow flowers that grew on these mountains. "Isn't this the most beautiful sight you ever saw?" she cried, moving her hands carefully over the tops of some.

"Beautiful," came the deep response.

Bella glanced up and discovered him studying her. *Oh, Luca*—what was he thinking? She would give anything if he'd tell her what was really going on inside him. There was a rightness in them being together like this again. He had to be feeling it too! But there was this great silence on his part. Again she was determined to find out if she was the only one in love.

They reached a forested area where they came upon a little family of stone marten foxes with white and gray fur darting around. Luca paused and took a picture with his camera. "Cute, aren't they?" he whispered.

"Delightful beyond anything."

"Isn't it interesting they're the predators of the forest these days, not the bears."

"It's sad isn't it," she murmured. "Vincenzo told me a bear did make it over a mountain pass from Italy into the Biosphere reserve years ago. They're monitoring it. I hope more are allowed to stay."

"We're lucky your brother and the conservation board are watching over the environment here."

She finished taking a picture that caught one of the foxes and Luca's profile. "Do you think your father knows?"

"I'm sure he does, but all the good Vincenzo does won't remove my father's prejudice against royalty. It's his flaw and I no longer care."

Bella wished she hadn't mentioned his father. After drinking some water, they left the forest and entered another meadow. Above it they would come to their favorite place.

Halfway there she noticed a bird cruising high in the sky. "Look, Luca—am I crazy or is that a bearded vulture?"

Luca had seen it too. "You have a sharp eye, Bella. That reddish color is a dead giveaway."

They both took pictures before he snapped one of her. Thrilled he'd done that, she moved faster to reach their favorite spot. Ten years had produced more grassy undergrowth and the tree branches above them had intertwined into a virtual solid roof forming their own cathedral.

They walked around underneath. "I don't see any sign of the hares, Luca."

"After ten years they've probably moved on to paradise."

"I think they must have been very happy here."

"I know I was," he admitted. "Do you remember once telling me and Vincenzo that you wished we lived right here?"

Heat swamped her cheeks. "I said a lot of foolish things."

"Not foolish," he came back. "I felt the same away. No rules or restrictions up here. No one to tell us what we had to do."

"Free," she murmured.

"Exactly. There's no feeling like it."

"That was how it was for me…before—"

"Before our fantasy world disappeared?" he interjected.

She took a deep breath. "I don't think it was such a good idea to come up here. The memories still hurt too much. Let's go back to the river and do some fishing." Her gaze swerved to his. "Did you bring your fishing license?"

"I brought one for both of us."

"You always think of everything." *There's no one like you, Luca Torriani.*

"Actually, I forgot the fishing nets you and Vincenzo used to take when you couldn't sneak poles out of the palace."

She laughed and started walking out into the late afternoon sun.

He caught up to her. "I want to hear more about your charity. How many children have you helped already?"

She looked over her shoulder at him. "Probably thirty-five, but there are so many more. They all need help from someone who has suffered the same way you did."

He shook his head. "My suffering ended in a few weeks. After I went to college in Ohio, my father talked to me about becoming an allergist so I could work with him. I told him I thought I might like to be an orthopedic surgeon like the doctor who operated on me."

"How did that go over?"

"Papa fought me on it. He gave me all the reasons why being a surgeon would be a bad choice. He said I would suffer burnout, depression and face malpractice suits. The education would cost too much when it wasn't worth it."

She eyed him. "Yet I bet he was thankful for the surgeon who fixed your leg."

Luca smiled. "*I* certainly was, and I reminded him of the same thing. For once he had no answer. Later I had to do rehabilitation and was sent to a sports medicine doctor for a few sessions of therapy. I liked his approach and he talked to me about other careers as a doctor I'd never considered.

"When I got into medical school and had to make a decision, you know what I did. My father wasn't thrilled about it. He never liked most of my decisions."

"You *did* become a doctor. Surely that had to satisfy him."

"To some degree. A doctor is still a doctor, just like a princess is still a princess, even if you don't want to be considered one."

No, she didn't, and she'd give anything if he'd drop the subject.

They reached camp and Luca pulled their fly rods out of the trunk. While she started the fire so they could cook their catch, he called to her. "What fly do you want?"

"Guess!"

He didn't have to and put on her favorite.

In a few minutes she hurried over to him and inspected it. "My mayfly nymph. It always brings me luck."

Luca grinned. "Don't I know it. You're the best fisherwoman I've ever been with."

One brow lifted. "Is that a *long* list, Dr. Torriani?"

"Probably not as long as the list of fisher princes you've entertained over the last ten years."

Fisher princes? A caustic laugh burst from her as she turned to him with that crushing hurt in her heart. "Just for tonight, could we be Luca and Bella who went through high school together, but never even got to attend the graduation dance?"

The pain in her voice echoed his own pain and ripped him raw. "Come on, Bella. First one to get a strike cooks the dinner."

Luca ran down to the bank ahead of her. She squealed and hurried after him. For the next half hour they fished their favorite spots. Plenty of fish filled the water this far upstream. Bella was a picture playing with her fly rod like it was a lasso ready to ensnare a bull at a rodeo with precision.

To his surprise they both caught a large trout at the same time and let out shouts of excitement. He walked over and took her fish off the hook. "Since it's a toss-up, I'll clean them and bring them to you to cook."

Within twenty minutes he'd set up their chairs at the small camping table and she'd cooked their fish to perfection. With fruit and a pasta salad he'd made and put in the cooler, he'd never had a better meal in his life. Bella was the unique ingredient that made tonight surreal.

By the time they'd finished eating and had done the cleanup, it had grown dark. She went to the tent with a lantern to get ready for bed. He locked everything in the trunk before approaching.

"Knock, knock." He waited at the entrance expecting her to unzip the opening.

Instead, he heard, "Have you forgotten the password?"

"No, but I wasn't sure if you remembered." Vincenzo had thought it up years ago when they were young and needed one in case of an emergency. *Winky.* He'd derived it from the name Arnold Winkelried, who'd been a legendary hero in sixteenth-century Swiss history.

"You go first," she challenged him.

A smile broke out on his face. "I don't think so."

"Luca—"

"It's okay you've forgotten. I'll just sleep in the car."

In a panic she cried out, "Winky!" and undid the zipper.

Nothing could have brought him more satisfaction.

He couldn't help laughing. Luca loved it that she ended up laughing with him.

Was there a woman more gorgeous than Bella standing there in the lamp light, her blond hair gleaming? She wore a black short-sleeved top with a Geneve-Suisse logo and Red Cross flag on the front. The black-and-white-plaid bottoms completed the outfit.

He wanted to crush her in his arms, but another prince would be in her destiny before long. "Do I need another password to come inside?"

Her eyes glowed a deep lavender. "Not a password, Luca. All I ask is that you remove that defensive armor and be the guy I knew before the avalanche. Is there no way under heaven you can look at me like I'm a normal woman? Or is this an excuse because there really *is* an important woman in your life? Believe me I would understand and be so happy for you."

Her earnestness could be his undoing. "Shall we go inside and get comfortable while we talk?"

"Of course."

He followed her in and zipped up the opening. "Close your eyes while I pull on some sweats."

She'd already climbed inside her bag. "I never used to."

He smiled. "Then enjoy the show."

"I saw many a sight when we were all together."

Bella. "I'm sorry to hear about it and don't think I want to know more."

Her laughter resounded in the tent.

Extinguishing his lantern, Luca only took a second to remove his jeans and put on his camouflage sweats. He left his boots on and subsided on his sleeping bag before turning toward her. The lantern next to her was still on and bathed her in a soft, beautiful aura.

"Your mother must have been inspired to call you Alectrona. The picture I see in my mind of her looks a lot like you, even if your hair is in a braid. Amazing."

"I never had one when we were young. My hair wasn't long enough. I liked it short, but mother felt it wasn't becoming on me, so I had to let it grow out. Yours hasn't changed."

"I grew it longer in Columbus."

She smiled. "Did you like it?"

"My parents came to visit and hated it."

"Why didn't you keep it long?"

"You never change, Bella. The truth is, my hair isn't curly and it kept getting in my eyes."

She chuckled and propped herself on one elbow. "Do you have a picture?"

"Somewhere."

"I'd like to see it."

"Why?"

Her violet eyes searched his. "I want to catch up on the ten years I missed. Do you realize that except for vacations, the three of us probably saw each other every day growing up?"

Yes, he did, and was trying desperately to forget. "We were quite the triumvirate."

"That's right! Vincenzo was Caesar, you were Pompey, and I was Crassus. You should have been Caesar. In real life my brother never wanted to be king, but I was afraid it would hurt his feelings if I voted for *you* to be our leader."

"That's what I like about you, Bella. Not only are you a flatterer, you're a loving sister, loyal to the end."

"Then why did I get the name Crassus?"

"That was easy. Like a politician, you defied the powers that be and had enough pocket money for us when we ran out of ours."

She fell back against her pillow. "Money means little when you're not truly happy. How's that for the world's worst cliché."

He felt her pain. "What kind of a statement is that?"

"A true one." She rolled on her side once more. "Is your life making sense to you? I'm not talking about your being a doctor. I'm talking about you as a man."

"That's a loaded question," he teased.

"I'm Crassus, remember?" She sat straight up. "Take off your helmet for one minute and look at me. Tell me what you think your life would have been like if I weren't a royal and we were a normal couple. When the avalanche was shooting down the mountain, you gave me a swift kiss and said, 'I love you, too, Bella. Always will.'"

He reached for a bottle of water and drank. "I meant it, Bella. But you were a princess. We were teenagers, a stage we had to outgrow to become sensible adults."

"That statement sounds like one from our parents you've had memorized for a decade."

"At that particular time, it had to become my mantra."

She got up on her knees. "No one knows that better than I do. But now that we're all grown up and have become reacquainted, the rules have changed. I'm old enough to be with the man I want."

His chest tightened. "If not with Prince Antonio, then another prince."

"No. That's my mother's expectation. Since seeing

you at my brother's wedding, I've rediscovered what it means to be with you. No one else will ever satisfy me." Tears trickled down her flushed cheeks. "I can't speak for you. If you haven't married because you haven't found the right woman yet, then that's one thing. But if you feel the same way I feel and don't want to be with anyone else but me, then I have a proposal."

His body started to tingle. He got to his feet. "What are you saying?"

"I'm no longer a princess. That part of my life is over no matter what lies ahead. I've already written to King Leonardo, telling him I've renounced my title to live the life of a commoner."

"You've done *what*?" Luca cried.

"It's true."

"But Bella—don't you realize that throwing your birthright away could be disastrous for you in ways you can't possibly imagine?"

"I don't know. I guess I'll find out."

"What if he won't grant it?"

"If he doesn't present it to the parliament, it doesn't matter. I've relinquished my title and told my mother. Vincenzo was allowed to marry a commoner, so why should I be denied the same right? I'm younger and further down the line of succession considering they want to raise a family. I plan to live a free life from here on out."

Maybe he was dreaming all this.

"All you have to do is say you want me too. Naturally if you can't because I'm not the one, it won't change a thing. If you decide you want me, we can be together any way you'd like for as long as you want."

"Bella—you don't know what you're saying."

"It's up to you," she kept on talking. "You set the parameters, *if* that's what you desire. I'll do whatever it takes to see you, meet you wherever, whenever you say. We'll work around your medical practice schedule. We could even *live* together if you wanted to. I'd do anything for you. It all depends on whether you're on fire for me too."

Live together... "Bella—can you hear yourself?"

"I've been thinking these thoughts for years!"

"Stop! You're going to regret what you are saying. It's up to me to protect you from yourself. Don't you see that?" he cried.

"Oh, I see all right." Tears gushed down her hot cheeks. "It appears my news hasn't set you on fire. I have my answer."

"What answer?"

"You don't feel the same way I do. You don't believe I can manage my affairs on my own. Well, that's too bad. Under the circumstances I'd like you to drive me back to town right now rather than stay the rest of the night."

She got out of the sleeping bag and stood up. "Let's pack up. I'm ready to go."

Luca watched her gather her duffel bag. Was she already regretting her decision to give up her title?

Suddenly she spun around. "After being with you again, that painful period of not acting on my feelings has come to a permanent end, Luca. When I go home, I'm going to move out of the palace and get an apartment with the money I've earned working.

"I'll get a job and continue to do charity work. As of today I intend to live my life as Bella Baldasseri from here on out—a normal citizen of Scuol with all the parts and passions of every child born into the world."

He couldn't believe what he was hearing. "I'll take you back, but I hope you won't be regretting your decision, Bella. What you're doing is like being born again. You don't know what you could be facing."

"That's the whole idea, Luca. Born again and free. Are you coming, or do I have to hike down the mountain? Remember I've got my bear spray."

He tossed her the car keys. "Go out to the car and wait for me."

CHAPTER SIX

BELLA HAD DONE it now. She sat in the car and waited for him to join her while he packed up the tent. Since seeing him at the wedding, she'd been the one to follow him out to the taxi, not the other way around. She'd flown to Saint Moritz and had shown up at his office unannounced. The campout had been her idea, not his. Worst of all, *she'd* been the one to suggest they could live together.

Once again, she'd thrown caution to the wind to entice him, praying he would reveal his true feelings. Well, she knew his true feelings now! Worse, she'd committed the cardinal sin. *A man liked to do the chasing.* But she'd taken the risk, and she'd found out he wasn't in love with her.

Still, she wasn't sorry. She would call Nonna Caderina and tell her she'd given Luca the ultimate test. And now he was taking her home because there was nothing more to say.

It hurt that Luca couldn't do the honest thing and simply reject her like he would a normal woman who'd proposed something he didn't desire. That was because he would always see her as an untouchable princess running around with him and Vincenzo.

The three of them had grown up in their own halcyon universe, but it was ten years later now. At this point she was the only one left in it. Both he and Vincenzo had moved on and were leading their own lives. Why did it take her until the age of twenty-six to grasp that fact?

Full of shame over such emotional immaturity, she stared out the window as he drove them down the mountain to the back of the palace. The guard stood at attention at the entrance. She'd send for her car at the station in the morning.

When Luca pulled to a stop, she grabbed her duffel bag from the back seat and got out of the car. "Thank you for the great campout. Being with you since the wedding has allowed me to express my sorrow for what happened ten years ago. You've been wonderful to let me relive some choice memories from our past. God bless you in the future, Luca Torriani."

She walked inside past the guard. If pain could burn you alive, she'd be ashes by now.

Once she reached her suite, she dropped the bag and ran for her bedroom. When she dived for her bed, her baseball cap fell on the floor.

"Bella?"

She turned over.

Her well-dressed mother picked up her cap and put it on the dresser. "We need to have a talk." She sat on one of the upholstered chairs and crossed her legs.

"What's wrong?"

"Several things. I've been on the phone with Mamma's caregiver in Sardinia. She has developed a bad cold."

"I thought as much. I talked to her the other day,

and her cough was much worse. I'm very worried about her."

"If she doesn't get better in a few days, I want you to go with me to see her, Bella. You'll have to plan a trip around your charity duties."

"Of course. Poor Nonna. What a terrible life she has lived since Nonno died. Of course I'll go with you. I love her."

"As I said, she's just one of my concerns. Considering you've been camping rather than carrying out official charity business, I should be thankful you came home before the weekend was over."

Bella took several breaths in succession. She'd known this was coming. "It's Luca you need to thank. You and his father did such a fantastic job on him, he's been programmed like one of the robots made by Constanza's family business. He's such a good little boy, he returned me untouched and pure as the gold from our family's King Midas Mine."

Her mother's brows furrowed. "I can't believe you're speaking to me this way."

Trying to tamp down her anger, Bella got to her feet. "I can't believe that you and Papa colluded with Dr. Torriani to permanently separate Luca and me after the avalanche. That move of his to Saint Moritz was pure genius."

She averted her eyes and clasped her hands tightly. "Did Vincenzo tell you?"

"No. *You* did. He's just a robot who took orders from the three of you. Luca and I figured it out for ourselves when we saw each other at Vincenzo's wedding."

"So, you *did* get together…"

"Several times since then actually, and you know it."

"What about Prince Antonio?"

"What about him?"

Her mother muttered something unintelligible, then said, "I forbad Vincenzo to invite Luca to the wedding, but he disobeyed me."

"That was probably the only time in his life he went against your wishes. Except, of course, for choosing Francesca for his bride before you learned the truth about Valentina's problems." She moved closer to her mother. "How could you expect him to obey your wishes when Luca has been his best friend for years?"

Her mother's features hardened. "You know why we—"

"I know exactly," Bella interrupted her while she undid her braid. "I *was* Princess Baldasseri who would have to marry the right prince. Those are the words you spoke to me at the hospital that night. Thankfully I'm no longer a princess."

Those blue eyes stared hard at her. "It's your destiny, Bella."

"Afraid not, Mamma. Phone King Leonardo if you want to hear that I rescinded my title."

She jumped to her feet. "That couldn't be true!"

"You'll find out, and you ought to stop obsessing about my future."

"You're being ridiculous."

"It's not ridiculous, just honest. The only man I've ever loved or will love is Luca. But of his own free will and no one else's edicts, Luca never wanted to marry me. If that had been his desire, he would have come after me years before now and talked me into running away with him." During tonight Bella had come to recognize the real truth of his feelings.

She walked over to her mother and kissed her cheek. "I love you more than you know. Because you're a princess and want me to have the same life as yours, I understand what motivated you and Papa back then. I hope you love me enough now that I'm a commoner."

A gasp came from her parent.

"I'll continue to do my charity work, Mamma, but beyond that I'm going to live a free life."

A tragic look crossed over her mother's face. For once she appeared at a loss for words.

"While I'm in the shower, why don't you phone Luca's father and let him know that the problem has been forever solved. Maybe then he'll stop trying to run his son's love life, let alone everything else. I'll say it one more time. Dr. Torriani's worries are over and so are *yours*."

She went in the bathroom and shut the door. It wasn't until the water was streaming down her head and face that tears of anguish poured from her eyes.

Bella cried herself to sleep that night, but by the morning, she'd wiped her tears away and had made a decision.

After college in England, Vincenzo had moved out of the palace for five years before their father died. It had given him the freedom to enjoy being a bachelor. Bella wanted that kind of freedom for a myriad of reasons. She could enjoy any man she wanted, or no man at all.

All she had to do was get on the computer and find a two-bedroom apartment here in Scuol. She'd make one room into an office to run her charity business.

That way she could invite people to meet with her when they could come.

Bella had some savings from her former job. She also had a car. Naturally she'd visit her mother and grandparents often and stay in touch. Of course, she couldn't do anything about her mother hiring security to keep an eye on her.

Pleased with her decision to become her own person, she dressed and went into her study to get on the computer. Two hours later she left her mother a message that she'd gone out but would be back by dinner. Starving at this point, she drove to a local drive-through for a meal before checking out the furnished apartments in Scuol.

She remembered that Vincenzo had rented a great condo at a location called The Spruces. Each condo was a separate home with a veranda and a view of the mountains. Bella had loved visiting him when she'd come home from Geneva for the rare weekend. He'd just bought Karl. She fell in love with his puppy. Those were joyous memories.

Bella wished she could rent the one Vincenzo had lived in, but now they were privately owned. That was okay. Within an hour she found a furnished two-bedroom rental on the first floor she liked at the Silvretta Lodge. She didn't want to climb stairs. It was perfect and had been modernized with simple furnishings. The landlady couldn't have been more accommodating. After living in a sumptuous palace, it was like a breath of fresh air.

Tonight at dinner Bella would tell the family her plans and move in on Saturday. Hopefully her grandmother would recover from the pneumonia and they wouldn't have to leave for Sardinia quite yet. Before long Bella would be inviting Vincenzo and Francesca over for *fondue au fromage* to celebrate. It would be the beginning of a new triumvirate that didn't include Pompey.

Bella got up early Saturday morning and dressed in jeans and a yellow crew neck top. She put her hair in a French twist so she wouldn't have to deal with it. Once she'd eaten breakfast, she was ready to go.

After a dozen trips to her car with her things, she left for her apartment. Rain had been forecast for today and the temperature had dropped. If she hurried, she'd miss the downpour.

The nice thing about a furnished apartment meant she didn't need furniture. Only her clothes, toiletries, a few items for the kitchen she'd already bought and everything for her office. A new chapter in her life was beginning that didn't include Luca.

She pulled in her parking stall at the side of the complex and turned off the engine. Ready to get busy, she grabbed the bag with her toiletries lying on the front seat. But when she opened the car door, a tall, hard male body prevented her from getting out.

Bella looked up into glittering, jewel-like green eyes she'd thought never to see again. It was a good thing he prevented her from standing up or she would have fainted dead away on the cement.

"Put your head down and take a deep breath, Bella." She did his bidding. Luca's deep voice kept her from losing consciousness. He rubbed the back of her neck. The touch of his fingers ignited her senses, bringing her back to life. She finally lifted her head. "Better now?"

"I can breathe again." She sat up straighter and gripped the steering wheel.

"That's something, but don't bother trying to get out yet." She heard the old familiar amusement in his tone. "The last time this happened, the snow buried us alive."

Bella struggled to comprehend what was happening. "How—"

"Vincenzo is back from their honeymoon. I was ready to phone you when he called. Your mother told him you renounced your title and planned to move to this apartment today," he broke in, reading her thoughts. "Rather than phone you, I came right over."

She shook her head. "What would we do without Vincenzo, but you've made a wasted trip."

He shifted his weight, drawing her attention to his cropped denims and navy pullover. It was her favorite color on him. "The night of our campout, you proposed that we live together. After living twenty-eight years without hope that I could ever be with you, I drove home in shock trying to comprehend that you'd actually proposed we live together."

Bella could grant that what she'd said would have stunned him.

"On the drive back to Scuol, so many thoughts bombarded my mind, but foremost was the courage it took for you to consider turning your entire universe around for me. A part of me wanted to protect you from yourself before you went too far and regretted it."

"I don't need protecting, Luca."

"I realize that now." One dark brow lifted. "You said

you'd do anything for me. It all depended on whether I was on fire for you."

"I did say that." Bella still clung to the steering wheel. She regretted those words now.

"I'm on fire for you, Bella. I've never been anything else. I love you with every breath in my body. You've always known how I felt."

She threw her head back to look up at him. "No, I don't, Luca. You drove me back to the palace without a word. Considering that I laid my life on the line for you, that was an amazing response for a man on fire."

He leaned closer. "After the night of our campout, I had many things to work out before I could come to you with my answer. It was my mistake not to stay in the tent and love us both into oblivion forever."

"No, it wasn't a mistake. You've never been spontaneous with me or come running to me, Luca. Only that one time on the mountain when I was in danger."

"Bella—" he whispered in a tortured voice.

"Your silence has been a good thing and gave me my answer. I've had this week to decide I like the idea of being on my own and independent. It's going to be fun to live the normal life of a commoner like millions of other women. But thank you for finally getting back to me, even if it wasn't necessary. Now I need to unpack. I have a lot of work to do."

"Bella—I realize my silence has condemned me. I've done everything wrong and am begging you to forgive me. I love you beyond anything in existence."

"I don't doubt you love me in your own way. We have a unique history. But we're not the right match and time has proven it."

"Nothing has been proven, Bella. Give me the

chance to convince you we're meant to be together. Do you feel strong enough to drive?"

She blinked. "Why are you asking me that?"

"My car is parked a few feet away. When you're able, I want you to follow me in your car. We don't have far to go, and then I'll explain why I don't want you to move into this apartment. There's so much I need to say to you."

"There you go again, putting off answers. It's your modus operandi."

"Please, Bella. If we leave now, we might beat the rain."

"I'm sorry, but my plans are set."

"You don't mean that."

Since he refused to go away, she started the car. He stepped away far enough for her to back out of her stall. Right now she needed sustenance in order to follow through with her resolve. A cup of coffee at the local drive-through would help. The rain started falling.

After her stop, she drove back to her apartment in a real downpour. She was still trembling from the encounter with Luca. The second she parked and got out of the car, she was caught around the waist from behind and let out a cry.

"Since you're no longer a princess, and I'm a normal man, I'm going to treat you like the normal woman you've always wanted to be. This is how we do it."

"No, Luca—" she cried out as he picked her up in his arms and carried her to his car. He ensconced her in the passenger seat and shut her door. Then he walked around and got behind the wheel.

"You want answers, *bellissima*? No more inaction. You're going to get them."

He drove down the road past the garage where he'd worked. When they reached The Spruces, he turned in and wound through the trees. It was like déjà vu after he pulled in the driveway.

"This is the condo my brother rented."

"A long time ago."

Luca parked the car and came around for Bella. He moved fast and had already unlocked the front door of the condo. She had no choice but to sweep past him, brushing the rain off her arms.

He walked in the living room for a throw and put it around her shoulders, squeezing them gently. "It's chilly all of a sudden. I'll turn up the heat. In fact, I could use a cup of coffee. I made a pot before coming to your apartment. Maybe you'd like another one."

"I want to go back to my apartment."

"Not until I've given you my full answer. Come in the kitchen and sit down."

She followed him and sat down at the table, still reacting to the feel of his touch. Bella had been in here before, but these furnishings were different. "Is my brother letting you stay in his condo?"

Luca brought each of them a mug of hot liquid and sat down across from her. "I don't suppose you know the story about this place. While I was in high school working at the garage, I would pass The Spruces. I thought it would be fun to live in one of the rentals and told Vincenzo.

"He thanked me for the heads-up and agreed it would be a great place when we were both on our own. On one of my few visits home while I was in medical school, he called me."

"You flew in from Ohio?" To think he'd been here in Scuol and she'd known nothing…

"It was my mother's birthday. I wanted to surprise her. Your brother had just returned from London. He told me you were away or I would have used him to see you. We drove over here and looked at this condo for rent. The lucky dude put down money and moved in."

How incredible, and it had all been Luca's idea. "I remember how upset our parents were." She took another long swallow of coffee while she tried to absorb the astonishing information.

"We decided that after I finished my residency, I'd move into a rental here too and we'd lead the bachelor life. But due to my father, my plans had to change and then your father died."

"Yes. My mother begged my brother to come home."

"He knew she needed him. Around that time the group that owns The Spruces put the condos up for sale. I bought this one for an investment a year ago."

A cry escaped her lips. "But you live in Saint Moritz—"

"Not since four days ago."

"What?"

"That's one of the reasons you didn't hear from me until this morning."

She gripped the empty mug tighter, unable to process what she was hearing.

"More importantly, for over a year the Lemond Institute here in Scuol has been asking me to join them. If my father hadn't mapped out my life after leaving Germany, I would have started working with them. This week I accepted their offer and informed the medical group in Saint Moritz that I had left. I did all this so you and I can be together."

She stared at him in disbelief. "You're serious…"

"Will this start to convince you?" He reached in his pants pocket and pulled out a white gold band with two round gems the color of a purple violet. "I've loved you since we were children. Your eyes were this exact hue the first time I met you. You've always been the bride of my heart. Forgive me if it took this long for my answer. I had to put everything in place first because I not only want to live with you, I plan to *marry* you and live here with you."

"Marry?" she whispered in absolute shock. Her eyes filled with tears. "Oh, Luca… If only you'd told me this while we were out camping."

His brows furrowed. "You know why I didn't."

"But that's the difference between us. I was ready to throw everything away to be with you right then. Yet you didn't tell me you were in love with me or hold me all night. That was your choice, but since then I've undergone a change. Not my love for you, but my perspective about you."

"What do you mean?"

"Your entire life you've always been free to make choices when the time suited you. I've never had that luxury about anything until I rescinded my title. I like the freedom it's given me—the possibilities. I want to explore it for a little while. To marry you has always been my hopeless dream, but—"

"But now that it can be a reality, you're not sure," he finished for her in a deep, grating voice.

"No, it's not that. I'd just like the chance to live the life of a normal woman."

The light faded from his eyes. He put the ring back in his pocket. Bella felt him close up. Maybe this was the greatest mistake of her life. Maybe she wanted him to hurt the way she'd been hurting since the campout. All she knew was that she needed time to think about it.

"Don't let me keep you from your unpacking. I'll run you back to your apartment."

There was nothing more to be said. She got up and walked out to his car. During the short drive, the silence between them was deafening.

Once Bella had gone inside her apartment, Luca took off for their Garden of Eden. The pain was so excruciating, he didn't know how to deal with it. Clouds sat on the mountain while thunder cannonaded from peak to peak. The temperature had plummeted. By the time he got out of the car, he could hardly see where he was going. After putting on his backpack and bedroll, he hiked through the rain the rest of the way, plodding through wet underbrush.

Relieved the garden interior had remained dry, he spread out his bedroll and collapsed inside it. He lay there for hours, bombarded with self-recrimination for his lack of bravery at the campout. Why hadn't he told her he loved her and couldn't live without her? She'd just handed him his heart's desire. But it had sounded so impossible, he'd gone into shocked silence and had only himself to blame for her rejection.

Fool of fools, he'd kept her waiting a week for his answer. And then he'd charged over to her apartment on his time frame, not hers. Was it any wonder she didn't melt in his arms? After what he'd done, how could she believe anything he had to say?

Bella had been dictated to all her life. After getting rid of her title in a courageous move, she'd planned their campout and proposed to him on the spot. And what had he done? Wounded her to the core.

He groaned as the hours wore on and fear started to creep in. Love could be a fragile thing. Maybe her independent life would change the way she felt about him. She might even want her old royal role back.

Not if he had anything to say about it!

Luca shot straight up. He realized he needed to show her his love all over again before that could happen. Filled with resolve, he got to his feet. Until she accepted his heart and ring, he determined to give her a taste of what it was like to be a normal woman, desired by a normal man.

The rain had stopped by the time he reached town. He stopped at a floral shop and bought a dozen long-stemmed red roses before driving to her apartment at seven. Relieved to see her car still in its stall, he parked and approached her door. He could have used the doorbell, but knocked instead several times.

"Who is it?" she called out.

"Luca."

After a wait she finally opened the door looking gorgeous in a stunning blue dress. In the background, a man he recognized as Prince Antonio sat on her sofa. Luca could hardly breathe. It felt like a slug in the gut to know she was with him. His eyes met hers as he handed her the box of flowers.

"I brought you a housewarming gift, something I should have done this morning. I've thought about everything you said. Since you're busy I'll call you tomorrow."

"I'm sorry, Luca, but I won't be available."

Luca could see a nerve throbbing in her throat. Was that because she would be spending more time with the Prince? He looked around, but didn't see a car that might belong to the other man. No doubt he'd flown in by helicopter and she'd picked him up in her car. "Sorry to have disturbed you. Another time, then. *Buna notg.*"

Luca knew that trying to win her back would be difficult, but he hadn't expected to see the Prince head-on. She'd wanted to be free. It looked like she was already making the most of it.

His jealousy worse than ever, he hurried back to his car and took off for his condo. Thank heaven the rest of his weekend would be busy filling in for two doctors away on a conference. Anything to deal with the pain.

No sooner had he parked his car in the driveway than Vincenzo phoned him.

"Did you find her?" his friend asked right off.

"I did." Luca apprised his friend of the situation. "She's enjoying her freedom with Prince Antonio tonight."

"Hang in there and give her time."

"I will." He had no choice. Bella was his whole life. He wouldn't give up. "Thanks for the moral support."

"Always. Just so you know, our *nonna* is ill, and Bella is worried."

"She told me. I'm so sorry."

"Me too. Call me anytime."

Luca hung up and went inside.

At six on Monday, he couldn't stand it any longer and called her to go out to dinner.

"I'm afraid I can't this evening. I have a ton of work."

Not to be daunted he said, "Then I'll bring you some pizza." He hung up before she could turn him down.

Within twenty minutes he stood at her door. She opened it wearing jeans and an oversize T-shirt. There was no Prince here tonight. Bella looked ravishing in anything, especially with her hair tousled. "You shouldn't have done this."

"Since I'm here, mind if I come in so we can eat while it's still hot? Afterward I can hang that picture you're holding before I leave."

She finally stood back so he could enter. So far, so good. He carried the box to the kitchen counter and looked around. "It looks like you've lived here a long time. I'm impressed." He opened the box. "Will you join me?" He sat on one of the stools and ate a couple of slices.

She put the framed picture against the wall. "This isn't going to work." The firmness in her tone twisted his gut.

"Because of Prince Antonio?"

"That's none of your business."

"Understood, but it's important you know I've come back to Scuol to live for the rest of my life. After talking to you on the campout, everything became crystal clear. I'm going to fight for us, Bella. If you're ready to give up on me, that's your call, but I'm never giving up on you. I'll let you get on with your evening now. I just wanted to make sure that was understood between us. Good night."

"Wait—" she called to him as he opened the door.

He turned to her. "What is it?"

"There is one problem that has me worried. I need your advice."

He heard concern in her voice. "What is it?"

"You know that boy Hasper Bazzell I told you about who lost the lower half of his leg?"

"Of course."

"His mother has said she doesn't want charity, but I felt something wasn't right so I phoned her today. We had a long talk. She said her son is afraid of everything. He won't talk to his school friends. He doesn't want to see any doctors and his depression is so bad, he just wants to stay in bed."

"That's not good."

"No. She's frantic and says raising money for him would be a waste. It's so sad. Because you're a doctor who has dealt with this kind of thing, do you have any ideas how I could talk to her and try to get through?"

"Why don't you let me try instead. Give me her number and I'll call tonight."

"I don't expect that, Luca."

"I know, but I'll do whatever it takes to help her son." *And hopefully show you I'll do anything for you, Bella.*

"That's very kind of you."

He added the number she gave him to his phone.

"Forgive me for being short with you earlier, Luca. I haven't even asked you how *your* work is going." It was the old Bella for a few minutes.

"Exactly as I had imagined."

"Are you glad about working at the Institute?"

"I am, but what is most important is that I'm home to stay. I'll get back to you after I've talked to Signora Bazzell. Get a good sleep."

The next night he phoned Bella, who picked up on

the second ring. "Luca?" She sounded expectant, which was a plus.

"I have good news. I spoke with Signora Bazzell and told her I'd fly to Glarus to talk to her son. I've arranged it for Friday afternoon. My work will understand since Hasper is going to be one of my cases on which I'm consulting."

"You're a miracle worker, Luca. When I last talked to her, she was so disheartened I didn't think anyone could get through to her. Come around to the back of the palace at noon on Friday. We'll fly to Glarus in the helicopter."

To fly with her was progress. He could make it to Friday after all.

He was still counting this blessing when he entered his condo. He showered and got in bed. For the next hour he answered half a dozen phone messages from his service. There was another message, this one from his father. It didn't require an answer.

There's no forgiveness for what you've done.

CHAPTER SEVEN

SUNNY SKIES PREVAILED over Glarus on Friday morning. Luca looked out the window of the helicopter at their approach. He liked the charming Swiss town of twelve thousand people located on the Linth River. The Alps surrounded it.

Before he and Bella had left the palace grounds, they made another phone call to Hasper's mother to finalize arrangements. She indicated that her boy refused to leave the house and meet them at the hospital. When Luca told Bella, she agreed with him they should rent a car and drive to the Bazzell farm.

"It's hard to believe that in a quaint, fairy-tale place like this, such a terrible tragedy happened to Hasper."

Luca reached for her hand without thinking and squeezed it. "Maybe this visit can turn his world around."

"I know you will find a way."

They followed directions up the hillside to the brown-and-white chalet. Signora Bazzell was waiting for them. She was a nice-looking, brown-haired mother probably thirty years of age trying to run the farm alone.

After introductions, she invited them inside and they went up the stairs. "Hasper is in his room."

"Does he know I'm coming?"

She nodded. "I told him a doctor wanted to visit him. That's all. He just turned away from me. I'm at my wit's end."

"Signorina Cusso and I would like to see him together." Bella knew all about the kind of guilt that played a big part in Hasper's problem. Her insight would be invaluable. "If you'll show us to his room, we'll introduce ourselves and talk to him."

"Speak to him in Romansh."

Luca nodded. They entered the boy's inner sanctum that contained a desk and chair. He noticed the slender, dark-haired boy lying on the bed fully clothed in shorts and a T-shirt. He was turned toward the wall away from them, minus a lower leg.

His mother brought in a chair from the kitchen. "Bless you for coming," she whispered. "I'll be in the kitchen if you need me."

Luca pulled the desk chair around so they could both sit near the bed.

Bella spoke first. "Hasper? My name is Bella. You remind me of myself. When I was sixteen and went skiing, I did something I was forbidden to do. A big sign warned of avalanche danger, but I didn't care so I started down the trail.

"A very brave eighteen-year-old guy chased after me to stop me. But I didn't listen to him because I was showing off in front of him. Suddenly there was an avalanche. It came crashing down and could have killed us. Later at the hospital I woke up just fine, but my mother told me the other guy would probably lose his leg. Worse, he was no longer at the hospital and I couldn't contact him."

If Hasper was listening, Luca couldn't tell, but hearing the emotion in Bella brought his old feelings of pain and despair to the surface.

"His name was Luca Torriani, the guy who'd been put on the Swiss ski training team for the Olympics. But he'd never be able to be an Olympian now because of me. His story was on the news and in all the papers."

To Luca's shock, the boy slowly sat up and turned around to look. He stared at her, then at Luca. A connection had been made.

"For years I wanted to die, Hasper, because I never did find out what happened to his leg. I'd lie in bed every night and sob over the terrible thing I'd done, until ten years later I saw him again. The man right here with me *is* Luca Torriani. He had to undergo an operation on his leg, but it changed his life for the better. Show him, Luca."

He pulled up his pant leg so the boy could see the scars. Bella was seeing them for the first time too. "I've got screws in there holding my leg together, Hasper. I don't ski competitively anymore, but thanks to the doctor, I can walk and move around like any other person."

Bella leaned forward. "You have no idea how happy I am that he can walk when I thought he'd lost his leg because of me. I realize you've lost your lower leg because your father told you never to drive the tractor. But you can be given an artificial one and—"

"And it won't require screws," Luca took over. "You'll be able to walk around just like your buddies. You can hike and do whatever you want. In long pants no one will ever know. When you're old enough, you'll be able to drive a tractor if that's what you want to do to help your mom."

"Hasper?" Bella joined in. "Your father wouldn't want you to lie around on this bed until you die. Neither does your mom. Pretty soon you'll get sick of it the way I did because that's what I used to do. Do you understand?"

The boy nodded.

"Your parents don't want you to feel bad. Your father is up in heaven proud of you for trying to help her. So there was a tractor accident. Accidents happen to everyone. All you have to do is get fitted for a new leg and you'll be better than ever. Show all your friends you're tough."

Luca moved to the side of the bed. "I'm a doctor, and I'll help you. Will you let me examine your leg?"

It took a minute before he said, "Okay."

The boy lay back down while Luca looked him over. He was satisfied there was enough soft tissue to cushion the remaining bone. The knee joint was intact and the skin on his limb was in good condition.

"You're a perfect candidate for a prosthetic leg and will have a lot of mobility."

"What does that thing look like?"

Thrilled they were getting through to him, Luca smiled. "A lot better than my leg. When you go to the hospital with your mom, the prosthetist will show you everything. I can tell you this much. The socket is the mold of your limb and fits over it. The suspension system is how it stays attached. It won't hurt."

"Will you be there?"

Luca and Bella exchanged glances. "We'll both be there all the way."

They could hear his mind working before he said, "I'll try it."

Bella got to her feet. "I'll go get your mom. She'll want to hear this wonderful news!"

More rejoicing ensued. Hasper's mother would make an appointment for the fitting and let Luca know when it could be done.

A half hour later, after more tears and hugs, they left the Bazzell home and drove to the hospital where the helicopter sat.

"A miracle has happened, Bella. It's all due to you. Today I relived our past and am in awe over your desire to help the unfortunate of this world. One day that boy will praise your name."

Her fantastic violet eyes looked into his. "The praise goes to the man who gave no thought to himself when he skied down that mountain to save me. I can't find the right words to tell you how…how grateful I am." Her stammer covered something else she would have said that gave him hope.

They traveled back to the town in their rental car, but en route she received a phone call from her brother. When she picked up, she turned on the speaker. "Vincenzo?"

"Thank goodness you answered. Where are you?"

"In Glarus with Luca. We've just been to the Bazzell farm so Luca could examine the boy Hasper for a prosthetic leg."

"Wow. That's fantastic. I wish I didn't have worrisome news."

"What's wrong?"

"It's Nonna. She's taken another turn for the worse. I think you'd better see her before it's too late."

Bella nodded. "I couldn't agree more. Let Mamma know I'll head straight to Innsbruck in the helicopter now. From there I'll fly to Sardinia."

"I wish I could be with you—"

"I'll go with her," Luca broke in. "I only wish there was something I could do to help. I like your *nonna*."

"Nonna thought the world of you too, buddy."

When they hung up, he stared at Bella. "Is it all right if I come with you? Tell me now if it isn't, and I'll arrange my journey back to Scuol."

"No, no. I remember how much she liked you. I think it will make her happy."

Little by little Luca felt that maybe he'd one day win his heart's desire.

The flight ended at five in the afternoon in Cagliari, the capital city of over one hundred and fifty thousand people. Many times Bella and Vincenzo had hiked to the hilltop *castello* during their visits and had explored the ancient walled old town overlooking the vista below.

Bella's grandmother had been put in a suite reserved for the Cusso royal family. The attending physician greeted her with enthusiasm. She introduced Luca as Dr. Torriani. "How is my *nonna*?"

"Princess Caderina is coming along from the latest bout of pneumonia, Princess Baldasseri." Bella moaned inwardly at the royal appellation. Certain things would never change. "If she continues to do well, I'll let her go home. It will do her good to see her granddaughter. Go right in. She hasn't had much of an appetite, but I know your visit will do her good."

"Thank you."

Luca followed her into the hospital room. She

walked over to the bed where her grandmother lay with her head slightly elevated. She'd been hooked up with oxygen. Her hair had turned white when it had once been red like the red hair Bella's mother had inherited. The two women had the same bone structure and had both been reputed beauties.

"Nonna?"

All Bella had to do was say the word and her grandmother's eyelids opened. "Bella, Bella—" she cried and tried to sit up.

"I came as soon as I could." Bella leaned over and kissed both her cheeks. "It's so wonderful to see you and I miss you so much. I'm sorry you've been suffering."

"I'm all right now that you're here. Bring the chairs around and sit so we can talk." Luca did her bidding. When they were seated, she studied him. "I'm a little worried, Bella. Am I seeing things or is it possible the man smiling down at me is Luca Torriani?"

"You're not wrong, Princess Caderina," he interjected.

"You've grown into an impossibly handsome man."

"He's a sports medicine doctor too."

Her grandmother knew everything, but she pretended otherwise. "Luca? I was crazy about you the first time I met you with Vincenzo and Bella. It was clear that my *bimba* was besotted with you all those years you were growing up."

"We both had it pretty bad back then." Luca laughed.

"And now?"

"We're just friends," Luca interjected again before Bella could say anything.

"Yes," Bella blurted. "He's helped with one of my charity cases. A little boy who needs a prosthetic leg."

"God's work. How wonderful! Come give me a kiss, Luca."

Bella watched through tears as her beloved grandmother and Luca embraced.

"*Bimba?* Did I ever tell you how much your mother loved your father? Before they married, he became so ill from the flu he almost died. She vowed to become a nun rather than marry anyone else if anything happened to him. I believed her at the time and still believe she would have."

"I didn't know that about Papa or her." Bella was shocked over the revelation.

"When he recovered, I'm sure she never wanted to think or talk about it again. But now I want to know about you and Luca. What's going on with your lives? Tell me everything. Leave nothing out."

Her love warmed Bella's heart. She and Luca leaned closer and they told her about their separate lives. They talked together until after ten when her grandmother finally closed her eyes and fell asleep. The hospital arranged for her and Luca to stay in the suite on cots so they could be near her. They set up their beds close together in the other room.

Luca propped himself on one elbow. "Your grandmother is a wonder, Bella."

"I know. No one has a kinder heart."

"She's like my mother," Luca confessed.

"I can't believe I've never met her."

"Maybe one day." He could pray for that.

"I'm just thankful Nonna is rallying from this latest

attack. I can leave tomorrow knowing she's all right for now."

Bella lay back on the pillow and slept all night facing the man she hungered for in secret. The next morning, they ate breakfast with her grandmother. When Bella leaned over to give her a kiss, her grandmother grasped her arm. "Don't worry," she whispered. "Everything is going to work out for you and Luca."

"I don't know."

"Yes, you do. Don't keep him waiting too long. A man like Luca only comes along once in a thousand years."

That was exactly what Bella thought too. "God bless you, Nonna. I'll visit again very soon."

Luca gave her grandmother another hug before they left the hospital for the airport. On the flight back to Innsbruck they talked about the revelation learned the night before.

"Nonna confirmed something for me I've always known, Luca. My father would have done anything for Mother. What I don't understand is why Mother never told me or Vincenzo that he almost died, or that she threatened to become a nun if he didn't make it."

"I think I do. If you don't know what she went through, you can't use it for leverage against her."

She turned to him. "I'm surprised you're not a psychiatrist."

"I did rounds in psychiatry before choosing sports medicine."

"And did it give you any insight into why your father has no use for royals? There has to be a reason."

"Lately, I've been wondering the same thing. The next time I talk to my mother, I intend to ask her what secret she has held back that she hasn't told me about."

They smiled at each other in mutual understanding before she turned away. Another second and she'd tell him she couldn't live without him.

Upon landing in Innsbruck, they boarded the helicopter and flew back to the palace in Scuol. They got in his car and he drove her to her apartment.

"I'm glad you came with me, Luca," she said in a trembling voice before getting out.

"So am I. It meant everything for the three of us to be together like old times."

Old times…

She rushed inside the apartment before he could see the tears streaming down her face. Before she got in bed, she phoned her mother.

"Bella? Where are you?" she asked in a strident voice.

"In bed in my room. Nonna was doing so well, I was able to leave this morning."

"We both know you were with Luca Torriani."

"Yes. Nonna remembered him and it made her happy to see him."

Her mother made a strange sound in her throat. "She's not in her right mind."

There was no point in arguing. "The doctor will send her back to the palace with her caregiver tomorrow. I'm so thankful, and I believe this crisis has been averted."

"But not the one you continue to create. When will you move back home and stop this nonsense?" she demanded.

"I'm in my new home."

"You've been neglecting your grandparents and Prince Antonio."

Bella gripped the phone tighter. "I've been doing

important charity work. I'll be over the day after to-morrow and spend time with all of you."

"You're not in your right mind either."

The divine right of kings Luca had once referred to about his father came to mind. Bella drew in a deep breath. "In that case I'll become a nun, the way you would have done if Papa hadn't survived the flu before your marriage. *Buona notte*, Mamma. Never forget that I really do love you."

The next evening at the condo, Luca phoned Bella.

"Are you alone?" he asked, barely able to keep the jealousy from his voice.

"You don't have the right to ask me that, Luca," she sighed.

"You're right, and I'm not going to beat about the bush. I can't go on like this. I told your grandmother that we were just friends, but the truth is that can never be true. You're the love of my life, Bella. Being with you on the campout, and in Sardinia, has made me hungry for all the things I've missed in the years we've been apart. I can help you with your charity work from a distance, but I can't be around you if I can't be with you. I love you. That's it. I don't want to play cat and mouse anymore. It hurts too much. Next Saturday after work I'll be meeting with some colleagues at the Wine Cellar for drinks. If you'd like to meet me there at seven for dinner, I'll look for you. In case you don't come, I'll know you've moved on with Prince Antonio, or another one, for good." On that note he hung up.

After what seemed like a month of torture, Saturday night arrived. Luca said good-night to his colleagues in the lounge of the Wine Cellar and waited for Bella to arrive. It was five to seven. He'd give her fifteen minutes. If she didn't show, he'd know everything was over.

When the clock said twenty after seven, he left the restaurant. Devastated that it really was over with her, he hurried down the narrow, outside stone staircase. Halfway to the ground he collided with a woman rushing up the stairs.

"Luca!" She clung to him. "Thank heaven I didn't miss you! My car has a flat tire and I had to call a taxi." Her voice shook.

When he could gather his wits, he realized he was holding the old Bella in his arms. "You should have phoned me. I would have picked you up."

"The important thing is that I'm here now. I love being independent, but the truth is, I hate this life without you. You're the man I've always loved and I don't want to lose you."

"But Prince Antonio…"

"I explained everything to Tonio that night you saw him at my apartment. Whatever was going to happen between you and I, or wasn't, he deserved the truth. And the truth is that there is no one else but you for me. There never has been. Tonio is a wonderful man and he'll make some lucky woman very happy someday. I wanted him to be free to find that as soon as possible."

Luca's elation knew no bounds, but people needed to get past them. "Come on. Let's go inside and talk about everything over dinner." He cupped her elbow and they climbed the rest of the staircase.

Her lips brushed his jaw as they made their way

inside the four-hundred-year-old restaurant. "Do you know I've never been here?"

"We both know why," he murmured. "Princess Bella wasn't allowed to dine in local establishments with locals like me. Thank heaven there will be no more of that."

The host recognized her immediately, but when Luca shook his head slightly, the other man remained silent. *"Vogliamo mangiare fuori."*

"Si, signor."

At Luca's request they were led to the patio. No diners sat out there yet. The air had warmed up since morning. Luca welcomed the mild temperature and knew Bella would enjoy the surrounding plants and flowers. After he helped seat her, a waiter came to bring them menus. They made their choices, then Luca examined the wine list.

"We'd like champagne first. Krug, I believe. Make it Clos du Mesnil."

"Subito, signor."

Luca smiled at the breathtaking woman seated across from him. "You've never looked more beautiful."

"If I said the same thing to you, I know you wouldn't like it."

"Try me."

"Oh, Luca." Above flushed cheeks, her eyes radiated purple. "I love you so much. I want to believe we will always be together, just like this."

"You do?" He reached in his trouser pocket and brought out the ring.

She stared at it in disbelief. "You still have it with you?"

"I never gave up on you, but are you sure you're ready for the next step?" he teased.

"I want it so much, I'm dying."

"Well, we can't have that." He reached for her left hand and slid it home on her ring finger.

At that moment the waiter came with the champagne and filled their glasses. Luca held on to her and lifted his glass with his left hand. "To the only woman in the world for me. *Ti amo, il mio tesoro.*"

She raised her glass. *"Ti adoro, Luca. Mio eroe."* She squeezed his hand hard. "My dreams began with you. No other man could make them a reality." He touched her glass and they began drinking the delicious champagne. "Shall we ask Father Viret to marry us?"

"Not if your mother hears about it, and she will."

"It doesn't matter."

"Even so, I have a better idea. Tomorrow is Sunday. We could request a meeting with Father Denis at the church. He was our family priest when we lived here. I imagine he'll be delighted to perform the ceremony."

While they smiled into each other's eyes, the waiter brought their salmon. Luca had also ordered *capuns* and *maluns*.

They both were starving and ate everything. "This food is marvelous, Luca. I love these crumbly potatoes and this sausage ball wrapped in chard."

"These are my favorite dishes."

"That's something about you I didn't know. I'll have to ask your mother for the recipes so I can cook them for you."

"We'll invite them to the condo and she'll show you. Nothing will thrill her more."

"Or me. Growing up I knew how much you loved her, and I always wanted to meet her." She finished her salmon. "Do you think your father will come with her once we're man and wife?" He heard a little tremor in her voice.

"We can hope his heart will soften one day. As for your mother, we'll just have to take it a step at a time. Maybe when our first baby is born."

She chuckled. "I love your optimism."

"Vuoi il dolce?" The waiter had just come to their table.

"Do you want dessert, Bella?"

"I couldn't. The champagne was all I needed."

Luca thanked him and asked for the bill. He put some money on the table.

"Let's go. Before I take you to your apartment and look at your car, I want to stop at the condo. It's going to be our home."

They left the restaurant. He helped her down the outside stairs and they headed to his car. Before long they'd wound their way back to his condo. After he walked her in the living room, he pulled her down on the couch. She lifted her eyes to him. "For us to be alone like this feels too good to be true."

"You took the words right out of my mouth, and I'm afraid it presents a problem."

She sat straighter. "What do you mean?"

"I have one rule. I want to be married to the woman I love when I take her to bed for the first time. Can you understand that?" he whispered.

Bella laid a hand against his jaw. "Yes, because I know you. Over the years you've proven to be the most honorable man alive. No wonder you left the tent on our campout."

"I've already made inquiries about getting married. I'm hoping we can find a way to make it as quick a process as possible."

"I hope so too. Perhaps being a princess will come in useful for something. I don't want to wait another moment to be your wife."

"Thank heaven for you, Bella." Luca's dark head descended and he kissed the life out of her before getting to his feet. "Come on. I'll run you home and change your tire. Tomorrow morning I'll come by for you at nine. We'll go to the church first, then I'll take you out for lunch and we'll make plans."

A half hour later, he walked her to her door. "Try to get some sleep."

She threw her arms around his neck. "I'll be waiting for you in the morning." Her tears started. "Thank you for being wonderful you. I'm the most blessed woman in the world to be engaged to you. When you drive away, I'm going to worry about you until I see you tomorrow. I'd die if anything happened to you."

"Don't say that. I promise we're going to have a perfect life together. *Buona notte, sposa mia.*" In his mind she already was his wife.

She gave him a final kiss that lit him on fire. After he got in his car, she waved. The sight of Bella standing there filled him with a jubilance he'd never experienced before.

He was still walking on air when he entered his condo. He showered and got in bed. For the next hour he answered half a dozen phone messages from his service. There was another message, this one from his father. It didn't require an answer.

I've heard about you joining the Lemond Institute. You've made the biggest mistake of your life. Consider yourself warned.

CHAPTER EIGHT

BELLA WANDERED AROUND the apartment, still having trouble believing that she and Luca were really, finally together. Once she'd showered and washed her hair, she got in bed and lay there for a long time dreaming of the wedding night to come. It felt like she'd been waiting forever to be alone with Luca and love him in every sense of the word.

On Sunday morning she got up and put on a navy print dress appropriate to wear to the church. She left her hair long and slipped on heeled sandals.

At five to nine she reached for her purse and walked out in front of the apartment to wait for him. The sky had few clouds and she noticed the air was much warmer. What a wonderful day!

At five after nine Luca pulled in the parking area. He jumped out of the car and hurried over to her. "You look fabulous."

"So do you." He'd dressed in a gray suit and tie. No man could compare to him.

His eyes played over her face and hair. "I can't fathom that you're going to be mine." He cupped her face and kissed her with a growing hunger. "How did you sleep?"

"I think you know the answer to that."

Luca chuckled and helped her into the car. "Tomorrow we both have to go to work and do our jobs. All I want to do today is make the most of it with you." He started the engine and they drove out to the main road. "Once we've talked to Father Denis, we can do whatever you'd like."

"I don't dare tell you what I'd rather do than anything else because I'm committed to your plan. I *can* wait until we're man and wife."

He gripped her hand as they made their way to the eighteenth-century church. The entrance to the office lay around the side. Once he'd parked, Bella jumped out and walked inside with him, eager to talk to the priest.

"Princess Baldasseri—" the receptionist exclaimed in surprise when she saw Bella enter the office with Luca. She got to her feet and bowed.

"Buongiorno, signora."

Luca walked over to her desk. "I'm Dr. Torriani and have made an appointment with Father Denis. Will you please let him know we're here?"

"I'm so sorry, but he was called away. He left word that any requests regarding you and Princess Baldasseri must go through Father Viret first."

So…the war had started. "I'm sorry too. He was my priest in my youth."

"He said as much. Would you like me to ring Father Viret?"

"That won't be necessary."

Luca exchanged a glance with Bella before he thanked the church receptionist and cupped Bella's elbow to leave. He continued escorting her back outside and helped her in the car. "I should never have underestimated them," he muttered.

"Who?"

Luca pulled out his cell and found the text. "This came from my father last night. I was going to show it to you while we ate, but you need to see it now."

When Bella read it, she groaned. "The team is at it again."

"Yes, they are, so let's pick a time to meet at the civic center tomorrow to apply for our marriage license. Then we'll find a local magistrate to marry us. I can get away from the office for a short time."

"We'll have to go first thing in the morning, Luca. I'm due in Chur on charity business at noon tomorrow and will be gone until Friday with more meetings in nearby towns." She put a hand on his arm. "Why don't we go home and change? I feel like a trip to the mountains."

"You're reading my mind." He winked at her before starting the engine. "We'll pick up food at the deli on the way."

"Even though I'm no longer a princess, it appears we're going to keep my security busy."

He grinned. "It's good for them."

"You know they're spying on us. I wonder if my mother pays them extra."

"I doubt it."

They drove back to her apartment. While she changed into jeans and a dark green pullover, she received a text on her cell.

Please come home, Bella, so we can talk about the situation. You've hurt Prince Antonio. How can you live with this man in Vincenzo's condo and forget you're a princess?

Bella shook her head. There was no situation, only the one with her mother, who knew nothing, thought the worst and created a nightmare by insisting Bella live her life as a royal.

After pocketing her phone, Bella put on her hiking boots and went into the kitchen. Luca was filling their water bottles. Once that was done, he drove them to his condo, where he changed into a dark brown turtleneck and jeans.

The man looked so gorgeous, she wanted them to go into his bedroom and never come out. Instead, she wrapped her arms around his waist from behind. "I feel like we're playing house."

"We *are* playing, and we need to keep playing until we say 'I do.' A man can only take so much."

"Why does a man always say that when in truth, a *woman* can only take so much too. Believe me."

"Bella..." He turned around and gave her a kiss to die for.

Breathless, she pulled away first. "We'd better go now while I can still honor your rule."

They left the condo and drove through town to the deli. "I'll run inside. What sounds good, *bellissima*?"

"Pasta? Salad? Whatever appeals to you."

"I'll bring a couple of colas too."

"Perfect. You're perfect." She kissed the side of his hard jaw.

Sometime later they found an ideal spot a little way up the mountain with a grassy slope ideal for a picnic. He locked up the car and they hiked until noon. She worried he had to be starving by now and suggested they go back to their spot to eat.

While she carried the blanket from his trunk and spread it out, Luca brought their food and drinks from the cooler.

"This is heaven, Bella *mia*." They'd both stretched out half raised on their sides to face each other while they ate. His expression grew thoughtful. "I heard at least half a dozen dings on your phone while we were hiking, yet you didn't answer. Why?"

"After what happened to us at the church, I knew these messages were from my mother. She sent the first one while I was changing for our hike. I didn't respond."

"What did she say?"

Bella pulled out her cell and let him read the text. "I was going to show this to you." They had no secrets from each other. "She assumes we're already living together in the biblical sense."

His penetrating eyes focused on her. "Only you and I know the truth. Your poor mother cares about your princess status deep in her psyche. Don't tell me this message doesn't bring you pain. I know differently."

She let out a sigh. "It all depends on your definition of pain, Luca. Yes, it pains me to disappoint her because she has loved being a princess. She wants that life for me. It has been her experience and I'm happy for her. But I'm my own person and never liked being Princess Bella. To continue any longer would mean living a complete lie. That's a pain I refuse to abide and you know the truth of that in your inner core."

"I believe you," Luca murmured. "You've just described life with my father. He's tried to turn me into a clone of himself. You don't have to be born a royal to have a fixation about your ambitions for your children. I don't want to disappoint him. He's a good man. Successful. But like you, I'm my own person and have hated living a lie that I feared would put me in an early grave."

Her eyes filled with tears. "Then we're in this no matter what."

"*No matter what.* It's one thing for them to have prevented us from being together ten years ago when they could see how we felt about each other. But we're adults now and this time they won't prevail."

He moved everything so he could gather her in his arms. The sun poured down on them while they gave in to their longing. Bella had forgotten everything in the ecstasy of his kisses when she heard a whistle. They stopped long enough to find out where it came from. Four teenage guys were out hiking and waved to them. The little monkeys.

She chuckled before Luca waved back and started kissing her again. She was dying to be closer to him. "I wish we could be put in a coma until our wedding day."

He kissed her throat, sending delicious chills through her body. "Don't think I haven't thought of it."

"Being out here with you is heaven."

"Except there's a forest service ranger coming up the road. I think we've provided enough entertainment for today. Let's leave and I'll drive you to see my new place of work."

She let out an excited cry and sat up once more. "Have you decorated it?"

"Not yet."

"Then let's stop at the condo for your things. I'll

help put up your diplomas. I want to inspect the office where my future husband will be spending his days while we're apart."

"It won't be that different from my office in Saint Moritz."

"Oh, yes, it will, unless Adele has been hired too." Both of them chuckled as they carried everything back to the car and headed for Scuol. "When word gets around that the famous, most attractive, drop-dead fabulous Dr. Torriani is there, he'll be deluged with admirers. It's a good thing you're getting married soon. I think I'll put a big picture of myself on your desk as an instant reminder that you're *taken*!"

Rich laughter rumbled out of him, a sound she could listen to forever.

Within an hour Bella learned that the Lemond Institute of doctors took up a portion of a building near the hospital. Luca had been given an office on the second floor. They carried two boxes from the car and got busy deciding where to put everything.

While she was hanging the last diploma on the wall, Luca went out to the car to bring in some extra cable cord for his computer. Suddenly she heard a knock and turned around.

Two men stood in the doorway. One had blond hair. The older one had dark hair with silver at the temples. Bella recognized him immediately from Luca's pictures at the condo, but she'd never met him. His nice-looking, distinguished father hadn't wasted a moment. She wondered if Luca knew he'd come.

The blond man smiled. "*Buon pomeriggio, signorina.* I don't believe we've met. I'm Dr. Raspar." She knew he had to recognize her, but he didn't act on it. "This is Dr. Jaronas Torriani. He's looking for his son."

"I'm Alectrona Cusso." On their hike they'd decided she would use that name around everyone. After their marriage, she'd be Signora Torriani. *"Che piacere incontrarla."* Except that she wasn't that happy to meet them at the moment. "Luca will be right back. As you can see, we're setting up his office."

Dr. Raspar grinned. "Luca didn't tell me you were coming in today."

"I'm not surprised. We only celebrated our engagement last night."

His father stood there frozen in place. Whether he liked it or not—and he didn't—she and Luca were in, *no matter what.*

"That sly dog. All the unmarried women in this building will be crushed when they find out. May I offer my congratulations. We're thrilled to have Scuol's famous young ski legend and soon-to-be wife join our staff at last."

The innocent comment was a reminder that would always cause her pain. "He's thrilled too, believe me. So am I."

"Well, I'll leave you here with your future daughter-in-law, Dr. Torriani." His gaze flicked to Bella. "I'm sure I'll be seeing you again soon. We're planning a dinner to welcome Luca and at the Hotel Belaval next Saturday evening and will want you to join us, Signorina Cusso."

"I can't wait, Dr. Raspar. Thank you."

When he disappeared, Luca's father moved inside the office staring daggers at her.

"We finally meet in person," Bella spoke first. "I've

always loved your son and am humbled that he wants to marry me."

His brows furrowed. "You still have the power to let him go before it's too late, Princess Baldasseri." His voice possessed a deep timbre like Luca's.

Just then Luca unexpectedly walked in on them holding a loop of cord. "It was too late the first time I met Bella."

His father turned to him. "You can't marry in the church. If you marry outside the church, it won't be a true marriage."

"It will be to God and to us." Luca walked around to hook up the cable to his computer. "That's what thousands and thousands of couples believe who are united in a civil marriage."

"I'm talking about you, Luca, and the way you were raised. You could marry any woman."

"I'm planning to marry the only woman I want forever, Papa. Bella was only eight years old when I met her. She was holding Vincenzo's injured dog Rex. When I told her we didn't have a dog, she said I could come over any time and play with him. She had a sweetness and genuine charm that captured my heart instantly. No other woman has ever come close."

"I felt the same way about you," Bella said in a trembling voice.

The conversation between father and son was no different from Bella's conversation with her mother. Right now she felt compelled to defend Luca. "We've already tried to plan for a private church marriage, Dr. Torriani. It's up to you and my mother to allow that to happen."

"No, it's up to you, Princess Baldasseri. You have the power to let him go, otherwise you will divide the entire Torriani family forever. Do the godly thing and give up this foolishness. Do you deliberately want to estrange Luca from me and his mother?" His cheeks grew ruddy. "If Prince Baldasseri were alive—"

"Bella's father is no longer with us," Luca broke in. "But if he were, it would make no difference." He walked toward her and put his arm around her shoulders.

"Trying to guilt Bella into getting your own way won't do any good, Papa. Her mother has her own strong feelings just as you do. Bella, who's no longer a princess, and I have our own strong feelings too and Mamma has given us her blessing. Any estrangement you've caused is with my mother and no one else. Let that be the end of it so we can all get along."

"Get along—" His father ground his voice to a thunderous pitch. "You truly have lost your mind."

Luca hugged her closer. "When Bella and I have children, you'll be their *nonno* and *nonna*. I know how much you long for grandchildren one day. Think about the future before you say anything else, Papa. You have the power to mend this estrangement that should never *ever* had happened."

"There'll be no royals in the Torriani family tree," his father pronounced like an edict. "I'll see to that." He wheeled around and left the office in a fury.

Bella eyed the love of her life, aching for him because of this impasse. "He's thrown down the gauntlet under no uncertain terms."

"My father did that ten years ago."

She brushed her lips against his chin. "I met Dr. Raspar."

"I know. We saw each other as he was coming out of

the building." Those lightning green eyes flashed between black lashes. "I asked him to avoid calling you Princess. He's still in shock over meeting you in person."

"He was very charming and mentioned getting together for a dinner next Saturday."

"You don't know what it will mean to have my fiancée there at my side. I'll be the envy of every man in sight."

"That's how it was when I was around you at school years ago. The girls hated me for having an in with the school's hero through my brother."

He shook his head and kissed her. "You didn't need an in. We were lucky he provided such great cover for both of us."

She kissed him back.

"Let's grab a bite to eat and get you home, Bella. We've both got a big week to get through. I know you have to leave for Chur. How would you feel about us going to the civic center first thing in the morning to nail down our wedding ceremony? It opens at eight thirty. I'd like to be there on the dot and get things settled. Otherwise, I don't think I'll be able to function."

"That makes two of us."

They left his office for the car. Darkness had fallen. On the way to her apartment, they stopped at a drive-through for takeout. A half hour later they were eating their dinner at her kitchen counter when Luca's phone rang. He glanced at the caller ID. "It's your brother."

She put down the last of her *croque-monsieur* and got up to stand next to him. "When you answer it, will you put it on speaker?"

Luca nodded. "I believe you're as curious as I am." He clicked on and pressed the button so they could both hear him. "What's up, Vincenzo? Bella is right here with me."

"Thank heaven. Now you both need to hear this. I've been at the palace to see Mamma and the grandparents. As I was leaving to go back to Zernez, I discovered your father has come there to see her. I hung around to find out what was going on. They're prepared to do whatever it takes to stop you two from getting married."

"We found that out at the church today," Luca muttered. Bella put a hand on his shoulder.

"Mamma has also put pressure on the regional chief magistrate to prevent a civil marriage."

Upon hearing that news, Luca's gaze fused with Bella's. "Thanks for the heads-up, Vincenzo. We'll do something else, even if we have to leave Switzerland."

"Let's not go that far. I'll think of something, but there's more I have to tell you. Bella?"

"I'm listening."

"According to Mamma, Nonna Caderina has grown worse again. Our mother wants you to fly to Sardinia with her and stay with her for a while. She plans to leave tomorrow. I'm sure you'll be getting a call from her in a few minutes."

Bella squeezed Luca's shoulder. "She was getting better when we left her. Do you believe she's suddenly a lot worse?"

"I don't know. I find the timing suspicious because of your plans with Luca, but you never know."

"Of course not. I love Nonna so much."

"Don't we all. Since I'm still at the palace, I'm going back upstairs to tell her I'm going to Sardinia with her.

I need to find out exactly what's going on. Francesca can't take off any more work so I'll be coming right back and report."

"I'm sorry you have to leave your wife."

"So am I, but I know she has you and Luca to lean on."

"Absolutely! We're crazy about her."

"She feels the same way about you two. I'll stay in close touch. Luca? Hang in there."

"Always." Luca had already gotten to his feet and put his arm around Bella. "We'll be waiting for your call. Come home safely."

He clicked off and pulled her against him, burying his face in her hair.

"My poor brother," she moaned the words.

Luca kissed her temple. "Maybe you should go again so you can see your grandmother and satisfy your worry."

She looked up at him. "I can't go yet since I'm leaving for Chur by helicopter tomorrow. I'll be gone until Friday and meeting with various people in other towns. But after I return, I won't plan anything else until after we're married."

"What if it's a true emergency?"

"Then I'll drop everything to be with her."

"In that case we'll go together."

"Do you have any idea how you've transformed my world? How much I'm going to miss you this week?"

"Tell me about it, *mia principessa*. I need to leave now or I'm in danger of breaking my promise."

She followed him to the door. "Take care, Luca. Life would mean nothing without you now."

"You're the one I worry about. Fly back to me, Bella. We'll talk on the phone this evening."

"I'm living for it." But one more breathtaking kiss from him would never be enough.

The week without Bella yawned wide for Luca. Vincenzo stayed in touch with him. On Wednesday evening he came by the condo. The two men hugged and sat down to eat some muesli cereal with milk, their favorite snack in the palace kitchen when they were young.

"I'll give you the bad news first. Our grandmother Caderina has pneumonia and it's growing worse."

"I'm not surprised." Luca finished his coffee. "What's the good news?"

Vincenzo sat back in the chair with a smile. "I've done some favors for Father Jaines in Zernez. He will be able to marry you up on the mountain. Francesca and I will bring him. All you have to do is be there with my sister."

"How can I ever thank you."

"You don't need to. You're my best friend, I'm happy to do it." He got up from the table. "I'm sorry for everything my mother has done to keep you two apart."

The second he left the condo, Luca called the love of his life. "Bella? Your brother just left. I'm afraid your grandmother is going downhill."

"I can believe it."

"He also gave us some good news. We're getting married by Father Jaines from Zernez, who will marry us up on the mountain. He and Francesca will bring him."

"You mean to our own Garden of Eden?"

"Where else? Rest assured your brother and Francesca will be our witnesses. Maybe the mountain hares will join us too."

"How did he accomplish that?"

"He did the priest a few favors."

"So, royals do have their uses once in a while." He smiled. "Your father would be scandalized."

"My mother will be delirious with joy."

Bella's cry of delight caused him to hold his phone away for a second. "I take it you're happy."

This time laughter bubbled out of her. "I'm in heaven."

"So am I."

"*Ti amo*, Luca."

"*Sei tutto per me*, Bella." She really was his everything. "I'll be waiting for you at your apartment on Friday night." He hung up and went to the kitchen for more coffee. The next order of business was to call Signora Bazzell. He needed to hear details about plans for her son.

CHAPTER NINE

FRIDAY AFTERNOON BELLA arrived in the helicopter behind the palace. Before driving to the apartment to meet Luca, she went inside to see her mother. The family were eating in the dining room. Bella walked around to give each of them a kiss.

"At last! Sit down and have dinner with us," her mother demanded.

"I can't, Mamma. I have other plans, but I just wanted to tell you I'll be flying to Cagliari again soon so I can spend a longer time with Nonna."

"Don't you dare fly there this time with Luca Torriani."

Bella took a quick breath. "He's my fiancé. We're going to be married."

"Oh, no, you're not! When will you be home again?" she demanded. "You've been neglecting your grandparents."

"I've been doing important charity work. I'll be over the day after tomorrow and spend time with all of you. Until after Luca and I are married, I won't make any more commitments to the charity."

"You're not in your right mind either. There will be no marriage."

Taking a deep breath, she said, "Love you all." Bella blew them a kiss and left the palace, driving over speed. Only one thing, one person, was on her mind.

"Luca?" she cried when she saw him waiting for her.

He caught her in his arms and they entered the apartment. *"Mia principessa!"* After swinging her around, he carried her to the couch where they tried to make up for nearly a week's deprivation. Half lying on him, no kiss could satisfy their deep hunger for each other.

She covered his face with kisses, pouring out her love. "I never want to be away from you this long again." Upset after seeing her mother, tears came to her eyes, causing Luca to lift his head.

"What's wrong, Bella?"

"I went inside the palace to see the family after I flew in. Mother is impossible."

"I expected as much." He kissed her hungrily. "Like my father, nothing she says or does is a surprise."

"But under the circumstances it still amazes me how totally inflexible they both are."

"Forget them." Luca caught her wet face in his hands and kissed her again. "Guess what? Hasper's mother has asked us to meet her at the Glarus hospital tomorrow at noon for his operation."

"Nothing could please me more than to hear her son is willing to go through the procedure."

"It's the best news." After a pause, "Now I have something else you need to know."

"What's happened?"

"Mamma phoned me on my way to work because my father was with a patient and couldn't hear her. Yesterday on the phone I told her I knew a secret about your mother and would tell her later. Then I kiddingly asked her what secret she knew about my father's dislike of royalty. I didn't expect an answer. This morning to my amazement, she told me something that explains so much, I hardly know where to begin."

Her heart began to thud. "Has she known this secret a long time?"

"Yes, but my father doesn't realize she knows anything."

Bella swallowed hard. "Am I going to like it or hate it?"

"Hate."

She cringed. "Please don't keep me in suspense—"

"Did I ever tell you about my great-grandfather Basil Torriani?"

"No."

"I never knew anything about him except that he was a tailor. But that's only a portion of his whole life story. It seems he was born and lived in Innsbruck, Austria. He attended medical school there."

"He was a doctor?"

"A well-known one," Luca informed her. "His career in ophthalmology led him to take care of your great-aunt Elsa Baldasseri in San Vitano."

"You're kidding!"

"There's something else you're not going to believe. She went blind after he operated on her eyes." Bella gasped.

"The King, Filipo Baldasseri, your great-great-grandfather, blamed him for causing his daughter's blindness. According to his *mamma*, who'd heard stories from her mother-in-law, he couldn't have saved her sight. In fact, he'd tried with all his might to restore it. But the King accused him and let it be known publicly. It ended his medical career and a humiliated Basil left Innsbruck in disgrace."

A groan escaped Bella's throat.

"It's no wonder my father became an allergist and didn't want me to be a surgeon."

"What a tragedy, Luca."

"Imagine having to give up his practice. He settled in Lucerne, Switzerland, with his family, where he worked in a tailor's shop until he died. It was his son, my grandfather Rudolfo Torriani, a doctor, who eventually settled in Scuol. His wife was born here and she wanted to be near her family. The Torriani family never forgave the King or anyone with the name Baldasseri."

"I don't blame them!" Bella cried. "How absolutely ghastly. No wonder your father holds such hate for me. It's a miracle he joined with Mother to fight you and me. Is there no way to prove that Basil wasn't responsible so his name can be cleared in a public way?"

"I don't know yet. The problem is, my mother learned about this years ago. She's afraid to cause any trouble, but she wanted me to know the truth because she loves us both."

"I love her more than ever."

"I feel the same way about you. Tomorrow I'll pick you up at eight and we'll drive to the hospital to take the helicopter. Let's pray it all goes well with Hasper." He eased away from her with reluctance and got to his feet.

She followed him. "How did I live this long without you?"

"I've asked that question about you thousands of times, but we're back together now and nothing will ever separate us again."

Those words rang in her ears throughout the night. The next morning she shivered in the cool air as they drove to the hospital to board the helicopter. Once strapped inside he grasped her hand. "We're a normal couple now. How does it feel?"

"I love it so much, I wish we were on our way to get married."

"A week from today I'll be able to call you Signora Torriani."

Together they flew to Glarus under darkened skies. After landing, they called for a taxi to take them to the hospital.

Hasper's mother met them in the main lounge. The doctor joined them and they went up to the operating room where they were gowned and masked. The prosthetist came in and soon Hasper himself was wheeled in. His mother hurried toward him.

Luca and Bella waited before walking over to him. "We're here for you, Hasper."

"They said it won't hurt very much."

"That's because they've given you a local anesthetic. It will wear off and you'll have a new leg."

"Will you stay right here?" The boy's brown eyes beseeched him.

"I promise."

"You can bet your father loves you and is watching from heaven," Bella murmured.

Luca put his arm around her waist, loving this marvelous woman beyond anything. She looked up at him before going over to sit by Hasper's mother and the procedure began.

Before long he'd been successfully fitted and was wheeled down to his hospital room, where they gathered round to celebrate. Bella presented him with a cell phone since he didn't have one. She programmed it with their numbers and his mother's. Luca showed him how to program the numbers of his friends.

At three that afternoon he and Bella left the hospital, excited for Hasper. He had a lot of rehabilitation to go through, but in time he'd be walking again. They took a taxi to the heliport. En route Bella had an idea.

"Luca? Since we're not in a hurry now, why don't we fly to Saint Moritz. Call your mother and tell her we'll be there for a while. I want to meet her."

"There's nothing I'd love more, but Dad will know and cause her grief."

"Not necessarily." He could hear her fascinating mind working. "You said she always grocery shops in the late afternoon. What store is it?"

"The Migros market."

"I know it's iffy, but could we rent a car and drive there? Maybe someone who works in produce or something could phone your mom and tell her about a sale that could get her over there right now. I want to get to know her. No doubt the spy network will inform your father, but not before the deed is done. He'll know it was our fault, not your mom's. What do you think?"

"You're brilliant, *bellissima*! I know the exact person."

Before long they arrived at the store and Luca introduced Signorina Cusso to Paulina, who ran the butcher shop.

"You're back in Saint Moritz already?"

His mother had been talking. Luca had an idea Paulina knew he'd moved to Scuol. Why not? They'd been friends for several decades. "Only for an hour. Would you do me a favor and call my mother? Tell her you've got a great sale on leg of lamb, my father's favorite. Tell her the deal won't last long so she'd better get over here now before it's all gone. Don't say anything else."

Paulina winked at him and made the phone call. To his delight she hung up and said, "Your mother will be right over."

Luca paid her for a leg of lamb. "I've included a bonus for you, Paulina."

The woman wrapped it and handed it to him with a broad smile. "If you need privacy after she comes, just go out the back of the store through the produce section. You know where it is."

Indeed, he did.

Bella had been watching the byplay. "Maybe you're beginning to understand why I like living a normal life so much."

"You mean because I get away with murder?" he teased.

"In a way." Her playful smile was so alluring, it was a good thing they were surrounded by dozens of people. "While we're here, I'll do a little shopping so we can drive straight to the condo and eat."

"I'll help."

Ten minutes later they'd paid for a few items and Luca spotted his mother at the meat counter. "Surprise, Mamma." He put his arm around her shoulders and kissed her cheek.

"Oh, Luca—" she cried in joyous surprise.

"Come out the back of the store with me. Your leg of lamb is there waiting with someone I've been dying for you to meet for years."

"You mean Bella," she whispered.

They hurried through the produce area and out the

door. Both women took one look at each other and hugged. For Luca it was one of the happiest moments of his life to see his two favorite women laughing and crying together.

He stood outside their circle while they got to know each other and communicated like mad. But after fifteen minutes, he tapped on his mother's arm. "I'm afraid if you stay here much longer, Papa will wonder what is keeping you."

She hugged Luca again. "Let him wonder. I'm getting to know my soon-to-be daughter-in-law. It should have happened years ago!"

"You're right, but now for your own sake, you *have* to leave." He pulled the wrapped meat from the sack and handed it to her. "Let's go back inside." With another kiss and hug, he and Bella watched her hurry through the store to the entrance.

He turned to Bella, whose beautiful face glistened with tears. Her violet eyes lifted to his. "She's so wonderful, I can't begin to tell you."

"You don't have to. It's written all over both of you."

"That's because we both love you so much."

After the drive home to Scuol, Bella fixed them a pasta meal he loved. But after one glass of wine, he got up from the table to kiss her. "I'm leaving now for the condo and you know why. We'll talk later tonight. Thank you for the delicious dinner and just being you."

Their marriage needed to happen soon or he wouldn't be able to honor his own rule. She knew it too and didn't fight him when he headed for the door. But before he opened it, Bella received a phone call from her brother. She put it on speaker.

"Vincenzo?"

"Where have you been, Bella?"

"In Glarus. One of the children the charity has helped was just operated on to fit a prosthetic leg. Luca and I just got back to my apartment."

"That's amazing what you're doing, but I have distressing news. Nonna Cusso might not make it this time. She's back in intensive care." Luca hugged her tighter. "The doctor says it's bad. Mamma left for Innsbruck and took the jet to Sardinia. Until we know more, Francesca and I are staying at the palace tonight to be with the grandparents."

Bella gripped her phone tighter. "I'm thankful you're there. Luca and I will drive over to the palace in a few minutes and we'll talk. Thanks for letting us know."

She hung up in tears. "Oh, Luca, I know it's coming, but you're never ready."

"At her age pneumonia can play havoc. I'm so sorry."

They cleared the dishes quickly, then left for the palace. "We can leave for Sardinia first thing in the morning, or even sooner if we have to, *bellissima*."

She nodded. "I should have stayed with her."

"But you didn't know she would have a relapse, and Hasper was counting on you. Surely you realize that because of your charity work, you were able to give him a new leg and pay for all the help he'll need. Did you see the love in his mother's eyes when she thanked you, Bella? None of this could have happened without you."

Her gaze met his. "I saw the love in Hasper's eyes when he asked if you would stay right there with him during the operation. You'll be his idol forever."

"I think his father holds that title. Today I couldn't help but imagine our own children one day."

"I thought the same thing. To have a family of our own would mean everything, but right now I'm so worried about Nonna."

"Let's not anticipate the worst." Except that being a doctor, he didn't have great hope she'd pull out of it this time. Her grandmother shouldn't have left the hospital the first time.

Bella clung to his hand all the way back to the palace. At close to nine they arrived and hurried inside. Vincenzo met them at the top of the stairs. "I'm glad you're here."

"I wouldn't be anywhere else." Bella hugged him.

Luca patted his shoulder. "I'm going back to the condo and get things ready in case we need to fly to Sardinia." He kissed Bella and hurried off so the two of them could be alone.

Bella turned to her brother. "In a way, I'm glad we're alone. I know a secret that you might or might not know. If you don't, it will blow your mind."

He held her upper arms and looked down at her. "What are you talking about?"

"Luca found out about it through his mother. What do you know about our great-great-grandfather Filipo Baldasseri?"

"That he was king and died from liver disease. His wife died from influenza. The Baldasseri line continued with our great-grandfather Alonzo, his son."

"What about his daughter Elsa?"

He thought for a minute. "She never married. She died of tuberculosis in a sanatorium hoping for a cure."

"You're telling me the whole truth?"

He frowned. "I swear it. What's going on?"

For the next few minutes she explained everything about Luca's great-grandfather and the awful tragedy that ended his career.

Vincenzo shook his head. "Poor Elsa, poor Basil."

"It's horrible, especially when the truth is that he tried to save her eyesight. It's the rea—"

"Oh, I get the reason," he broke in. "It explains the hate Luca's father has always felt for me."

"And me," Bella added. "Why do you think the King said his daughter had tuberculosis?"

"Probably because she needed care and a sanatorium would accomplish that," Luca reasoned. "Remember that his wife had died the year before."

"I can't bear to think about it. Elsa was blind and didn't belong in an institution. All she needed was love and attention."

"Let's face it, Bella. Our great-great-grandfather ended an honorable man's career out of anger because he needed someone to blame. Like you, I understand Dr. Torriani's rage against us and I'm going to look into it. Don't worry. Luca's mother needn't be concerned that secret can be traced back to her."

Bella hugged him. "Thank you, brother dear."

"Come on. Let's go in the drawing room until we hear from Mamma."

They walked inside and sat down. She pulled out her phone and sent Luca a text.

Darling? My brother knew nothing about Filipo and Elsa. He's horrified and will look into it without your mother ever knowing.

No sooner had she finished sending it than her brother got the call from their mother they all dreaded. At this point she phoned Luca, begging him to come back to the palace with his suitcase packed.

Luca arrived in lightning time and put his arm around her. "Tell me what happened, Vincenzo."

"Mamma spent the last few hours with her. They talked and suddenly Nonna didn't say anything more. The doctor rushed in, but she was gone. If it's any consolation, it was a very peaceful passing."

"I'm thankful for that," Luca murmured. "Do your grandparents know?"

"I just told them. They're in bed. The news was hard on both of them."

"Your poor mother. She shouldn't be alone."

"I agree and have made arrangements to fly us in the helicopter to Innsbruck in the next few minutes. We'll leave for Sardinia from there and help her plan the funeral. She wants it to be on Wednesday, four days from now. Francesca has to work Monday and Tuesday. Then she'll fly overnight to Cagliari with Rini and Luna. He loved Nonna too."

"We all loved her." Bella turned to Luca, and he caught her in his arms. Now came the hard part.

"Bella—I'm not going to the funeral with you."

Her face fell. "What do you mean?"

"This is one time when I refuse to intrude."

"But—"

"No *buts*." He kissed her lips. "We're not married yet. This is a family affair. I know your mother is grieving and I don't want my presence to disturb her while she mourns her mother. She'll want you and your brother at her side."

Her eyes filled with tears. "I can't bear the thought of going without you."

"*Bellissima*—I already had my chance to say my goodbyes to your *nonna* when we flew there. Once we're married, we'll do everything together, but now we need to do the right thing."

She clung to him. "I'm afraid."

He looked at her. "Why?"

"I don't know. I've got this terrible feeling something will go wrong."

"What could go wrong? A week from now we'll be married."

Fear broke out on her features. "What if there's some kind of surprise we hadn't counted on that prevents us?"

Luca hugged her tighter. "Nothing can prevent my marrying you. *Nothing.* Now come on. I'll help you out to the helicopter with your luggage. Let's hope you can get some rest on the flight."

"You think I could rest knowing we're going to be separated for the next five days and nights? I won't be seeing you until Thursday. Luca!" she cried in agony.

"Bella—what is it?"

"I'd die if we couldn't be together."

"We will be," he ground out, sucking in his breath. "It's only five days, then no more separations ever."

"But you can't guarantee it."

"After ten years we found each other again. If that isn't a miracle, then I don't know what is. Believe in it. *I* do. I'll be here when you step out of the helicopter on Thursday and sweep you in my arms."

"What about your work?"

"I'll start my vacation on Thursday. We'll have ten days to honeymoon and do whatever we want."

"Do you have a place in mind?"

"I do, but I'll tell you after the ceremony."

She stared at him. "You have so much strength and faith."

"That's because your love gives me both. I'm the luckiest man alive. Now let's get you out to the helicopter, *mia amata*."

CHAPTER TEN

LATE WEDNESDAY NIGHT, Luca was just ready to phone Bella when he received an unexpected call from Vincenzo.

"Hey, buddy. I'm surprised you're phoning me now."

"This can't wait."

Luca got a sick feeling. "What's wrong?"

"It's fantastic news in the midst of this sadness. I don't know how it will affect your father, but it makes me love my great-uncle Leonardo more than ever."

"What did *he* do?"

"As you know, my cousin Rini is like a brother to me, the same way you are. I told him about your mother's secret. He did a lot of digging and a journal was discovered with all Basil's notes regarding his operation on Elsa. The truth was there, proving that he'd tried to restore her sight, but at the time King Filipo refused to listen.

"Rini was so appalled over the injustice done to Basil, he went straight to his grandfather with the journal. They pored over it together and the King actually wept when he had the proof in hand.

"He has already made a royal apology in front of the San Vitano parliament for the harm done to Dr.

Basil Torriani and the entire Torriani family. He went further and sent letters to the medical society in Innsbruck explaining the miscarriage of justice. Lastly, he wrote a special letter of apology to your family in care of your father. It will be delivered to him by personal messenger from the King himself."

Luca sat on the side of his bed in absolute shock.

"Leonardo has also promised to make reparations to all living Torriani descendants for the damage done to your relative's reputation. I don't know if this will be enough to satisfy your father for all the hurt in your family, but it's a start in the right direction."

At the moment Luca was reeling. "A start in the right direction? It's a miracle only *you* could have brought about. No man on earth ever had a better friend!" Overcome with this news, Luca had to fight tears.

After they hung up, he phoned Bella.

"I've been waiting for your call. I love you so much and can't wait to see you."

"It's a good thing our long wait is almost over. Right now I have something utterly incredible to tell you, *mia principessa*."

"You sound really excited. Tell me before I burst with curiosity."

"I have the most amazing news. But I'm trying to be sensitive because the grandmother you love has just passed away."

"I knew her death was coming. Our last phone call and all that coughing told me a lot I didn't want to admit. You sound different. Please tell me what's going on."

"You have a saint for a brother. I just got off the phone with him. He's done something I can never repay him for. He said that if I married his angel sister, that was all the payment he would ever want."

"He had to say that. Now tell me."

For the next little while Luca related what he'd learned from her brother. "I can't believe he called your cousin Rini to help him uncover the truth about Basil. They're both remarkable men I'm honored to call my friends."

She broke down and had to clear her throat. "Vincenzo has loved you all his life. He'd do anything for you. I felt the same way after I met you, and I love my great-uncle Leonardo with all my heart for what he's done. Rini's a saint too."

Luca nodded. "He's amazing. If my father can't overcome his hurt and anger after all King Leonardo has done, then I don't suppose there's any hope for him in that regard."

"When we get back from Sardinia, you and I can visit your parents and find out your father's reaction."

"I'll see you tomorrow, Bella. I'm living for it."

CHAPTER ELEVEN

BELLA CLIMBED IN the limousine Thursday morning taking all of them to the airport. The funeral had been beautiful. Her mother had taken charge of Caderina's household. She'd handled everything with aristocratic grace and efficiency.

Both Bella and Vincenzo marveled at the way their mother was holding up. They knew her grief had to be unbearable without their father there to sustain her. They tried to help her, but she wanted to do everything herself. All they could do was stand by and offer comfort if she would let them.

When Rini had arrived with Luna and Francesca, their mother greeted them, but it was as if she were living in her own world, detached from everyone. Before long Bella got the feeling her mother wasn't living in reality. None of them could understand the change that seemed to have come over her.

Early Thursday Bella called Luca and told him her mother acted like a robot. "I don't know her like this, Luca. She stares at me with such a strange expression every time she looks at me."

"I'm sure your mother is in shock. She needs to get

through all this before she can function normally. She'll recover soon and be herself," he consoled her.

"I'm sure you're right, but I've never seen her so... so unnatural."

"Give her time."

Bella had only been thinking of herself. "Luca—what about you? Did you tell your mother what the King has done?"

"Of course, and she's so overjoyed she can hardly talk."

"What about your father? I'm almost scared to ask."

"I'm driving to Saint Moritz now, but will return to Scuol at noon. Mamma said Papa received the couriered letter from the King yesterday and went into his office. She says he hasn't spoken about any of it. In fact, he's hardly speaking at all." A groan came out of Bella. "When he comes out for coffee, he walks around like he's in a daze."

"He didn't share any of it with her?"

"Not yet."

"No doubt that letter has sent him into shock."

"I'm surprised it didn't knock him unconscious."

"Oh, Luca—I can't wait until this is over and I can be with you. I need you desperately."

"Come home to me before the day is out, my love. Only a little while longer."

After they hung up, he made himself a bite to eat in the condo kitchen when the phone rang again. His mother's name came up on the caller ID. Now he could tell her he was driving to Saint Moritz.

He picked up. "Mamma? I'm just leaving to be with you."

"Thank heaven. I'm so glad you're coming, *figlio mio*. You must get here at once."

He'd never heard her this upset and his spirits plunged. "Are you ill?"

"No, but I'm going to be if your father doesn't come out of his office. He's been in there all night. He refuses to eat, won't talk, won't answer me, and the door is locked."

"I'm leaving now and will be there within the hour."

"Bless you."

Luca flew out of the condo and headed for Saint Moritz at top speed. The King of San Vitano had done everything in his power to make amends to their family for King Filipo's cruelty to Basil. Luca's father was a proud man, no doubt about it. But not to talk to his loving mother about this great blessing to their family really threw Luca.

As soon as he arrived at their house, he rushed inside where his mother waited for him in the living room. He hugged her, but could tell she'd been in pain. Together they walked through the house to his office.

"Papa? I just got here and I want to talk to you. Please open the door."

"Go away!" his father bellowed.

Luca had never heard him this out of control. He shared a worried glance with his mother.

"We need to talk, Papa."

"This is all your friend Vincenzo's doing! Damn him to hell and his interference! If you think this letter from King Leonardo changes anything, you're very much mistaken.

"How typical of this family to try and gloss over Basil's tragedy with meaningless words and money thrown at the problem. It's another case of the Baldasseris trying to force through what they want no matter what. Should you dare to marry Princess Baldasseri, your mother and I will disown you. Do you hear me? It will be as if you never existed on the face of this planet!"

His father sounded out of his mind for real.

Luca's mother grabbed his hand and shook her head. "There's no reasoning with him right now."

"I can see that. You're coming back to Scuol with me right now to spend the weekend. Grab the things you'll need and we'll leave."

"I can't, Luca. He's my husband."

She was noble and loyal to the end, but it would be her ruination to stay with him right now. "He has crossed a line, Mamma. Come with me and let him find out what it feels like to be without the love of his life."

"Oh, Luca. I can't believe this is happening."

His fists clenched. "I can, and now his behavior is hurting you."

"I shouldn't have called you."

"Oh, yes, you should have, and I'll always be here for you, Mamma."

"I know. I'm so sorry he's having such a difficult time accepting the inevitable."

Luca nodded. "A difficult time hardly describes his state of mind. It's clear he's going to take my marriage out on you if I go through with it." He walked around the living room for a few minutes, then stopped. "I can't allow that, not with you the sacrificial lamb for the rest of your life.

"I know Bella. She'll want you to live with us for the rest of our lives. We'll find a large place to live where you can have your own apartment. For a little while I believed we could make it all work, but now I know differently. Papa will have to live alone with what he's done."

"*Luca*—don't you think this will pass? Your father is a good man."

"I don't know. It may not be permanent, but I'm not letting his tantrum ruin everything. Go on and get packed. I'll help and we'll drive back in time to meet Bella's helicopter."

"But your father didn't used to be like this at all."

"That's true, but the situation has changed. I love you too much to watch him punish you because of my actions. He thinks he can stop this wedding, but he's going to find out differently."

An hour later they were ready to go. He walked through the house to his father's office once more and knocked on the door. "I'm leaving, Papa. Just so you know, Mamma is coming with me. Bella and I will be taking care of her from now on."

"I forbid it!" he yelled.

"Forbid all you want. If you only knew what a lucky man you really are. You married the woman of your dreams, a woman who's both saint and angel. She has loved you through all these years and put up with your anger and venom. Well, no longer."

They went out to the car with her luggage and left for Scuol. En route they stopped for groceries and a bite to eat. But they reached the condo much later than he'd anticipated. After getting his mother settled, he texted Vincenzo to explain what was going on.

Dear friend, an emergency has come up. I'll explain later. I can't talk to Bella right now and won't be able to pick her up when you land in the next half hour. Keep her with you. I'll call her later.

"I don't see Luca's car," Bella whispered to Vincenzo after they all climbed out of the helicopter. Her mother had already gone inside the palace with Francesca.

Her brother put his arm around her. "Luca just texted me about an ongoing emergency. He said he'd call you in a little while."

"I just don't understand it."

"He's a doctor, remember?"

"I know, but—"

"Come on," he spoke over her. "Let's go inside. Mamma said she wants to have a talk with you. Since Luca can't come yet, now would be a good time."

Bella shook her head. "She wouldn't talk to me the whole time we were in Sardinia. *Now* she wants to talk? I can't take any more. After I go inside to change, I'm driving over to his office and wait for him."

She rushed inside the palace and hurried straight to her suite. After a quick shower and shampoo, she dried her hair and brushed it out, leaving it long. Then she put on her pleated white pants and a silky lavender blouse. Once she'd applied lipstick and slipped on her sandals, she was ready.

But when she whisked out the door, her mother stood there waiting for her with that strange look in her eyes.

"Mamma—I can't stay to talk, but I'll be back later."

Tears filled her mother's eyes. "You mustn't go until you've heard what I have to say."

Bella shook her head. "I've heard it all."

"No. You've never heard any of this. I only came to my

senses in the last few hours before Mamma died. Let's go in your bedroom where we can be strictly alone."

What? "I can't right now. I have to find Luca."

"And I want you to. When you do find him, tell him that I'm no longer against your marriage. Luca *is* a wonderful man. I've done a terrible thing trying to keep you from being with him. I thought I was being a good mother and guiding you to your destiny. Now I know that was wrong."

Something was seriously wrong with her mother.

"Mamma made me see things clearly for the first time in years. She spoke from her soul and told me how wrong I was to impose my will on you. She loved you so much, and she loved Luca. In him she saw all the attributes of a true prince. I was blinded by my own willful aspirations. Marcello went along with my wishes, but I know deep inside your father always approved of Luca and would want you two to marry."

All Bella could do was gasp.

"Mamma made me realize that I had no right to plan out your life. Being your mother didn't give me carte blanche to decide your path. Our long talk was an illuminating revelation that has made me see everything differently. More than anything in the world I want your marriage to take place in the church here."

"Y-you're serious—"

"Yes. I promised her that I would talk to Father Viret and ask him to marry you in front of our friends and family on Saturday. I called him before she took her last breath, and I've already spread the word so everything is set for your ceremony at ten a.m."

Bella stood there blinking in confusion. "What has happened to you, Mamma? I know Nonna's death has devastated you. But what you're talking about now doesn't make any sense. I simply don't understand you."

"Please believe me, darling. I'll be asking God's forgiveness forever after what I did to you following the avalanche. Luca has always made you the happiest girl on earth. I could see that, and resented it because it didn't go along with my rigid idea of what your life should be. I can only hope and pray that in the years to come, you'll forgive me and let me be a part of your life with Luca. Forgive me."

Bella broke down and embraced her mother. Joy filled her soul. She remembered Nonna's final words to her. *Everything is going to work out for you and Luca.* Bless her dear grandmother for her big heart and her wisdom. If Bella and Luca had a girl, they'd name her Caderina in honor of her.

Half an hour later, a shaken, overjoyed Bella left her mother in the bedroom and raced out of the palace for her car. She called Luca, but it went to his voice mail. In a panic, she drove to his office and rushed inside, only to learn he hadn't come in to work because of an emergency. When she called the hospital, they hadn't seen any sign of him either. Vincenzo swore he knew nothing except for the text Luca had sent him.

This meant that Bella's earlier premonition had come true. Something was horribly, horribly wrong. She rushed to the condo, but his car wasn't there, nor was he parked in front of her apartment. In a final moment of desperation, she phoned his mother in Saint Moritz. Again, all that greeted her was the call-forwarding message.

Not being able to find Luca took her back to the day

when she'd tried to reach him after the avalanche and couldn't. This was a thousand times worse than déjà vu.

Bella got the feeling his disappearance had everything to do with Luca's father. Instinct told her he'd gone to Saint Moritz to confront hm. This time Bella knew exactly where to find him. Together they'd face the bitter man who had the most marvelous son on earth.

Fifty minutes later she approached the door of the Torriani home in Saint Moritz. Luca's car wasn't around, but that didn't matter. She was here now and she would force him to tell her where his son had gone.

After knocking half a dozen times, the door opened and she faced the man who'd done so much damage to all their lives. "I'm looking for Luca. Do you know where he is? He was supposed to meet the helicopter earlier, but my brother received word there'd been an emergency. Have you any idea what that was about?"

He just stood there with his hand on the door handle looking dazed. In a way he reminded her of her mother while they'd been in Sardinia. "He was here hours ago. I have no idea where he is now."

"Is your wife here?"

His expression closed up. "No."

"I see. Well, just so you know, my mother has had a change of heart. Luca and I will be married at the church on Saturday at ten by Father Viret. There's absolutely nothing you can do about it. Only you have the power to change the situation with your son. He's always loved you and always will.

"I'd like the chance to love you too. After all, you're the man along with your wife who gave him life and molded him into the sensational human being he's become. Any father on earth would give the world for a unique, marvelous son like him. How sad if you can't see what a blessing he is in all our lives. I'll love him forever."

Bella fought not to break down until she reached her car and headed back to Scuol. She'd go to his condo and wait for Luca. Then, as if it was a sign from the heavens, Bella's phone rang and Luca's face appeared on the call screen.

Luca had been watching for her from the window while his mother was getting comfortable in the guest room. The second he saw her car, he ran out of the condo and pulled her from the driver's seat. They threw their arms around each other, kissing each other hungrily. This long five-day wait had been the hardest of all.

"Forgive me for not being there when you flew in, Bella. I have so much to tell you. Mamma is inside with me. My father has turned into a madman, so she's going to be living with us from now on."

"That dear woman. I want her with us always. I knew something awful had happened between you and your father for you not to be there when we set down."

"Mamma called me early and told me to come to Saint Moritz quickly. I drove there as fast as I could. Papa wouldn't leave his office. He said the letter from King Leonardo meant nothing. He damned Vincenzo for his part in everything. Worse, he told me that if you and I married, he and my mother would disown me."

"Oh, no, Luca—"

"Oh, yes. I knew he'd take our marriage out on my mother since she'd given us her blessing. I had to have a long talk with her and convinced her to come with me. It took time to get her packed. By the time we reached

Scuol, we weren't going to be able to meet the helicopter. I texted Vincenzo that there's been an emergency and that I'd explain later."

"I knew something ghastly had happened. When I couldn't find you anywhere, I drove to Saint Moritz."

"You're kidding—"

"I saw your father. He opened the door and he looked as dazed as my mother did back in Sardinia. He said he was alone. Now I know why. I gave him a piece of news that probably did blow him away completely."

He looked troubled. "What news?"

"My mother has undergone a total change of heart, all due to my *nonna* before she died." For the next few minutes Bella told him everything. "Mamma has begged my forgiveness and wants our marriage. She's a changed person, Luca. You won't believe it when you see her next."

"I think I'm having a heart attack, *bellissima*."

"I know. I only wish the same transformation would happen to your father. I told him you loved him, and that I wanted to love him too. I told him we'd be married by Father Viret at the church on Saturday, just so he was informed."

Luca crushed her in his arms again, trying to take it all in. Bella's love for him washed over him like a giant ocean wave. "I've missed you so terribly that there were nights when I wanted—"

"To die?" she cut in. "Every night was like that for me. When you weren't there at the helicopter pad waiting for me, I knew my worst fear had been realized."

He grasped her shoulders and stared at her. "Your mother really has turned our world around. I'm out of my mind with joy."

"So am I, Luca. Maybe in time your father will have a change of heart too. But let's be thankful your mother is with us. I love her so much."

He threw his arm around her shoulders. "Let's go inside and discuss all our plans with her."

"You need to call Vincenzo too and ask him to be your best man. Tell him we'll never be able to thank him enough for everything he's done for us."

"I already did ages ago."

Once inside the condo, Bella looked around. "We won't be married with the hares as witnesses after all."

"We'll go up there on our first anniversary. How does that sound?" He pulled her down on the couch and started kissing her, forgetting his mother, let alone forgetting that they weren't married yet. A long time passed before Luca lifted his head. "Two more nights and you're all mine."

Her smile illuminated his world. "I've been all yours since I was eight years old. How does it feel to be holding an ordinary girl in your arms?" she teased.

He traced the line of her lips with his index finger. "Princess or not, you were never ordinary, thank heaven. We'll never let it matter to our lives again."

"Amen, *caro*."

"Bella? Luca?" They both shot up at the sound of his mother's voice.

She laughed heartily. "Sorry to intrude."

Bella jumped and ran over to hug her. "You could never do that. I'm so thankful you're here. Luca has told me everything. Maybe your husband will have a change of heart in time."

"I'm wishing for that."

"Of course. We all are."

Luca walked over. "Bella drove to Saint Moritz looking for me, Mamma. Papa answered the door, still unreachable, but let's not allow that to ruin our happiness right now. Come in the living room and sit down."

It was like music to his ears as he listened while Bella told his mother of her mother's change of heart.

His mother laughed in a way he'd never heard her do before. "I'm elated and I can't wait to see you two get married on Saturday at the church."

"What about Papa?"

"What about him? While you were in here, I was in the guest bedroom talking to Bella's mother on the phone. Neither of us is worried. He'll either come around, or he won't. We both agreed men can be impossible."

Incredulous, Bella and he stared at each other before they burst into laughter.

"Wait—you've talked to Bella's mother?"

"Of course, Luca. Bella's bodyguard told her where we were and she called me, begging my forgiveness. I told her there was nothing to forgive. A mother tries to do the right thing for her child. In the end it is all working out. Both of us are looking forward to grandchildren. We agree you two can't get married soon enough. Do you have any other questions?"

CHAPTER TWELVE

THE REST OF Thursday and Friday were a scramble to get ready for the wedding. Bella called Constanza to be her bridesmaid along with Luna. Constanza would stay at the palace.

She asked her friend to come early to help her buy a wedding dress. It turned out to be a long silky white dress. No train and a short mantilla. Nothing a princess of the realm would wear. That was the way Bella wanted it.

Luca made calls to a few colleagues in Saint Moritz and Scuol to invite them to the wedding. Vincenzo went with him to buy a dress suit and take care of the flowers. On Saturday morning he drove Bella and his mother to the eighteenth-century church where both their families worshipped. The interior had been filled with flowers and scented candles.

To her joy, Rini and Luna arrived early. He'd been very close to Bella's father Marcello and planned to walk Bella down the aisle in his place.

As the church started to fill with family and church friends, Bella's grandparents arrived. The Visconti family flew in from Bern, including Francesca's brother, Rolf, and his fiancée, Gina.

Bella waited out in a room off the foyer in her wedding dress, delighted to see Francesca's boss, Dr. Zoller, and his wife enter the church. Two other people she worked with closely at the charity had also come. So far everyone she loved had arrived.

She kept watching and waiting. Only one person was missing. But she couldn't let it ruin this glorious day when she would become Luca's wife.

Vincenzo came in the little room at the last second with her bridal bouquet. "You're a vision, Bella. I hope Luca can handle your radiance."

She kissed his cheek. "I love you."

"The war has been a long one for you, but it's over today and your new life of joy is beginning. If ever there were two people made for each other..."

"I feel the same about you and Francesca."

He squeezed her. "Rini is right outside."

"What a magnificent friend he's been." Her eyes filled. "Because of him, a terrible wrong has been righted."

"He's the best. So is Luca, but I don't have to tell you that."

"No. There's no one like him. If he hadn't become your best friend, I would never have known him. I can't even imagine it. Not to have known or been loved by Luca Torriani—" Her breath caught.

"Say no more. I understand completely." He kissed her cheek and left the room.

Bella picked up her bridal bouquet of roses and gardenias and walked out to join Rini. He looked every bit as dashing as Luca in a navy-colored dress suit.

"Dr. Torriani is one lucky man, cousin."

"I'm the lucky one to be walked down the aisle by you. The great service you have done to restore Basil Torriani's reputation will never be forgotten by me or

Luca. My father loved you. More than ever I understand why. Thank you from the bottom of my heart for standing in for him today."

"It's my greatest pleasure, Bella. You were always more like a sister to me than a cousin. Are you ready?"

"The truth is, I've been ready for years."

He flashed her a beautiful smile. "The organ music has started. Let's go."

But before she could take hold of his arm, another person entered the church. A man. She took one look at him and almost fainted.

It was Luca's father!

He'd come! Luca wouldn't believe it. She could hardly believe it and looked up at Rini. "Do you know who that was?"

Rini smiled. "Oh, yes. It seems the miracle we wanted just came true. After you, Bella."

She took his arm and they walked through the foyer into the church. Bella felt as if she were floating in a dream. Luca stood near the altar with Vincenzo next to him. Her beloved wore a gorgeous dark blue suit with a gardenia in the lapel.

If a person could die from loving someone too much, she was the prime candidate for all time. His eyes had focused on his father, who'd walked up to the front and sat next to Luca's mother. She'd been seated with Bella's mother, who sat next to her parents, Alfredo and Talia. *Incredible.*

This was a day out of time like no other. A miracle *had* happened. Her heart was bursting with joy. She could only imagine Luca's.

When she could gather her wits, she saw Luna and Constanza standing on the other side of the altar in beautiful ivory-colored gowns. Father Viret stood in the middle in his ceremonial robes.

Rini led her to the priest, who smiled at her. They'd been friends for years.

"What a beautiful sight," he began. "Two choice spirits who've worshipped here since they were born, wanting to be united in marriage. Two exceptional human beings whose love has brought them to God's house. Two sets of remarkable families all united as one on this glorious day."

Bella felt like this just couldn't be happening.

"Luca? Come and take Bella's hand."

Her gaze fused with his incredible green eyes for this first time since entering the church. She saw a light in them that had taken away the last shadow. To realize his father had come around had made all the difference in the marriage they were going to have.

Father Viret nodded to Constanza, who relieved Bella of her bouquet. Luca gripped her hand and held it fast.

"You two beloved people don't need a sermon in constancy or devotion. Others could learn from your example of how to love and never give up hope. Having said that, I'd like to marry you as soon as possible since I know you can't wait any longer."

She loved Father Viret.

"Bella Baldasseri? Do you take this man, Luca Torriani, to be your husband, to honor him, to keep him in sickness and in health, to love him with all your might, mind and strength?"

"I do!" she cried.

"And you, Luca? Do you take this woman to be your wife, to honor her and protect her, to keep her in sickness and in health, to love her with all your might, mind and strength?"

"I do and I will love her through all eternity."

"Then by the power invested in me by the Church, I now pronounce you husband and wife. You may kiss your beautiful bride, Luca."

"Bellissima," he cried softly before covering her mouth with a husband's kiss. There was something different about it from all his other kisses. It was like a promise of things to come that sent sparks of desire through her entire body.

After he let her go, Father Viret said, "The congregation may congratulate Dr. and Mrs. Torriani out on the lawn in front of the church."

Suddenly the bells of the church rang for the whole town to hear. Luca hurried down the aisle with her. They reached the outside first. He kissed her again, almost taking her breath away. "I'm glad we're not having a reception. I need to be alone with you."

"You know I feel the same way. Where are we going?"

"To your brother's chalet in the mountains."

"Are you serious?"

"We'll stay there overnight before we do anything else. I can't handle the thought of being in flight twelve hours."

"I never wanted to go anywhere. All I want is to be alone with you as soon as possible." She rose up to kiss his mouth once more and heard a deep voice say, "Luca? Bella?"

She turned her head and stared straight into the eyes of his father. His were a darker green and piercing. "I don't expect either of you to ever forgive me for what I've said and done."

"It's forgiven, Dr. Torriani," she cried. "You've come. It's the greatest blessing we could have. We'll never talk about it again."

Tears filled his eyes. "You mean it?"

"She means it," Luca spoke in a tear-filled voice. "Thank God you're here, Papa."

Bella watched father and son hug while she embraced Luca's mother, who said, "I prayed he'd come around. It just takes him more time than some people."

"Oh, I love you," Bella whispered. "Bless you forever."

Soon Bella's mother came over. "This was always meant to be, but I couldn't see it. Forgive me, darling."

"You couldn't help anything, Mamma. You've been such a wonderful mother to me. I can't wait until I have a baby who will fall in love with you."

"It would be my greatest joy."

They kissed before everyone else came over. After dozens of hugs, Luca told the crowd he and Bella had to leave.

Everyone laughed, especially Father Viret, who watched from a distance with Father Denis. He knew both their hearts and had done everything in his power to make the nonroyal ceremony short and sweet.

Twilight had fallen over the mountains. Luca hadn't noticed the time. His honeymoon had started eight hours ago. He'd made love to his wife all day and could have gone on all night. But it wasn't fair to her since she needed to eat. So did he when he thought about it.

Francesca and Vincenzo had done everything to supply them with food and comfort. They wanted for nothing. While she slept for a few minutes, he slid out of bed and threw on a robe. Before long he'd brought her dinner and put it on a table near them.

Could there be anyone more delectable than his new wife? Her long wavy hair swirled around her on the pillow. His eyes played over her body partially covered by the sheet, a miracle of feminine beauty. He was thankful he'd managed to remain true to his promise. Their wedding night was sheer rapture and worth the long wait. She gave and gave, filling him, completing him, with her love over and over again. If a baby resulted, nothing would make him happier.

Suddenly she opened her eyes and rose up on one elbow. "Where did you go?"

"I brought our dinner. May I serve you?"

"Oh, Luca. Yes." She sat up straighter.

He brought the tray over to the bed and got in, placing it between them. "Francesca takes the honors for our meal."

"My favorite, chicken scampi. Vincenzo must have told her."

"I love it too."

They ate while smiling into each other's eyes. "Could you believe Father Viret? He performed a quick, modern, commoner ceremony."

Luca drank some wine. "He loved doing it, you could tell."

She sipped her wine. "I saw your father come in the church while I was waiting with Rini. I came close to fainting."

"So did I when he walked down the aisle." They continued to eat. "Mother had a lot more faith in him than I did."

"That's because their love is true and she knows him inside and out."

"The way you know me." He leaned over to kiss her cheek.

"Did it really surprise you when I phoned you the day after Vincenzo's wedding?"

"Yes. I wanted you to. I prayed for it, but after ten years... Since then I've learned a lot more about you.

When you proposed to me in the tent and told me you'd given up your title, I began to hope that your love was here to stay forever."

"It is, and I want you to love me all over again, day and night. Do we have to go anywhere else on our honeymoon?"

"Not if you'd rather stay here."

"You know I do. But how do you feel? Tell me honestly, Luca."

"I've been waiting for you to beg me to stay right here until we have to go home." He moved the tray to the table and got back in bed, half covering her with his body. "I'm addicted to you, my wife—every part of you. *Ti amo!*" he cried.

Luca devoured her with his mouth and rolled her on top of him. He needed to feel her arms and legs around him again, enclosing him as they once again began the age-old ritual that sent them soaring as one.

The hours passed. "You're so beautiful, no words can describe you. Love me, Bella. Always love me. I'm nothing without you." He covered her face and throat with kisses. "These past weeks of waiting came close to driving me mad. I've always had to love you from afar. But now we're married for eternity, and I can worship you with my body until the end of time."

"I love *your* body, Luca Torriani. I love your heart, your mind. Out of all the women in the world, I'm the most blessed one of all to be your wife."

He kissed her hungrily. "You're my very soul, Bella."

* * * * *

WHISKED INTO THE BILLIONAIRE'S WORLD

NINA SINGH

MILLS & BOON

To all those still trying to find where they fit in best.

CHAPTER ONE

SHE JUST COULDN'T do it. She couldn't allow this couple to tie the knot.

Clairey Robi knew she would lose her job for what she was about to do. But the two people in question had no business getting married. The results would be too toxic.

And there was a child involved.

She'd been on the fence until she thought about the child. Given what Clairey had herself dealt with growing up, how could she risk what might happen to the little girl? Still, what she was about to do was rather daunting. And she was just starting to like this job. Plus, she needed it badly. Really badly. Clairey was at the level of broke where she was actually being charged for it. The bank kept imposing fees on her measly account for insufficient funds. What a racket that was.

Determined, she brushed all those annoying thoughts aside and continued across the resort lobby, aware that the havoc that she was about to cause was sure to wreak havoc in her own life for years to come.

The sound of sharp, pointed heels sounded behind her. Tessa Gilman was striding next to her a moment later.

"You still determined to go through with this?" the

other woman asked. They'd discussed Clairey's quandary at breakfast in the resort's outdoor café by the pool area.

"I wouldn't be able to live with myself if I didn't." That was the absolute truth. How different might her own life have been if someone had ever bothered to step up for her? If there'd been someone who'd cared enough?

But there hadn't been.

She couldn't just stand by and watch another child potentially go through what she herself had.

Tess frowned but Clairey didn't slow her steps. If she hesitated now, she might not go through with it at all. "I hope you know what you're doing." Tessa elongated the final word into three syllables.

"Of course I don't. I tossed and turned all night with the decision. Agonized over it." That was no exaggeration. Clairey's eyes stung, red from her restless night.

"Okay," Tessa answered. "As long as you're prepared for Louis's reaction. He's going to be livid."

Clairey cringed at the mention of her boss's name. The man was a grump in a sales-rack suit on the best of days.

"I know," Clairey answered, but she kept walking at her steady rate toward the secondary conference room.

Tessa for some reason felt the need to drive home her very obvious point and kept talking. "He is absolutely going to fire you. And it's not like he'll give you any kind of recommendation to help you get another job."

Clairey sighed. Why was Tessa repeating all this? They'd gotten into all of the unpleasant outcomes this morning at breakfast. The fact that she'd be out of a job with no real prospects of finding another one anytime soon was one of the major reasons for her hours-long insomnia last night.

"Why do you feel so strongly about this?" she asked.

The question gave Clairey pause. Tessa knew why. Maybe not the full story but enough of the overall gist.

Clairey had no interest in dredging up the devastating memories. Especially not now with what she was about to do.

To make matters worse, the timing was just so off: just when she thought she might be able to save enough money to be able to stop crashing on Tessa's couch and find a place of her own. That clearly wouldn't be happening anytime soon. Not with all the student loans she had to pay off.

Best to just get this over with. She made it to the double doors of the meeting room by the concierge desk and pulled them wide open, then stepped inside with a deep, fortifying breath. Seven pairs of curious eyes immediately whipped in her direction.

Okay. Maybe the entrance had been a bit dramatic. But even a moment's hesitation might have caused her to delay or perhaps even change her mind altogether.

She turned to Tessa for some support and courage but only saw her friend's back as the other woman made a hasty retreat down the wide corridor back toward the main lobby.

So much for friendly support. With another deep breath, Clairey stepped into the room and pulled the doors shut behind her.

The seven in attendance sat around a conference table, various binders and loose papers strewn about its surface. Seven? Why was there someone else among the group? The bride, her mother, the groom, the photographer, the florist and their wedding planner. As for the other gentleman, Clairey couldn't guess who he was. She'd never seen him before.

Clairey's gaze fell to the one unexpected attendee. And she had trouble regaining her focus.

The man was almost unnaturally handsome. Jet-black wavy hair that framed a face of tanned olive skin, his eyes the color of warm amber. His suit jacket hung over the back of his chair.

And he was staring right at her with intense scrutiny.

Who in the world was he? She'd thought she'd met every member of the wedding party. And she absolutely would have remembered meeting this man.

"Clairey?" Emma, the bride's mother finally addressed her. "I'm sorry. I didn't realize we were expecting you for this meeting."

Clairey managed to somehow tear her face away from Mr. Tall Dark and Handsome. Not that it was easy.

"I'm not here for the meeting," she finally answered once she'd found her voice.

"Then, why are you here?" Danielle, the bride, asked.

Here it was. The moment of no return. "To tell you that I strongly believe tomorrow shouldn't happen."

The woman certainly knew how to make an entrance. Drexel Osoman stilled in the act of signing his name to yet another check, made out to the florist this time, and studied the meeting-crasher.

She looked more than ready for a fight.

And what she'd just said certainly qualified as fighting words. Had she really just declared that tomorrow's wedding should not go forward? His soon-to-be sister-in-law scowled across the table. "I'm sorry. Is this some kind of joke?"

Drex realized just how anxious the young woman was. *Clairey* the bride's mother had called her. She was shaking visibly, her fists clenched tight at her sides. Her eyes were wide with apprehension.

Yet, she was clearly still determined to go through with what she'd come in here to do.

Drex couldn't help but be impressed.

She shook her head now with a brisk movement that sent her wavy chestnut curls bouncing. "No. It's no joke. I've come here to say I strongly object to the two of you getting married."

An audible and collective gasp echoed throughout the room. Her eyes seemed to have landed on him as she finished her sentence. As if looking for some confirmation or support from his direction. As much as Drex agreed with her, it wasn't as if he could actually say so.

She continued. "I think doing so would be a terrible mistake that would only lead to unnecessary suffering."

Wow. That was rather direct. Another round of gasps followed her words.

Drex took a moment to study her. She was…striking. It was the first word that came to mind. Her long dark hair cascaded down her elegant shoulders. Grayish-blue eyes outlined in dark charcoal. Smooth, tanned skin. She looked like she could be an extra in one of those old Hollywood films about Cleopatra.

No. Strike that. This woman was no extra. She

would definitely be the lead. He gave a shake of his head. What was wrong with him? He had more pressing matters at the moment than this woman's notable looks.

Drex leaned back in his chair and scanned the others in the room. One by one, they all seemed to turn in his direction with clear expectation.

How and why had he become the decider on exactly what to do about the current scenario? He'd only arrived at the crack of dawn this morning, for heaven's sake.

The meeting with his overseas partner-to-be had not gone well. The man was culturally traditional and didn't want to budge on any of the more modern ideas for the project. It had taken all of Drex's wits and willpower to maintain a steady resolve with the negotiations. All he wanted now was a long shower and a chance to catch up on some of his other demands. He really was in no mood for any of this.

But seeing as he'd found himself in the middle of some kind of strange standoff with no real resolution in sight, it was clear he was going to have to take the lead here. Putting his pen down with a resigned sigh, Drex cleared his throat.

"I've just arrived, Miss...?"

"Robi. My name is Clairey Robi," she supplied.

"Ms. Robi. I'm Drexel Osoman. The groom's older brother."

She made some sort of small movement with her shoulders, not quite a shrug.

Drex continued. "I was due here earlier but have been busy with a rather complex business deal and couldn't get here until near dawn this morning." If the irritation he felt was evident in his voice, there was nothing for it. He didn't need all this drama on top of everything else happening in his life at the moment. "May I ask, what exactly is the issue here?"

She sucked in a breath. "It's like I said earlier, Mr. Osoman."

"Call me Drexel, please. Or Drex."

She visibly swallowed. "It's like I said earlier," she repeated. "I strongly object to the marriage moving forward. I know I'm merely a stranger here—"

Drexel cut her off once more. "Indeed, you are."

She flinched ever so slightly. "I'm aware. But I needed to let my feelings be known."

Drexel steepled his fingers in front of him on the table. Clearly, the woman had some sort of delusions about her opinion mattering to anyone in the room. Nevertheless, Drex was slowly starting to put the puzzle pieces together to form a comprehensive picture. Starting with that easy corner piece. That piece being how well he knew his brother.

She really was quite attractive. It didn't take a genius to surmise that his brother must have indulged in one last dalliance before his impending nuptials. And now the codallier was too enthralled and smitten to see Chase tie himself to another woman.

Chase never did make anything easy on himself. Or on Drexel for that matter.

"Objections are usually reserved for the ceremony, are they not?" he asked. "When the officiant asks whether there are any. You know, *Speak now or forever…*well, you know." Not that doing it that way would have been less disruptive. But Drex was trying to get a feel for what exactly her thinking was.

Another brisk shake of her head. "Of course I know. But I'm not invited to the wedding. I have to do it now."

Drexel couldn't help the curious spark of admiration he felt at her answer. She was determined to go through with this calamity, despite how nervous she clearly was. "I see."

She forged ahead. "Obviously, no one has to listen. And obviously, people have the right to do what they want." She motioned to his brother and his bride. "But I have to say my piece. And hope someone listens."

"And that is what, exactly?"

Maybe he was being too indulgent: he really should politely but firmly take her by the elbow and escort her out at this point. But heaven help him, he wanted to hear what she had to say.

Clairey tried to clamp down on her nervousness. She hadn't expected another person to be in the room, but he was clearly in charge. The others seated around the table seemed to think so, anyway. They were all staring at him, waiting for his direction. Even the bride and groom themselves.

"Ms. Robi," he prompted her now.

Oh, yes, he'd asked her a question, hadn't he? What was it again? Seeming to sense her struggle, he repeated it. "Perhaps you'd like to tell us exactly what your concerns are with regard to this union." He motioned to the couple seated across him.

Clairey noticed for the first time the wide-eyed panic in the bride's eyes. She'd gone a marble shade of pale. The look she directed at Clairey was clear: *Please don't do this.*

Once again, Clairey felt the inklings of doubt and

hesitated. She didn't want to ruin anyone's reputation, but the things the bride had told her last night in her drunken state could not be ignored in good conscience. Still, she wasn't going to divulge the other woman's ramblings outright. She had to tread carefully here.

She licked her lips, which had suddenly gone desert-dry. She scrambled to find the right combination of words. The things the bride had told her last night had been divulged in confidence, as awful as they were. Clairey hated to think she was betraying that confidence, but what choice did she have?

As common a cliché as the horrible stepmother was in various fairy tales and folklore, life was more complicated than that. Danielle really seemed to be in over her head as far as the prospect of parenting a young child.

Unlike Clairey's own stepparent, the woman didn't seem to harbor real ill will. Rather, Clairey sensed she was nervous and apprehensive about the vast responsibility about to be foisted on her.

"Um… I don't think the couple have thought through exactly what a life change marriage might be for everyone involved. *Everyone.*"

Dear God, she knew she sounded downright ditzy.

A peal of laughter erupted from the bride's mother. The photographer coughed into his hand. As loud as it all was, Clairey could hear the nervous breathing from Danielle.

Clairey swallowed and forced herself to continue. "It takes more than a wedding ceremony to make someone a stepparent. I'm not sure the couple has thought that through." It was as close to specific as she was willing to get at the moment in front of everyone.

"This is ridiculous," the bride's mother declared. "Drexel, surely you don't intend to indulge this…this… twit any longer."

Ouch. That one hit home. Being called names was nothing new for her. She'd been called that and many other similar slurs throughout the years. Only, right now, she did feel rather like a twit. Albeit a twit with good intentions.

"Look," she began, "I just think these two would be better off maybe rethinking the wedding. I would just hate to see anyone hurt." Particularly one five-year-old girl with strawberry-red corkscrew curls and a wide smile with two missing teeth.

The man who called himself Drexel rose slightly in his chair at her last word. "What do you mean by *hurt*?"

She should have used a different word. She clearly had his attention. Before, he'd been eyeing her with a mild curiosity. But there was nothing mild about the expression he had right now.

At her silence, he added, "That's quite a thing to say, Miss Robi. Surely, you don't mean *hurt* in the physical sense?"

"No!" she answered right away. Though there really wasn't any way to be certain, now, was there?

Besides, physical hurt wasn't the only way a child could be severely damaged. As she knew firsthand.

Someone in the room swore; another released an exasperated sigh. Neither one being the groom. Surprisingly, he wasn't saying much at all, just glancing over at his brother as if seeking guidance. For heaven's sake, the man couldn't even come up with anything to say. He really had no business getting married without considering all the ramifications.

Clairey summoned all the courage she could muster. She had to get through this. "I've simply ascertained, over the course of my dealings with both the bride and groom throughout the week, that perhaps they are rushing into this marriage. I'm not sure either one has really thought it through. And there is a child to consider in all this."

Drexel's eyebrows rose ever so slightly.

The bride's mother shot up out of her chair, so abruptly that she nearly knocked it over behind her. "I'll hear no more of this nonsense. I don't know why anyone here is indulging this woman." She shot an accusing glare in Drexel's direction. "She should be shown the door. I will have no part of it." Huffing, she stormed out of the room.

The bride's eyes darted from her mother's retreating back, then to Clairey, as if debating whether to follow. Seemingly making a decision, she stood and caught up to the older woman. Before walking through the door, she turned with both hands on her hips. "I don't know what this is, but it's obvious Clairey is not exactly credible. I wouldn't believe a word that comes out of her mouth." With that, she stormed off after her mother, leaving the door wide open.

Clairey almost guffawed out loud at that last statement. Danielle had sounded very different about her last night. In a drunken stupor, she'd been slurring her words as she unloaded about how much she didn't want to become a stepmother. That she didn't even particularly like the groom's five-year-old daughter from a previous relationship. She didn't like children in general and really resented having to be saddled with a child for the rest of her life simply because she was marrying its father. *Its* being the actual word Danielle had used.

But all that was almost secondary. The really troublesome thing, as far as Clairey was concerned, was the clear animosity in her voice and in her eyes as she talked about the girl. Marnie was an innocent and unsuspecting child. She had no real say in any of this. No voice at all.

Clairey had no idea who or where the girl's biological mother was. But it was clear the woman was not involved in the child's life whatsoever. In that way, she might have considered herself lucky. At least Clairey had enjoyed the benefit of having both parents in her life for the early part of it. Before everything had fallen apart and her life had shattered when she'd least expected. Clairey pushed the memories away. This wasn't about her.

No, Marnie had no one who really seemed to be concerned about her welfare. No one to speak up on her behalf.

So Clairey would have to do it.

Despite the two dramatic exits, it appeared the strange little standoff continued. Drexel glanced at his watch. He was due on a conference call with a client overseas in under an hour. And this conversation, as unbelievable as it was, seemed to be going nowhere.

Quickly signing his name on the last check—there was no real indication that the wedding would be called off, after all—he rose from his seat.

As Drexel expected, Chase immediately followed his lead and stood as well. The photographer still sat with his mouth agape. The poor man hadn't said a thing since this Clairey had barged in. Drexel pushed the last check in his direction across the table to reassure him that he would indeed be getting paid despite the strange call to cancel the wedding.

Not that it had any credence. But something had compelled Ms. Clairey Robi to do what she just did. Drexel had always trusted his instincts. They'd served him well and had gotten him rather far in life. If there was anything he'd learned throughout his adult years, it was that he should heed his gut feelings.

His intuition was telling him to get to the bottom of whatever had caused all of this drama. She'd mentioned concern for Marnie, his niece. That was worrisome.

But for now, it was high time to end this. This meeting was neither the time nor place for it. Though, he'd have to find Clairey Robi at some point and figure out exactly what had her so agitated about his brother's wedding.

What exactly had she meant about Chase and his bride not being ready to coparent? How in the world would she possibly know that? Was it just some kind of a ruse to cover her true motives?

Again, it occurred to him she was yet another of Chase's jilted flings. But something about that theory didn't sit right the more he studied her right now. For one, she'd barely glanced in his brother's direction this whole time. They hadn't so much as made eye contact, not that he'd seen from where he was sitting.

Which would be rather odd if a wayward fling was the reason for the woman's outburst. No, upon further reflection, Drexel was almost certain he could rule out that this scenario might be due to an ill-timed love affair. For some strange reason, that brought an odd sense of relief coursing through him.

Which made no sense. It really was none of his business if his brother had indulged in one last rendezvous before tying himself to one woman for the rest of his life.

Though, heaven knew, for Drexel even the very idea nearly made him break out in hives.

To each his own.

He crossed his arms in front of his chest and leveled his gaze on Clairey who was now chewing her bottom lip quite aggressively. She was certain to draw blood at any moment.

"You've said your piece, Ms. Robi. I believe you should leave now, as I need to go about my day."

A flash of clear anger shone in her eyes. "Are you dismissing me? Like some sort of—"

"Employee of the hotel?" he finished for her. As callous as his words were, Drexel really had more pressing matters to deal with. He just didn't have time for her anymore. Not if she wasn't going to be specific about what she was here to say. "Precisely."

She bristled and uttered something under her breath. He'd barely made it out but suspected she'd called him a rather unseemly body part. Without another word, she turned on her heel and stormed out of the room.

Everyone remaining in the room stared silently at the door after she'd left. Feeling uncomfortable, someone cleared their throat. Suddenly, Chase bolted out of his seat.

"I'm going to go find Danielle."

Not so fast. Drexel stopped his brother's exit with a

raise of his hand. "Hold on for a minute there, bro. I'd say we need to have a chat."

The others in the room apparently took that as a sign for their own departure. One by one, they gathered their things and took their leave, uttering excuses about having to be somewhere else.

What a mess!

His brother started to protest as soon as they were alone. "I'd really like to go find Danielle. She's bound to be upset after what just happened."

Drexel clicked the tip of his pen up and down. "What exactly just happened, Chase?"

His brother released an exasperated huff. "You think I know? I have no idea why that confounded woman just did what she did."

"None whatsoever? No idea at all what might have compelled her to barge in on a private meeting and make the declaration that she made?"

Chase merely shook his head, his eyes wide.

"Think hard, little bro. Is there anything that might have triggered her actions?" He paused before adding, "Perhaps there was something you did to trigger them?"

Chase blinked at him. "You think I'm responsible for this?"

"I'm merely asking."

"You're asking in a very accusatory way there, brother."

"She's very attractive."

His brother's eyebrows snapped together. "Yeah? So? What's that got to do with anything?"

Drex sighed and pinched the bridge of his nose. Nothing was ever smooth or easy when it came to his little brother. Not even a simple prewedding meeting. "Let's start again. Do you have any idea what the woman might have been talking about?"

"What's with the third degree? I already told you I don't know."

Drex ignored that. "Why did she mention your daughter?"

"She happens to be your niece."

Drex was hanging onto his patience by a mere thread. A thread perilously close to snapping at any moment. "Answer the question."

"Look, Danielle's a talker. Maybe she mentioned something to this woman about Marnie."

"What might she have said?"

Chase released a deep sigh. "She's a little apprehensive. About being a stepmom. If you must know."

"Isn't it a little late for that? She knew you were a father when she met you."

Chase shrugged. "Yeah. But Marnie was with Mom most of the time back then. Her being with me full-time is rather new."

Drexel felt the now-familiar pang of loss and sadness settle deep in his gut at the mention of their mother. Up until several weeks ago, Alice Osoman had been a fairly active woman. One that could take care of her granddaughter despite her disease. She'd been managing her relatively mild symptoms well enough. Then she suddenly got worse. Now she was merely a shell of her former self. A shell who probably wouldn't even recognize the girl anymore. The doctors were very sympathetic when they'd explained that she had one of the rare cases of the disease that progressed particularly rapidly.

That was an understatement. It was as if her symptoms had magnified overnight.

Drex pushed away the distressing thoughts and turned his attention back to his sibling. "If that's the case, then I dare say this Miss Robi was right."

Chase's shoulders slumped, and he rubbed his eyes.

Drex continued, not ready to spare any sympathy given the import of the matter. "You need to figure this out before you and your bride say your *I do*s."

CHAPTER TWO

WELL, THAT HAD gone well. *Not!*

Clairey plopped down in her office chair and waited for the inevitable reckoning. Sure enough, mere seconds later, a loud knocking sounded from the other side of the door. Actually, *pounding* would be a better word. Louis didn't bother waiting for an answer before barging into the room.

"Clairissa! What in the world did you just do? Are you out of your mind?"

Clairey made certain to not so much as flinch. She wouldn't cower. And she certainly wouldn't apologize. She'd made her decision and had acted on it. She would lie in the bed she'd made.

"What in heaven's name were you thinking?" Louis demanded to know. "To interfere in a paid event! A wedding, no less."

She swallowed, lifted her chin and looked the man straight in the eye. "I had my reasons."

He scoffed dismissively. "That's all you have to say for yourself?"

"It's all I have."

He glared at her. "Well, it isn't much."

"I'm sorry, Louis." It was all she could say at this point.

His eyes grew wide. "You're sorry? That the bride and her mom both read me the riot act? They want their pound of flesh for what you just pulled."

"I had no doubt that they would."

"Did you? Did you really think it through? Did you consider that they would trash us online with negative reviews? That they would consider suing and demand refunds? Because that's exactly what they threatened to do."

Clairey squeezed her eyes shut. Louis had a right to be angry. None of this was his fault in any way. She couldn't very well do much about the litigation part. "I'll respond to each online comment. And I'll post on every travel site that it was all me."

He pointed a thick, stubby finger in her direction. "That's not going to do squat, and you know it. We'll be dealing with the fallout from your foolish actions for months to come. Maybe years."

"I'm sorry," she repeated, completely at a loss for anything else to say. She certainly wasn't about to get into her motivations for acting so brashly. Or how much of a kinship she'd felt for the little girl involved. Clairey hadn't even confided more than the bare basics of her childhood to Tessa. She certainly wasn't about to confide in her furious boss.

Anyway, something told her Louis wasn't the type who would understand. There'd be no sense in explaining to him that the cliché of the evil stepmother could be all too true in real life. Or stepfather, in her case.

He ignored her apology. "And apparently the brother is some type of hotshot businessman with considerable clout. The very type of person who can ruin a business with a couple of phone calls to his myriad of friends in high places. Even a place like a high-end resort in Cape Cod, Massachusetts, that's been around for years."

"Then, you have no choice but to place the blame squarely on a low-level employee, I suppose."

Louis rubbed his eyes. "You bet I will. Not that it will do much good."

Clairey hadn't any doubt his plan had been to do just that all along—throw her to the wolves. "I really am sorry," she repeated. "I did what I thought was right."

He shook his head. "Huh. Pack up your desk. In case there was any doubt, you're fired." Sneering at her, he turned away. He slammed the door on his way out, hard enough that her smock fell off the hook. Not that she'd be needing it any longer. As activities manager, one of her duties was to come up with crafts and other ways to keep the younger resort guests occupied and happy. This morning's activity had been to paint paper kites, then try to fly them on the beach. She'd really miss that particular part of the job.

Clairey inhaled and resisted the urge to give in to the sting of tears behind her eyes. She could do any crying once she'd packed up all her stuff and got out of here. She'd be darned if Louis, or anyone else for that matter, might happen to return and see her cry.

She was impulsive and reckless, and what had it gotten her in the end? She'd only managed to jeopardize the reputation of the resort and the jobs of her coworkers, who happened to be some of her dearest friends. Not to mention, she hadn't changed anyone's mind. The wedding was sure to go forward.

Maybe she could talk to the brother. Drexel. The hotshot businessman. Explain to him why she'd done what she had. Convince him not to retaliate. After all, she'd only been doing what she thought was right. She'd been trying to protect his very own niece. Did he know how resentful his soon-to-be sister-in-law felt about becoming a stepmother? He would see her reasoning when she explained. No doubt he would try to dismiss her. But Clairey would find a way to make him understand.

Though, she had no clue how to go about doing that. There was no time. In a matter of minutes, she would be escorted out of here by one of the resort's security personnel. Louis was probably at the guard shed by the entrance right now, posting her picture on the wall with clear instructions that she never get past the gate ever again.

No. Clairey wasn't going to be able to explain anything: she'd probably never see Mr. Drexel Osoman again. It wasn't as if they ran in the same circles.

But she had to try. A little girl's well-being depended on it.

Drexel was distracted. More than a little. Uncharacteristically so. A pretty sorry state of affairs, given how much he had to get done today and how far behind he was. It also didn't help matters that he was completely out of his usual environment. Trying to work on international deals while stranded on a family-oriented resort was challenging, to say the least. And *stranded* was the perfect way to describe his situation as far as he was concerned. He'd commissioned use of one of the main conference rooms and set up a temporary office but still found it hard to concentrate. Every few moments or so, a shrieking child would run down the hallway outside or a service person would run a vacuum in the hallway while he was trying to update a spreadsheet or manage an overseas call.

One of those calls came through at that very moment. His potential deal partner calling from Abu Dhabi, Sheikh Farhan.

Drex sighed with resignation and tapped to accept the call. The man barely gave him a chance to say hello before beginning to speak.

"Haven't heard from you in a while, my friend. Was wondering if you would even answer the phone."

They'd spoken less than forty-eight hours ago.

"Just getting ready to attend and celebrate my younger brother's nuptials."

"Ah, yes, the wedding. Please send our family's congratulations to your brother."

"Thank you. I will let him know."

He was back to business immediately. Not that Drex could blame him. A lot was riding on their potential collaboration. For him especially. Much more so than the sheikh. "You'll be available for the conference call on Tuesday, correct?" he asked Drex, not for the first time.

"Absolutely," Drex reassured him. "With updated documents and figures for you to go over beforehand."

Mollified for the moment, the sheikh bade him goodbye and hung up.

Drexel leaned back in his chair and sighed. Despite what he'd just told Sheikh Farhan, he wasn't fooling himself. He *was* having trouble focusing at the moment. He cursed himself for it internally. Given the importance of this deal, he couldn't afford to botch it up now. He'd come too far in life, accomplished too much, to risk a deal of this magnitude falling through.

The real reason he couldn't concentrate was because he couldn't get a certain wavy-haired brunette out of his mind. The determination in her voice, the rigid set of her spine. The strength blazing behind her eyes. Every time he tried to answer an email or focus on a new development, his mind started wandering to Clairey Robi and exactly what her motivation had been.

Chase might have acted offended when he'd been questioning him, but they both knew that what Drexel was asking him was not beyond the realm of possibility.

But he'd been right. Chase and this Clairey hadn't actually been romantically or physically involved. Or in any way, for that matter. She'd said she was worried about Chase's daughter. Why exactly was she so invested? Was it simply out of the goodness of her heart? If that was the case, she would truly be a rare breed. Most people didn't stick their necks out for others they didn't even know. Not even for children.

If Chase's bride and her mother had anything to say about it, the young lady would find herself in the unemployment line. Yet, she'd taken that risk without hesitation. Heaven knew, Drex himself hadn't met many such people in his lifetime. Most people turned a blind eye or pretended not to notice when something was amiss in a household.

Not Clairey Robi.

He was more curious about her than he could explain or wanted to examine.

When was the last time he'd found himself so intrigued by a woman? If it had ever happened before, he couldn't remember.

An email marked *Urgent* popped up on his laptop

screen, but this time he knew better than to try to address it. With a curse, he slammed the cover shut and stood. Technically, he was on vacation, after all. Not that any of his colleagues or clients were heeding that fact. Several matters required his immediate attention, but he knew when to call it a day. He wasn't going to get anything done until he found her.

A brief visit to the front desk told him exactly where to find Ms. Robi's office. "But I'd hurry if I was you. She won't be there long," the desk attendant warned him before he left.

Apparently, Drexel was right about that too. Her antics this morning had indeed gotten her fired.

Her desk was packed up. Nothing left to do now but turn in her badge and leave. A knock sounded on the door as Clairey took one last look around the small office. For one insane moment, she had the heartwarming thought that perhaps Louis had changed his mind. But no such luck. The person who opened the door a moment later was Matt, the bar manager who also happened to be her rather casual boyfriend. If she could call him that. Well, they'd gone on more than a few dates. But Matt had made it clear they were not exclusive. More than clear, in fact. Yeah, he definitely wouldn't consider himself her boyfriend. Especially not now, when she was unemployed and completely broke.

"So, you heard," she said as he stepped inside the room.

"Yeah. Sorry, babe. But what were you thinking?"

"I've been asking myself that all day. Oh, and Louis wanted an answer too."

"He came into the bar area after. Red as a beet and mumbling under his breath."

"He does that when he's angry."

"Then, he's downright incensed. Did you really try to stop the Osoman/Traynor wedding? Barged in on them in the conference room?"

Clairey felt her chin tremble. When he put it that way, what she'd done sounded super unreasonable. "I'll tell you all about it over dinner tonight at the Crab Shack."

Matt ducked his head. "Yeah…um…about that."

Oh, no. She should have seen this coming. Matt wasn't exactly the loyal type. He had more than a healthy concern about each of them paying equally whenever they went out. And now that she was out of a job…

"I forgot there was something I had to do tonight. Sorry. Totally slipped my mind."

Right. What a lousy liar.

She'd been right. Matt wanted no part of her now that she was unemployed. Said a lot about her worth in his eyes. The chin tremble suddenly got worse.

She wasn't surprised. Life had shown her more than once that people could be quick to turn a cold shoulder. Even those closest to her.

No job. No romantic prospects. No hope of anything getting better anytime soon.

"I understand," she said simply. She certainly wasn't about to beg or plead with him to keep their date. She'd seen that sort of desperate act up close countless times as a teenager. Her mother never considered herself above begging when it came to her stepfather. Even before they'd gotten married. It still brought tears to her eyes when Clairey remembered all the various times she'd done so. For a man who didn't deserve her. A man who had torn their lives apart.

And her stepfather's actions had demonstrated to her just how little Clairey had meant to her remaining parent.

Clairey tossed off the memories and focused back on Matt. "Maybe you should just go," she told him instead.

He shrugged without so much as a pause. "I'd help you carry your stuff out, but I have to head back. The bar is getting slammed 'cause of the rain."

She shook her head. She wouldn't accept his help anyway. Besides, it was only a couple of boxes and her wilted plant. She could be out of here in two trips.

"Then, you should probably just leave, Matt."

He did so without another word. What a day it had turned out to be. She'd lost her job and her boyfriend—who wasn't actually even her boyfriend. So why did she feel like she'd just been kicked when she was already on the ground? Well, it didn't pay to feel sorry for herself. That wasn't going to do anything for her. Clairey blew out a breath and grabbed the bigger box to take to her car. Walking by the front desk, she managed to keep her head high and not make eye contact with any of the other employees. The so-called Walk of Shame. At least no one from Security had shown up to escort her out. If she rushed, she could get out of here without having that added indignity thrust upon her.

Within moments, she was back from the parking lot to grab the remaining box and the precious philodendron which she balanced on the lid. Heavy footsteps sounded in the hallway leading to her office. Clairey bit out a curse.

A security officer, no doubt. She'd taken too long. But there was still a chance she could evade him if she rushed out the other direction. In her haste to leave the room and avoid the newcomer, she turned on her heel. Too fast. The plant went flying off the box and flew in an arch through the air to squarely hit the midsection of the man who'd just appeared at her door.

And it was no security officer. Drexel Osoman stood there covered in soil, a look of utter annoyance on his face.

She had thrown a wet, dirty plant at him! Drexel squelched the urge to swear out loud. It wasn't easy. Before this morning, he'd had no idea this woman even existed; now she was the bane of his existence. She was the reason he'd gotten absolutely no work done today. And she was the reason he was now standing here with mud plastered on his tailored silk shirt.

"Oh, my God!" she cried, still holding the cardboard box. "I'm so sorry. I guess I overwatered it this morning."

Drex looked down at the mess of mud covering his torso. "I'd say."

"It's just that you surprised me. I wasn't expecting anyone and—" She eyed him with a narrowed gaze. "What are you doing here, anyway?"

She had to ask?

"I wanted to talk. Do you have a minute?"

Her shoulders slumped in a gesture of complete and utter defeat. For just a moment, Drex felt the slightest bit sorry for her. But then a glob of mud fell off his shirt and landed on his Italian leather loafers.

"I guess I owe you some answers."

She had that right. He pulled over the chair sitting in the corner of the room and sat. "You stirred quite the hornet's nest down there earlier today."

She dropped the box on her desk and stared at him. "Did I?"

"Yes. For what it's worth."

"That's the question, isn't it? What was it worth? From where I'm standing, nothing has changed. The wedding will go on, won't it?"

"Indeed, it will."

She nodded once. "Right. So the only thing I managed to accomplish is to steer myself out of a job. With no real hope of finding any kind of adequate replacement."

"Yet, something tells me you'd do the same thing if given the opportunity to do it again."

She studied him before answering. "You're very observant. I was going to try to find a way to contact you. See if you could help. Apparently, you're fairly well-known in certain circles. Not that I had any sort of clue how to go about it."

That surprised him. She was thinking about turning to him with all this? "Why?"

She shrugged. "You were clearly the one in charge in that room. And it wasn't as if the bride's mother was going to be of any help. I'm pretty certain she was ready to toss me into the waves out there." She motioned with her head in the direction of the ocean outside her window.

If he had been curious before, now he was totally intrigued. He wouldn't be able to sleep until he got to the bottom of her motivation for doing what she'd done.

"And what exactly would you have me do?"

She threw her hands in the air. "I don't know. Stop the wedding, at least temporarily. Your brother and his bride have a lot they still haven't considered before tying the knot."

"And you know this how?"

"I suppose I have to tell you."

"Indeed, you do. You said it involved Marnie. My niece."

She rubbed her forehead, expelling a weary sigh. "It does. I was at the bar last night, to visit my boyfriend. Well, not that he was ever really a boyfriend. Which doesn't even matter. He just broke up with me. If one even can break up with someone they weren't really dating. Not technically, as he kept reminding me."

Drex lifted his hand. "If we could stick to the matter at hand?"

"Right. Well, Danielle, your soon-to-be sister-in-law, was sitting there on one of the stools. She'd already indulged quite a bit by the time I got there. I was actually going to recommend to Matt that they cut her off. The Sea View has rules about such things. I can't imagine why they let her continue on the way she did. Just ordering drink after drink. Some of the cocktails were pretty heavy drinks too."

Drexel tried not to let his irritation show. It wasn't easy. "Again, Ms. Robi..."

"Sorry. Well, she started talking about how she was ready to get married but not to be a stepmother."

Ah, so that was indeed the problem. Just as Chase had offered earlier. "I see."

Clairey blinked at him as if expecting him to say more. She went on when he didn't. "She continued about what a brat her future stepdaughter was. Which

I don't understand. I've had little Marnie in the activity room all week, and she's an absolute doll. So creative. And full of humor. She makes me laugh at least once a day."

"Ms. Robi," Drexel said to redirect her. It was so very hard to keep this woman on track.

"Oh. Sorry."

"You do realize that all her talk may have just been the drunken ramblings of a completely inebriated woman."

She rolled her eyes at him. "Of course. But she still said those things. After all, doesn't alcohol usually diminish one's inhibitions so deeply that the speaker's truth emerges?"

She had a point there. Not a chance worth taking when a child was involved.

Clairey inhaled deeply, as if bracing herself before going on. "There's more. Danielle said she couldn't wait to find a way to get rid of the child. One way or another."

Drexel released a deep sigh. That was another matter entirely. Being apprehensive was one thing. But if the woman had plans to actually find a way to toss Marnie aside somewhere, it was clearly a serious matter. Marnie was much too young to be displaced once again. The little girl was barely processing the abrupt and unexpected loss of her grandmother as her primary caregiver.

Clairey may have gone about it in a rather reckless way, but she clearly had reason to be concerned. Though, clearly Danielle had overindulged in drink. Maybe all this was much ado about nothing. There was a chance she didn't mean all that she'd said to Clairey last night.

"I know I'm a stranger, but I'd hate to think that an innocent little girl is about to be thrust into a bad situation and that I did nothing to try and stop it."

Drex had heard enough. "Thank you for your concern, Ms. Robi. Don't give the matter another thought. You've done enough."

She stood abruptly. In a flash, she was at his side and had him by the elbow. The woman could move quickly. Drex's gaze fell to where her small hand rested on his arm. An inexplicable rush of warmth spread over his skin where she touched him. She hastily removed her fingers.

"Wait. You're just going to ignore everything I just told you?"

"On the contrary," he answered. "I'm going to go find my brother." Though, he would stop in his room to change clothes first. "It appears he and I need to have another talk." This time, Drex would demand some real answers.

CHAPTER THREE

HE SHOULD HAVE known things weren't going to go smoothly down here. Matters relating to his brother seldom did. Now, said brother was about to marry a woman who didn't want any part of raising his child. Drexel bypassed the elevator and made his way to the stairs. Even though he was uncomfortable with a mess of mud on his shirt, he figured he'd need some kind of physical exertion after the conversation he'd just had. He didn't know his young niece very well; that was on him. It was too late now, but Drex should have spent more time and effort getting to know his niece. He should have checked in on her well-being after his mom had taken seriously ill. And he should have made sure Chase was adjusting to becoming a full-time parent to an active, curious little girl.

He felt a pang of sympathy for her now. No child deserved to be stranded with someone who didn't want them. How ironic that Chase of all people would put his own daughter in such a predicament, given the way they'd had to grow up. Chase knew all too well how damaging such an existence could be for a child. They both did.

Bad enough the girl's own mother had abandoned

her when she'd been barely more than an infant. Chase didn't even know what had become of his former fling. Drexel snorted a humorless laugh as he rounded the stairway turn on the third floor. He wondered if Chase even remembered the woman's full name. The kids these days would call her Chase's baby momma. But heaven knew the woman had never done any kind of momma-ing.

Marnie had mostly been brought up by Chase and Drex's mother up until she'd finally succumbed to the disease that had plagued her for years. His mom couldn't even take care of herself now, let alone a dependent child.

Drex had wondered how Chase would adjust to having his daughter back full-time. Ms. Clairey Robi had just told him the answer. When he finally reached his hallway, Drex could see that he wouldn't have to hunt down his brother, after all. Chase was waiting for him at the door.

Chase looked awful. His hair was a disheveled mess, as if he'd been running his hands through it. Half of his shirttail was untucked and hanging over his hip. His pallor was an odd shade of gray. And he looked nervous. He almost laughed at the spectacle they made together with Drex covered in drying mud and Chase looking as sloppy as he did.

His brother did a double take as he noticed Drex's attire as he approached. "What the heck happened to you?"

"You wouldn't believe me if I told you," Drex answered as he pulled his key card out to unlock the door. "And I could ask you the same question."

"Danielle and I were doing some talking. Things got a little heated."

Another curious turn to the sordid saga. Drex didn't really want to know what their conversation might have been about. But with resignation, he opened the hotel-room door and motioned for his brother to enter.

Chase began speaking immediately, not giving Drexel even the moment it took to take his shirt off to change. "So I need you to take Marnie."

Drexel gave his head a brisk shake. He couldn't have heard him correctly. "I thought Danielle's mother was going to take her until the two of you got back from your honeymoon."

Chase inhaled deeply. "I mean long-term."

Drexel stilled in the process of walking to the wash-room to clean up. "Come again?"

Chase thrust his fingers through the hair at his crown. "Danielle came clean about why that resort employee barged into the meeting this morning. It's because Danielle confided in her. About not wanting to be burdened with a kid through marriage."

Drexel knew all that already. But what did any of that have to do with him taking Marnie for any amount of time, let alone long-term?

Studying the desperation clear on Chase's face, the answer began to dawn on him. His brother's bride had given him an ultimatum. And Chase was choosing his bride over his daughter.

"It's probably going to be temporary."

"What makes you think you'll be ready to take her back later? If you don't want to parent her now?"

Chase blinked at him in confusion. "I don't mean me."

"Then, who?"

He shrugged. "I mean, Mom might recover and take her back, right? You've got her set up with the top doctors in one of the most renowned institutions in the country to make sure she gets the best care."

Drex closed his eyes briefly. Chase knew better. Was he trying to fool himself, or did he take his older brother for a fool?

"You know she's not going to get better."

Chase looked down at his shoes. "Then, you can set Marnie up with a slew of nannies."

Drexel knew he shouldn't be surprised. Much too often in their life, his younger brother had shown himself to be an utterly selfish and narcissistic type. Maybe Drexel was a fool for ever expecting anything different from his younger sibling.

He could kick himself for not having seen this coming.

"You have to do this, man," Chase said, his voice tight yet determined. "There is no one else. You have to take her."

Clairey knew she was tempting fate. If she was smart, she'd be off this resort by now. Her office was packed up and locked. All that was left to do was to surrender her employee badge and walk out the double doors of the entrance.

But she couldn't bring herself to leave without stopping by the kids' activity room just one last time. The hours she'd spent in there had been the best part of her job, the responsibility she would miss the most by far, now that it was all over. The smiling faces of those kids as they painted or danced or worked on various crafts had brought joy to her days. She'd take the company of the children over the adult resort guests any day. Spending time with those children reminded her of the good times from her own childhood. Before it had all fallen apart with the tragic loss that had changed everything. And now she was losing that forever.

To her surprise, a parent strode into the room with a tot in tow, followed by another mother with her son. And then a dad trailed by with a set of twin boys. They each sat down at a station and stared at her expectantly.

Louis hadn't even thought to cancel the afternoon's crafting class. Well, she wasn't about to disappoint all the kids who'd shown up. There was no way Louis would set security on her when she was entertaining a roomful of children. And besides, she may have been technically fired, but she was on the clock until the end of day. Louis had told her this was the last date of her employment. No one had said anything about the hour it was to end.

As she greeted the children, another girl ran into the room and took a seat at one of the stations up front: Marnie.

Clairey hadn't even seen who had brought her down. Usually, Danielle or her mother did it. Neither one stuck around after dropping the child off. No different today. Now, the little girl gave her a wide smile and a small wave.

A dull pain throbbed in Clairey's chest at what the poor child might be dealing with in a few short days. She could only hope Drex had talked to his brother and found some kind of resolution.

Drex.

Since when had she considered herself familiar enough with the man to think of him by a shortened moniker? She cringed inwardly thinking about the way she'd accidentally flung a plant pot full of mud in his direction and made a mess of his shirt. Somehow, he'd still managed to look distinguished and handsome, despite being covered in mud. For an insane moment, she'd thought he might take his shirt off and give her a look at what was sure to be a chiseled, muscular chest.

Clairey gave her head a brisk shake. What was wrong with her? She had a class to run here, had no business thinking about Drexel Osoman's looks or the way he might look shirtless.

Half an hour later, the children were elbow-deep in molding clay. Most of the parents had chosen to leave, so Clairey did her best to bestow ample attention to each child as they attempted their foray into the art of sculpting. Though, she couldn't seem to help hovering over Marnie just a bit more than the others.

She sensed him before she saw him.

Sure enough, when Clairey looked up, Drexel Osoman was standing in the hallway outside the classroom. She had to suck in a breath at the sight of him. Though he was dressed much more casually than when she'd first seen him this morning, the man still emitted a clear aura of authority and command. No wonder everyone in that room this morning had been waiting for him to decide their cue.

He wore a short-sleeved Henley shirt that brought out the contours of his clearly muscular chest. No one should look that formidable in pressed khakis. A silver and gold watch adorned his left wrist. Heavens! How was she supposed to get through the remaining minutes of her class with him standing out there looking so very…masculine?

Curiosity had her chest tightening. Why was he the one here for Marnie?

Finally, the hour was up, and parents slowly trickled in to pick up their children. Marnie made a beeline for her uncle as soon as she saw him. Drexel looked hesitant as the child hugged him around the knees, as if unsure how exactly to greet her.

"Hey, sport," he said, tousling her hair. That earned him a wide grin.

"I made a bunny rabbit!" She pointed to the glob of clay at her desk that resembled nothing akin to a bunny rabbit.

"I see that. Well done!" Drexel told her, the corners of his mouth lifted.

Clairey forced away her trepidation and made herself walk to where they stood. She had no reason to feel so anxious around him. She didn't even know the man, for Pete's sake. Still, everyone else had gone, and she was essentially alone with him—the presence of Marnie notwithstanding.

She cleared her throat before she could say hello. And there was something else she wanted to say to him. "I wanted to thank you," she blurted out before she lost the nerve.

"For?"

"For caring enough to find me earlier. For asking why I did what I did."

Marnie, seemingly bored with the conversation, left them to go play some more with her mound of clay at her station.

Drexel lifted his chin. "You're welcome. I'm glad you told me."

"And?"

He crossed his arms in front of his chest. "You're wondering how my conversation with my brother went."

She nodded. "Yes. Has the situation about Marnie been resolved?"

His lips tightened before he answered. "Not exactly."

His instincts were kicking into gear again. They'd been triggered when he'd walked down to pick up his niece and seen Clairey with the children. Chase had flat out announced that Drex might as well be the one to do it, seeing as he'd be her guardian soon. Not that Drexel had willingly agreed, exactly. But for all practical purposes, he had to, didn't he?

What choice did he have? He couldn't very well allow his niece to fall into the foster system just because her father was a dolt. Sure, there were plenty of foster families out there who were kind, caring and competent. But he knew from personal experience it was no way to live. Bouncing around from home to home, never truly belonging in any. The experience could be soul-crushing. Plus, there were also those families who had no business taking in a child. He and Chase had been bounced around to enough of those. No, Marnie wouldn't go into the system if Drex had anything to say about it.

Nor could he risk demanding that Chase man up to his parental responsibilities and keep Marnie, thereby leaving her with two people who resented her existence. Nothing damaged a child more than dealing with parents who resented them. As he very well knew.

There was really only one viable option. He would have to take her and make sure she was okay. He just had to get her situated with a competent nanny. But that was going to take time. And time was a precious resource he didn't have much of at the moment. There were a million things requiring his immediate attention as soon as he returned to his penthouse apartment back in Manhattan. The deal with Sheikh Farhan was currently at a tipping point. What Drex managed to accomplish in the next few weeks would be crucial to its success. Or failure.

He didn't have a spare moment, let alone the amount of time and effort it would take to locate and interview qualified candidates for a reputable nanny. He glanced over at his niece. The youngster was about to lose yet another parent. Kids were resilient, but Marnie was well aware of the fact that she didn't have a momma. And her *mimi* had suddenly been taken away from her. Now, the only father she knew was about to walk away from her as well. Drex knew Marnie was particularly sharp so he couldn't rush this process. He had to make sure to get it right for her sake.

The woman standing before him may very well be the answer to the quandary he'd so recently found himself in. She might be the key to it all, in fact.

"Listen, can I buy you lunch?"

She blinked at him in confusion. "Lunch?"

He almost wanted to laugh at her expression. Clearly, she hadn't seen that coming. Frankly, neither had he up until a few moments ago, when he'd watched her with Marnie and the other children. Every one of them seemed to adore her. She'd certainly held their attention, no small feat with a group of toddlers.

"Yeah. It's typically the midday meal." He made

a show of looking at his watch. "And it happens to be midday."

She rolled her eyes. "I know what lunch is. What I don't know is why you'd ask me to join you."

"You'd be joining me and Marnie both. She clearly has a fondness for you. I think she'd like it if you came along." That was the absolute truth. He would get into his ulterior motives later over the meal.

Her eyes traveled to where Marnie sat gently holding her ostensible bunny. They held clear hesitation and no small amount of suspicion.

"Come on, let me buy you lunch. It's the least I can do for the way you tried to stick up for my niece earlier."

She scoffed. "Not that it did any good."

She had no idea. Well, he was about to tell her exactly what her actions had led to. And exactly how she could play a part in going about fixing things for the girl. As well as for him.

As if on cue, Marnie suddenly dropped her art project on the desk. The clay landed with a resounding thud. "Uncle Drex, I'm hungry."

Maybe it was low of him, but he would use her declaration to his advantage. "How about some pizza?" A hungry child could be a powerful motivator for anyone.

Marnie nodded enthusiastically. Drexel walked over and lifted her into his arms. "I've asked Ms. Clairey to join us. What do you think of that?"

Marnie clapped her hands. "Yeah! Miss Clairey can come too!"

Clairey tilted her head and gave him a clearly knowing expression. "Why do I get the feeling I've just been played here?"

"Did it work?"

She sighed and brushed back her hair with her fingers. "I suppose it did. I'll come to lunch with you two, but only because Marnie would like me to."

Well, that was a bit of a bruise for the old ego. She walked over and tickled Marnie under the chin, earning a peal of giggles. The scent of Clairey tickled his nose. An enticing scent of roses that reminded him of the first days of spring.

"It has to be off the resort, though. I'm not really supposed to be here."

"Say no more." He held his elbow out to her, Marnie still tucked in the crook of his other arm. "My car is out front."

Less than fifteen minutes later, they were being seated at a homey, rustic Italian restaurant that Clairey had directed him to.

"This place has the best pizza on the peninsula. If not the entire state of Massachusetts," she said, unfolding her napkin and placing it on her lap. Marnie sat next to both of them in a booster seat.

Drex couldn't remember the last time he'd had pizza. When he went out, it was usually to Michelin-star restaurants to entertain clients. Otherwise, he was heating up a prepared meal late at night or grabbing a granola bar at his desk. Meals out at restaurants often were simply to negotiate a deal or acquire new business.

Not that this was any different. Despite having a five-year-old in tow, this was simply yet another business meeting—one he had to close. So much depended on it.

Not unlike his other pending negotiation with the sheikh.

Their waiter arrived and poured them some water.

Clairey took a sip before speaking. "So. Let's have it, then. What's this little lunch outing really about? I'm guessing I'm not usually the type of woman you ask out, so what's up?"

She was sharp. And direct. He wasn't sure how to respond to the second part of her question. What she'd said was accurate. Drexel usually did date more glamorous types. His last fling had involved a well-known actress he'd accompanied to Cannes. But the relationship had gone sour when he'd refused to drop everything to attend every movie premiere and red-carpet event she wanted him by her side for. No, Clairey didn't strike him as the type to demand ultimatums.

In that sense at least, she wasn't his usual type.

Clairey had to wait to get her answer. The waiter chose that moment to come to take their orders. They went with the house special, a margherita pizza loaded with basil and lots of fresh, homemade mozzarella. For Marnie, her uncle ordered a small cheese pizza off the children's menu along with a bowl of applesauce.

Normally, simply being in this place made Clairey's mouth water. But she was much too distracted right now to be thinking about the food. Her gut told her this little outing was about more than discussing how Drexel's conversation with his brother had gone. As curious as she was about what had transpired during their conversation, she couldn't very well argue that it was really any of her business. So why exactly was she here?

"So tell me," she prodded once again after the waiter had left. "Why'd you ask me here? I'm guessing you have a slew of eager women who'd be ready to jump at a chance to have lunch with you. You're a handsome, successful man."

He gave her a mischievous smile. "Are you coming on to me, Ms. Robi?"

A flash of heat rushed to her cheeks. "What? Of course not! I would never do such a thing." Why in the world had she just said all that?

He dramatically clasped his hand on his chest. "You scar my ego yet again." Clairey didn't know what he meant about *again*.

"Relax. It was a joke," he added, taking another bite of his pizza. "Apparently a rather poor one." Clairey was still too nervous to eat. Although, she had no real idea why.

Drexel's next words did nothing to alleviate her anxiety. "I asked you here because I want to discuss a proposition I have for you."

Her skin began to tingle in alarm. She couldn't fathom what kind of proposition he might be referring to.

"You asked how it went when I spoke to my brother earlier. About his bride's reluctance to become a stepmother."

She could only nod.

He let out a long, weary sigh before answering. "The gist of it is that I'm now my niece's sole guardian."

Clairey didn't bother to hide her surprise. The pieces started to fall into place. Drexel's brother had tossed his young daughter aside in order to please his bride. Clairey glanced at the little girl. A smudge of marinara sauce marked her chin. She had applesauce all over her fingers. How could anyone turn their back on such an adorable child? A pang tugged inside her chest. Poor Marnie.

"I see," Clairey answered, though she didn't really. Danielle's position was tough enough to comprehend. She couldn't understand for the life of her how anyone could do such a thing to their own child. But she knew. All too well. She had a very good idea about not being wanted by your only parent.

Drexel continued. "There is no one else. Marnie was being looked after by our mother until very recently, and she isn't able to do so anymore. So it's up to me now." A flash of pain shone in his eyes, and he looked off to the side.

"That's a lot to ask of you."

He shrugged. "Let's just say I'm used to cleaning up my brother's messes. And really, what choice do I have?"

"I'm really sorry, Drexel," Clairey said because it seemed an appropriate thing to say given what he'd just had thrust upon him.

"Thank you."

"But I still don't understand what any of that has to do with me."

"Until I can find an acceptable nanny, I need someone to help me take care of her. I don't know the first thing about parenting a kindergartner."

Clairey's mouth went dry. He couldn't be asking her what she thought he was asking.

"Wait. Are you saying you'd like me to do it?"

He nodded once, his gaze fully fixed on her face. "I'll make it worth your while. She already knows and likes you."

"But I'm not a child caregiver. I'm a manager at a

resort." At least she was up until a couple of hours ago. "I'm not qualified."

"On the contrary. I saw you with those kids today. You were great with them."

She shook her head. He had to see how wrong this all was. "Leading the activity room wasn't really part of my responsibilities. I simply took it over because no one else wanted to do it, and I enjoyed it."

He smiled at her. "That sort of proves my point that you're good with kids, wouldn't you say?"

She'd walked right into that one. Drexel leaned closer to her over the table. "I'm guessing you went through a background check with the proper authorities before being allowed to run a children's activity room."

"Yes, but—"

He cut her off. "That already makes one task easier for me. I just have to verify with the resort rather than go through the whole process myself."

He'd really thought of everything. How? She hadn't even laid eyes on the man until this morning.

"And you do happen to be out of a job," he added, throwing out the proverbial ace card.

He was certainly right about that. Not only was she unemployed now, she had no idea how to go about finding another position anytime soon. The resort had been her first real job out of college. Any prospective employer would be curious as to why it had ended so soon. Louis wasn't going to be of any help with a reference on her behalf either. She had loans and bills and no other source of income whatsoever.

Still, this wasn't right. She felt disoriented by his ask, not sure how to respond.

He was asking her out of desperation, not because

he really even wanted her for the role. She should just say no.

Marnie dropped her pizza to the ground with a splat and leaned over to stare at it. "Uh-oh. My pizza fell down." She looked up to give Clairey a gummy grin, her lips smudged with red sauce. Another pang tugged in Clairey's chest.

"I'll have to think about it," she answered instead.

CHAPTER FOUR

"PLEASE TALK ME out of this," Clairey told her friend as she adjusted her helmet and climbed on her bicycle. It was the perfect day for a long, peaceful bike ride. Not too hot or steamy, the air light with a cool ocean breeze. Cape Cod had miles and miles of pristine bike paths that afforded some of the most breathtaking scenes of the ocean and various ponds and lakes. It was one of the few activities one could do on a budget around these parts. All you needed was a rented bike and a bottle full of ice-cold water.

Tessa gave her a pointed look before pushing off on her left pedal. "I'll do no such thing," she threw over her shoulder as they began to ride. "You've been handed a golden opportunity just when you thought you were down-and-out. You should be thanking the man," she added.

They rode in silence side by side for several moments before Clairey found the courage to admit what was really nagging at her about Drexel's offer. "There's something I haven't shared with you about all this," she began.

"What's that?"

She was just going to come out and tell her. "I feel

so disoriented around the man. Out of my element. Working for him is bound to be awkward."

Tessa shrugged. "You're attracted to him. I've seen the man. Who can blame you? He's devilishly handsome."

Clairey didn't have it in her to argue that. She'd be lying.

"Besides," Tessa added, "you wouldn't be the first woman to be attracted to a drop-dead gorgeous employer."

"I suppose not."

"I know you're a true professional who can handle it."

If only she could be sure of that. That point was precisely where all her doubts lay. She could easily imagine making a fool of herself over someone like Drexel Osoman. Not to mention, the little girl in his care was already well on her way to capturing Clairey's heart.

After they'd ridden about three miles, Tessa motioned to pull over. Clairey wasn't surprised. They'd been on enough rides together that she knew this was typically the point when Tessa would need a break. They pulled up next to a wooden park bench that faced an opening in the greenery with a perfect view of a small swamp pond. A family of five was crabbing in the water with plastic pails and small shovels. It made for an idyllic scene. The Cape attracted so many families this time of year. Their presence always made Clairey feel a longing for the sense of familial acceptance she'd never experienced herself.

Tessa pulled her out of her melancholy thoughts. "Aren't you excited about the prospect of living in Manhattan for a few months?" she asked, taking a long sip of her water. "I've always loved New York City. Wouldn't mind living there."

"I've never really thought about it." Growing up right outside of Boston in the rough streets of Southie, she'd never really lacked for the experience of city life.

"I think you should do it," Tessa declared. "I don't know why you're even on the fence about it."

Truth be told, Clairey couldn't really explain her hesitation. Drexel really had handed her a chance to overcome the monumental setback of losing her job.

"Ask for more money, if that will make the decision easier," Tessa suggested.

Clairey toyed with the buckle on her bike helmet. "I can't justify doing that. The salary he offered was more than generous."

"Then, I don't really see why you're not jumping at the chance. You have no job. And not that I don't love having you there, but your primary residence is my pull-out sofa."

"It's my only residence. In my defense, I just haven't been able to find an affordable place yet. The Cape isn't exactly cheap this time of year, at the height of tourist season."

"All the more reason to say yes to this Drexel."

"There's a lot to consider, Tessa."

Tessa turned to stare at her for a couple of beats, then slapped a hand to her chest. "Oh, my! It's more than just surface attraction, isn't it?"

Clairey tried not to react to the truth in her friend's words. "I don't know what you're talking about."

"I think you do. You're genuinely drawn to him. You can't stop thinking about the man. And it's got you scared."

"That's ridiculous. I've had two whole conversations with him." But she'd lain awake all night unable to get the image of him out of her mind. Scenes replayed in her head of the way he'd looked at her when she'd barged into the conference room. The utter look of shock on his face when her plant had gone flying into him. The way he'd lovingly lifted his niece into his arms and wiped the pizza sauce off her face after their lunch.

"Me thinks doth protest a tad too much."

Clairey couldn't help her amusement. "You have just botched that line so marvelously. Shakespeare is sure to be rolling over in his crypt."

"Yeah, well, the overall idea still stands."

Clairey didn't have the words to deny what her friend was saying. Tessa was right. There was something about Drexel that had her unnerved about the way she reacted to him. He was the type of man that could have a woman head over heels before she knew it. Only problem with that was that he was way out of her league.

"Tell me more about him," Tessa directed. "You must have looked into him after he made his offer."

She had. She'd spent most of the night looking him up online right before she'd crawled into bed and then tossed and turned thinking about him nonstop. There were no shortages of write-ups about him on business sites.

"What did you find out?" Tessa prompted.

"Well, in addition to being handsome, he's wildly successful. He's in mergers and acquisitions. Started with a well-known international firm, then struck out on his own. He's also widely recognized for his near-genius instincts when it comes to investing. He's gone early into everything from popular websites to new tech start-ups. Everything he's touched has grown exponentially. He's Midas."

Tessa let out a low whistle. "Impressive."

Clairey left out the other details she'd read about. The more gossipy sites that covered Drexel's private life. Every picture had him side by side with a myriad of different beautiful women. He'd been snapped with everyone from models to actresses to Olympic-level athletes.

She had no idea how to fit into a life like that.

They sat silently, simply admiring the view until Tessa jumped up and straddled her bike. Clairey followed her lead, and soon they were back on the bike path and pedaling at a steady pace.

An hour later, after they'd circled back to their starting point, a voice-mail alert pinged, and Clairey pulled her cell phone out of the bike basket.

Drexel. Clairey's stomach did a little flip: she had no idea what she might say when she returned his call. Despite discussing little else with Tessa while they rode, she still had no idea what to tell him about his offer. Every time she'd decided and made up her mind one way or the other, a mountain of doubt emerged and stopped her from following through with an answer.

She needed more time. She was about to call and tell him that when he beat her to it. Her phone rang, and his contact number popped up on her screen. May as well get it over with and tell him she had no answer for him just yet.

Clairey clicked on the call without giving herself a chance to hesitate.

"I'm not calling to pressure you," he said over the phone before she could so much as get a word out. "But I could use your help with something else."

Okay. Drexel's voice was tense and anxious. He sounded like a man at his wit's end. What was this about, then?

"Hello to you too."

She heard him utter a low curse. "I'm sorry. It's just that I have a very bored and confused little girl on my hands. Her father left this morning on his honeymoon, and it's just the two of us."

"I see."

"So far, we're off to a rocky start here. I could really use some assistance, Clairey. I could really use you."

What a fool he'd been. Drex had actually thought that he could handle a little girl by himself for one or two days until Clairey came to her senses and accepted his offer. His plan was to keep upping the salary and increasing the benefits and incentives until he reached an offer no sane person would refuse. But they hadn't even made it past late morning with no less than three tantrums. Marnie wanted to know where her father was and why he hadn't taken her along. Apparently, no one had explained to the poor child that she wouldn't be accompanying the couple on their next journey.

"What have you tried so far?" Clairey was asking him now.

"Everything from snacks to walks to attempts at a nap."

Clairey paused before answering. "She needs to be reassured that she's going to be all right. That you know what you're doing and you know how to take care of her."

Drexel grunted in frustration. "Well, that would be a bit of a fib, now, wouldn't it?"

"She just needs to believe it, Drexel."

The way she said his name, softly and with a clear note of respect, registered in his heart. Damn, she sounded sexy over the phone. And wasn't this a fine time to be thinking such a thing?

"I'll try my best."

"She also needs a distraction. Something to occupy her mind. She can't just sit there and busy herself while you try to get some work done."

Huh. That's exactly what he'd been doing. How in the world had she figured him out in such a short span of time?

"What do you suggest?"

"Marnie mentioned several times in class how much she loves the water. Maybe take her swimming."

He shook his head even though she couldn't see it. "No go. I asked if she wanted to head down to the pool. She said she hates the way the other kids splash around in there and get her all wet." His niece was upset about the prospect of getting wet. In a pool. Heaven help him, what world had he woken up in?

"I think she meant the ocean."

He hadn't thought of that. "Oh." Striding to the window, he took a peek outside to the Atlantic a few acres away. "The beach, huh? I've never taken a little girl to the beach before. It looks pretty windy out there. The waves aren't exactly smooth."

"Do you know if she has floaties?"

"Is that some kind of kids' cereal or something?"

He could practically hear her chuckling at him. "No. Safety floaties. They're meant to keep kids safely afloat in the water. She really should have a set."

"If she does, I have no idea where they are."

"You can get them almost anywhere. Even the grocery stores on the Cape carry them."

When was the last time he'd stepped foot in a grocery store? He couldn't even recall.

Clairey was saying something else. "There's a small, secluded area of beach off Old Silver. Only the locals know about it. It would be the perfect spot to take Marnie. I can send directions to your phone."

He rubbed his forehead. He was a grown man who'd been wildly successful in his area of business and had taken on more than his share of bullies, both in the corporate and the real worlds. But the prospect of spending the day alone on the beach with a five-year-old made his blood run cold with fear. "Listen, Clairey. Half a minute ago I didn't realize kids needed floaters or that they even existed."

"Floaties," she corrected.

"Right. My point is, this all sounds rather daunting. I'm ready to yield to you half my worldly possessions if you'll just come with us." He was only partially joking.

She paused long enough that Drexel had a moment of sheer panic. He was not above pleading with her if that's what it would take. "I'm willing to pay you for your time."

Several more moments of silence passed with Drexel holding his breath. Finally, he heard her heavy sigh over the tiny speaker. "That won't be necessary. I'll meet you at the location I'm about to send you. And I'll pick up the floaties that work best on my way there."

Drexel felt the tension loosen its grip on his shoulders. "You are an angel sent from Heaven above."

Her only reply was to say she'd see him in about half an hour.

Drexel hung up the phone just as Marnie let out another shriek of frustration, this time because her cartoon had just ended on TV.

How in the world was he supposed to do this? Especially if Clairey turned down his offer? The very idea sent a shudder through his entire being. He had no idea how to raise a young girl. All his success in the business world meant naught in this particular situation. He could provide for a child, sure. But that was about it. As for the rest, Drex was absolutely clueless.

Nevertheless, he had to appreciate the small victory. The immediate crisis was averted. For now.

Releasing a long sigh of relief that the tantrums would be over soon, he flopped onto the bed and rubbed his weary eyes. He'd known Clairey would know what to do. Thank the heavens above he'd been right.

Over the phone he'd referred to Clairey as an *angel*. But the way she looked in a tankini top and swim shorts was downright sinful. He forced himself to look away and focus on the task at hand, setting up the large beach umbrella that Clairey had thought to bring.

"It never even occurred to me we'd need a sun umbrella," he admitted. "Thank you for thinking of it." He had so much to thank her for, he didn't even know where to begin.

"Us locals know what's needed on a beach trip."

That was sure true. She'd thought of everything really. Whereas he'd simply grabbed sunscreen, a towel, and Marnie's sun hat, Clairey had brought a canvas beach bag loaded with everything from juice boxes and snacks to sand toys.

Marnie clapped her hands in delight when they pulled out the latter. Clairey gave the girl a wide smile. "Are you ready for a fun beach day?"

Marnie squealed in delight before answering, "Yeah!"

Satisfied that he'd dug the umbrella post deep enough that it wouldn't lift off in the oceanside wind, Drex finally allowed himself a calming breath.

But now Clairey was putting her hair up in a twist and then rubbing sun lotion on her shoulders, and he had to remind himself to keep breathing. Her dark wavy hair complemented her golden tanned skin. Her cat-eye sunglasses lent her a bohemian look. Dear Lord, was that a small tattoo over her hip bone? Drexel had never considered himself a fan of body art, but the tiny rendering of a star and moon that peeked out from the waistband of her shorts made him think thoughts he had no business entertaining. Not about the woman he hoped to hire as a temporary nanny.

Luckily, Marnie drew his attention before he got caught gawking. She pointed to the ocean waves. "Water!"

Clairey laughed and tapped the little girl's nose. "Yep. That's water, all right. Would you like to swim first or dig in the sand?"

Marnie seemed really torn about the decision. Finally, she reached for the bucket and shovel. In no time, she was knee-deep in sand.

Drexel tore his gaze away from his niece to stare

at the woman who'd helped to turn his disastrous day around. She really made quite the picture stretched out on one of the towels she'd laid down for them. Her bathing suit was modest by most standards, but she looked more sexy and enticing than he wanted to acknowledge.

Without warning, she looked up to catch him staring at her. Drexel made sure not to squirm under her gaze.

"What?" she asked.

He did his best to look innocent. "Nothing. I'm just not one to sit idly on a towel, that's all. What does one do exactly on a so-called beach day?"

She chuckled and looked out over the water. "Precisely what we're doing."

"Making small talk?"

"Relaxing. Enjoying the ocean air. The sunshine." She flashed him a wide smile. "Aren't you enjoying all that? I am."

He was certainly enjoying her company. That he couldn't deny. But she was only here because he'd asked. "Listen, Clairey. I realize we've taken you away for the day. It's only fair you're compensated for your time."

"Compensated?"

He nodded. "I'll pay you for the hours you're spending with us."

She shook her head. "Oh, I won't accept your money. That's not what this is about."

What in the world? "I don't understand."

She shrugged. "Simple. I'd like my payment in the form of a dare."

A mischievous glint appeared in her eyes, and it took all he had not to reach for her the way he so badly wanted to.

All right. He'd play along. "What kind of dare are we talking about here?"

"Do you like ice cream?"

At no point in this conversation would he have guessed that would be her next question. "I don't particularly go out of my way for it. But I don't dislike it. Why?" What was she getting at? Whatever it was, the playfulness in her voice was amusing him to no end.

"There's an ice cream I'd like to see you try."

He had to laugh at her. "If you want ice cream, you can just say so, Clairey."

"This would be for you. But I get to pick the flavor."

This sounded like it could be ominous for him. "And what flavor would that be?"

"There's a sweet shop in the center of town. They have the best chocolate and the best ice cream. And they're the only place I know that serves lobster vanilla caramel."

She couldn't mean real lobster. "You mean candy, right? Gummy lobster of some sort?"

She shook her head. "Nope. Not candy. Real Maine lobster pieces served up in a cone of vanilla with drops of hardened caramel."

Drexel felt his stomach roil in offense. "You're kidding. That flavor actually exists? And you'd like me to eat it?"

She nodded with clear humor. "You said you owed me for today, right?"

That was neither here nor there. "That's a real flavor? You're not just pulling my leg?"

She batted her eyes in mock innocence. "Would I ever do something like that?"

"And that's the payment you're asking for joining us today? That I try this atrocity of gastronomical insult?"

She chuckled, a soft delicate sound that seemed to hover in the air. "It's a delicacy. Tourists from all over the world visit that shop just to try it."

Drexel grimaced at the thought. "Are you sure I can't just give you half my worldly possessions? Like I mentioned on the phone?"

She shook her head. "Nope. My terms are my terms. You eat the lobster ice cream. The whole cone. And I'll consider us squared."

He rubbed a hand through the stubble at his jaw. Of course he was going to take her up on her silly dare. But he wasn't going to acquiesce so easily.

"What do you say?" she asked. "Do we have a deal?"

"Fine," he finally said after making her wait several more moments. "I'll eat this affront to gastric sensibilities. If it will make you happy." He held out his hand for her to shake on the strange barter. Even though what he really wanted to do was pull her in his arms and kiss her senseless.

Half an hour later they were strolling through the center of town. Clairey had been there countless times, but today she seemed to be seeing it with fresh eyes. Maybe it was due to Marnie's influence. She was enthusiastically running into every tourist-trap gift store and making her uncle buy countless worthless baubles that would no doubt end up in the garbage can within a month's time. Or maybe it was being here with a charismatic and tall, dark and handsome man who seemed to make both male and female heads turn. Clairey had thrown on a sundress over her beachwear, then helped

Marnie get herself dressed in a dry top and fresh pair of shorts. As for Drexel—well, all she could think was that no one should look that appealing in a pair of swim shorts and casual loose T-shirt. His dark olive skin was just sun-kissed enough. And the shirt did nothing to conceal the muscles of his chiseled chest. The watch adorning his wrist further accented the pure masculine look of him.

As busy as he was, the man obviously worked out regularly. She wondered if he did any particular sport. He certainly seemed athletic.

Stop.

Marnie grabbed her hand just then and dragged her into yet another shop, this one much higher-end than the others. A clothing boutique that sold designer women's clothing and hand-crafted purses, as well as other fairly pricey items. Pricey enough that Clairey had only stepped foot in the place once, before walking back out within minutes. The little girl pulled her over to a glass display case full of jewelry made from rare colors of sea glass.

"Pretty," Marnie announced, her nose pressed up against the case.

"Yes, they are," Clairey agreed. "Very pretty."

Marnie looked up at her uncle. "Can I get that? Please?" She pointed to a choker necklace set atop a mound of cream-colored satin fabric. The kid had taste.

Without hesitation, Drexel turned to the saleslady who had come to stand next to them. "We'll take that necklace as well as the one next to it."

"Of course," the woman answered with a dazzling smile aimed only in his direction. "May I put it in a velvet box for you? It's only a small additional charge."

Drexel nodded.

Marnie hugged her uncle around the knees when the woman walked away. "Thank you!"

"You're welcome," he said, tousling her hair with affection.

Clairey couldn't help but feel touched by the scene. Sure, such an expense might be somewhat extravagant for a little girl. But the pieces would be something Marnie would treasure forever, along with the memory of how she came to acquire them. During such a time of confusion and upheaval for his niece, she didn't think it was unreasonable of Drexel to make such a purchase.

Despite Marnie's rather tumultuous young life so far, the little girl had certainly lucked out in the uncle department.

The saleslady was back within moments with a decorated paper bag that she handed to Drexel. She still hadn't so much as looked in Clairey's direction.

Upon leaving the store, Clairey stopped dramatically and slapped her hands on her hips in mock seriousness. "Enough stalling. The sweet shop is two doors down."

Drexel tilted his head in resignation and held out his hand. "Lead the way."

Clairey walked them to the store and ordered strawberry for Marnie, at her request, mocha chocolate chip for herself, and the dreaded lobster vanilla caramel for Drexel.

She handed his cone to Drex with a somewhat naughty wink. Who was this unfamiliar woman? She hardly recognized herself, teasing a man she barely knew in such a manner.

He eyed the cone with an exaggerated shudder. "I have to eat the whole thing, huh?"

Of course, she wasn't going to make him if he really didn't want to. But she wasn't going to tell him that just yet. And so far, Drexel was being a good sport about the whole thing. Besides, everyone she'd seen have it for the first time was pleasantly surprised, herself included.

She watched as he took the first bite. His lips tightened into a firm line. Then his eyes grew wide. "Huh! It's not half bad."

She couldn't help her chuckle. "You see? Sometimes it pays to try new things."

He took another, larger bite. "I guess you're right. I don't know if I'd order it again, but I'm not sorry I tried it."

"Right. Now you can say you've had a dessert that contained a crustacean."

Marnie held her ice cream up without a word and rubbed her eyes with clear exhaustion. She was too tired to even finish her cone.

Drexel lifted her up with his free arm, and she immediately tucked her head on his shoulder. "I think our girl's battery is running low. We should probably start heading back."

She had to force herself not to react to his use of the word *our*. It was just a figure of speech. He didn't mean anything by it. Certainly, he wasn't inferring anything that might mean the three of them were any kind of unit.

"She has done a lot today."

"I'll drive you back to your car."

When they made it back to the beach where they'd

left his rental—a sporty convertible that had probably cost her whole month's salary to rent for the week— Clairey settled Marnie in her booster and buckled her in. The child then promptly fell asleep before Clairey had even clipped on her own seat belt. Drexel pulled out and started driving out of the parking lot.

Looking at the girl sleeping soundly in the back seat, Clairey had to come clean to herself.

There was nothing for it. Clairey couldn't deny how much she'd enjoyed herself today. Spending the day with Drexel and Marnie had comprised some of the most enjoyable hours she could remember in a long while. In fact, she couldn't recall a time she'd so thoroughly felt joy. Certainly not after she'd been so unceremoniously forced out of her home by her mother. Not that the days she'd lived in that house before her banishment could be described as anything resembling happiness.

On top of it all, Drexel had needed her today. He and Marnie both had.

It was a heady feeling, and she knew she had to tread carefully. No one had actually needed her before. Not really.

How in the world could she turn her back on that? She couldn't. She had to help Drexel get settled back in New York with a little girl in tow, and she had to help Marnie get adjusted to her new life. Clairey would accept his job offer, but she'd do it on her terms. Drexel needed to know that she only planned to take this job as a temporary assignment.

She turned in her seat to tell him before she could change her mind. "I'll do it," she blurted out without giving herself a chance to think any more on it. "I'll take your offer to be your nanny for Marnie."

Drexel's eyes grew wide, and a smile appeared on his lips. "You will?"

She could only nod. Then, before she knew it, his arm was around her shoulders and his mouth was on hers. Heaven help her, every inch of her body responded, and she returned the spontaneous kiss.

CHAPTER FIVE

HOW IN THE world had she ended up here? Clairey stared at the early-evening Manhattan skyline as it slowly began to illuminate and come to life. Five short days ago, she'd been tossed out of a job with barely enough money in her bank account for a sandwich.

Now, here she was. In a penthouse apartment in New York's Upper East Side, overlooking Central Park. A hefty advance had been deposited into her bank account. And she no longer had to sleep on her friend's couch at night. Drexel's spare bedroom he'd had her move into was the size of Tessa's whole apartment. All in all, some pretty life-altering developments.

The only problem was she couldn't seem to help but develop feelings for the man responsible for it all.

She felt his presence behind her before he began to speak. "Are you settling in okay? Anything you need?"

She forced a casual smile on her face and turned to face him. "Quite well, thank you." So far, they were doing a jolly good impression of playing the ultimate professional duo of boss and employee.

If that kiss they'd shared in the parking lot a few days ago entered Drexel's mind, he sure wasn't showing any indication of it. While she couldn't get it out of her mind.

Though, she really had to. Clearly, it had meant nothing. Just a spontaneous, knee-jerk reaction he'd had in a moment of relief that she'd be taking the job. She had no business reliving the sensation of having his lips on hers from the moment she woke up in the morning until she closed her eyes at night. And pretty much every moment in between.

But Drexel obviously had forgotten about the whole thing. A sharp pang of disappointment ran through her chest before she swatted it away.

"Did you have enough dinner?" he asked her, courteous beyond need. "Sharon's gone home for the evening, but there are plenty of leftovers in the fridge."

"Oh, no. I'm quite full. Sharon is a genius in the kitchen. Dinner was delicious."

"Good. That's good."

Why in the world were things so awkward between them now? Such a far cry from that day back on the Cape when she'd made him try lobster ice cream.

"Marnie seems to be settled in, as well," she added, just for something to say. He knew very well how Marnie was doing. He'd seen to it himself that the girl had everything she needed.

He nodded once. "I just checked on her. She's setting up the new dollhouse. I told her she could do that for an hour or two. Then she has to go to bed."

For someone who had no experience with kids, the man sure seemed to be getting the hang of having one around. He was a natural. "I'll go read to her in a bit and tuck her in. Will you be stopping by to say goodnight to her later?"

"I've already said good-night. I'll be heading out for the evening."

It was then that she noticed what he wore. With him standing somewhat in a darkened corner of the room, she hadn't realized before just how formal his attire was. A crisp white shirt and tailored black trousers appeared to be the pieces of a tuxedo with the jacket yet to be added. Along with gold cuff links that had probably cost a fortune.

No doubt his plans for the evening involved a glamorous night out with an equally glamorous woman who'd probably been waiting with bated breath for him to return to the city.

The disappointment she'd felt earlier turned to a throbbing, searing ache. This was why she'd hesitated in coming here. She had no business feeling as wounded as she did simply because he'd be spending the evening with another woman. What of it? It really was none of her business whatsoever. Despite the gnawing ache in the pit of her stomach.

Dear heavens. She was developing real feelings here. Feelings she had no right to. But who could blame her? Drexel Osoman was a prize by any standard. Not just because of his looks. Or his wealth. That was all surface level, as far as Clairey was concerned. No, it was more the way he behaved around his niece. Or how he made sure Clairey had everything she needed to settle into her new surroundings. He was attentive and considerate and a truly loving uncle. How was Clairey supposed to guard her heart around all that?

But the truth was she had no claim to him at all. Their arrangement was nothing more than a business one. She had to get that through her head and learn to live with it.

Maybe if she repeated it to herself over and over, it would gradually sink in.

"I hope you have a lovely time," she told him with a lightness she didn't feel.

He should never have kissed her. Hell, he should never have so much as touched her. Drexel bit out a curse as he strode down the hallway to grab his jacket and take the private elevator down to the waiting car in the street.

Things were so awkward and tense between them now. Gone was the easy and light camaraderie they'd shared the other day back on the Cape. So much so that he hadn't even been able to give her the necklace he'd gotten for her at that small boutique before they'd gone for ice cream. It still sat in its gift box on top of his dresser.

It would be much too awkward to give it to her now.

He half hoped she'd just come out and ask for it. She had to know he'd gotten it for her. Why did she think he'd bought two, for Pete's sake?

Well, he didn't have time to ponder any of it right now. He'd been unable to get out of the charity dinner he'd signed up for weeks ago. As much as he'd rather stay home and tuck Marnie into bed and then perhaps share a conversation with their newly hired nanny, he had to attend this shindig. Tara, his office administrator, had informed him in no uncertain terms when he'd offered to make a sizable donation instead of going, that it didn't work that way and that it wouldn't do to not make an appearance and afford the charity the type of publicity only a young billionaire could provide. He'd do his best to make it a quick night. Drexel would make an appearance, then he'd make his exit.

Would Clairey be waiting up for him when he returned?

Snap out of it.

He gave his head a quick shake and chastised himself for the thought. He had no business thinking of her that way.

There was only one reason Clairey was here at his penthouse, and that was to help Drexel with his niece. Heaven knew he needed her assistance. On top of running a demanding international business, making sure his mother had the best care, and dealing with all the other pressures on him, he was absolutely in over his head. Clairey was an absolute blessing—and one perfect for the role. After all, she'd stuck her neck out for Marnie before she'd even really known her.

But he couldn't forget her true purpose in their lives.

She wasn't there as his companion to greet him with a cup of tea or a glass of wine after he'd suffered through a boring night of speeches and fake haggling over bids.

There was no denying, however, just how much that image appealed to him. Then his imagination took it a step further. He pictured what she might be wearing at that time of the late evening as she joined him in a nightcap. Perhaps a well-fitting silk shirt she liked to sleep in with matching shorts that showed off her shapely figure. Maybe a revealing negligee.

Drexel sucked in a breath and swore yet again. Not quite under his breath and just as the elevator doors slipped open on the ground floor. The attendant at lobby desk gave him a startled look.

"Rough day, Mr. Osoman?" the man asked with a slight smile.

"Something like that," Drex answered as he made his way out to the waiting car.

His evening wasn't going to be any less rough, for that matter. Not if he couldn't stop thinking about one dark-haired and beguiling temptress who just happened to be sleeping in his apartment. And she would be for the foreseeable future. So he had to get over this fixation on her that he seemed to be developing, whatever it was.

He settled into the back seat and greeted his driver. Sure enough, within a block, his thoughts turned back to Clairey. Was she still reading to his niece? Or had she tucked the little girl in already? Maybe she'd crawled into bed herself right after. The image of her under satin sheets sprawled on the mattress invaded his mind.

Get a grip!

He had to stop these wayward thoughts once and for all. As far as he was concerned, he couldn't view Clairey any differently than Sharon, his housekeeper. They were both in his employ and had to be considered the exact same way.

He grunted a laugh at that, earning him a sideways glance from his driver. Sharon was a grandmother of seven cut right out of central casting if anyone needed a matronly type. And Clairey was about as far from matronly as *A* was to *Z* in the alphabet.

"Just confirming we're not picking up anyone else, correct, sir?" Tom asked, breaking into his thoughts.

"Correct."

He hadn't had a chance to ask Charlotte or anyone else to accompany him tonight before leaving for the Cape for his brother's wedding. And he hadn't the inclination to call and ask any of his past dates once he'd arrived. He had to wonder if that was due to a certain resort employee he'd met his first morning there. Too bad he couldn't have brought Clairey along. She might have enjoyed the pageantry of it all. The over-the-top decorations and extravagant canapés. But of course, that would have been inappropriate.

Wouldn't it?

Nothing said they couldn't attend events such as auctions together simply as friends. He rubbed his forehead and stared out the window at the passing scenery of the city. That was wishful thinking. Not to mention a slippery slope.

He couldn't risk getting close to Clairey in any way. For one thing, she deserved much more than he had to offer. The men in his family didn't exactly have a stellar track record as far as stable, loving relationships were concerned. He had several projects at work he couldn't allow himself to be distracted from. Oh, and there was that whole new development where he was suddenly sole guardian of a little girl. It wouldn't be fair to date any woman with so much on his plate, let alone a woman as dynamic as Clairey.

No. She deserved much better than the likes of him.

There was someone else in the apartment. Clairey awoke with a start at the sounds coming from down the hallway. A glance at the digital clock on her bedside table told her it wasn't particularly late. Way too early for Drexel to be back already.

She'd been so tired she'd crawled into bed with a paperback bestseller right after tucking Marnie in. She must have drifted off. The sounds coming from outside her room had woken her up.

Maybe Marnie had woken up and was shuffling around. That could be dangerous. Half-asleep, the girl might not know her way around the penthouse at all. Clairey had turned off all the lights. Alarm shot through her at the thought of Marnie moving around in the dark in an unfamiliar apartment. She bolted out of bed and flung the door of her bedroom open, flying toward the kitchen area.

The sight that greeted her when she got there halted her in her tracks. Drexel with his jacket off, his shirt sleeves rolled up, and the front of his shirt unbuttoned halfway down his chest. So ruggedly handsome, for a moment she forgot to breathe.

He looked up in the process of pulling a covered dish out of the refrigerator, appearing as shocked to see her as she was to find him there.

"Drexel? What are you doing here?"

He shrugged. "Just got back, came looking for those leftovers I mentioned earlier."

Was he deliberately being obtuse? "I mean, why are you here? In the penthouse?"

The corners of his mouth lifted. "I live here. Remember?" He looked her up and down, and a current of heat arose as his eyes traveled over her body. "Are you sleepwalking or something?"

She threw her hands up in frustration. "You know what I mean. I wasn't expecting you back so early." His date must have not gone well. Not that it was any of her business. Absolutely no reason for her to feel any sense of relief mixed with a strange headiness. "I'll leave you to it, then," she added to spare herself the risk of gawking at him. The man sure looked good in an unbuttoned tuxedo shirt.

He stopped her before she'd gone more than three steps. "Do you like kittens?"

Maybe she was sleepwalking. Because his question made absolutely no sense. "I'm sorry. Did you just ask me about kittens?"

He nodded. "Do you like them?"

What kind of person didn't like kittens? And why in the world was he asking? "Yes. I like kittens. They're very cute. Why do you ask?"

He set the plate he'd been holding down on the counter and shoved his fingers through his hair. "I thought maybe Marnie would like a pet. To help her adjust to moving in with me. I never had one growing up. I figured a kitten might be easier than a puppy in a high-rise."

Something tugged in her chest right around the vicinity of her heart. Drexel had obviously been giving this some thought. He really wanted to do right by his niece. Maybe Chase had done his daughter a tremendous favor in leaving her to his brother to raise. Harsh as that sounded, he certainly hadn't been there for his child when she'd needed him the most. He'd practically abandoned her. Whereas Drexel was doing everything he could to make sure Marnie was all right.

Kittens! Drex certainly wasn't making it easy on her to ignore her growing attraction.

She went and stood across the kitchen island from him. "I think that's a wonderful idea."

The smile he sent her way nearly had her swooning. "You said that first day I had her that kids needed distractions," he reminded her. "What better distraction than a playful little cat?"

"I can't think of anything. I can call around to see about finding one. I'll start with nearby rescue shelters."

"You would do that for me?" he asked. "I mean, you'd do that for us? It doesn't exactly fall within the job description."

She nodded. "Then, consider it a friendly favor."

His lips grew thin, and something she couldn't name flashed behind his eyes. "Is that what we are? Friends?"

Clairey's heart skipped a beat. It was such a loaded question. Somehow, they'd gone from speaking about cute little kittens to discussing the defining parameters of their relationship.

"I'd like to think so," she answered as honestly as she could. Though, it wasn't one hundred percent honest because deep down she knew she wished for more.

"Then, I could have asked you to come with me tonight. As a friend."

"On your date?" she blurted out without thinking.

He blinked at her. "What?"

It occurred to her that she really had no idea exactly where he'd been or who he'd been with. "I just assumed... I mean, the way you were dressed. So formally. And you've been out of town." Oh, for goodness' sake, now she was just blabbering.

"What made you think I was out on a date?"

"I just assumed you probably had someone waiting for you while you were off on the Cape for your brother's wedding."

"Did it occur to you that there was a reason I was sans one at the wedding?"

Of course it had. But she wasn't about to admit it. "I hadn't given it much thought."

Liar.

His lips quirked into a small smile, and he looked at her as if he might be thinking the same thing.

"I'm not dating anyone right now," he announced, taking a bite of a sandwich he'd efficiently put together during their conversation. "I have too much happening at the moment."

She would have thought men like him always had time for romantic relationships. Someone with all the qualities Drex had wouldn't have to put too much effort in. "Oh?"

He nodded, took another bite, chewed and swallowed. "My life was crazy enough with some major work projects coming due. Now I have to adapt to becoming a fill-in parent all of a sudden."

He slowly put the sandwich down on a plate and wiped his hands, as if he'd suddenly lost his appetite.

For the life of her, Clairey couldn't come up with anything to say to try to reassure him. The turn his life had unexpectedly taken really was rather daunting. His words rang in her head. He didn't have time for any kind of relationship. Not that she'd thought she ever had any kind of chance with him, but here he was making it quite clear. He didn't want to be romantically involved with anyone. Certainly not the woman he only saw as a caretaker to his niece. She had to squelch the disappointment that swelled in her chest.

After several silent moments, he snapped his head back up to look at her. "I asked you earlier if you liked kittens. Do you happen to like fireworks, as well?"

She had to chuckle at the sudden change of topic. "Yes. I like kittens, puppies and fireworks. Though, one of those things just doesn't belong here." The last phrase she sang to the tune of the well-known children's song that accompanied the matching game played in nursery school.

He crooked a finger in her direction. "Come here. I want to show you something."

Clairey stood off the stool and followed him as he walked down the hallway to the main living area. Where could he possibly be leading her after speaking of fireworks? She'd never met anyone like Drexel Osoman. Every moment was an unexpected adventure of some sort. "Kittens and fireworks. Sounds rather magical." And exciting, she added silently.

Just like the man himself.

The conversation was getting too loaded back there. He'd been too tempted to pour his soul out to her. And that just wouldn't do. Drexel knew what parts of his life he needed to keep guarded. For his own sake as much as for Clairey's. No need to burden her with the darkness that was his past.

So he'd thought of a distraction. He led her to the living area with its walls of glass that offered a sweeping panoramic scene of the Manhattan skyline. It was beautiful enough this time of night with the lights of the skyscrapers glowing brightly all around. As well as the brightly lit Brooklyn Bridge in the distance.

But tonight there'd be even more. The show should start in a matter of minutes.

"This view takes my breath away," Clairey said next to him as they took in the night.

"There'll be more to enjoy in a bit."

As he said the last word, a distant bouquet of light bloomed in the sky to the west. He pointed that way. "Did you see that?"

Clairey's mouth fell open. "Well, I'll be darned. Fireworks? The Fourth was two weeks ago."

He nodded. "It was rainy in New York. The city itself never cancels, rain or shine. But a few of the boroughs postponed to tonight."

"And we have a perfect view."

He pulled the love seat around to face the window, motioning for her to sit. "I say we enjoy the show. Would you like a glass of wine?"

She hesitated. "I really shouldn't. I have no idea how early Marnie will wake up tomorrow."

"Your choice. But I checked on her when I got in, and she was out like a light. I'm guessing she'll probably sleep in. She's had a rather harrowing and exhausting few days."

"You think so?"

"I do. If not, I have some really strong Jamaican Blue Mountain blend I always keep on hand."

"Sounds strong." She gave him a reluctant smile. "Maybe just one glass, then."

He walked over to the bar to open one of the barrel-aged merlots a client in Napa Valley had gifted him. He didn't know a thing about her wine tastes or coffee tastes, or anything else she found pleasurable, for that matter.

He had to suck in a breath. Bad direction for his thoughts to have taken.

Nevertheless, the merlot was sure to please. He'd bet on it.

Clairey had settled on the love seat with her legs tucked under when he handed her the glass of wine.

She didn't tear her eyes away from the window. By this point, another set of fireworks could be seen in the distance, this one clearer and a bit closer in the sky.

She took a small sip of her wine, and her eyes grew wide. "This is really good."

He'd been right. A rush of pleasure surged through his chest. He liked pleasing her. "I'm glad you like it."

They sat in silence for the several minutes. It was over all too soon.

She set her half-empty wineglass on the floor by her feet. "That was lovely, Drexel. Thank you for thinking to show me."

"I'm glad you liked it," he repeated. *Way to go, fella. Keep dazzling her with your witty conversation.*

"I really did. I had to work on the Fourth and missed the fireworks on the Cape. I'd actually been kind of sad about it. Before this job, I'd make sure to catch them in Boston. They have theirs over the harbor. I would take the T into the city with friends and spend the day in the commons until it grew dark and was time to head over to the Green Line."

She sounded wistful. He said, "Sounds fun. There's something about watching them in the sky over water. I've seen the ones in Atlantic City a couple of times."

"Oh?"

He nodded. "I grew up in New Jersey. Right outside of Hamilton."

"I've never been to Atlantic City. Or anywhere in Jersey for that matter."

"You haven't missed much. Atlantic City is a smaller version of Vegas. With a disproportionate slew of seedy areas." He cringed thinking about all the seediness he'd been exposed to in his life.

"But the casinos must be fun."

She was wrong there. Casinos weren't much fun if your dad happened to have an addiction to gambling. "I didn't particularly care for them. I still don't."

He wasn't about to get into the reasons for that opinion and wished he could forget them himself.

No, the days and nights Drexel had found himself in a casino had never been any fun. Far from it.

CHAPTER SIX

WAS IT SOMETHING she'd said?

Clairey watched as the muscles along Drexel's jaw tightened. He stiffened where he sat on the love seat. Suddenly, their light and easy conversation seemed anything but.

She grasped for something to say to get some semblance of it back. "There's something very unique about watching fireworks from a distance like this, in a high-rise apartment. It feels so…intimate somehow."

He sucked in a small breath. Wrong choice of words. One that could be taken in so many ways.

"I just mean it feels very private. The Fourth of July festivities I've gone to in Boston attract thousands of people."

He shot her a warm smile. "Sounds fun."

"One of my favorite days of the year when I was a kid. My dad would get us up early to take the T into the city." She laughed as the bittersweet memories stormed her mind. "Honestly, he acted more excited than me. My mom just sort of tolerated the long day and night in the city. She isn't one for crowds. My dad and I, though, we both loved every minute of it. I still do."

"And what about your father now?"

A sharp stab of hurt. "I'm afraid I lost him years ago, around middle school." In a very real sense, she'd lost her mother then too. Never the very motherly type, Nora had become increasingly distant after the loss. Then she'd met Frank and had become a completely different person altogether.

"I'm very sorry to hear that. It must be very hard on you and your mother not to have him around any longer."

Her lips trembled. Dad's loss had hit her mother hard, but she'd gotten over it surprisingly quickly. "My mother has moved on. She remarried several years ago, and they moved out to Arizona. I hardly see her anymore." Or hear from her, for that matter, she added to herself.

"Again, I'm sorry," Drexel said on a soft whisper. He leaned her way, and for one crazy instant, she thought he might touch her. But he stood instead. "I could use some more wine," he announced, lifting his goblet, his fingers tight around the stem. "How about you?"

She shook her head. "Definitely not. Though, it's delicious, I must say."

Clairey watched as he poured from the bottle. He appeared uncomfortable, strained. Maybe she shouldn't have shared so much about her past with him. She'd clearly made him uncomfortable somehow.

He remained silent as he sat back down next to her, his gaze fixed on the distant night sky. Clairey didn't think he was even looking at the view anymore. He seemed lost in his own thoughts.

This was all so confusing. She had no idea how to communicate with this man. The parameters of their relationship still needed to be worked out. In a very real way, Clairey was the catalyst that had led to this drastic change in his life. Though, judging how quick Chase was to toss his daughter to her uncle, she suspected eventually the end result would have been the same. It had simply been a matter of time. If that meant that Clairey had somehow saved Marnie so much as a day of feeling unwanted and unloved, she would consider it a win. Marnie deserved to feel both those things. All children did.

All that aside, Drexel made her more than a little nervous. Still, for the life of her, she couldn't figure out what she'd said to cause yet another awkward silence.

Finally, she could stand the silence no longer. At the risk of overstepping her bounds, she forced herself to ask the question burning in her mind. "You seem to have drifted off somewhere. Feel like talking about it?"

When he slowly turned his head to face her, his eyes were clouded with clear pain.

"I'm sorry to be such poor company. It's just been… a lot, these past few days."

There was more to it, she knew. And now she'd gone and insulted him. "I didn't mean to imply you were being poor company. I don't expect you to entertain me, Drexel."

He tilted his head and saluted her with his wineglass. "I'm not used to seeing a friendly face after a long day."

She chuckled. "I'm not sure how friendly I could have looked. I wasn't expecting you and panicked at first, hearing noises."

"Still. Arriving home tonight felt rather different. In a good way. It was a pleasant experience not to walk into an empty apartment. Something I haven't really had the pleasure of too often in the past."

It was all she was going to get, no doubt. Nevertheless, a feeling of gratifying warmth spread inside her at his words.

He stopped her before she could set foot over the threshold with a gentle touch on her elbow. Gentle or not, she felt a current run through the tips of his fingers all the way through to her chest. "Just one more thing."

"Oh?"

"There's something that's been on my mind. Something I think we need to discuss."

Well, that sounded rather ominous. Had she done something wrong with Marnie? Great, barely a moment on the job, and she was being reprimanded already. "What is it?"

"The day I kissed you back there on the Cape, when you first accepted my job offer."

"Yes?"

"I've been meaning to apologize for that. I shouldn't have so much as touched you without asking."

Her mouth went dry. Dare she admit that she'd liked it? That far from having to be sorry, he'd given her a moment of pleasure she couldn't stop thinking about?

The courage escaped her. She gave a brisk shake of her head with a nonchalance she didn't feel. "It was nothing."

His lips tightened, and he nodded once. "Be that as it may, I offer my apologies." The way his moods seemed to switch from warm and giving all the way to ice-cold and formal was going to give her whiplash.

"I'll bid you good-night, then," he added.

Without another word, he turned on his heel and

strode down the hall to his own suite. Clairey thought about calling after him to tell him how much she enjoyed watching the fireworks but hesitated too long in her indecision.

Just as well.

Something about the woman made him act all kinds the fool.

It was nothing.

Her words echoed in his ears. He had no business feeling disappointed that she'd referred to their kiss as if she'd already forgotten it had even happened. What a fool he was to have brought it up again.

In his defense, when he'd arrived home, he hadn't expected a beautiful woman to come running out into the kitchen in sleep shorts and a loose-fitting T-shirt. An outfit that somehow looked sexier on her than any negligee.

He bit back a curse. Great. Now he was thinking of her in a negligee. Drex pounded the pillow under his head and tossed for the umpteenth time onto his other side. He'd crawled into bed almost an hour ago and was still nowhere near falling asleep. His mind kept replaying the scene with Clairey earlier tonight. The way she'd opened up to him about the loss of her father. How he'd gone silent in response. Discussions about the past, his past, made him uncomfortable. He hadn't wanted to risk the tables turning and having his own past become the topic of discussion.

She may have opened up to him, but Drex wouldn't do the same in return. How would he begin to explain the pressures that had been put upon him since he was barely more than a teen? Pressure to keep the family afloat, to keep food on the table, to pay the bills by working several manual-labor jobs and hiding his pay before his dad got ahold of it so that he could feed it to the slot machines.

He cringed at the memories and forced them away. If anything, the pressures had only grown as he'd gotten older. Now, he had to make sure his mother's care facility was paid for. He had to ensure Chase had a chance to reach his full potential. And now there was a little girl to support.

All of the many reasons this deal with the sheikh was so important.

No. Clairey couldn't understand, but Drexel had made the right move in clamming up and then walking away. It had taken almost all of his will, but he'd made sure to maintain a distance like a true professional would with someone in his employ.

So why did it feel so wrong that this restless insomnia plagued him now?

He didn't have an answer, and he didn't know what to do about it. Those questions still bothered him about six hours later when he finally gave up and shoved the covers off. It was no use. He was pretty much going to be shot for the day, given his intermittent bouts of sleep. He couldn't have gotten more than an hour or so combined.

Not bothering to grab a shirt, he flung his door open with disgust and made his way out to the kitchen…to find that now it was his turn to be startled by Clairey the way he'd surprised her last night.

She was already up and puttering around the kitchen. He didn't need to glance at his watch to know it was barely past dawn. She'd changed into loose-fitting gray sweatpants and a scarlet tank top that fell just above her hips. Above the low-waisted sweatpants, it afforded him a glimpse of half an inch of skin and sent his blood shooting hot through his veins.

When she noticed him, she stilled in the act of pulling a pot out of one of the lower cabinets.

"You're up early," he said, stating the obvious.

She yawned in response before speaking. "Tell me about it. But I wanted to get a head start on Marnie's breakfast and begin planning her day. I want everything to be smooth sailing from the start."

Huh. "That was smart. I'm sure she'll appreciate it." As did he. "Thank you."

She shrugged. "No need for thanks. Just doing my job."

Drex didn't bother to tell her what he was thinking. Not every nanny would wake up at the crack of dawn to ensure the day went smoothly for their charge. But he was grateful for it. The fates had certainly smiled on both of them where Clairey was concerned. One of the few things in his life he could say that about.

The sadness he'd taken note of in her eyes last night still swam in their depths. It made him want to take her into his arms and hold her tight against his chest to comfort her. He should never have brought up her parents last night.

"Look, I didn't mean to pick at old wounds last night, when I asked about your father. I'm sorry if our conversation made you sad in any way."

She gave her head a vehement shake. "Please don't apologize. I don't mind talking about him. Of course it's sad that he's gone." Drexel didn't miss the hitch in her voice and the slight pause before she could continue. "And I miss him terribly, but his memory truly brings me comfort. He really was a great man. A great dad."

"I'm glad one of us can say that about either parent." Drexel flinched as soon as the words left his mouth. He hadn't meant to say that part out loud.

"I'm guessing you didn't get along with one or both of your parents. Your father?"

Childish as it was, he made the motion of a finger-gun in her direction. "Bingo. Second guess gets the prize."

She chewed the bottom of her lip, hesitated before continuing. "Drexel, I want you to know that I'm a really good listener. I'm all ears if you'd ever like to talk. Now or any other time."

There was nothing but sympathy in her eyes. Her facial expression flushed with concern and worry for him.

But all he could see was pity.

He felt every muscle in his body tighten. This was exactly what he'd been trying to avoid last night. Somehow, he'd walked straight into the same perilous territory mere hours later. Something about Clairey had him acting uncharacteristically unreserved and with his guard down all too often. It made him annoyed with himself. So he took it out on her.

"Look, I don't really have time to stand here and participate in any kind of deep conversation. I have an international call to make soon, and it's nonstop meetings and deliverables after that until late evening."

What a cowardly way to say he didn't want to talk about it.

She jammed her hands on her hips and blew out a

puff of air. The first gesture of frustration he'd ever seen from her. He had to wonder if he'd pushed her too far.

Though he desperately wanted to take back every harsh word, he knew he'd deliberately lashed out at her. In fact, it was better this way. This was good. Better she knew exactly what a son of a bastard he could be and not expect any better.

Doing so would only cause her hurt in the long run.

CHAPTER SEVEN

YET AGAIN WITH the emotional whiplash.

Clairey watched as Drexel poured himself some type of coffee from a complicated-looking machine on the counter near the fridge.

"Help yourself," he uttered to her before walking away to his suite of rooms.

Then she watched his retreating back, the rigid set of his shoulders, the stiffened spine. Clearly, he was having trouble adjusting to having people in his apartment. Despite what he'd said last night about coming home to a friendly face. Apparently, waking up to one was a different matter.

She huffed out a frustrated breath. That would teach her, wouldn't it? This wasn't exactly a piece of cake for her either. Clairey was the one who'd abruptly found herself in a new city and a new residence. Not to mention a job she barely had the experience for. She had some of her own adjusting to do.

Well, one thing was for certain. She'd learned her lesson. She refused to put herself out there again where Drexel was concerned. No more personal conversations, no more friendly chats. From now on, she would be the utmost professional. Every discussion would center around Marnie or something that might affect her.

Clairey was done. With a capital *D*. From now on, her sole and only focus would be the five-year-old girl sleeping down the hall.

Now, what might said little girl like for breakfast?

Clairey certainly had options when it came to making that decision. Drexel's housekeeper had the pantry and fridge fully stocked. She'd been told the woman typically had Mondays off. It was all typed up neatly for Clairey on a long document that she'd pulled up on the laptop Drexel had provided in her room. Everything she'd need to know about what he may require of the nanny he'd hired. Laid out in very clear terms in digital pixels on a master file he'd entitled *Marnie Osoman*.

So very efficient of him.

Her ward woke up and entered the kitchen just as Clairey flipped the last pancake onto a serving platter. She'd also cut up some berries and poured a tall glass of milk.

"Perfect timing."

Marnie clapped her hands together. "Pancakes!" Pure delight rang in her voice.

"I remembered one morning back at the Sea View. You were eating nothing but pancakes at the breakfast buffet," she explained.

"I'm glad you remembered that."

Clairey helped her get settled on a counter stool and set up plates for them both.

"Where's Uncle Drex?" the little girl asked after taking several bites and downing half the milk. "Isn't he going to eat with us?"

"He's a little busy at the moment. I'm sure we'll see him later, though," Clairey answered. Hopefully, she wasn't lying.

Three hours later, she was starting to suspect she might have done just that. They'd already spent the morning coloring and working on her letters and over an hour playing with the intricately designed doll-house in Marnie's room. The girl had asked about her uncle often enough times that Clairey had lost count.

For Marnie's sake, she would venture into the pro-verbial lion's den and ask if Drexel planned to perhaps have lunch with the girl. Or even say a simple hello.

His office door was slightly ajar, and he didn't appear to be on the phone. Drexel noticed her before she could knock.

"Was there something you needed?" he asked, clearly distracted. Clairey figured it would seem less intrusive if she just spoke to him from the hallway.

"I understand your days are certain to be busy. I just thought maybe you could break away, given it's her first full day here and all."

He shook his head. "I'm afraid I can't. And it's not just days. I'm afraid my evenings and weekends are pretty full as well. I have a lot of international clients who expect me to be available at all hours. When I'm not dealing with them directly, I'm prepping for the times I will be." He waited a beat, then added, "I also do a lot of traveling."

"I see." She swallowed, forced herself to continue to say what she had to say.

"Don't you think that might be a problem? I mean, long-term?"

He blinked at her. "Problem? What kind of problem?"

"Marnie's certain to get bored and tire of me if I'm the only one she sees all day. Day after day."

"She'll be going to school in the fall."

"It's still mid-July. That's still several weeks away."

"Fine. I'll make a call." He pivoted on his heel and walked back to his desk before she could ask him what he was talking about.

A call? What kind of call would address the fact that he'd ignored his niece all day?

She found out the answer to that question fifteen minutes later when Drexel called her into his study. He was seated at his U-shaped dark mahogany desk with four large monitors facing him. He didn't bother to look up or stop typing when she entered the room.

"You called for me?"

Drexel continued pounding on the keyboard as he answered. "The lobby desk downstairs informed me that most of the families with small children are at their summer residences until school starts."

Now she understood. Enough to have her heart sinking a little.

Drexel continued. "But there's a family on the fourth floor with a daughter around Marnie's age who had to stay in the city, something having to do with their house in the Hamptons being renovated. I had the desk call to set up a get-together between the girls. They should be here after lunch."

"You set up a playdate."

He paused long enough to glance at her, eyebrows raised. "Is that what they call it? I suppose I did."

Clairey opened her mouth to explain that wasn't exactly what she'd had in mind but snapped it right back shut. What was the use? He clearly wasn't going to tear himself away from his study anytime soon. And this girl would be here within a couple of hours. Plus, Drexel looked rather pleased with himself. "I see," she answered instead.

"Maybe they'll even stay for dinner."

"Dinner?"

"I'll be out. I have a dinner meeting in the financial district. You should ask them if they can join you and Marnie."

"I might do that."

"Get something delivered. Or you can all head out. I've provided a list of my favorite nearby restaurants."

"Yes, I know. It's all right there in the Marnie file on my computer."

He nodded once. "That's right."

Clairey tried to quash the feelings of disappointment that flushed through her. Was this how things were going to be for her and Marnie? Finding ways to keep themselves busy with playdates and other distractions while Drexel spent all his days glued to his desk and all his evenings out and about?

If that notion made her feel lonely, that was solely her problem. But this wasn't about her. The bigger concern was, of course, Marnie. The girl needed another anchor in her life besides her nanny, for heaven's sake. Clairey had to somehow make Drexel see that. And she had to do it in a way that wasn't overstepping her bounds. After all, Clairey couldn't stick around forever. This job was a temporary one: she had a career she'd studied and worked hard for. As much as she was growing to care for the little girl, Clairey being here wasn't meant to be a permanent solution.

Drexel had to know that, didn't he?

If he didn't, he was in for a rude awakening when the time came. Clairey would have to do everything she could to make sure little Marnie didn't bear the brunt of it.

When the door buzzer went off just after three o'clock, Clairey realized with no small amount of surprise that she was rather nervous. She'd never entertained anyone who was successful enough to live in a building such as this one.

Smoothing out her skirt and adjusting her ponytail, she went to answer. Her sigh of relief was audible after opening the door. She should have guessed. The woman standing there, holding the hand of a smiling girl, was about the same age as Clairey and wore black denim jeans and athletic sneakers, her auburn hair secured in a large clip. Clearly, this was a babysitter too.

"Please, come in."

The little girl bounced through the door ahead of her sitter and announced, "Hi, I'm Sara." Definitely not a shy one.

By contrast, Marnie was hovering hesitantly by Clairey's leg, chewing on her thumbnail.

"And I'm Lana," the young woman said with a smile, following her charge inside the apartment.

Clairey gestured toward Marnie and introduced her to the two newcomers. "Thank you so much for taking the time to meet us. And on such short notice too."

Lana clasped a hand to her chest. "Oh, thank you for thinking to contact us. It's been so boring around here for Sara with all her friends away for the summer. We're usually at the Hamptons this time of year, but the house is being renovated, and it's taking so much longer than they thought."

"I see. Well, how fortunate for us that you happened to have stuck around this season!"

"Thank you. What's keeping you from heading to your summer place, then?" Lana asked.

Now, there was something to consider. It occurred to her that Drexel probably had multiple other residences. As successful an investor as he was, his holdings had to include real estate. She would have to find a way to ask him about it.

Clairey motioned for them all to follow her inside to the sitting area. "Actually, I don't quite know where that might be or even if there is one. See, this is literally one of my first days on the job."

Lana's eyes lit up with interest. "Oh? What service are you with? This penthouse has been occupied for a while. How did we never know there was a little girl Sara's age living here?"

"It was a private arrangement," Clairey answered simply, avoiding the second part of Lana's question and hoping it would drop the subject. As innocuous as the question was, she didn't feel comfortable discussing Marnie's situation with strangers, friendly as they were.

Lana glanced around the apartment and walked over to the glass wall to look out at the skyline. The girls were already ankle-deep in coloring books around the center coffee table.

"Wow," the other woman said, taking in the view.

"This place is even grander than I thought. What do your employers do, again?"

Drexel chose that moment to step out of his office. He'd unbuttoned the top two buttons below his collar and rolled up his sleeves. A slight layer of stubble had begun to appear on his chin. The man looked like he could have stepped out of a cologne ad. Lana must have thought so too. Her expression when she turned and saw him could best be described as awestruck.

He looked from Clairey to the two girls with crayons and coloring books strewn all around his floor, and for a brief second looked completely, utterly confused. Then clarity washed over his features. Clairey felt a pang of sympathy for the poor man. What a life change he was experiencing. Barely two weeks ago, he was living the life of a bachelor with no responsibility to anyone but himself. Now he was suddenly living with a woman and accommodating the needs of a small child.

"Hello," he said to the other babysitter. The girls hadn't even bothered to acknowledge him, too engrossed in their activity. He waved to Lana and introduced himself.

"I see the playdate is in full session," he remarked, waving a hand toward the girls.

"It is indeed."

"Good. That's good. Well done." Drexel excused himself to head to the kitchen.

Lana blew out a breath and uttered something that sounded like it might have been *hubba-hubba*.

She turned to Clairey, her eyes wide. "Oh, my... Is that who you work for?" She patted her hair. "Someone should have warned me. I would have at least put some makeup on. That man could tempt a mother superior with those looks."

Something twitched in the center of Clairey's chest. Something she refused to examine as any kind of jealousy.

Lana continued, "His wife must be something. What's she like?"

"There is no wife."

"Oh? Then, how—?"

Clairey cut off her question. She was not about to get into any of that with someone she'd literally just met. Drexel deserved to have his privacy protected. She would discuss with him at an opportune time how much he wanted to reveal to his neighbors about who Marnie was.

She deftly changed the subject. "It's a long story. I'm hoping this won't be our last visit together, and I can tell you all about it sometime. But before I forget, I was wondering if you could help with something. Do you happen to know where we might be able to get a kitten?"

Lana still stared in the direction of the kitchen. "I'm sorry. What'd you ask?"

"I asked if you knew where we might be able to go about finding a kitten to adopt."

The other woman blinked with a small shake of her head and finally turned her focus back to Clairey.

"A kitten." She smiled wide. "You're in luck. My sister happens to work for a rescue in Westchester. I can ask her, if you'd like?"

With the uncomfortable conversation about Marnie's past diverted for now, Clairey walked over to the couch and motioned for Lana to join her. As soon as Drexel was done in the kitchen, she'd go brew them some tea. In the meantime, she would go about finding a pet for Marnie as they'd discussed last night.

She just might be getting the hang of this nannying thing.

Drex tiptoed carefully out of his office two hours later in an effort to avoid running into Marnie and Clairey's guests if they were still there. Nothing against them personally, he just wasn't any good at small talk. And he especially didn't know what he might possibly say to a sitter and her small charge. Hell, he barely knew how to speak to the child he was now responsible for.

The apartment was quiet: no giggling little girls and no sound of grown-ups' voices chattering in friendly conversation. Looked like the coast was clear. Except, as soon as Drexel had that thought and took a few steps, a small blur in a pink tutu shot toward him and hugged him around the knees.

"Hey there, kiddo."

Clairey rounded the corner after his niece.

"Uncle Drex!" Marnie squealed with excitement. "I made a new friend. And she was so nice, and she colored with me, then we played dollhouse, and we had a snack. She was so nice!" she repeated.

Clairey laughed softly. "Marnie had a lovely visit with Sara."

"I can see that."

Marnie barely let him finish his sentence. "Oh! And she told me about the other kids that live here. She says they're so much fun to play with too. They all go to the same school, and they say the teachers are really nice, and it has a great playground." The child paused just long enough to take a quick breath. "Sara says I have to go to that school too. Can I please? Please, Uncle Drex. Can I?"

Drexel crouched down to her level. "I don't see why not. We'll make sure you go to the same school all your new friends will be at."

Marnie hopped excitedly. "Yay! Thanks, Uncle Drex." She gave him a tight hug around the neck, and Drexel could swear he felt a slight loosening in the tightness that always seemed to be gripping his chest. He returned her hug.

"You're welcome."

Marnie gave him another squeeze before unwrapping her arms. "I'm gonna go look at all the pictures we colored."

Drexel stood up to find Clairey staring at him. She was looking at him like he'd just slayed a dragon. For what? Returning his niece's hug? He was probably imagining it. "She seems very excited about going to this new school."

She nodded. "I'll call Sara's nanny to get the details. She gave me her contact info."

"Uh, thank you. That would be great."

Clairey pulled her cell phone out of her pocket. "In fact, I'll do it right now. No time like the present. Right?"

"I suppose."

Drexel waited while Clairey placed the call and asked about the school. Then he watched as her smile faded.

"Oh. I see," Clairey said into her phone. She looked like someone might have just deflated her birthday balloon and beaten her to blowing out the candles on her cake.

"Well, thank you for the information. I'll relay it all," she added, then disconnected the call.

"What did she say?" he asked, though he was fairly certain he didn't want to know the answer. Clairey's words and her expression did not bode well.

"As it turns out, that school is one of the most popular and esteemed ones in all of New York."

"Isn't that a good thing?"

"Sure. In the sense that anyone who's planned enough in advance to apply and interview for a coveted spot in one of their classes is guaranteed a great elementary education."

"Six weeks isn't enough advance to apply?"

A sound escaped from her lips that could be described as a combination of both scoff and chuckle. "I'm afraid not."

Drexel felt a surge of disappointment pummel his core. He hated to think about how Marnie would react to the disappointing news. He'd practically promised her she'd be able to attend this school with her new friend and the other building neighbors her age.

He rubbed his eyes. "All right. We'll make sure to explain to Marnie that she just has to wait until next year. And that we'll find her another school she'll like just as much. She might not even want to switch from whatever school she attends by then."

Clairey's lips tightened. "Well, that would indeed be a good thing. I'm afraid next year isn't going to work either, for the school in question."

"What? Why?"

Clairey pressed her fingers to her forehead. "Lana just told me that the wait list is long. Really long."

"How long would that be?"

She wrung her hands together. Yet another bad sign. "Drexel, parents apparently apply upon their kid's *birth*. They go through years of communication and a rigorous review process. I'm afraid there's no hope of getting Marnie into the Hammond School. Not based on what I just heard."

Great. Now he would have to break the news to his niece that would break a promise he'd made. He swore out loud. How could he have been so stupid as to reassure her of something he had no clue about? He didn't want to be yet another adult who'd let Marnie down. He should have been more careful with his words.

His mind flooded with all the times he'd been let down by a distracted and uncaring father. Promises broken. All the lies about finally changing his ways. Drex had sworn throughout his life never to behave that way himself. Especially not toward anyone he cared about. And here he was on the first few days with his niece about to break a pledge he'd made to her.

Clairey's next words somewhat helped to mitigate the storm of self-recrimination rushing through his core. "Except she did mention one thing. A small possibility we might still be able to get Marnie enrolled."

He stepped toward her. "What kind of possibility? Whatever it is, we have to try."

"Lana said she'd forward me all the info via email. But apparently the Hammond School holds an event every summer."

Drexel stifled the urge to groan out loud. He was already up to his ears in functions and charity events to appease one client or colleague or another. "What kind of event?"

"Apparently it's a huge gala of some sort. Centered

around an auction to benefit their sister school in San Juan. The final event is a draw."

"A raffle?"

She nodded once. "Exactly. The buy-in is an exorbitant amount, from what I understand."

That wasn't surprising. "What's the prize?"

"A coveted spot for one lucky student who can afford the tuition at the Hammond."

Drexel ran a hand over his face. It was clear what he had to do. Anything he could to help Marnie transition into her new life and ease the hurt of having her father abandon her without any regard whatsoever.

"Tell me exactly what the email says," he directed Clairey. "If there's any way we can purchase a lottery ticket, let's do it ASAP. I don't want to risk them selling out or anything."

"Aye, aye," she responded, with a mock salute, just as her phone pinged with an alert of some kind. Clairey glanced down at her screen. "Huh. Looks like she's already sent the info. I'll go download the document on the computer."

He started to follow her to her room.

"I hate to ask," she said over her shoulder as they made their way down the hall. "Lana said the price was *exorbitant*. Her exact word."

He shrugged. "Doesn't matter. I'll pay whatever it costs."

At this point, the expense was inconsequential. He'd made what amounted to a promise to Marnie out there. He didn't want the start of their time together to begin with a broken one. Kids were resilient, he knew. Heaven knew he'd had to be, growing up. But they could become weary all too easily. He didn't want his niece to feel that way about him.

When they reached Clairey's room, he hesitated before stepping inside. These were her private quarters. But she made no move to stop him, so he went to stand beside her as she sat down at the French antique desk he'd had set up for her with a laptop. But not before he had a chance to notice how much she'd made the place her own. Several framed photographs of her and various friends smiled out at him from every corner of the room. A painted tapestry hung on the wall by the door.

No one in any of the pictures seemed much older than she was. She had no photos with her mom.

Before he could even register what it was, his gaze traveled to a wire rack sitting right by her bathroom door. Various delicate lingerie items were hanging on it. A silky, lacy number in scarlet red made his pulse quicken. For as straitlaced as she appeared, Clairey Robi's taste in undergarments ran toward the boudoir variety. No use for it: he couldn't help but imagine the way she'd look wearing it. The pleasure that would come from taking it off of her.

He had to swallow down the rush of desire coursing through his veins and yanked his eyes away. The last thing he needed was to be caught ogling his nanny's underwear.

In the file he'd prepared, he'd made sure to include the laundry service he used as well as where to find the washer and dryer. So why hadn't she used either, for heaven's sake? Now he would never be able to get the image of her wearing...*that* out of his head.

Taking a deep breath, he bent over the desk next to her and made himself focus on the laptop screen as she clicked the mouse. She had several windows open. A few of the article titles caught his eye: "Helping Your Elementary-aged Child Thrive." "Reading-skill Levels for School-aged Children." "Ensuring Your Child Is Eating Right."

She'd been reading up on how to best take care of Marnie.

First week or not, he was already thinking about giving her a raise. The woman was clearly dedicated.

Loyal and affectionate. How many such people had Drex met throughout his life? Not enough. Then again, Clairey was one in a million. Someone a man could easily find himself falling for if he wasn't careful.

He would have to make sure he was careful.

Drexel found himself staring at her profile as she navigated the computer screen. She really was strik-ing. Her dark hair brought out the bright hue of her eyes. The mass of curls complemented her patrician nose and soft chin.

"Here," she said after a few moments and pointed at the screen. "The charity ball is next week. Says you can purchase the raffle tickets online but have to be present to claim the prize. We have to hurry, though. There are only a handful of tickets left."

She turned to stare at him, and he realized just how close their faces were. Was it his imagination, or did she pause ever so slightly when their eyes met? Several beats passed as neither one of them moved. Finally, she cleared her throat. "What do you think?"

Think? Drexel was finding it rather hard to do that at the moment. What exactly was she asking him about? Pulling himself together, he straightened, then winked at her. "Might want to think about what you'd like to wear. Looks like we're going to a charity ball."

CHAPTER EIGHT

THEY'D BE ATTENDING a ball together. A social event. Like some kind of real couple. Drex was still contemplating the ramifications of that bright and early the next morning when his phone vibrated with a call alert.

He muttered a small curse when the caller's profile picture appeared on his phone screen. Any time the sheikh called for an unscheduled conversation, it usually meant bad news. Another snag in their ongoing negotiations, no doubt.

With a resigned sigh, Drex tapped on the Accept button.

"Sheikh Farhan. To what do I owe the honor?"

There was a long enough pause at the other end that Drex braced himself.

Drex gave him a prod. "Did you have a question about the latest specs?"

He heard the other man sigh through the tiny speaker. "It's not that, Mr. Osoman."

Another bad sign. The sheikh usually called him Drex. "Then…?"

"I've been hearing things."

"What kinds of things?"

"Your personal life is obviously none of my concern."

Yet it seemed it was. Drex racked his brain to figure out what the other man might be referring to. He hadn't been tied to anyone famous in quite a while. What could the gossip sites possibly be saying about him?

The other man continued. "I believe you've had a major life change recently, correct?"

Marnie. He meant Marnie.

Drex cleared his throat. "Yes. I'm taking care of my niece for a while. I assure you it will have no impact on any of my professional duties."

"I would imagine having custody of a small child would lead to significant distractions. At this stage of the deal, we can't afford that, Mr. Osoman."

"We have a nanny. She's highly qualified."

"I see," the sheikh replied. Though, he didn't really sound like he did. Not at all. "Just one nanny, then?"

"For now."

"Tell me. Does this woman never require any time off? She will never have a personal matter to attend to? What if she suddenly quits?"

"She's a live-in," Drex answered, knowing full well how lame that sounded. How it didn't really answer any of the questions the sheikh had just fired at him.

Drex rubbed his forehead. This was a very competitive deal. Numerous others were waiting in the sidelines to pounce if things went sour between him and the sheikh. On the surface, he had to admit that the other man was right. One live-in nanny hardly appeared as a permanent solution, especially for someone as traditional as the sheikh. More than another employee, what Drexel could really use was a true partner. A wife, almost.

He wanted to laugh out loud. He wasn't even dating anyone at the moment. There was no one who even came close he might consider.

Except maybe there was. Drex stopped short. It was a preposterous idea. Wasn't it? He and Clairey weren't romantically involved. But there was no doubt she already meant more to him and Marnie than a simple employee. There was a world of difference between, say, Sharon, his chef slash house manager, and Clairey.

Romantic or not, he and Clairey were more than boss and employee. And she was certainly more to Marnie than a simple caregiver.

Or maybe he was simply justifying what he was about to do.

"Your Highness, I can assure you the lady in question will not quit."

"How can you be so sure?"

Before he could give himself time to think, Drex found himself uttering a truly remarkable sentence.

"Because we've fallen in love. I intend to ask her to marry me."

The sheikh gasped in response, and Drex went on. "I'm about to present her with a ring any day." What in the world was he doing? Of all the spontaneous, potentially disastrous moves, this one could really bite him in the behind.

But the words were flowing out of him now. Almost unstoppable.

"I was just waiting for the right time and the perfect setting. She's very fond of Marnie and would make an excellent stepmother to her." Technically, all that was true. Not that Drex felt any less deceptive.

"Well, why didn't you say so from the beginning?" the sheikh asked with a pleasant laugh. "Congratulations, my friend. I can't wait to meet your soon-to-be fiancée."

"Meet her?"

"Yes. With the sheikha. I plan on being in New York early next month. For the premiere of a blockbuster I happened to invest in. That superhero franchise. We would love to have you and your lady join us as our guests."

Well, that was certainly an unexpected turn. There was nothing to it. Drex was too far in. He had to accept. He couldn't risk losing his potential business relationship with the sheikh. It was way too important. Especially now. Drex couldn't fail when he'd come this far. "We would consider it an honor."

"Excellent. We shall see you both in a few weeks."

"I look forward to it," Drex said, which this time was indeed a lie. With another muttered curse, he tapped off the call.

What had he just done? And how was he going to present it to Clairey? But was it really that ridiculous a notion? He and Clairey just had to pretend until he could close this deal. Two months at the most. Plus, there was the charity ball next week at the prospective school for Marnie. Wouldn't it look better if they presented themselves as a family unit there? Raffle or not, Marnie had a better chance at being accepted, both literally and figuratively, at a school like that if they didn't have to explain that she was living with a bachelor uncle who barely had time in his life for his own personal needs, let alone the needs of a child.

The ball could be a practice run for their pretend engagement before they met with the sheikh during his visit.

On the surface, what he'd just done made perfect sense. For him, anyway. He just had to hope Clairey would go along with his latest gamble.

Clearly, she hadn't gotten out of bed this morning. She must still be asleep, and this was all some kind of strange dream. Because there was no way Drex was standing in front of her asking what he appeared to be asking.

"You want to pretend I'm your fiancée?"

"I know it sounds ridiculous."

That was one way to describe it. Clairey focused her gaze to the view of Central Park outside the glass walls. She had to look away. There was no way she could process what was happening if she had to look at Drex. He wanted to take her to some movie premiere. Which was unbelievable enough in itself. But to attend such an event with him as his fiancée—well, that was downright fantastical.

Drex continued. "It's just to appease the sheikh."

She nodded. "Yes. Your client."

"More like *potential business partner*. I really need this deal with him to go through. I know it's a lot to ask."

She held up a hand. He'd been doing his best to explain the reasoning behind such an outrageous ask. But somehow it wasn't quite sinking in.

Her. Clairey Robi. Pretending to be Drexel Osoman's fiancée.

"Tell me again why."

Drex rammed his fingers through his hair. "As you might guess, the sheikh is from a culturally very conservative part of the world. When he heard I was the new charge of a little girl, he became concerned it would impact my business dealings. That I'd be distracted."

"So you told him you would soon have a wife."

He nodded. "And, more importantly, a stepmother for a little girl."

"I see."

"Will you do it, Clairey? For the premiere? And maybe also the charity auction for the school? Then we can decide how to go on from there."

She blinked at him. "The auction too?"

He shrugged. "In for a pound and all that. I figured we'd look better as a couple who's trying to get their daughter into a good school. Whether we win or not."

Couple. Parents. Fiancée. The words sounded foreign and strange to her ears. A foolish part of her wished that somehow it could all be real. But that was pure fantasy. Men like Drex didn't fall for women like her. She was small-time. Plain and too ordinary. Of course she wouldn't get any kind of real proposal from a worldly, successful business tycoon.

"If we're lucky, there'll be some media there to leak photos of us together," Drex added.

"You've really thought this through, haven't you?"

He shrugged. "It all seemed to fall into place as I was talking to the sheikh."

What world had she found herself in? Less than a couple of weeks ago she was sleeping on a worn-out couch. Now, she was being asked to play the part of a billionaire's future wife.

Drex went on. "Of course, I will completely understand if you say no."

Except he didn't look like he would. He looked completely crestfallen at the possibility she might refuse. And what would become of his crucial business deal if he had to explain to the sheikh that he didn't in fact have a fiancée? How would he even begin to explain it? The amount of embarrassment he would face made her shudder. Could she do that to him? After all he'd done for her?

There was only one clear answer. She shrugged, feigning a nonchalance she didn't feel. "Why not? It's just a couple events. I'll do it."

Drex's mouth widened into a large grin. Without warning, he picked her up and spun her around in his arms. "For Marnie," he said with a chuckle above her head.

Clairey had trouble catching her breath when he finally put her back down on her feet. She felt dizzy and light-headed. Couldn't even tell whether it was due to the spin, the feel of being in Drex's arms or the enormity of what she'd just agreed to. Probably all of the above.

For Marnie.

CHAPTER NINE

CLAIREY RESISTED THE urge to pinch herself as she stared at her image in the mirror. As cliché as it was, she felt like Cinderella on her way to the ball.

It was hard to believe the image in the glass was actually her. Her dress was unlike anything she'd worn before. A slinky midnight-blue number that draped over her body with a low-cut back. Low enough that Clairey had almost hung it right back up on the rack, but Lana had insisted it was perfect and jokingly hinted that Clairey was acting a tad prudish.

For the third time that day, she thanked her lucky stars for having met Lana when she'd first arrived. Being a native New Yorker, Lana knew where to go to find a formal dress at a relative bargain. The two of them had taken a cab to the fashion district with their two little charges in tow. Marnie had been delighted at the adventure.

She'd also borrowed a pair of dark velvet stilettos from the other woman, who luckily had the same size feet. The only shoes Clairey had brought with her were sensible and practical ones that someone chasing after an active little girl would need. Added to all that, now

Lana was watching Marnie for the night so that she and Drexel could attend the charity auction together.

Looking at herself now, Clairey knew she'd never be able to adequately thank the other woman who was swiftly becoming a true friend.

Heavy footsteps sounded outside in the hall. A moment later, there was a soft knock on her door.

"Come in."

Her door slowly opened, and Drexel stepped in, preoccupied with adjusting his cuff links. Clairey had to swallow down a gasp. The tuxedo he had on was clearly tailored especially for him. The suit fit him like glove. His hair was tidier than usual with a hint of gel. He looked like a prince straight out of a fairy tale.

Her very own Prince Charming. Except he wasn't really hers. And he never would be.

"Almost ready?" he asked, still tooling around with his left cuff link.

"Yes."

He finally looked up at her. His eyes snapped open wide, then traveled the length of her body. "Wow!"

Her pulse jumped. Clairey made sure not to react in any way. Though, it was so very hard. It wouldn't do to act pleased at his reaction.

"You look…uh…"

Huh. She'd left him speechless. A twinge of feminine satisfaction hummed along her veins.

"So this will work?" she asked, running a hand along her midsection down toward her thigh.

His response was a very slow nod. "Oh, yeah. That all works. Really, really well."

This time, she couldn't hide her smile.

He blinked a couple more times before giving his head a slight shake. "Oh, before I forget…"

Clairey watched as he reached inside his jacket pocket and pulled out a small square object. A velvet box. Without any kind of preamble, he handed it to her.

"Can't be engaged without a ring."

For a brief moment, she couldn't so much as breathe. Of all the ways she'd imagined receiving an engagement ring, this scenario hadn't entered the realm of her imagination. With trembling fingers, which she hoped Drex didn't notice, she flipped open the cover. Inside on a cloud of white satin fabric sat an oval-cut diamond on a simple gold band. It was beautiful. Suddenly, unexpected tears stung her eyes at how little it really meant. As exquisite as it was, the ring was nothing more than costume jewelry. A prop.

"I guessed on the size," Drex told her. "There's a jeweler next door if it doesn't work. We can do a quick swap." He glanced at his watch. "We'll have just enough time."

Clairey swallowed past the lump in her throat and slid the ring onto her finger. "It's a little snug. But it should work."

"Excellent," Drex said, offering her his arm. "Shall we, then?"

Within minutes, they were down on the street, and Drexel helped her into the waiting limousine.

She studied his profile as the car moved through the city streets. The man was the very definition of drop-dead gorgeous. So handsome in a tux, she was having trouble keeping from gawking at him.

Just for a few moments, she let herself pretend there was more to their relationship than trying to win an auction or a tricky business deal. That she and Drexel were a real couple, that there was no reason for the pretense. The man that would take her back to their shared apartment at the end of the night and kiss her good-night was really hers. Heaven help her, but she did want him to kiss her again. And not just the spontaneous, unplanned kiss he'd planted on her, back on the Cape when she'd accepted his job offer. A real kiss. She wanted to feel his firm lips on hers. To discover how he might taste. The way his caress would feel.

Stop it.

Clairey could pretend all she wanted. But reality was what it was. This wasn't some kind of real date with her real fiancé. Just like they weren't really engaged. Tonight they were doing all this for Marnie's sake. To try and win her a spot at the school that so many of their building neighbors would be attending. She had absolutely no business fantasizing about the man sitting next to her. He might have paid her a compliment or two, but no doubt Drexel was simply being a gentleman. He was solely focused on the task at hand. As she should be.

Next to her, Drexel cleared his throat. "You look lovely. That dress is very flattering."

So why wasn't he even looking at her as he said so? Regardless, Clairey felt a warm flush creep into her cheeks.

"Thank you. You look quite nice too."

He glanced down at her hands, clasped tight in her lap. She hadn't realized she was holding them so tightly, the new ring biting into the skin of her palm. "Something wrong?"

"No. I'm fine."

He raised an eyebrow. "Are you sure? Because you look like you're on your way to face an inquisition of some sort."

"Okay, I have to admit to being a tad nervous. What if I say the wrong thing to someone or hold my wineglass wrong or something?"

"How in the world might you hold your glass wrong?"

She shrugged. "I don't know. Is my pinkie supposed to be up a certain way?"

"Your pinkie?"

She lifted her hands and waved her two pinkie fingers at him. "The closest I've come to attending an event like this would be the weddings or birthday parties I've worked back at the resort. And for those I was there as an employee."

He reached for her then, gave her hand a reassuring squeeze. "Trust me, no one will be looking at your pinkies. Not in that dress." Clairey inhaled a small gasp at the heat that swam in his eyes as he said the last words. Giving her hands another reassuring squeeze, he dropped them and looked out his window.

It took a lot of willpower to not reach for him again.

The champagne must be going to her head. Because despite being so nervous upon arriving, Clairey was actually starting to have fun. Though, she had to admit, right now that probably had much more to do with the man currently leading her across the dance floor than the bubbly she'd been imbibing. He'd surprised her soon after they'd arrived by asking her to dance. Then surprised her further by proving to be quite competent with his footwork.

Now, they were doing a fast-paced foxtrot across the dance floor. Another couple they passed actually applauded.

"You know your way around a dance floor, Ms. Robi. Is there no end to your talents?"

"With all the weddings I've had to work, you pick up a few things. You should see my electric slide."

He winked at her, and a strange feeling of euphoria shivered down her spine. "I look forward to it."

"And I could say the same for you. Are you just a natural, then?"

"Hardly. I dated a competitive ballroom dancer for a while. At the time, I thought it was a nuisance when she guilted me into learning the steps. Now I have to admit it's come in quite handy over the years."

It was silly, she knew. But the idea of him dancing with another woman, holding her the same way he held Clairey right now, had her dispirited.

She had to remind herself that none of this was real. She was simply pretending. He'd dated and been involved with more women than Clairey wanted to think about. In real life, a man like Drexel wouldn't be interested in any kind of relationship with an ex–resort manager who he'd simply hired to look after his informally adopted niece.

One waltz and a tango later, they decided to take their seats. A server stopped by with a tray of the evening's specialty cocktail. Clairey didn't know what was in it, but it tasted like sweet ambrosia and honey combined.

From then on, tray after tray arrived with delicious hors d'oeuvres and tiny dessert tarts. Clairey picked a glazed fruit tart to go with her cocktail. A burst of flavor exploded on her tongue at the first bite.

She looked up to find Drexel staring at her, a whimsical smile on his face. "What is it? Do I have something on my face?"

He chuckled before answering. "No. Just enjoying how much you're enjoying that tart."

A flush warmed her cheeks. "I've always had a sweet tooth, I'm afraid."

He leaned toward her on the table. "Well, don't keep me waiting. How does it compare to lobster ice cream?"

Clairey playfully looked upward, as if concentrating. "It's a tough call. I might have to have another tart before I can answer."

Before Drexel could respond, the applauding couple from the dance floor approached their table and asked to join them. Drexel nodded without hesitation and motioned for them to pull out a chair. Silly as it was, Clairey had to squash a surge of disappointment. It was rather fun having Drexel to herself, and the intrusion felt like a rare and precious gift had been taken away from her.

She forced a smile on her face as the introductions were made.

"You don't look familiar," the woman said now. "Is your child new to the school?"

"No. We're hoping she will be," Drexel answered.

"Ah, you're here for the raffle, then."

"We are."

"Well, best of luck to you," the husband said. "I hope your daughter gets in."

Drexel didn't bother to correct the other man. Instead, he pulled her ever so slightly closer, his arm tightening around her shoulders. A shiver of heat ran down her spine at the contact. Along with a thread of excitement. There was something oddly enticing about the fact that this other couple, as well as the other people in the room, must assume they were married with a child of their own. She had no business feeling so fond of that idea, but she couldn't deny that she was.

Her phone pinged with a text message right at that moment. "Excuse me, but I must check this," she said to the table at large and pulled out her phone.

"It's Lana," she said to Drexel a moment later.

Tight lines of concern immediately etched his face. "Is everything all right, darling?"

Clairey's heart quickened at the endearment. She nodded, brushing aside the longing that had bloomed in her chest at the name he'd called her. All this pretending was starting to feel all too real for her emotions. "Yes, yes. Everything is fine. She says the girls are asking if Marnie might spend the night. They'd like a sleepover."

His outward breath of relief was audible. "Fine by me."

Clairey sent a quick text response to Lana.

"Your sitter for the evening?" the wife asked.

I'm actually the sitter was the first thought that popped into her head, reminding her of reality once more. "She's more a close friend," Clairey answered, which was the absolute truth.

The woman gave her a soft smile in response just as the lights dimmed. A bolt of excitement lanced through Clairey's chest. It was time for the raffle. A large screen drew down on the wall behind the stage. Digital icons scrambled around and around until eventually one lit up as the winner.

Clairey gasped with delight as she read two words on the screen. *Marnie Osoman.*

Before she knew it, Drexel stood at her side, pulling her chair out. His excitement was palpable. "We won. Marnie won!"

"I know! I can hardly believe it." Had that really just happened?

"We did this together." Clairey gasped as he picked her up off her feet and twirled her around just as he had three days ago when he'd first proposed his outrageous fake-engagement plan. Her pulse, already pounding by the time he put her back down, skyrocketed at his next words. "We make a good team, my love."

Everything Drexel had ever acquired throughout his life had come from hard work and sheer drive. Having something he'd wanted so badly randomly come to be through mere chance was a heady feeling he hadn't been adequately prepared for.

Now, as he escorted Clairey into the back of their waiting limo, a disquieting thought occurred to him. One some deep level, he might begin to understand the temptations that could have led his father into a life of excessive and destructive gambling.

The thrill he'd just felt in there when Marnie's name was announced, the chances he took in boardrooms—hell, look at the huge gamble he'd taken by fibbing to the sheikh. Was he more like his old man than he might have thought? Drexel pushed the disturbing thoughts aside and strode to the other side of the car to slide into the back seat next to Clairey. He refused to entertain any unpleasant thought at the moment. What had just happened in there with the draw was cause for celebration.

He turned to tell Clairey exactly that. Her smile hadn't faded in the least. She was humming with excitement and happiness. He might even say she was happier for Marnie than even he was.

"I say this calls for champagne. What do you say?"

"She'll be so happy when we tell her the news."

Drexel had to laugh. Her focus was squarely on Marnie. As well it should be at a time like this. But had she even heard what he'd asked about celebrating?

"Well?" he prodded.

She nodded with enthusiasm. "Yes. Let's toast to Marnie's good luck this evening. I'm guessing you have a good bottle of champagne back at the apartment."

She'd be guessing right. But Drexel had something else in mind. He'd been thinking since that first night about how much she'd enjoyed watching the Manhattan skyline out of his penthouse glass wall.

"I was thinking we'd stay out a little longer," he answered her.

Her eyebrows lifted slightly. "You were?"

"Seeing as Marnie's settled for the night. There's a place I wanted to take you. I think you'll enjoy it."

Within minutes, they'd arrived at the spot. Drexel escorted Clairey out of the car and to the lobby of the five-star restaurant they'd pulled up to.

They were greeted immediately upon walking through the revolving glass doors.

A familiar smiling face approached and led them to the hostess stand. "Will you be dining with us tonight, Mr. Osoman? Your table can be set up in moments."

"Just here for a nightcap, Kristen."

The young woman returned the thick leather menus back to their slot. "Enjoy your night."

"The restaurant has rooftop seating," he explained to Clairey. "As well as a fully stocked bar. And given that it's a Saturday evening, there should be live entertainment."

Drexel led Clairey toward the elevator with a hand to her back. He had to suck in a breath at the touch of his skin against her bare back. The low-cut dress she wore screamed temptation, and he couldn't seem to resist touching her. Having her up against him on the dance floor had given him a taste of the way she felt in his arms. Heaven help him, it had felt right. He wanted to dance with her again, to touch her again.

He wanted it very much.

This was a mistake. Drexel knew he was bound to regret it as soon as the night was over. But was it so wrong just to live in the moment for once in his life? A look at the excitement on Clairey's face as the elevator lifted higher and higher gave him a clear answer to that question.

It was confirmed when they reached the part of the ride up where the steel walls gave way to glass. She gasped as the view of the city below and Central Park in the distance burst into view. She actually pressed her palms against the glass and studied the scene below as they continued to rise up. "Oh, my."

He'd seen the view from this elevator countless times in the past. Something about the way Clairey was reacting to it now made him wonder just how much he'd actually seen it. The way the greenery of the park stuck out like a portrait landscape within the gray tone of the city. How the horse-drawn carriages looked like miniature toys from this height. How the lights from the neighboring buildings lit up the sky. He'd never really looked at any of that before.

That was the thing about Clairey: she made him appreciate things he might not otherwise even notice. Like she had with helping his niece adjust to her new life. It would have never occurred to him that she might need a friend her own age until school started. Nor would it have occurred to him to research some of the items he'd seen on her computer that day about Marnie's developmental or nutritional needs.

"This is breathtaking," she said now, her gaze still fixed on the glass panel. "I can see why you come here often."

"What makes you think I come here often?"

"The hostess down there said you had a regular table."

He didn't bother to correct her. He happened to have a table because he owned the restaurant. In fact, he owned the commercial building itself, which housed everything from boutiques and jewelry shops on the first floor to some of the most upscale apartments in New York City.

But none of that was the reason he felt like a fortunate man tonight. That feeling was due to the woman he'd be lucky enough to spend the evening with.

CHAPTER TEN

SHE'D STEPPED INTO another world. How could this possibly be the top of a building? Clairey felt as if she'd somehow taken an elevator to an island in the Caribbean. Trees two to three times her height outlined the square area. Across from where they stood, the bar Drexel mentioned was a U-shaped high-top structure about thirty feet in length. It was surrounded by throngs of people. A four-piece band right next to it played a bouncy, jazzy number that had her tapping her feet. A lit pool complete with a waterfall completed the picture.

The only thing missing was a sandy beach and the ocean.

She lost count of the number of times she'd felt awestruck this evening. A server approached them almost immediately.

"The usual, Mr. Osoman? And what can I get for the lady?"

He really must come here a lot. But who could blame him? The place was beyond entertaining. She'd come here every night if she could. Though, something told her she wouldn't be able to afford it. Not if she wanted to continue paying down those student loans.

Drexel ordered a bottle of something that sounded French before leading her to a high-top table by the pool.

"This is bigger than the pool deck area back at the Sea View," she said as he pulled out a stool for her and helped her sit.

He took the other stool across from her but removed his tuxedo jacket first. Then he proceeded to roll the sleeves of his shirt up to below his elbows. Something about his bare arms sent a shiver of electricity over her skin. He'd already unbuttoned the top of his collar midway to his chest. The man looked downright dashing whenever he loosened his collar and rolled his sleeves up that way.

Clairey made herself look away and focus on the small crowd of dancers in front of the band. The server from earlier arrived and ceremoniously uncorked a sweating, green-tinged bottle with a foreign label. The only word she could make out was *champagne*.

Drexel lifted his glass to hers after the young woman was done serving and had walked away with a slight bow. "To Marnie and the new life she's about to embark on in New York."

Clairey tapped her flute to his and added, "And to the luck of the draw."

"I'll drink to that."

She took a small sip. Tiny bubbles burst on her tongue and a wave of exquisite flavor rushed her taste buds. She held the glass out and examined it. "Wow."

"You like it?"

That was an understatement. It was downright shocking just how much she liked it. "I've had sparkling wine before. The real thing is quite a whole other level, isn't it?"

"Nothing compares to the real thing. Good or bad."

It sounded like a very loaded statement. Though, for the life of her, she couldn't guess what he might be referring to.

He continued before she could so much as think of how to go about asking.

"So, tell me about yourself, Ms. Robi. It occurs to me that I don't know all that much about you."

That was rich. At least he knew where she was from and how she'd come about to lose her coveted job. She didn't know a thing about him. Only that he'd grown up in New Jersey somewhere near Atlantic City.

She tapped a finger to her chin with mock seriousness. "Let's see. Upon the time of our meeting back in Cape Cod, Massachusetts, I'd foolishly risked my job which led to all sorts of financial instability. But you know all about that."

"Ah, but there's a lot I don't know."

She eyed him over her glass. "For instance?"

"For instance, is there anyone back on Cape Cod who might feel slighted if they happen to catch a photo of you on the arm of someone claiming to be your fiancé?"

Clairey had to chuckle at the question. "Is that your roundabout way of asking me if I'm involved with anyone?"

He ducked his head with a sheepishness that only seemed to add to his charm. "Guilty as charged."

She swallowed another sip of her drink. "There's nothing to tell. I haven't been serious with anyone. Not really. Just a few dates here and there." She squeezed her eyes shut before divulging the rest. "And there was a certain Casanova in college who said all the right things, then ghosted me."

Clairey cringed internally at the memory of her college crush. For the first time since losing her father, she'd thought when she'd met him that maybe she'd found someone who might be able to love her. She'd been so naive.

"Then, he was beyond a fool," Drex said, his voice thick. He raised his glass. "And look where you are now."

In some kind of fantasy, apparently. One where she got to pretend she might actually become this man's wife in some unknown universe.

There was a thing or two she was curious about too. She braced herself to ask the question that had been forming on the tip of her tongue since they'd first sat down. "What did you mean before, when you said what you did about things that are real being good or bad?"

He shrugged. "Take Marnie, for instance. I'm not her real father. One might argue she's unfortunate in that she's stuck with an uncle when her actual dad is fully capable of parenting her. So she's stuck with second best."

"You can't honestly feel like you're second-best where Marnie is concerned."

He swirled the liquid in his glass, took another sip. "Chase wasn't perfect as a father. But he is her real dad. That's just a matter of fact."

Her heart tugged a little in her chest. She'd had no idea he was harboring any sense of inadequacy as far as Marnie was concerned.

"Oh, Drexel, you can't think that way. Look how much you're doing for her. And she's thriving in New York."

"But she misses her dad. Tells me so every night when I tuck her into bed."

She'd been telling Clairey as well. "That's only natural and to be expected. Her longing for her dad in no way diminishes all that you've done to make her feel settled here."

His response was a tight frown. He was second-guessing himself. And he really had no cause to. Clairey would have never pegged Drexel Osoman as the insecure type. But apparently, at least in this one area, he was.

"I hope you're right, Clairey. I really do."

Without thinking, she reached for him then. Leaning over the table, she took one of his hands in both of hers. His gaze followed to where they touched, and heat swam in his eyes.

Yet she couldn't bring herself to pull away.

Her hands felt good on his. And it felt good to sit here with her now, simply chatting. Drexel hadn't intended to reveal any of his feelings about being unexpectedly responsible for his niece. But it felt good to get it off his chest. Something about Clairey felt familiar, put him at ease talking about things he'd normally keep close to his chest. He'd grown to feel affection for her. It was more than merely sharing a living space. Which reminded him...

"I've been meaning to tell you, and I hope it goes without saying, you're welcome to have visitors at the penthouse. There must be friends or relatives you'll be missing. Invite whoever you'd like. Whenever. This is your home now too."

Clairey smiled at him. "That's very kind of you. Thank you. There is someone I might have come see me."

"Oh?"

She nodded. "A friend. Tessa would get such a kick out of staying in New York for a few days." Her eyes widened slightly. "Though, I'm not quite sure what I would tell her about this." She held her hand up to indicate the fake-engagement ring.

"I'll leave that up to you. She's your friend. You decide what you want her to know."

Her shoulders sagged with relief. "I'm glad you feel that way. I wouldn't feel right lying to Tessa. And I know I can trust her."

"Then, I trust you to make that call."

"Thank you for that," she said, her smile warm. "Wait until she gets a load of the penthouse. She won't believe what luxury I'm living in."

He had to chuckle at that. Sometimes Drexel forgot just how much he had to be grateful for and how much he took for granted in his life.

"So just Tessa, then?"

She teased her bottom lip with her tongue. "I think so. For now."

"What about your mom? You said you haven't seen her in a few years. You might have a reunion of sorts."

Drexel felt like a heel as soon as the words left his mouth. Though he was sincere about welcoming any guest of Clairey's, the truth was he was curious about her. He wanted to know more. Like exactly why she hadn't seen her mother in so long.

"My mom will be too busy to visit," she answered after a long pause, her voice laced with pain.

Yep, he definitely was a heel to pick at her scab that way.

Clairey continued. "She and Frank do a lot of RVing and camping. They don't have much room in their lives for anyone else."

Or room in their hearts, it sounded like. "The nomad life."

"Something like that."

"Sounds like you miss her."

She ducked her head slightly. "I did at first. I've grown to accept it over the years. My mom was never the nurturing type to begin with. She certainly didn't really have much use for me after my father passed."

"How long have you been on your own?"

She swallowed. "I felt alone from the moment my dad died. But things really came to a head in our household once I turned eighteen."

"How so?"

"Frank always acted like he resented me. I can't recall a single instance where he was kind. In fact, he seemed to go out of his way to be cruel."

Drexel itched to take her into his arms and soothe some of her pain away. He had no doubt that she would accept his comfort. But right now, at this moment, it was more important that she say as much as she wanted to tell him about her past. "In what ways?" he asked.

"He'd comment about my hair, my clothing. Make disparaging remarks about my looks. Say things like I definitely didn't take after my mother as she was pretty and I was...well, the opposite of that."

Anger surged in his chest. Something told him her stepfather had less than innocuous reasons for noticing and commenting on her looks. Drexel never felt such animosity toward a man he had never met. This Frank had better hope the two of them never happened to cross paths. "He'd always object if I wanted to bring friends home. And if any came to the house, he'd make sure to make them feel unwelcome and uncomfortable. I started to lose touch with the few friends I had, thanks to him."

"What happened when you turned eighteen?"

Clairey closed her eyes and blew out a slow breath. "He woke up in a particularly sour mood. Grumbling about how I was always in his way, I wasn't doing enough around the house. You get the picture."

He certainly did. And it had him nearly shaking with rage.

Clairey went on. "I had the audacity to talk back. I said something like how the house was a mess because he never picked up after himself, leaving dirty dishes and filthy ashtrays all over the place." Her hand tightened around the stem of her flute. "My mom came in then. I knew she wouldn't defend me, she never had. But I still had some small smidgen of hope." She huffed out an ironic chuckle.

"What did she do?"

"My stepfather just said it. He told her he wanted me gone. That I was of age now, I had no business in his house. Never mind that it wasn't his house at all. He'd moved into the house my parents had bought together when they were first married."

Drexel had to lean back in his chair. He couldn't help but imagine his own niece in such a situation. How close had the girl come to experiencing such an existence? What would have happened if he hadn't been around when Chase's new wife made her wishes clear about not wanting a child underfoot? But this was about Clairey. He waited silently for her to tell him the rest.

She took another small sip of wine before doing so. "I remember thinking, *This is it.* We'd finally be rid of him. My mother wouldn't let him give such an ultimatum."

His heart sank for her as he could only guess what must have played out afterward. "I take it that's not what happened."

"You'd be guessing right. My mother's reaction was not what I'd expected. Though, I see now how naive I was to be shocked."

It took several moments, but she went on. "She turned to me and said five simple words. 'You need to go, Clairey.'"

She immediately turned away, but not before he noticed the wetness flooding her eyes. "That was the last night I spent in my childhood home."

Drexel bit back a curse. She deserved so much more than the hand she'd been dealt. No wonder she felt such a connection to Marnie and was so quickly forming a bond with her. Clairey could relate to the little girl. She'd essentially been abandoned herself.

Clairey toyed with the bangs on her forehead. "Well, that was quite a trip down memory lane," she said with an unconvincing smile. "I didn't mean to dump so much sad history on you. On such a pleasant night too."

"I'm glad you told me, Clairey." People didn't tend to confide in him. He was glad Clairey seemed to be an exception.

Several wisps of hair had come loose and blew softly in the wind. It took every ounce of willpower he possessed not to reach over and tuck those strands back into place. Then he'd run his finger down her cheek, trail his hand lower toward her chest. The round table between them was small enough that she was easily within reach.

The band behind them started a new number, and Clairey turned her head in their direction. "I really like this song. Are you up for any more dancing tonight?"

He knew an attempt to change the subject when he heard one. After all, he was a master at it himself.

He stood and extended his hand out to her. "I'd be honored."

Clairey tried not to react to the electricity that hummed through her as Drexel took her by the elbow to lead her to the square dance floor. She couldn't believe how much of herself and her past she'd just shared with him. Not even Tessa had heard as much about her life before she'd moved out of her childhood home. It wasn't something she particularly enjoyed talking about. But something about Drexel had made her feel open and comfortable enough to share it all with him.

Ironic, really. Of all the ways she could describe how she felt about the man, *comfortable* would probably not even make the list.

Excited. Aware. Attracted. Those words definitely would.

Now, as they moved together to the bouncy song, she noticed how in sync they were, how well they moved together. She felt lighter, somehow. As if a weight had been lifted off her chest. Talking to Drexel about Frank and her mother had been freeing. Cathartic. She'd had no idea how much she'd wanted to share it all with someone. Although she'd never felt the need to do so before. Something had told her that Drexel would understand, in a way that she was certain even Tessa wouldn't be able to.

No. Drexel was unlike anyone she could think of.

Without even meaning to, she found herself voicing her thoughts aloud. "You're not like any man I've ever met." She cringed as soon as the words left her mouth. Of all the cliché-sounding... Made all the worse as she'd yelled the words over the loud music. She could have sworn she heard someone on the dance floor behind her snicker.

Clairey wanted to somehow take the words back and simultaneously disappear into a sinkhole. She ducked her head as heat rushed to her cheeks.

Drexel apparently noticed. "Don't be embarrassed, Clairey. I was thinking the very same thing about you."

She blinked. "Me?"

As luck would have it, the current song ended right at that moment. The next tune was much slower. Drexel didn't seem to hesitate. She found herself in his arms, nestled against his chest as he moved with her to the music. The scent of him, now so familiar, washed over her. A combination of some kind of aftershave that reminded her of moonlit summer nights along with the distinctive masculine scent that was his alone.

"Yes, you," he said against her, ducking slightly to accommodate their height difference.

He had to be patronizing her, trying to make her feel better, given what she'd told him. The man had dated supermodels, actresses and world-renowned dancers. Clairey was certainly different than any of those types, but not in any kind of impressive way. "You don't have to do that, Drexel. You don't have to try and indulge me with platitudes."

He sighed, his breath hot against her cheek. A shudder ran through her at the feel of him so close.

"You beautiful, silly little fool. You don't believe me, do you?"

"I can't say that I do," she admitted.

She felt his arms around her tighten ever so slightly. Her heart pounded double-time in her chest at the closer contact.

"Then, let me try to explain," he said. "For one, you made it by yourself after losing everything you'd known to become the manager of a world-class resort."

She scoffed. "I lost that job, remember?"

"I do. I recall you lost the job because you stuck your neck out for a little girl you didn't even know. You're doing everything you can now to make sure that little girl thrives and flourishes."

"Many others would have done so. Doesn't make me special in any way."

"You can't believe that." He tilted her chin with his finger, staring into her eyes. "Listen. I have no idea what I would have done without you. Finding the school for Marnie. Enabling her to make a friend. Helping me keep this business deal going by pretending to be in love with me."

Her voice caught at his last few words. He might be pretending. But the imaginary line for her was becoming more and more blurry by the instant.

"So yes, in my eyes that makes you one exceptional, impressive young woman."

He sounded so genuine. The words he said were beyond touching. So why did she feel like crying? She couldn't come up with anything to say in response.

Because she wanted more, heaven help her.

"Thank you, Drexel," she said softly when she finally found her voice.

"For what? Telling you the truth about yourself?"

The truth as he saw it, anyway. She still wasn't convinced she was as impressive as he'd just made her sound. "Yes," she admitted. "I had no idea how badly I needed to hear it."

"You're welcome," he answered simply. They danced together in silence for two more songs. Clairey allowed herself to fully indulge in the sensations she was experiencing: the feel of him against her body, his heartbeat pulsing against her upper chest, the strength she felt emanating from him and somehow bolstering her own.

By the time she looked up, the night had grown much later, and the crowd had considerably thinned. The band played their last song and said their goodnights.

A sense of sadness washed over her: she didn't want this night to end. "Looks like most people are heading out along with the band. Maybe we should call it a night."

Drexel glanced at his watch. "Nonsense. The night is just beginning."

When they returned to their table, another chilled bottle had been opened, and the ice bucket filled with fresh ice. Additionally, a bowl of fresh berries had been placed in the center with a small pitcher of chocolate sauce.

He must be quite a favored customer, the way the

staff seemed to be catering to him. Drexel took one of the larger berries and dipped it in the sauce. He held it out to Clairey. She opened her lips and accepted the treat. The flavor of the fresh fruit mixed with deep rich chocolate had her taste buds celebrating. "Hmmm. That's delicious."

Drexel picked up the bowl of fruit and sauce and walked over to an area by the pool with a set of chaise longues.

Clairey indulged in a few more of the berries, admiring the view of the starlit sky. For several moments, they simply relaxed there, lying side by side.

When she thought to look, there was no one left but staff. And they seemed to be clearing up the place. "Shouldn't we be going too? They seem to be closing up shop."

He nodded his head. "They won't mind if we linger."

They certainly didn't seem to mind at all. In fact, no one was even paying attention to them.

Maybe it was the champagne. Or maybe it was the way he'd made her feel back on the dance floor. But a courageous part of her seemed to rise to the surface.

She wanted Drexel to kiss her. For once in her life, she was going to ask for what she wanted.

She summoned all the courage she could. "You apologized to me that day. About kissing me."

He turned to fully face her. "Yes. I shouldn't have done that."

"I liked it, Drex," she admitted, her heart ready to pound out of her chest. Heat darkened his eyes. "I'd like you to kiss me again. Now."

He didn't hesitate. With a gentle grip on her forearm, he pulled her toward him. Then his lips were on hers.

This kiss was entirely different than the quick, chaste one he'd planted on her back on the Cape. No, this one was far from chaste. It was fire and desire and pure passion.

It would take a while to calm her racing pulse.

CHAPTER ELEVEN

CLAIREY AWOKE WITH a start as the first rays of predawn sun landed softly on her face. Heaven help her, somehow she'd fallen asleep. Not only that, she'd done so in Drexel's arms, lying next to him in the very same lounge chair. They were the only two people left on the roof. His tuxedo jacket covered her middle, his arms wrapped around her shoulders. She bolted upright.

What in the world had come over her to fall asleep like that? That did it: she was never drinking champagne again. Then the other memory rushed through her mind. The kiss. She'd nestled up against Drexel after that mind-blowing kiss. No wonder she'd lost all her senses.

He stirred next to her now. She waited with bated breath as he finally opened his eyes.

His eyes widened when they landed on her face. "What's the matter? You look like you've been caught with your hand in the cookie jar."

"What do you mean, what's the matter? We fell asleep up here."

An alarming thought shot through her and turned her blood ice-cold. What if something had gone wrong during the night and Lana had tried to reach her? They might have been fast asleep when Marnie needed them. She rummaged around for her handbag until she located it hanging from the armrest of the lounger. Luckily, her phone displayed no missed messages when she pulled it out and looked at the screen.

Relief rushed through her, and she let out a long sigh. "I can't believe we might have missed a call from Lana."

He lifted an eyebrow. "Did you intend to stay up the whole night back at the penthouse in case she called?"

"Well, no, but…"

"How is falling asleep here any different?"

Well, when he put it that way… "I don't know."

He leaned back against the chair and pulled her back along with him. "Try to relax. Look," he said and pointed to the horizon.

Clairey glanced at the sky, then had to rub her eyes to get a better look. The sight took her breath away. The sun rising in the distant sky sat among a burst of orange and red. The view looked like it could have been hand-painted by a gifted artist. At this height, it was as if they were aligned perfectly with the magnificent sight.

"Wow," was all she could muster.

Drexel's hand tightened around her shoulder. "The view of the sunrise from a New York City high-rise is a wonder to behold. And you would have missed it if we hadn't fallen asleep up here."

She couldn't tear her gaze away from the sky. "Still, it feels wrong to have stayed up here all this time. Won't anyone say anything?"

He shrugged. "They'd have no standing to. I own the place."

Had she just heard him right? "You own the restaurant and the bar?"

"Sort of."

What did that mean? He either owned the establishment or he didn't. "I don't understand."

He tapped her nose playfully before standing up and stretching. "I own the building. As well as everything in it."

Clairey watched in awe as Drexel pulled a key card out of his wallet and used it to summon the rooftop elevator. A whirring, mechanical sound echoed from the floors below. Moments later, the double doors slid open, and Drexel gestured for her to step inside.

He owned the building. And the businesses and apartments within. That certainly explained the deference he'd been shown by the staff all night. As well as how comfortable he was to stay here overnight.

Why was she even surprised?

He used the same key card to engage the panel of buttons on the wall of the elevator. Within seconds they were on the ground floor and exiting to the street.

They summoned a taxi to bring them back to his building. The events of the past several hours ran through her mind like scenes from a movie as they entered the lobby. If the doorman and desk attendant noticed they were still clad in evening attire, they had the grace to look away with just a brief, friendly smile.

Had she really just lived through such a romantic and magical night? Had she really had the nerve to ask Drex to kiss her? And he'd obliged. She rubbed her fingers along her lips summoning the feel of his mouth against hers.

Clairey knew it had all indeed happened. But she also knew she couldn't let any of it go to her head. Not even the kiss. Especially not the kiss.

It didn't mean anything. Not to him. The fantasy and magic of the evening, along with all the pretending, had gone to both their heads. As soon as Marnie returned to the apartment, Clairey would go right back to being the hired help. The kiss last night and everything that had happened both before and after were merely her living out fantasies she had no business entertaining in the first place.

She had a more pressing matter to deal with when the elevator doors opened to reveal a familiar face. Lana did a double take when she saw them.

"Oh, hey."

"Um…hello."

"My *Sunday Times* wasn't outside the door," she said. "I just popped down to see if any papers had arrived at the building. The girls are still sound asleep," she added after several silent beats.

"Oh," was all Clairey could come up with to say. No doubt, she'd face a barrage of questions from the other woman as soon as the two of them found themselves alone. For the life of her, she had no idea what she might say in response. How could she address Lana's questions when she didn't know the answers herself?

Drexel seemed to be shifting his glance from one woman to the other, a curious expression on his face. He was the one who finally broke the awkward silence.

"I take it the girls had a fun night together?" he addressed Lana with a charming smile.

Lana blinked as if confused. Then she seemed to pull herself together. "Oh! Yes! Yes, they had a lot of fun. They can't wait to do it again sometime." She waved a hand in their general direction. "We'd love to have her. You know, if you two want to go out again."

Drexel's smile widened. Clairey cringed where she stood. She knew her friend meant well, but her words made for the most awkward of moments. "I'm sure that won't be ne—"

Drexel cut her off before she could finish. "We just might take you up on that. Thank you."

Now she was practically gawking.

Lana blinked some more before giving her head a brisk shake. "Well, I guess I'll go see about my paper, then." She brushed by them but then suddenly turned again. "Oh, I chatted with my sister yesterday. She says a new litter of calicos just arrived the other day. They're looking for fosters or adopters."

It took Clairey a moment to shift her focus to the sudden turn in the conversation. Kittens. She and Drexel had promised Marnie they'd get her a pet.

"Oh, that's good news."

Lana nodded. "You and Marnie can even head down there later today to take a look. They're open for a few hours after lunch on Sundays. Sis said she'd personally introduce them to you."

"That's very nice of her," Clairey answered.

Drexel rubbed a hand over the dark stubble on his chin. "Wait a minute. I have a small objection."

Clairey's stomach fell. He'd changed his mind about the pet. Marnie was going to be heartbroken. "You do?"

He nodded at her solemnly. "Why should you ladies have all the fun? I'd like to meet these little creatures too."

It was Clairey's turn to blink in confusion. "You want to come with us? To look at kittens?"

He narrowed his eyes. "Why's that so hard to believe?"

Lana guffawed, then coughed into her hand to try and cover it. She was thinking exactly what Clairey was. In no sense whatsoever did Drexel Osoman give off the impression that he might waste away the afternoon playing with a litter of kittens.

"You're just always so busy on Sundays," Clairey answered. "Getting ready for the work week ahead."

"Yes, well. Some things a man should make time for."

He was going to make time to help them pick out a kitten.

How in the world had he found himself here?

Drexel knew the answer, and he had to acknowledge it. Sure, he wanted to be here for his niece. But the real reason for his motivation currently stood off in the corner of the room. She'd changed into a sundress that draped her curves in all the right ways. Her sandals showed off rainbow-painted toenails.

Not nearly as splashy an outfit as what she'd worn last night, yet somehow just as tantalizing. The woman could wear a straw bag and it would look tantalizing on her.

But there was more to her that drew him.

He had to admit he wanted to continue spending time with Clairey. He'd enjoyed himself last night more than he had in a long time. As long as he could remember. In fact, he couldn't recall ever previously feeling so carefree, so content just to live in the moment and enjoy the company of the woman he was with.

She brought out a playful side of him he'd thought he'd lost years ago. Drex couldn't even explain why. He just knew he felt lighter around her, less like the whole world rested on his shoulders.

Drexel picked up the small mound of fluff trying desperately to climb up on his shoe only to fail miserably. If someone had told him a month ago that he'd be at a city animal shelter as small kittens tried to climb on him, he would have laughed at the image. The tiny thing wiggled in his palm, waiving his little stub of a tail. Drexel didn't think anything could feel quite so soft.

"Do you like that one, Uncle Drexel?" Marnie asked, her own arms holding a bundle of squirming mewing furry babies.

"I do. And he seems to like me."

Clairey stood off in the corner, her arms crossed and an amused smile on her face. She was taking it all in and seemed wholly entertained. "They all seem to like you," she said. Then her smile faded. "Except this one." She walked over to one of the kittens shivering by itself in the corner. The poor thing looked scared to death. It was barely half the size of the rest of the litter. Clairey gave its tiny head a gentle rub with her thumb.

"That one is dealing with a bit of a health issue," the lab tech, who was also Lana's sister, informed them.

Clairey looked up at her with alarm. "What kind of health issue?"

"She was born with a congenital defect. An umbilical hernia. She struggles to eat. It's why she's so much smaller."

"Is there a way to cure her?" Clairey asked the other woman.

"We're hoping she'll grow out of it. She's on some meds in the meantime. Otherwise, she may need surgery at some point."

Marnie gently put down the three kittens she'd been holding and immediately walked over to the ill one with Clairey.

"Oh, the poor thing," his niece cried, a hitch in her voice. "She looks so frightened." She ran a hand softly along the cat's back.

Clairey looked ready to cry herself. She helped Marnie pick up the kitten and gently hold her against her chest. The cat immediately started to purr.

One look at the two human and one feline females, and Drexel knew what he had to do. "That's the one we'll take, then."

As soon as the words left his mouth, another little one scurried over to Clairey's sandaled feet. Though still low and soft, its mewing had definitely grown in intensity.

Marnie glanced down at the new arrival, and her eyes welled up with tears. "They don't want to be separated."

The lab tech tilted her head. "You're a very insightful little girl, Marnie." She nodded toward the two kittens. "Those two are nearly inseparable. They cuddle together for naps and cry whenever the other is being handled."

Drexel studied the scene before him. Clairey rubbing a hand down Marnie's back to comfort her in her distress over the plight of the cat siblings. The shivering little one mewing desperately for his sister. Then he glanced down at the wiggling ball of fur he still held in his own hand.

Again, the decision was clear. There was nothing for it. They would have to get all three.

The moment of truth was here. Or the moment of falsehood. Clairey couldn't even be sure which. All she knew was that in a few short minutes she'd be meeting a real-life sheikh and his wife. And she'd have to do so while pretending she was about to become a wife herself.

If she was nervous before the school auction, what she felt now was close to sheer panic.

She should be excited, she really should. After all, she was currently sitting in the back of a stretch limo next to Drex en route to Times Square. For an exclusive screening of the latest installment of a major superhero franchise she'd barely paid attention to in her past life as a resort manager. Most women would be giddy. But all she could think about was saying or doing the wrong thing and blowing the whole charade completely.

Drex must have sensed her trepidation. "Try to relax, Clairey. Everything will be fine. The sheikh and his wife are actually lovely people. If a little sober."

"I'll try," was the only response she could utter.

Drex reached over and gave her hand a reassuring squeeze. "Just trust me."

She did. She just wasn't sure if she could trust herself. Within minutes they'd reached the long line of luxury cars being directed toward the entrance of the theater. Finally, the limo came to a complete stop, and an attendant immediately appeared near her door and began to open it.

Drex turned to her. "Ready?"

"As I'll ever be."

He'd reached her side of the car before she'd so much as stepped foot outside the vehicle.

A roar of noise greeted her ears once they were outside. Throngs of people had gathered across the street which had been cordoned off. Clairey's steps faltered as she took in the size of the crowd.

"It's okay, sweetheart," Drex said in her ear calmly. "They're here to see the real talent. The stars haven't arrived yet. No one is paying attention to us."

The attendant motioned for them to follow and quickly led them past the crowds and inside the building. By the time they reached the lobby, Clairey thought her heart might very well beat right out of her chest.

Before she could so much as try to take a steadying breath, they were immediately approached by an elegant-looking older couple dressed in traditional ceremonial dress. The sheikh and his wife. They were surrounded by a quartet of burly-looking men in tuxedos and earpieces. She'd never met anyone who'd needed bodyguards before.

She mimicked Drex's slight bow of his head in greeting just as he'd instructed her to do.

"Lovely to see you, Drex," the sheikh said before turning to her. "And so lovely to meet you."

Clairey could barely keep from trembling with apprehension as the formal introductions were made. But by the time they'd taken their seats and the theater lights dimmed around them, the sheikha had completely charmed her. The woman was warm and genial and more relatable than Clairey would have ever guessed.

It took a while, but eventually Clairey even managed to relax enough to enjoy the movie. Surprising, as her tastes usually ran more along rom-coms and less action-packed entertainment.

But then she lost all sense of focus again when she felt Drex's arm come around her shoulder. He gave her a gentle squeeze and surprised her further by dropping a series of gentle kisses along her cheek, then lower along her jaw.

She couldn't help her gasp as heat curled low in her belly and spread through her limbs. The man's touch did things to her that she couldn't begin to understand. If they were alone at that moment, she'd have half a mind to jump on his lap and kiss him until they both lost all sense.

She felt his breath against her cheek as he leaned close to whisper something in her ear. When he spoke, it took her a minute to process exactly what he was telling her. "I just got a text on my phone during that last quiet scene. Sheikh Farhan wants to move forward. Says he's ready to sign off on it all. I have you to thank, Clairey."

Clairey's skin grew cold. So that's what the show of affection had really been about. Drex was merely doing it all for the sheikh's benefit. To show him that they were indeed a besotted couple in love and that he could be comfortable with the decision to do business with Drex. His tenderness, the loving caress and gentle kisses had nothing at all to do with her.

The night of the auction, she'd been the one who'd asked him to kiss her. This time, it was a ruse for the benefit of his potential business partner. What did that say about the way he felt about her?

A brick of disappointment settled in her stomach, and her eyes began to sting at the crushing realization. She would have kicked herself for it if she could.

It looked like Drex's plan had worked like a charm. Too bad she'd forgotten for a moment that plan was the only reason she was here with him in the first place.

CHAPTER TWELVE

Three months later

DREXEL CALLED UP the calendar on his laptop and his eye caught on the date it so often did lately. He'd simply marked it with a digital icon as a reminder. Next month was Clairey's birthday. He'd gathered that bit of knowledge out of her by chance last week. Birthdays called for celebrations. He would use that celebration to come clean with her once and for all about finally addressing the proverbial elephant in the room.

For months, ever since the night of the premiere, they'd been the utmost professionals. Which meant they'd tiptoed around each other.

Was it so wrong that they'd enjoyed each other's company? And that kiss they'd shared—things between them had certainly turned awkward afterward. He refused to allow himself to regret it. It may have started out for the sheikh and sheikha's benefit. But it had quickly turned to something much more. Her lips against his, the taste of her. He still thought about it every night, couldn't get it out of his mind.

Yes, she was his fiancée in name only. Realistically, she was Marnie's nanny. But she was so much more than that. Both to him and Marnie. It was about time one of them acknowledged that fact. Being in his employ, Clairey was probably hesitant to broach the subject. Plus, he struck her as simply shy at times.

So it was up to him. They were both adults. Adults didn't ignore what was so blatantly obvious. And it was obvious the two of them had loads of chemistry. It was high time he did something about it. He'd take her out for her birthday to do just that.

He was pulled out his musings by the alert of an incoming call from his administrative assistant. He glanced at his watch. The woman lived on the West Coast and very rarely called him before noon.

Unless it was urgent.

He tapped to answer before the second ringtone. "Drexel. There's a matter of concern you should know about. There's been a gentleman who's been calling for weeks now. I think you need to talk to him."

Drexel's mouth went dry as he listened to the rest of what she had to say. In less than two minutes, he'd heard enough to have alarm bells sounding loudly in his head.

"I can try and get him on the line now," Alyssa offered.

As much as he wanted to avoid the conversation that would ensue, Drexel had never been one to put off the inevitable, no matter how unpleasant. And this was definitely going to be unpleasant.

"Put him through."

"Mr. Osoman, my name is Bill Thomas."

"What can I do for you, Mr. Thomas?" Drexel asked, though by now he had a pretty clear idea. And even the thought of the possibility had ice running through his veins.

The other man sighed into the phone before he answered. "I believe my daughter had a relationship with your younger brother about seven years ago. I think there are some things we need to discuss."

Seven years ago. The daughter this man had just referred to would be Marnie's mother. He was speaking with his niece's maternal grandfather.

"What kinds of things?"

"We have some concerns about our granddaughter."

Drexel felt his hands clench at his sides. "And those concerns would be?"

"Mainly that she's living with her single uncle."

"I'm engaged to—"

The man was abrupt. "We've read all about it. You've taken up with the girl's nanny, it appears. None of the sites mention any kind of planned wedding or date. You've had plenty of relationships before that went nowhere. It's all out there in black and white. In fact, you were engaged once before, it seems."

The man had certainly done his research. He'd clearly come prepared for this call.

For the umpteenth time in his life, Drex cursed the tabloids that made such fodder of his life. His previous so-called engagement had been nothing but a publicity stunt for the actress he'd been dating at the time. She'd fed the rumors to countless gossip sites worldwide. They'd reported on the fake story relentlessly, plastered his picture with the starlet all over the internet. Drex had been too much of a gentleman to deny the misinformation. At the time, he couldn't be bothered: it all seemed so trivial. He regretted that now.

The other man continued. "Your lifestyle is not very stable, Mr. Osoman. I understand my granddaughter has already been displaced from one home with her other grandmother and again after staying with her father for a while."

"Be that as it may, she's settled now."

"I believe she'd be better off with us." That was certainly blunt.

Drexel listened with minimal restraint to what the other man had to say, offering little in return.

"We are her blood, Mr. Osoman," he finally finished.

Somehow, Drexel kept himself in check and managed not to laugh out loud at that statement. As if blood was enough to ensure love and security. What mattered was love and affection and respect. Marnie had all that and more here in New York with him and Clairey.

He'd heard enough. "I'll be in touch, Mr. Thomas," he said, then ended the call without waiting for a response.

Suddenly, all his plans for the next few weeks, including ones about Clairey, had to be relegated to secondary importance. All the pressing work projects would have to wait, as well. Thank heavens the sheikh had finally signed on all the necessary dotted lines.

His one focus now was to do well by his niece. Without any doubt, Marnie's best interest was to remain exactly where she was. With him and Clairey.

As soon as Drexel hung up, he made another call. This one to his personal attorney.

It was time for a serious conversation. She had to do it before Marnie got home. Marnie never allowed Clairey to say a cross word to any of these three. She approached the three felines, Georgie, Porgie, and Pumpkin Pie as they swatted around their scratching post.

"Which one of you knocked over all the plants? Or was it all of you?" she asked.

Six bright green eyes blinked at her before ignoring her completely and returning to their batting and clawing. She waved a finger in the air to all of them and none of them in particular. "Don't let me catch you doing it again. You made a horrible mess on the carpet. It took me forever to clean it up."

That was a slight exaggeration. But the cats didn't need to know that. Clairey had to chuckle at herself and the picture she must make. At the ripe old age of twenty-six, she'd somehow become a cat lady. And they weren't even her pets!

Drexel chose that moment to fling the door of his study open and stride over to where she stood reprimanding the heedless cats. Whoa. After all these months, the sight of the man still took her breath away. He was dressed in his usual work uniform of silk shirt, baby-blue today, and pressed tailored dark pants. He was due for a haircut soon, but it had been a particularly busy month so his dark hair fell in soft waves over his forehead. Her fingers itched to run her fingers through it. She longed to feel his lips on hers again.

But she'd never gotten the courage to ask the way she had the night of the raffle. They were both doing a spectacular job of pretending they'd never kissed at all. Not the night of the auction. And not during the movie premiere.

It couldn't go on. Sooner or later, something had to give. But she hadn't found a way to ask the questions that plagued her. Had either of their kisses meant anything to him? The night of the premiere, when he'd touched her and caressed and softly brushed his lips against hers, was all that solely for the benefit of the sheikh? Could there possibly have been anything more to any of it?

Would she ever find a way to get any answers from him?

But all those thoughts fled her mind when she got a good look at his expression. The look he wore on his face had Clairey's pulse quickening. Something was very, very wrong.

"What is it?"

"Marnie's still at school?"

She nodded. "For hours still. And she'll be even later today. There's a rehearsal for the fall play."

"Good. It will give us a chance to talk. Do you have a minute?"

"Of course." She followed him into the sitting area.

Though he motioned for her to sit, Drexel continued standing and pacing. She'd never seen him so agitated. It took all her will not to jump up, give him a good shake and demand that he tell her what was happening already.

"I got a rather unwelcome phone call earlier today," he finally began.

"Oh, no. Was it about your mother? Is she okay?"

He blinked at her as if confused. "No. I speak with her doctors twice a week. And I was just there to visit her the other day, as you know. There's been no change in her condition."

That was a relief, at least. "Then, what is it?"

"The phone call was about Marnie."

Clairey's heart began to thud in her chest. "What about her?" A horrifying possibility came to her. "Was it her father?" She couldn't bring herself to voice more of her fears.

"No. Not her father. Not Chase."

"Then, who?"

Drexel finally sat down. With clear weariness, he braced his forearms on his knees and stared at the floor.

Okay. Now she was starting to get a little spooked.

"Marnie's maternal grandparents only recently found out about her. They've been estranged from their daughter due to the woman's addiction issues. By chance they came upon one of her friends who happened to let it slip that their daughter had had a child about six years ago."

Clairey could hardly hear him over the pounding in her ears. She knew where this conversation was headed.

Drexel continued. "They've been trying to locate her ever since. Apparently, a family friend of theirs who happens to be a retired police detective finally managed to do just that about three weeks ago."

She swallowed past the brick that had suddenly lodged itself in her throat. "Maybe it's not so bad. Maybe they just want to visit the granddaughter they've never seen."

He shook his head with a sadness she'd never seen him display before. "They don't just want to visit her, Clairey. They think it's in Marnie's best interest to have her live with them. Permanently."

Clairey's mouth went dry. "Oh, no. They can't truly mean that. Did you explain to them how much she's thriving here? Her school, her friends, the city she's grown to love?" Not to mention the guardian uncle who clearly loves her and dotes on her? She didn't say that last part aloud, however.

"I could tell there was no use. On the contrary, he said he was concerned about his granddaughter living with a known bachelor who's been linked to several high-profile women and has been photographed more than once at various parties."

"But that's just not true. The only parties you attend are for charity or work events."

"He didn't seem to think that matters. I'm technically a bachelor, and he can offer her a steady home with her grandmother and grandfather. That's the argument they plan to make if any of this gets to court, anyway."

"Did you tell them you were engaged?"

He nodded. "He doesn't seem to care. Thinks it doesn't mean much, given my past liaisons."

Clairey chose to ignore the pang that particular phrasing caused in her chest. Her panic was slowly beginning to turn to ire. These grandparents had no idea what they were doing. Marnie was happy here. She had everything a little girl could want. Including an uncle who loved her like any father would. And Clairey loved her too. She'd come to that realization without any kind of big revelations. It was just the truth that became more and more obvious with each passing day. To take Marnie away from all that would be heartless.

"I can't bear to think of her being uprooted yet again," Drexel said, echoing her thoughts.

"Maybe we can compromise with them. They can

have her over the summers. That way she'll get to know her grandparents and not give up her life here."

"All options are on the table. I spoke with my attorney immediately afterward," Drexel said. "Of course, he's going to do what he can from a legal standpoint, file all the necessary paperwork. But he had some guidance as a friend also."

"What kind of guidance?"

"He thinks there's a card I might be able to play. A rather unconventional one. There might be a way to stave off the threat of any kind of custody battle. You might be able to help me to do that."

For the first time since Drexel had mentioned the phone call, Clairey felt a ray of hope. "What is it? What can we do?"

"I know how much this will be asking of you, Clairey. But I have to ask."

"Ask what exactly?"

He took her hand, held her gaze. "No more pretending. I'm asking you to marry me. It has to be real. You would have to be my real wife. In every way that counts."

Clairey stared at him as if he'd just spoken a foreign language. Maybe he shouldn't have blurted it out that way. But he'd never been one to beat around the bush. She gave her head a brisk shake.

"I'm sorry," she chuckled into her palm. "I must be hearing things. It almost sounded like you just proposed. To me."

"That's exactly what I did. Our best hope to keep Marnie here where she belongs is for us to get married."

He'd rendered her speechless. Not that he could blame her.

"Think about it. Their biggest argument is that Marnie is living with a bachelor uncle with no roots. We could counter that with the image of a family, including an adopting mother who happened to have been taking care of her for the past several months."

She sat motionless on the sofa. "I see."

"It wouldn't be a real marriage, Clairey." Was it his imagination or did she just flinch ever so slightly? He continued. "We're just doing this for appearances. To give Marnie the best chance possible to stay with us. As her guardians."

She remained silent, wringing her hands and staring at the carpet between her bare toes. If she didn't say something soon, Drexel thought he might very well lose his mind. Or his nerve.

But he couldn't do that. There really were no other options. He carried on in an attempt to fill the silence. "In the meantime, we have to be seen doing things that engaged couples do."

She looked up at him then, slight panic in her eyes. "Like what?"

He shrugged. "Spend time together. Both as a couple and as a family with Marnie."

"Seen by who, exactly?"

"The people who mostly pay attention to such things. New York–society gossip pages. Websites and rags that depend on prying into others' lives for sales and clicks."

She visibly swallowed. "We're going to be the subject of sales and clicks?"

He moved from his position to sit next to her. Gave

her a playful bump on the shoulder with his own. "Just for a little while. They'll lose interest soon enough. By then, we'll have gotten plenty of photos that prove how much in love we are."

Her head snapped up as he said the one loaded word. "Come on," he said, teasing. "You can pretend you love me for a while, can't you?"

She ignored the question.

He pressed on. "Of course, you'd be compensated. I don't expect you to go through all this for nothing."

Her head snapped up again, anger clear in her eyes. "You don't have to bribe me, Drexel. If I do this, I'd be doing it for Marnie. Not for some monetary reward."

Great. Now he'd made her mad. She'd gone from confused to angry in the blink of an eye because he'd mentioned payment. Maybe that was crass. But what did she expect from him? He was flying blind here. He'd never faced the prospect of having to fight for custody of a child before.

"I'm sorry," he told her sincerely.

This time, she was the one to nudge his shoulder. "Apology accepted."

"Of course, you'd be doing this for Marnie's sake."

But just as much for him.

She'd asked if she could sleep on it. Which was laughable, really. As if she'd be able to get any sleep. Clairey tossed over to her other side on the mattress yet again.

Up until now they'd simply been pretending. Now, Drex wanted to make it legal. A fake engagement was one thing. But a true marriage on paper was a whole other ball game.

What would it mean for her to go through with it?

More importantly, what would it mean for her heart? The idea of a real marriage wouldn't have even occurred to Drexel if it wasn't for that blasted phone call he'd received from Marnie's grandfather. And if that fact left a small hole in her heart, well then, that was her problem.

For Marnie. She'd be doing this for Marnie. When she thought about the impact her decision would have on the little girl, Clairey really had no choice. She had been fooling herself to think she might possibly turn him down.

She would do it. She would accept Drexel's sham marriage proposal. Even though her heart was going to slowly shatter at how fake it all was. When she yearned to have it be real, somehow.

With her decision made, sleep finally began tugging at her, and she managed to drift off.

The dream came sometime toward dawn. In it, she wore a long white bridal gown of the finest lace. A bouquet of pink roses graced her hands. With excitement and anticipation, she slowly walked down the aisle. But when she reached the altar, there was no one there waiting for her. No groom to meet her. The bouquet fell out of her hands, the once-fresh roses now wilted and dry.

She was alone.

Clairey woke with a start. It was no use. She had no hope of getting back to sleep. Crawling out of bed, she went to make some much-needed coffee.

Apparently, she wasn't the only one plagued with insomnia. Drexel was already at the counter, impatiently drumming his fingers as he waited for his own coffee to brew.

He tossed an expectant look her way when he noticed her entrance.

"I'll do it, Drexel. I'll be your fake wife."

His features flushed with relief, and he tilted his head back, releasing a deep sigh.

A twinge of guilt nudged her chest at his reaction. He'd really been worried she might say no. Now that she was sure, Clairey realized she'd never even really considered the alternative. Her mind had just needed the time to process it all.

Drexel leveled a loaded gaze at her. "Thank you, Clairey. Someday Marnie will understand just how much you're doing for her."

She pulled out a stool and sat while Drexel prepared a cup for her. By now, he knew exactly how she preferred her morning latte. "As long as it works."

"It has to. There's no plan B."

"So how exactly do we start?"

He set her cup down on the counter and slid it with precision into her waiting hands.

"Thank you," she said and took an appreciative sip.

"You said Marnie's at school for a few hours later today at rehearsal again, right?"

"That's right."

"That leaves us free to set some of this in motion." He pulled out his own stool and sat down next to her. "I figured we'd start with brunch."

It couldn't be that simple, could it? "That's it? We're going to be a couple who do brunch? That's how we'll convince people?"

He winked at her. "You'll see."

He was right. Four hours later, Clairey had the answer to her question. The brunch Drexel had planned for them involved a 1920s luxury yacht set to sail along New York Harbor. The menu included seafood omelets, truffle pancakes and bubbly mandarin juice mimosas. There were about seven other couples onboard.

"This is quite the excursion," she commented as they took their seats. Servers immediately appeared at their table with crystal flutes full of the cocktail and trays of steaming, mouthwatering food.

"That's the financial district," Drexel told her as they sailed past a square of tall buildings and steel structures. Minutes later, in the distance to her left, Clairey could see the Statue of Liberty standing majestically over the wavy water.

"I never thought one could see so much of New York via boat." But Drexel wasn't listening. Without warning, he ran the back of his hand down Clairey's cheek and leaned closer to plant a soft kiss along the base of her neck. She couldn't help the shiver that ran down from her spine clear to her toes. How often had she relived their kisses?

Then she realized what was happening. One of the other couples sat across the hull, their food completely ignored. The man had a cell phone aimed square in their direction.

"I believe they're from *Billionaire* magazine." Drexel said softly so that only she could hear, though he made it appear as if he was whispering sweet nothings in her ear.

"There's something called *Billionaire* magazine?"

He nodded at her. "Yup. They have a ranking system and everything. I was at the top once or twice."

She didn't find that hard to believe. "How did they know you'd be here?"

"An anonymous tip strategically placed to various outlets."

Wow. He really wasn't leaving any of this to chance. Proving her point, he leaned over and dropped another kiss, this time closer to her lips. He was certainly putting on a show. All the while, heat suffused her body, and longing surged through her core. She had to get a grip. Yet again, none of this was real. Drexel was here for one reason and one reason only. It was the only reason he was touching her, caressing her, just like that night back in the theater.

She'd be a fool to forget that. Even if his fake kisses were having a very real effect on her soul.

How many times could she make the same mistake, anyway?

CHAPTER THIRTEEN

IT WAS A beautiful day for a wedding.

Clairey stared out her suite window at the bright shining sun as it rose above the Manhattan skyline. By this time tomorrow, she'd be a married woman.

On paper, anyway.

In every other way, she suspected her life would pretty much continue as it was. Aside from the four-karat diamond on a plain gold band on her finger, there'd be nothing different about her. She'd still essentially be the nanny Drexel employed. Not really his wife in any way that meant anything.

A soft knock on her door pulled her out of her thoughts.

She released a pent-up sigh and turned away from the view to answer. Tessa was early, it appeared. She was due in an hour to help her get ready for the big day. Maybe Tessa had caught an earlier flight. Lana would be helping her to get ready too. Her bridesmaids. They were both beyond excited for her. Clairey still hadn't decided how much of the truth she would tell her two friends. For now, they believed that she and Drexel were tying the knot for all the right reasons. Though, they couldn't figure out why the two of them were rushing the wedding.

But it wasn't Tessa standing outside her door when she opened it. Drexel stood there with his arm braced against the doorframe.

"Oh, it's you." Even now, she felt the tingle of thrill that she experienced every time she laid eyes on the man. In as drab an outfit as a cotton T-shirt and loose sweatpants, he somehow still managed to exude pure masculine sex appeal.

"Can I come in?"

She stepped aside and motioned for him to enter.

"I know it's supposed to be taboo to see the bride before the wedding," he said, brushing past her. "But I figured in our case, the usual superstitions don't apply. And not on the day before."

Because none of it was real. "I think that mostly refers to the bride in her wedding gown, anyway," she said, turning to face him.

He reached inside his pants pocket to pull out a long rectangular box. Clairey immediately recognized the logo on the top cover. The designer boutique on the Cape.

"I've been meaning to give this to you ever since that day. There never seemed to be a good time."

She reached for the box and opened it. Inside resting among soft velvet fabric sat a glittering glass necklace. One of the two she'd watched him purchase that day.

"I figured this was as good a time as any."

She blinked up at him, confused. "I thought you got this for Marnie."

He shook his head. "No, I bought it for you. It was always meant for you."

Clairey felt touched beyond words. Even back then he'd been thinking of her enough to get her something sentimental. "I... Thank you."

"I debated that day about the appropriateness of getting you a gift. We'd just met, after all. So I held onto it."

"Until today."

"I figured the flower girl and the bride could wear matching necklaces."

She pulled the piece of jewelry out of the box and admired it. The way it caught the sunlight from the window, the beauty of the design. "May I?" Drexel asked.

She handed it to him, and he gently unclasped the small gold fastener. Then he stepped behind her. His fingers felt warm and firm against her skin. A current of heat traveled down her neck to her center as he put the necklace on her. Was it her imagination, or did his hands linger along her neck a moment or two longer after he'd fastened the clasp?

"It's beautiful," Clairey told him when he was done, fingering the delicate glass. "Thank you."

He'd have no idea just how much the gift meant to her. When he'd given her the diamond for their fake engagement, she'd known how unreal it was. That ring was only for show, pretense.

This felt so much more genuine. Ceremonial. Drex had gotten this necklace especially for her. The sentiment made a world of difference.

Their upcoming wedding might be a farce, as was

their pretend engagement. But as far as Clairey was concerned, this moment was genuine.

And so were her feelings for her soon-to-be so-called husband.

He hadn't expected to feel quite so nervous. None of this was real, after all. They just had to go through this sham of a ceremony so that the gossip sites would do their write-ups and publish a few photos and he would have concrete proof that he was a married man.

Nothing in his life was about to change in any real way. Except that, technically, he'd have a wife. That wife being Clairey.

On paper, anyway.

Things had been so different between them the last time they'd been on this rooftop the night of the school raffle. She'd fallen asleep in his arms on a chaise longue. They'd woken up to see the sunrise the next morning. He would have never guessed that night that in a few months' time he'd be waiting for her at a makeshift altar for an impromptu wedding.

The ding of the elevator signaled her arrival. Clairey exited the doors soon after.

Drexel's breath caught in his throat at the sight of her. Even through the veil and from this distance, she was heart-stoppingly beautiful. A vision. There was no other way to describe her in her wedding gown. It complemented her figure and hugged her curves in a way that made him imagine taking it off her later. He pushed that thought aside.

Marnie walked slowly in front of her, dropping delicate rose petals along the aisle. Clairey's two friends flanked her as bridesmaids and in lieu of the father she'd lost who would have given her away.

Drexel couldn't tear his eyes away from her as she made her way down the runner. He had to remind himself this wasn't any kind of authentic wedding. They'd rushed the ceremony and just needed to get it over with.

So why was there a rush of emotion surging through him at the moment?

Clairey reached his side and gave him a small smile through her veil. Her brown hair a dark contrast against the white fabric, adding to the striking allure of the overall picture she made.

The officiant began speaking, but his words barely registered. Not until Drexel heard him say, "You may kiss your bride."

He hadn't so much as touched her since the wedding. Now, over a week later, Drexel was holding her hand. Only because they were in a very public place. He was only doing it for show. Their little charade continued now that they were among others. Behind closed doors, however, nothing had really changed between them. They still kept their separate living quarters. Drexel hadn't invited her into his suite even once.

Clairey tried not to let the hurt of that ruin her mood as they took their seats in the school's auditorium. Marnie could barely contain her excitement this morning about her role as a small gourd in the Hammond School's autumn performance of "Harvest Moon," a play written by the children themselves. So far, the little girl was surprisingly oblivious to the dynamics in her household. Clairey had to wonder if she found it odd that her uncle and nanny were currently husband and wife, yet they behaved exactly as before with each other.

Drexel gave her hand a squeeze and pulled it over onto his lap. Her pulse quickened at the rather intimate action. Funny, no one was watching them now. In fact, the lights had dimmed. There was no need to put on such a display. Still, he made no move to let go of her. Probably just a reflexive action at this point. Clairey decided not to question it. A girl could get used to such tender gestures, regardless of motive.

Moments later, the curtains drew open to reveal several children on stage dressed as fall vegetables in colorful costumes. The first act did not go smoothly. All the children flubbed their lines, earning amused laughs from the audience. One little redheaded boy completely forgot what he was to say and stood frozen until the teacher walked onto the stage to help him out. Marnie, for her part, only missed a word here and there. Her bright smile told Clairey she was enjoying herself.

At the end of the performance, the little thespians received a standing ovation. Drexel seemed to be clapping louder and more enthusiastically than most anyone else. He even blew out a loud whistle when Marnie took her bow.

"I'll admit, I enjoyed that more than I thought I would," he said when the curtains were drawn and the houselights came on. Marnie came running out from backstage moments later.

Drexel lifted the girl in his arms and twirled her once. "There she is. You were a star up there, sweetheart."

Marnie giggled. "Silly Uncle Drex. I was a baby pumpkin."

"The best baby pumpkin to ever grace the stage."

Drexel put her back down, and Marnie immediately ran over to give Clairey a tight hug around the waist. "You were the best pumpkin I've ever seen."

A ringtone sounded from Drexel's pocket. She heard him utter a soft curse as he pulled out his phone and glanced at the screen.

"Excuse me, ladies. I need to take this call."

Marnie gave her one more tight squeeze around the middle before dropping her arms and jumping in place.

Clairey had to laugh at her exuberance. "You are so excited, little one."

"I'm gonna go back to my friends now. We're making sundaes to celebrate our great show." With that, she ran back to her teacher and group of classmates.

Clairey found Drexel in the hallway just as he ended the call. The dark expression on his face told her the conversation had not been a pleasant one.

"Where's Marnie?" he asked, looking behind her for the little girl.

"Off with the rest of her class. They're having an ice-cream party back in their classroom. We can pick her up in a couple of hours."

She pointed to the cell phone in his hand. "What was the call about?"

"That was my attorney," he told her, repocketing the phone.

An icy dread washed through her veins. The call had to be about Marnie. "The Thomases have requested a visit. They're planning on flying into New York within the next week. They want to meet Marnie and see for themselves her exact living situation."

She reached for him without thinking. "We have to let them, Drexel. And we'll just have to deal with whatever the fallout may be."

He released a heavy sigh and crammed his fingers into the hair at his crown. "I know. I can't keep her grandparents from her completely. She has a right to know who they are."

"I couldn't agree more. I would have given anything to have a set of grandparents around after losing my father. But they were all gone by the time I was born." Clairey knew this wasn't about her. But having two other people in the world who cared for her might have made a mountain of difference in the lonely way she'd had to live her life. No matter the older couple's intentions, Clairey knew the meeting was inevitable. She was surprised they hadn't made the request before.

"I'm glad you're being reasonable about this. We have to think of what's best for Marnie when we make these decisions."

He nodded, and a darkness settled over his eyes she'd never seen before. Clairey got the feeling she was getting her first glimpse of the self-made successful businessman who went after what he wanted and made sure to get it. His words when he answered served to confirm that thought.

"I can be reasonable, Clairey. But only to a degree," Drexel said between gritted teeth. "Grandparents or not, I know Marnie's better off with us."

She couldn't argue that, thinking of how happy Marnie had been up on that stage and of her excitement about having ice cream with all her new friends.

Drexel continued, "I'll fight them with all I have if they try to take her."

The Thomases looked like they could be models for a cooking-magazine photo spread. Or in a Norman Rockwell painting. Muriel Thomas had bluish-gray hair she wore in tight curls. Dressed in a smart cream-colored knee-length skirt and flat loafers, she gave every impression of the cookie-baking, Sunday-roast-preparing, matronly grandma. Bill Thomas had lost most of his hair. He had wide shoulders and large hands that had clearly helped him make his living.

Drexel had led them into the living room when they'd arrived two minutes ago. They were waiting for Clairey to go get Marnie from her room. "My wife will be right out with Marnie. She's just finishing getting dressed."

Bill gave him a suspicious look. "Wife, huh?"

Drexel lifted an eyebrow in question. "Something you'd like to get off your chest, Mr. Thomas?"

Muriel placed a cautionary hand on her husband's forearm, but the man ignored it.

"I just think it's mighty convenient how you happened to get married sometime after our first phone call." Apparently, Bill wasn't one to pull any punches.

It took plenty of restraint, but Drexel somehow managed to clamp down on his ire. These people may have Marnie's best interest at heart, but so far, he was less than pleased with their approach.

Clairey entered the room at that moment with Marnie practically clinging to her leg. The girl was nervous. Drexel could hardly blame her. Two strangers she'd never seen before had made a trip from halfway across the country to visit her. It didn't help that Marnie knew nothing of her mother, let alone the type of people her maternal grandparents might be.

Clairey rubbed the top of Marnie's head in reassurance. "Marnie. This is your grandmother and grandfather."

Not for the first time, Drexel said a silent prayer of thanks that Clairey was here to help him through this. He'd faced countless adversaries both on the streets as a teenager and in the boardroom. But he was certain he'd be handling all this much more poorly if it wasn't for her support and understanding. Not to mention her presence now.

He needed to keep his wits about him. And he needed to stay calm and even-keeled. With Clairey's help, he just might be able to.

"Would you like to go say hello?"

Marnie hesitantly let go of Clairey's leg and took a small bow. "Hello. I'm Marnie."

Muriel clasped a hand to her chest and let out a small cry. "Oh, my. She's utterly precious. Becky looked so much like her as a little girl." Her eyes suddenly flooded with tears before she turned away and pulled a tissue out of her purse.

Marnie looked up at Clairey in question. Clairey gave her a reassuring smile and a gentle nudge. Drexel felt a tug in his chest at the picture the two of them made. The Thomases had to see what he was seeing. In the previous months, Clairey had been more of a mother to Marnie than anyone else in the girl's short life so far. They'd have to be blind to miss that even in the brief time they'd been here.

Marnie finally dropped Clairey's hand and walked over to stand between the older couple on the couch.

"May I hug you?" Muriel asked.

Marnie nodded her answer. Drexel watched as the two embraced. Then Bill joined in and put his large, burly arms around the two of them.

A slew of conflicting thoughts rushed through his head. Marnie's grandparents were clearly affectionate and caring people. They were already showing how much love they'd bestow on their grandchild. The scene before him was genuine and heartfelt, there was no doubt.

Drexel tore his eyes away from the three of them and made his way to where Clairey stood. Her eyes had grown rather misty, as well. Without hesitation or thought, he pulled her tight up against him and held her against his length. The scent of her calmed him. She felt like a steadying anchor to his storm of conflicting emotions.

He needed her more than he knew. And it had somehow happened when he hadn't even been paying attention.

A week later, after half a dozen more visits between Marnie and her grandparents, Bill Thomas rang from the lobby asking to meet with Drexel. When the man arrived at his office, he had a look of resignation on his face. Yet, Drexel could read something else in his expression as well. Relief.

"I'm going to be honest with you, Mr. Osoman."

"Please call me Drexel."

The other man nodded. "Drexel. My wife isn't in the best of health. She's fighting a recurrence of a battle we thought she'd won long ago."

"I'm very sorry to hear that."

"But we had to make sure our grandchild was all right."

Why couldn't he have just said all that from the get-go? It could have saved everyone so much angst and worry. Drexel kept the thought to himself.

"We had to see for ourselves," Bill added. "Bad enough we lost our daughter to her addictions, we couldn't not know our grandchild."

"I understand."

Bill scratched at his head. "I think we've seen and heard enough. I'll admit to speculating on your sudden marriage. But the end result for Marnie seems to be a well-adjusted household where she's well taken care of. It's all we wanted to know."

"Thank you for that."

"Our only ask is that we can come visit her. And maybe have her come stay with us and meet some of her cousins."

Drexel made sure not to react in any kind of celebratory way. The whole dilemma was working out the way he'd hoped. But he couldn't feel any satisfaction at the struggles these two people were dealing with. "You're welcome here whenever you'd like," he assured the other man. "You and your wife and any cousins who might want to make the trip. In fact, the flight and lodgings are on me."

Bill immediately shook his head. "We don't accept any kind of charity."

Drexel held a hand up to stop him from saying any more. "It wouldn't be charity. I'd be doing it for my niece. The more people she has in her life who love her, the better for her."

Bill rubbed his jaw. "Well, in that case, I'll take it up with the wife."

They shook hands on it before Bill turned to leave. Drexel watched the door shut behind the other man and gave in to the surge of relief that flooded through every cell in his body.

He wouldn't celebrate alone. After all, there was one other person who shared this victory with him. Clairey. His wife.

CHAPTER FOURTEEN

"So, to what do I owe this honor, big brother?" Chase sat across from him sipping the fine brandy he'd taken upon himself to order along with his dinner. Drexel figured it was a small price to pay if this little get-together accomplished what he intended.

Chase continued after several more sips. "Did you invite me here and fly me in for a belated bachelor party or something?"

Drex took a moment to study his only sibling. Chase's cheeks were ruddy, his eyes slightly bloodshot. He'd guess the glass he held wasn't his first one of the day. "Not exactly," he answered.

"Then, why am I here? I've left my wife all the way back in Maine to come. We're still technically newlyweds, you know. Though, not as new as you and what's-her-name."

Drexel somehow held onto his temper, although it wasn't easy. "Her name is Clairey. Clairey Osoman now." He wouldn't bother to ask Chase if he wanted to see Marnie. It hadn't even occurred to his brother to ask about his only child.

Chase held his glass in the air in a mock toast. "Ah, yes. Clairey. How did you two come about getting married again? Didn't you just meet the woman a short while ago when she tried to destroy my wedding?"

He would ignore the jab. Never mind that Clairey had been absolutely right to try and intervene. He shuddered to think of the life Marnie might be subjected to now if Clairey hadn't stormed into the meeting room that morning.

Remarkable, really, the impact she'd had on his life since then. Somehow, when he hadn't been looking or paying attention, she'd become a true partner. A support and anchor he hadn't even known he'd needed. Or wanted.

A small twinge of apprehension itched in his chest at those thoughts, but he didn't have time to examine that right now.

He answered his brother, steepling his fingers over the table. "We've grown quite fond of each other since then." Best to just get this over with. "Marnie's quite fond of her, as well. They're at Central Park right now enjoying Shakespeare in the Park."

Chase cut into his steak, took a bite and chewed. "What's any of that got to do with why I'm here?"

"There's some paperwork I'd like you to sign."

Chase may as well have rolled his eyes, his boredom was so clear. "What kind of paperwork?"

"I got a phone call a few weeks ago. From Marnie's maternal grandparents."

That seemed to get his attention. "Oh? What'd they want?"

"Mainly to meet Marnie. But they were also concerned."

Chase set down his knife and fork and leaned back in his chair. "About what, exactly?"

"They were thinking about having Marnie live with them until they saw how well she's taken to her life here."

"Huh."

"I don't want to risk something like that happening again."

Chase had to know what he was thinking. Now that Marnie's grandparents were appeased, the only one who still posed any kind of threat that his niece might be taken away from Drex and Clairey was sitting across the table.

"It might have gone differently if it wasn't for Clairey. We might have lost Marnie to her grandparents."

Chase tilted his head to the side. "Yeah?" His brother may have been reckless and lazy, but he'd never been stupid. Chase put the pieces together almost immediately. A knowing smirk formed along his lips. "That explains it. It's why you married her, isn't it?"

Drexel didn't bother to try to deny it. It wasn't as if Chase's thoughts on his marriage meant anything to him. That wasn't the kind of brothers they were, and it wasn't what this meeting was about.

He got right to the point. "I want you to sign over custody. I'd like to begin the process of adopting Marnie. It will go much more smoothly if done with your cooperation."

Chase took another sip of his drink. "Why would I do that?"

He had to ask? Drexel took a steadying breath. He wasn't going to let his brother goad him into losing his composure. "Because you don't want to be a father. Not to Marnie, anyway."

"I might change my mind about that at some point in the future."

"And what would happen if you do change your mind? You would pluck her from the life she's grown into and take her away from all that she loves?"

"I'm her father."

He'd hardly acted like it. "You'll always be part of her life. But I think it's in her best interest for Clairey and me to adopt her."

"You wanna adopt my kid? With your fake wife?"

Drexel clenched his fists under the table. Chase didn't give him a chance to respond before continuing. "You're a real piece of work, big brother."

"What's that supposed to mean?"

He leaned forward and drained the rest of his drink, motioned for a refill to the bartender across the dining room. "It means you always thought you were better than us. But the truth is you're not so different than the old man."

The blood pounded in his ears at the unwarranted accusation. Chase had some nerve. "I'm nothing like him. I never had to have a teenager come drag me away from the slot machines in the middle of the night. I never got beaten to a pulp because I cheated the wrong man at an underground card game. And I never lost money over and over again only to gamble more away the next day. Losing money that could have gone to feeding my impoverished family and keeping my sons off the streets."

Chase's eyes narrowed on him. "Maybe not. Or maybe you're just better at winning than he was."

"You're not making any sense."

"Face it, bro. The games might not be the same. But you do whatever it takes to win when you play. Like how you conned a young woman into a loveless marriage just so you could win yet again."

Drexel saw red as his brother's words echoed through his head. Chase didn't know what he was talking about. He'd married Clairey for his niece's sake. Not for some ego-driven desire to succeed or to best anyone else.

And he certainly didn't have to explain himself to anyone about it.

"You know what?" Chase bit out, pushing away from the table and crossing his arms over his chest. "Sure, I'll sign. But there's a price."

You can do this.

Clairey gave herself the same pep talk she'd been repeating since she'd woken up this morning. Sometime over the course of the past several days she'd come to a gradual realization. She was tired of waiting for Drexel to make the first move. Or any kind of move, for that matter.

As anxiety inducing as the Thomases' visit had been, it had led to Clairey reaching a profound conclusion. She wanted that kind of relationship for herself. Bill and Muriel had grown old together, faced hardships together, and were now surrounded by loving family and grandchildren they adored.

They'd been true partners in their marriage. Unlike the selfish love that Clairey had witnessed between her mom and Frank, what the Thomases had was enviable to witness.

If there was even a chance that she might be able to achieve that with Drex, she would never forgive herself if she didn't take the chance to find out.

She was in love with him. There was no denying it

any longer. And she wanted her marriage to be a real one. In every possible way.

No, Clairey had no idea what the future held for them. But right now, she wanted the type of intimacy that true couples shared. With the only man she'd ever fallen in love with.

He had to want this too. She could feel it in her bones. In the looks he gave her when he thought she wasn't watching. The way he touched her fingers in the mornings as he handed her the latte he'd prepared. The way his face lit up when he walked in and found her waiting for him in the kitchen. All that had to mean something.

Maybe she was about to make a fool of herself. Maybe all of this was simply wishful thinking. But one way or another, she was going to find out for certain if Drexel wanted her the same way she wanted him. As his authentic, legitimate wife in every way. Their union might have started as a means to an end. But tonight Clairey was going to try to make it a real marriage.

She wanted to make love to her husband.

Marnie was already at Sara's. Lana had agreed to take her for another sleepover. The silky red dress she'd purchased hung ready in the closet. She'd already done her hair.

The home-cooked meal she'd prepared simply needed to be popped in the oven when he came home.

Clairey had thought of everything.

But her plans hit a serious snag when two hours had gone by and Drexel still wasn't back. She glanced at her watch. It was already past nine. Where was he?

An hour later, panic was beginning to set in. Maybe there'd been some kind of emergency. Clairey's heart pounded against her chest as she reached for her phone on the glass coffee table. Straight to voice mail. A short text message went unanswered for another hour.

Just when she was deciding where to start trying to look for him, she heard the penthouse elevator ding.

Clairey scrambled off the couch to her feet and met him halfway in the kitchen. "You're home. I've been waiting for you."

He took one look at her and raised both eyebrows. Then his gaze traveled the length of her body, lingering at her plunging neckline. Clairey felt heat rise to her cheeks.

"Did we have plans? I didn't realize."

Hot tears sprang to her cheeks, but she refused to let him see. He hadn't realized because she'd taken great care to surprise him.

"Where have you been, Drex? I was worried sick."

He loosened his collar and undid several buttons on his shirt. Clairey wanted to kick herself for her reaction. Even now, given her distress, she wanted nothing more than to stride over to him and touch her fingers to the bronze skin at his chest. She wanted him to hold her, to tell her he was sorry for making her wait.

"You shouldn't have been worried. I just jumped into a quick round of cards at the gaming hall by the airport."

A card game? "I thought you hated those places."

His lips tightened. "Sorry you were worried, Clairey. But there's hardly need for all these questions. I just needed to blow off some steam after seeing Chase."

Of all the turns she might have expected this conversation to take, that had definitely not been on her radar. "Chase? You saw your brother?"

"Yes. I asked him to relinquish custody of Marnie to me."

Me. Not *us.* He was throwing her all sorts of curve balls. Clairey was having trouble processing.

"You didn't tell me."

"I didn't want to say anything until I was sure Chase would sign."

"I see." But she didn't. Not really. She didn't see why he'd gone ahead and made such a huge move without so much as mentioning it to her.

"He signed."

Well, at least that was one less thing to worry about. Marnie's future with them was secured, at least.

A bloom of hope blossomed in her chest at the thought. Maybe they had something to celebrate tonight, after all.

But Drexel didn't appear celebratory. His expression told her there was more he had to say. Clairey's mouth went dry. She wasn't sure how much more she could take.

"There's something else, isn't there?"

He fingered his collar, clearly weighing his words. "There's been a development with the Abu Dhabi acquisition. It's going to require me to give it my full attention."

"What kind of development?"

"There's been a lot of unexpected glitches trying to break ground. I'll have to fly down there and stay until everything falls into place with the project. I took the liberty of calling a nanny service so that you'll have some help with Marnie while I'm overseas."

Okay. Yet another huge revelation. What in the world was happening right now? Clairey felt utterly unprepared. She somehow swallowed past the boulder that had lodged itself in the base of her throat. "When do you leave?"

"As soon as possible. Within the next twenty-four to forty-eight hours."

Clairey's stomach took a nosedive. A day or two? "How long will you be gone?"

"A year. Maybe more."

Her knees went weak as his words sank in. Despite his roundabout way of announcing it, she finally understood what was occurring right before her. He was leaving them. Leaving her. What a fool she'd been! While she was sitting here hoping to bring them closer together, he'd been setting all sorts of things into action that would do just the opposite.

"I know it's a lot to take in," he told her. "But it seemed to come together all at once."

If that wasn't the understatement of all time.

Drex made a move toward her but stopped himself. "Clairey? Say something."

What did he expect her to say even if she could make her mouth work? Finally, somehow, she found the words to sum up what she was hearing. "So you arranged to have me replaced as Marnie's primary caregiver, and you plan on moving thousands of miles away for the foreseeable future. And you did it all without me having any kind of say in any of it. Do I have all that right?"

Clairey hated the tremble in her voice, hated the way she was shivering where she stood.

And she absolutely hated what Drexel had to say in response. "It's all for the best, Clairey."

Drexel shut the door of his suite and leaned up against the door with his eyes shut tight. A moment later, he heard the elevator door ping open then shut again.

She'd left the penthouse.

Go after her. Try to explain.

He reached for the doorknob to do just that before he stopped himself. There was no use. What was done was done. His brother's accusations had rattled him enough that he'd felt the need to test himself at the run-down casino by the airport near downtown. No, he hadn't enjoyed himself. Not even when he'd run the table and won. Thank goodness for that small assurance.

But that minor victory didn't make the rest of Chase's words any less relevant.

His brother was a thankless clod who'd just ransomed custody of his only child. But he'd also given voice to the misgivings that had plagued Drexel since he'd hired Clairey back on the Cape.

Her working for him was only supposed to have been temporary until the situation with Marnie was sorted and Clairey was back on her feet. Instead, he'd roped her into a sham marriage for his own needs.

Maybe with him gone and Marnie set up with a nanny service, Clairey would finally get a chance to pursue her own goals and go after her ambitions in life. He'd even make some calls, see what was out there for someone with her skills and experience. New York was the world's hub for tourism and hospitality, and Drexel had no doubt she would shine wherever she found herself. She might even meet somebody who deserved her for who she was and not simply as a way to use her for his own selfish needs. A stabbing pain shot through his midsection at the thought, but he had to ignore it.

As much as it pained him to walk away, he had no right to hold her back any longer.

CHAPTER FIFTEEN

"I TAKE IT your romantic evening didn't go as planned," Lana remarked upon opening the door to Clairey's knock. "The fuzzy socks and baggy sweatpants are a big clue if you're wondering how I know."

A hiccup of a sob escaped Clairey before she could stop it.

Her friend immediately stepped over the threshold and put her arms around her shoulders. "Oh, sweetie. Come in. Tell me what happened. Do I need to go over there with my heavy skillet?"

Clairey sniffled. "No. I mean, maybe. Maybe I need the skillet."

She followed Lana to the living room, and they both plopped down on the couch.

"The girls are engrossed in a movie they're streaming, and the Wallaces are at a dinner party. You have plenty of time to cry on my shoulder." She handed Clairey a full box of tissues.

Clairey hiccuped yet again and wanted to kick herself for it. She hated coming across so weak, so wounded. But that's exactly how she felt. Like she was about to lose something precious and coveted. Or she'd never had it in the first place.

"Tell me," Lana gently prompted.

Clairey struggled with how to start. Then she simply blurted the whole story as best she could relate—from Drexel showing up late to the fact that he'd been at a casino the whole time to all the bombshells he'd dropped on her when he'd finally turned up.

"Wow." Lana's vague response almost made her chuckle. Almost. "That's a lot."

"He's leaving, Lana. Thousands of miles away. For months on end."

Her friend tucked her legs under her on the sofa cushion. "I'm missing something."

"What's that?"

"Well, for one, what did he say when you told him everything you had planned? How you wanted to finally make it a true marriage?"

That gave her pause. Clairey stopped in the act of wiping her eyes to stare at her friend. "You knew?"

Lana shrugged. "I knew something was amiss. One day you two are employer and nanny, and the next you're engaged. Then suddenly you're rushing a wedding, just as Marnie's grandparents show up. Something didn't add up."

Great. Now she could feel guilty on top of everything else. "I'm sorry I didn't tell you the truth from the beginning."

Lana patted her knee. "That's a conversation for another time. Now, tell me how he reacted when you tried to seduce him."

Clairey cringed at the wording. Lana was right, though; there was no better way to describe it.

"I never got the chance. I was so taken aback at all that was happening."

"Huh. So you have no idea how he might have reacted if your plans had come to fruition tonight? If you'd told him exactly how you feel about him?"

Clairey wrung the tissue in her hand so tight her knuckles began to hurt. "No, I don't." She threw her hands up in frustration. "But what difference does it make?"

"I'd say it makes all the difference," Lana declared, handing her another tissue.

"He's leaving, Lana," she repeated. "He seems very determined. And I don't think there's anything I can do to stop him."

"Oh, honey, aren't you even going to try?"

She wasn't back yet.

Drexel picked up his phone for the umpteenth time to call Clairey, only to toss it back in disgust. He had no idea what he would say to her when she answered. She might not even pick up. Which would be more than he deserved. Maybe it was better that she wasn't here. A clean break left fewer scars.

But he was going to slowly go crazy if he stayed up here in the penthouse any longer, rehashing the same pointless thoughts over and over. His half-hearted attempts to pack for Abu Dhabi were going nowhere and only added to his overall frustration. He couldn't even find his toiletry bag. And where the hell was his passport?

Drexel swore and tossed his bottle of aftershave so hard against the wall, a chip of paint fell to the floor. He rubbed a hand down his face and tried to calm down.

As happy as he was about the deal, being a huge business success, he knew he'd paid too much for the property. An impulsive move made on a whim due to his confusion and self-recrimination. Yet another gamble. Maybe his brother was right about him in more ways than one.

He had to get some air. A walk might do him some good, despite the late hour. Not bothering to grab any kind of jacket, he made his way down to the first floor.

Drexel did a double take when the elevator doors slid open down in the lobby. A familiar figure stood over by the entrance. He rubbed his eyes to make certain he wasn't seeing things in his agitated state. His eyes weren't tricking him.

"Chase? What are you doing here?"

His brother shoved his fingers through his hair. "Working up the courage to come up and try to see you."

"You were?" Drexel could guess the reason. Chase had no doubt rethought the amount he'd asked for earlier for Marnie's custody agreement. He was most likely here to renegotiate what he'd already signed off on.

So be it. Drexel would write him another large check. What his brother didn't understand was that he'd have given him the money outright merely for the asking. Custody or not.

"Got a minute to talk, big brother?" Chase asked now, his hands jammed into his pockets.

Drexel answered with a nod. "Walk with me. I was just going out to get some air."

The air was crisp and breezy when they stepped onto the sidewalk and started walking in the direction of the park.

"Listen, man," Chase began, "our conversation at the restaurant earlier didn't sit well with me."

That was unexpected. Drexel tried not to let his surprise show and made sure to maintain his steady stride.

Chase continued. "Look, I lashed out and said some things I knew better than to say."

This time Drexel did pause. He turned to face his brother. "Chase, are you actually trying to apologize?"

His brother gave him a chagrined smiled. "Well, duh. What do I have to do? Write you a card? Buy you flowers?"

"Huh," was the best Drexel could come up with in response.

Chase rolled his eyes and looked up at the sky. "All right, fine. I'll go ahead and say it all. We know you're better equipped to take care of Marnie. You're obviously more successful, you can offer her a better life. It's why I sent her off with you in the first place. I know I can't be a good father right now. But when confronted with the reality of all that, I let my insecurities get the best of me. And I took it out on you."

Drexel truly felt at a loss for words. Especially at his brother's next comments. "I know I have a lot to thank you for. You were the lifeline Mom and I never had with Dad. You were there to fix things whenever he broke them. Guess that's why I asked you to help me fix what went wrong with my daughter."

A ball of emotion welled up in his throat. To hear his brother say such things made him realize just how much he could use his own lifeline right about now. And how he'd pushed the one person away who was serving that very purpose.

Out of his own fear and insecurities. What a self-ish fool he'd been.

His brother carried on. "I'm still trying to get my act together. We both know you make a better father than I do. And you're married to a woman who stuck up for Marnie when she didn't even know her. I know she'll help you take good care of her."

Drexel squeezed his eyes shut and bit out a curse.

"What is it?" Chase asked.

"I might have messed that up."

Chase narrowed his eyes on him. "Already? What'd you do?"

"I pushed her away." He wouldn't divulge the fact that he'd reacted as a direct result of taking everything Chase had said to him to heart. It wasn't as if he could lay the blame at Chase's feet. No one was responsible for his actions but himself.

Chase blew out a low whistle. "Well, you gotta fix it, man. 'Cause from the look on your face, I'd say you have no choice. That's the look of a man in love."

Drex exhaled a deep breath. Chase was right. It was so obvious: he'd fallen in love with Clairey. He just hadn't allowed himself to admit it. "I don't know if she'll forgive me."

"Guess there's only one way to find out, big brother. And you should get started—pronto."

Drexel couldn't help but huff out a small laugh. "How did you get so wise all of a sudden?"

A look of softness washed over his features. "Believe it or not, married life has been good for me. Danielle has been good for me. We have our individual issues we need to work on. But together we make a pretty good team."

Drexel gently cuffed his brother's shoulder. "I'm glad to hear that. Really."

"Besides, trust me. I have selfish reasons."

"Yeah, how so?"

"You can't let a woman like that get away," Chase said, waving a finger at him. "The way she made sure Marnie wasn't stuck where she wasn't wanted—only someone with a heart of gold and a boatload of courage would do something like that. And I'd want nothing less in a mother for my—" he caught himself and corrected the last word "—*our* little girl."

Drexel pulled him in a brotherly embrace.

Chase was right.

They had more in common as brothers than appeared on the surface. Just like Chase, Drexel had let his insecurities and doubts get in the way of his true shot at happiness. As a result, he just might have ruined the best thing that had ever come his way. The best chance he'd have at a life full of love.

He could only hope he wasn't too late.

Clairey awoke with a start and bolted up in bed. She hadn't even bothered to change into her night clothes or crawl under the covers. Drexel was gone again when she'd come back to the apartment last night. She'd fallen asleep waiting for him to return.

But she heard him now. In fact, two distinct voices could be heard coming from the hallway by the entrance elevator.

Clairey forced herself to take a fortifying breath and summoned all the strength she could. When she left her room, she found Drexel crouched in front of Marnie, speaking to her very intently.

He must have picked her up from Lana's earlier this morning.

Her stomach dropped when she realized why. He was saying goodbye to his niece. Several bags of luggage sat in front of the elevator doors. He certainly hadn't been kidding about leaving ASAP.

Drexel took Marnie's hand in his and must have asked her some kind of question as the little girl bobbed her head up and down in answer.

Clairey couldn't guess what they might be discussing, but Marnie clearly didn't understand exactly what was happening or the gravity of the situation, for she appeared to be giggling happily.

"You were gone late, last night," Clairey ventured from her position several feet away from where the two of them stood, afraid to get too close for fear of him seeing the sheen of tears in her eyes.

He straightened immediately upon hearing her voice. "Chase stopped by. We realized we had a lot of things left unsaid between us."

Another goodbye he'd gotten out of the way, then. She had to wonder if he'd planned on bothering to do so with her. A boulder of hurt settled in her stomach. She felt as if she were drowning in deep, choppy water with no lifeline in sight. For she'd fallen in love with this man when she hadn't even been paying attention. And now he was shattering her heart into a million pieces.

"Well, good. That's really good. I'm glad you two cleared the air."

"Me too."

"So you're packed and ready to leave, I take it?" How her mouth even worked, she wasn't even certain. She felt as if she could be a puppet, her strings being pulled by an unknown entity as she went through the motions.

"Sort of," Drexel answered. Clairey wasn't sure what that meant and didn't know how to go about asking.

Several beats passed in absolute silence. Why in the world was Marnie still smiling? For such a usually perceptive child, she certainly didn't seem to be reading the room correctly.

There was something else about what she was witnessing that didn't sit right. Clairey couldn't quite put her finger on what it could be. She was one big ball of jumbled emotions and bitter disappointment. And tremendous hurt. But there was more to it. Her mind screamed at her that there was something she was missing, something she had to pay attention to. It was important. Something about the scene in front of her didn't compute.

Then she realized what it was. The pile of luggage included three pink and purple Polly Pony bags. Bags that belonged to Marnie. He'd packed for his niece as well as himself.

Her blood turned to ice in her veins. Was he planning on taking Marnie with him? On leaving Clairey here completely alone? Without either of them and only three kittens to keep her company?

That would certainly explain the girl's giddy mood. But she couldn't even think about what it meant for her. Day after day and night after night sitting here by herself. Alone. With no one around who loved her or cared about her. Once again. A roaring began to sound in her ears, and her vision grew cloudy.

Marnie had walked over to her and was tugging at

the hem of her T-shirt. "Uncle Drex has something to ask you."

Clairey did her utmost to smile at the child, but inside a part of her was slowly dying. Clairey had to be strong for her sake. She couldn't risk upsetting Marnie simply because her life was being shattered.

Drexel cleared his throat. "I do, at that. Actually, we both do."

She watched as he seemed to approach her in slow motion. Then he completely confounded her by dropping to one knee in front of them both. He slowly pulled a box out of his front pocket.

Clairey lost the ability to breathe. "Drex," she whispered through lips that had gone desert-dry, "what are you doing?"

"Marnie and I are proposing to you. A real proposal, this time."

Clairey felt her jaw drop. She couldn't have heard him correctly. "You're doing what?"

"Clairey Robi, would you do the honor of marrying me? And Marnie? In a real ceremony with all our friends and loved ones in a dress of your own choosing and a real honeymoon to follow?"

He opened the box to reveal a glittering ring.

"You already have the diamond," he explained, a mischievous glint in his eyes. "This one is glass," he pointed out. "To match your paired necklaces."

She had to be dreaming this. Clairey was certainly still back in her room. She'd never awakened this morning, never crawled out of bed.

None of this was really happening.

"What about the bags? You're all packed to go to the Middle East."

Drexel made a show of looking around. "Oh, these bags are for all of us. And we're not going to the Middle East. Not even close."

"We're not?"

"No. See, there's this wonderful resort on the Cape that hosts the most extraordinary weddings. They even allow pets, believe it or not. I believe you're familiar with it."

"Oh, Drexel."

"It's all been arranged. We just need you to say yes."

Clairey finally allowed herself to breathe. She wasn't being deserted. She was being proposed to!

Her heart felt as if it must have swelled to twice its size in her chest. She pulled Drexel up to standing and allowed herself to fall into his arms. His lips found hers in a heady, deep, soul-shattering kiss. A set of skinny arms could be felt around the tops of her thighs a moment later.

She'd been right. This really was a dream, one come true for her. One she never wanted to wake up from.

"Clairey, what's your answer?" Marnie asked in a muffled voice.

Clairey laughed with all the joy and love overflowing in her heart. "Yes!" she declared, looking from Drexel and then down at Marnie's smiling face. "My answer to both of you is absolutely yes!"

EPILOGUE

"I think that last one was called a sparkler."

Clairey nestled up tighter against her husband, her back to his chest as they watched the stunning fireworks display from the deck of their flybridge boat. The moonlit night was perfect for the stunning show. As was the smooth, calm water of Cape Cod Bay.

"I believe those are Marnie's favorite," she said, reveling in the warmth of his embrace. Her adopted daughter had only left for Colorado three days ago. But Clairey missed her already.

"She seems to be having fun at Bill and Muriel's," Drexel remarked.

"And all those cousins. I think she mentioned about five or six."

Drexel laughed. "At least. Not a bad way for a little girl to spend part of the summer. Running around a ranch with a host of cousins and two doting grandparents."

"And I believe several horses and sheep."

Drexel tightened his arms around Clairey and nuzzled the top of her head with his chin. "She'll be off to visit Chase and Danielle soon too."

Drexel's brother had come far in the past year. He'd

been sober for months and was now even sponsoring others. Drexel was rightly proud of him.

"But she misses Sara," Drexel added. "And her other friends from school."

He'd just given her the perfect segue. Clairey couldn't imagine a better time to tell him the news. She tilted her head and planted a soft kiss on his jaw.

"Speaking of which, I grabbed an application from the Hammond School when I picked her up on the last day. We'll need it soon."

He gently turned her to face him. "An application? Don't tell me we have to renew for Marnie every year. That seems excessive."

She shook her head slowly. "It's not for Marnie. We can't be too early."

He lifted his eyebrows in question. "Not for Marnie. Then, who—?"

Clairey watched with bated breath as his features lit with understanding. His gaze slowly fell to her belly.

"You mean—?"

She couldn't hide her smile. "I don't want to have to try to win another raffle."

She'd barely got the last word out when she felt herself being lifted off her feet and spun around.

"Are you sure?" he asked when he set her back down.

She nodded. "Confirmed twice. There's no doubt."

He took her lips in his then. Even a year later, it took her breath away every time he kissed her. A year ago, they hadn't even met. Now, the man holding her was the center of her world. And soon they'd be adding yet another source of joy and love to their union.

Clairey couldn't have dreamed she'd ever be so lucky

MILLS & BOON®

Coming next month

BAHAMAS ESCAPE WITH THE BEST MAN
Cara Colter

The smile that had been tickling the wickedly attractive curve of his mouth formed fully, revealing the full straightness of his teeth, as white as the towel around his neck.

Then he threw back his head and laughed. The column of his throat looked strong and touchable. The sound of his laughter was more intoxicating than the rum.

She, Marlee Copeland, had just made a very attractive man laugh. That felt like a cigar-worthy reason for celebration!

"The cigar matches your start on your career as a criminal. People sometimes lick them before they light them."

"What?"

"They're usually wine-dipped."

She flicked the cigar with her tongue.

"Here," he said, gently. "Let me take that."

And just like that, his hand brushed hers, and a few more rocks crumbled from that cliff.

He took the cigar.

His eyes lingered on her lips.

A fire leaped to life within her.

"I wonder if there's really a wild, train-robbing outlaw under all that green fluffy stuff."

"It's not green." Her voice was hoarse, a choked whisper. "It's sea foam. Chiffon."

He held up the cigar and his tongue slipped out and licked it, exactly where her own tongue had been. His eyes were steady on hers. It was shockingly sensual.

"I need to get out of this scratchy dress," she said. What had made her say that? It was totally inappropriate. Did it sound as if she wanted to get out of the dress with him? Did it sound like an invitation?

Why did she always have to be so socially inept, blurting things out awkwardly?

Why did men like this always make her feel like a tongue-tied teenager?

Fiona had been right. This dress did suit her.

On the other hand, what would a train-robbing, cigar-loving, rum-drinking outlaw do? She could be that. For just a few minutes in time, she could. Maybe just for one night.

She took a deep breath. She felt as if she was on the edge of a cliff, trying to build up her nerve to jump.

"Want some company for your swim?"

Continue reading
BAHAMAS ESCAPE WITH THE BEST MAN
Cara Colter

Available next month
www.millsandboon.co.uk

COMING SOON!

We really hope you enjoyed reading this book.
If you're looking for more romance, be sure to
head to the shops when new books are
available on

Thursday 9th June

To see which titles are coming soon, please visit
millsandboon.co.uk/nextmonth

in love. She lifted her face to her husband to tell him exactly that.

Just as another burst of colorful fireworks lit the night sky.

* * * * *